WITCHBLADE

PUBLISHED BY
TOP COW PRODUCTIONS, INC.
LOS ANGELES

For Top Cow Productions, Inc.

For Top Cow Productions, Inc.

Marc Silvestri - CEO

Matt Hawkins - President & COO

Elena Salcedo - Vice President of Operations

Henry Barajas - Director of Operations

Vincent Valentine - Production Manager

Dylan Gray - Marketing Director

To find the comic
shop nearest you, call:
1-888-COMICBOOK

Want more info? Check out:
www.topcow.com
for news & exclusive Top Cow merchandise!

WITCHBLADE, VOL. 1. First printing. JULY 2018. Published by Image Comics, Inc. Office of publication: 2701 NW Vaughn St., Suite 780, Portland, OR 97210. Copyright © 2018 Top Cow Productions Inc. All rights reserved. Contains material originally published in single magazine form as WITCHBLADE #1–6. "WITCHBLADE," its logos, and the likenesses of all characters herein are trademarks of Top Cow Productions Inc., unless otherwise noted. "Image" and the Image Comics logos are registered trademarks of Image Comics, Inc. No part of this publication may be reproduced or transmitted, in any form or by any means (except for short excerpts for journalistic or review purposes), without the express written permission of Top Cow Productions Inc., or Image Comics, Inc. All names, characters, events, and locales in this publication are entirely fictional. Any resemblance to actual persons (living or dead), events, or places, without satirical intent, is coincidental. Printed in the USA. For information regarding the CPSIA on this printed material call: 203-595-3636 and provide

WITCHBLADE

CAITLIN KITTREDGE
WRITER

ROBERTA INGRANATA
ARTIST

BRYAN VALENZA
COLORIST

TROY PETERI
LETTERER

ERIC STEPHENSON
EDITOR

ROBERTA INGRANATA & BRYAN VALENZA
COVER

CHAPTER ONE

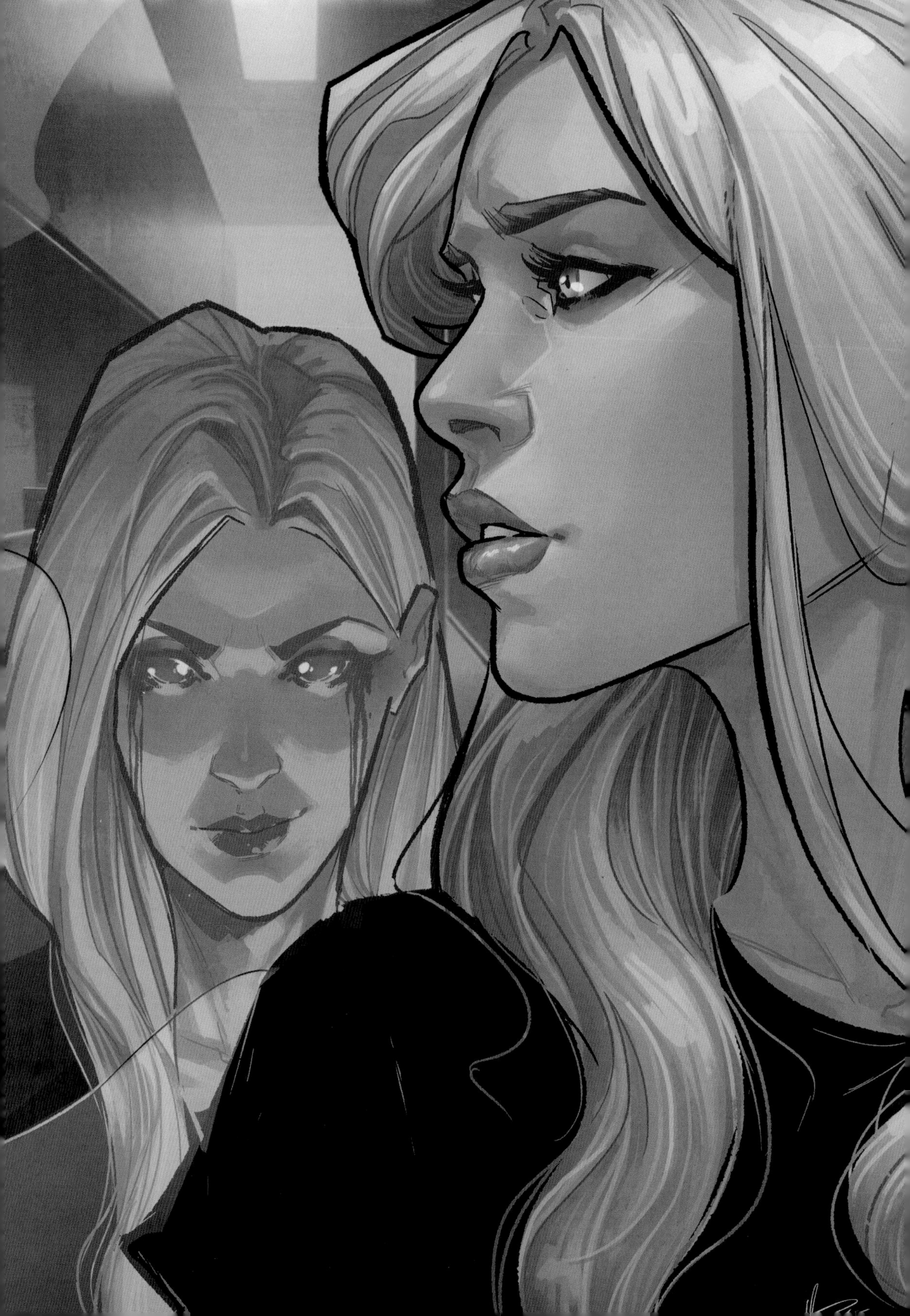

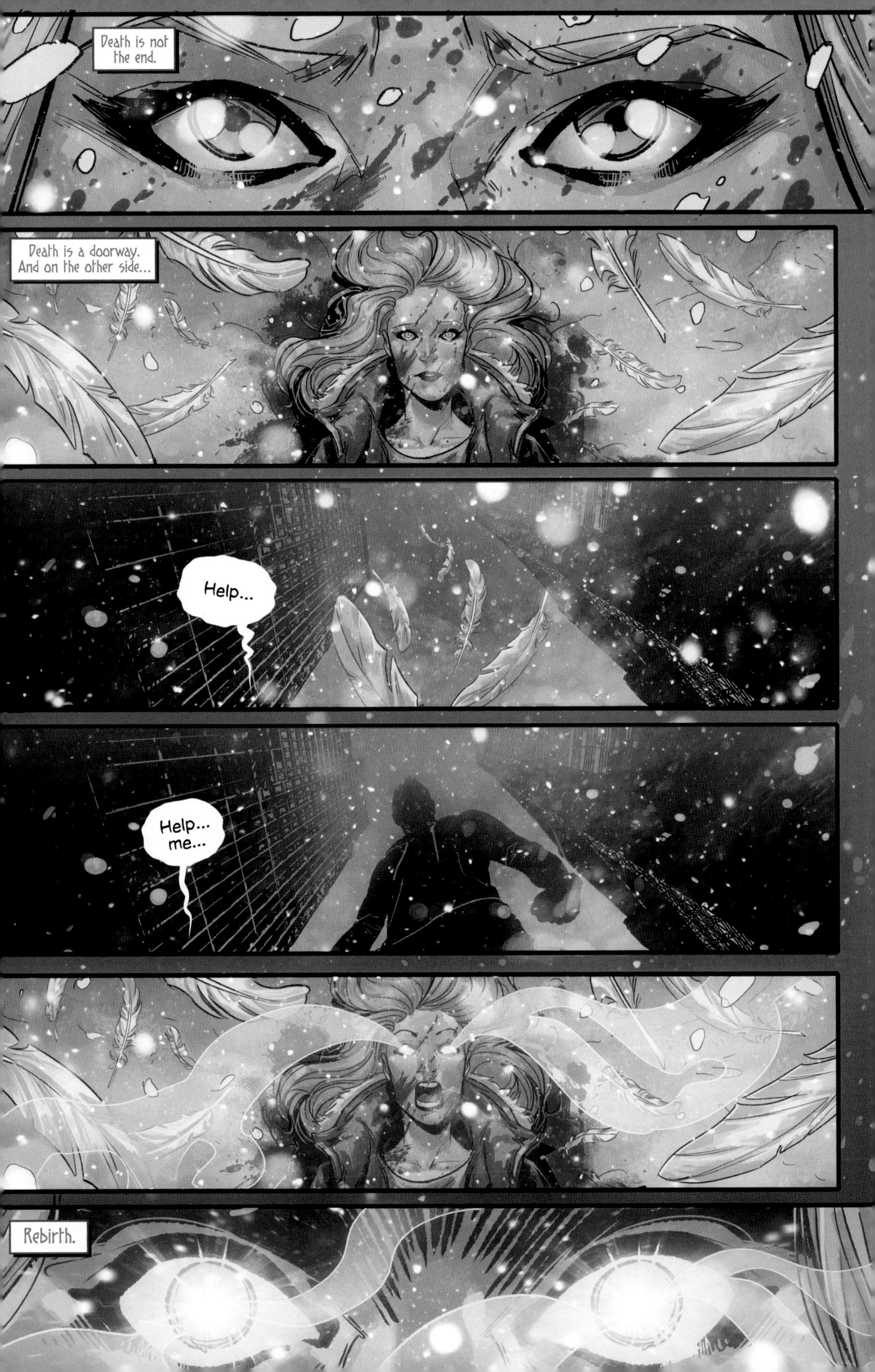

Death is not the end.
Death is a doorway. And on the other side...
Help...
Help... me...
Rebirth.

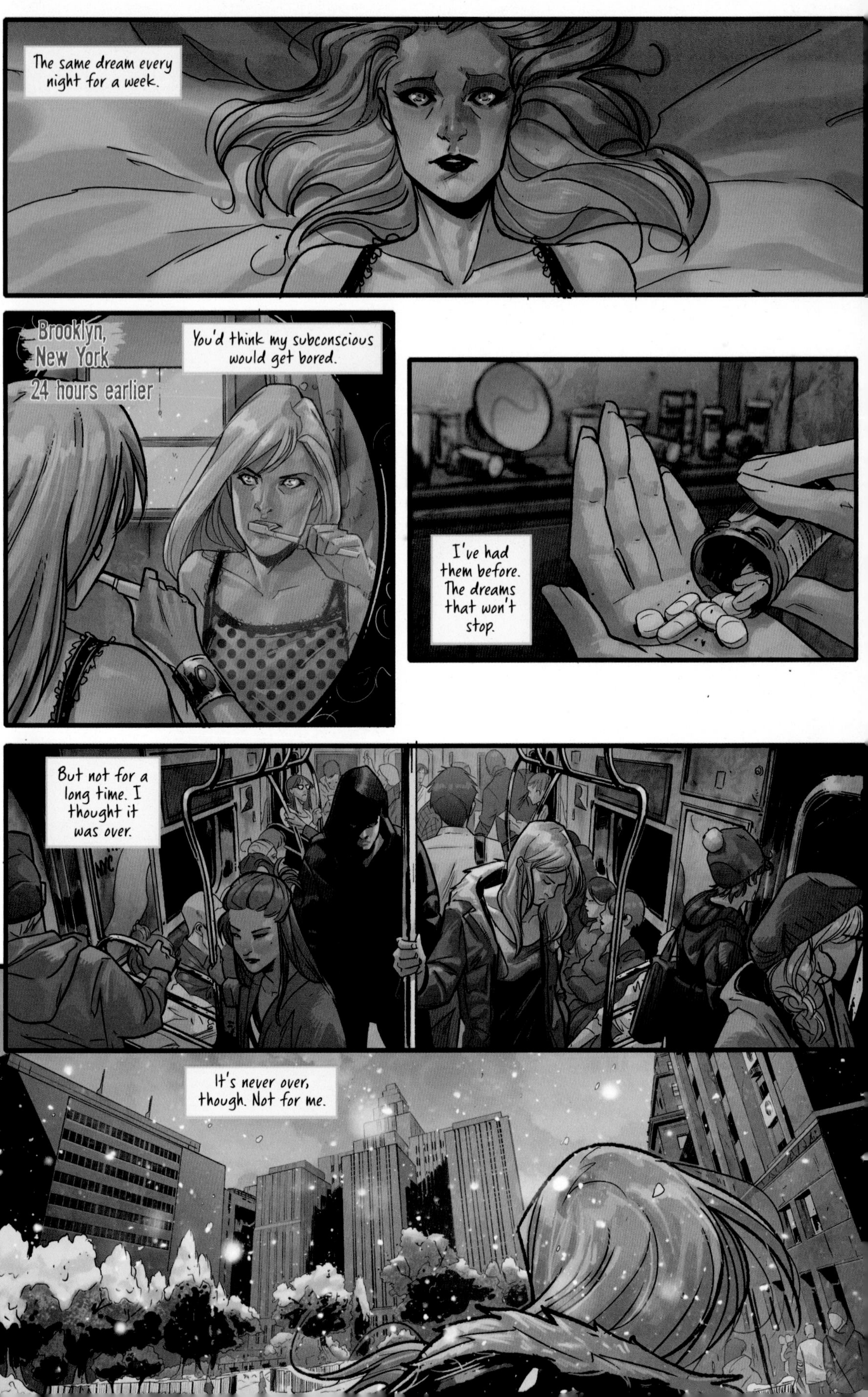
The same dream every night for a week.
Brooklyn, New York 24 hours earlier
You'd think my subconscious would get bored.
I've had them before. The dreams that won't stop.
But not for a long time. I thought it was over.
It's never over, though. Not for me.

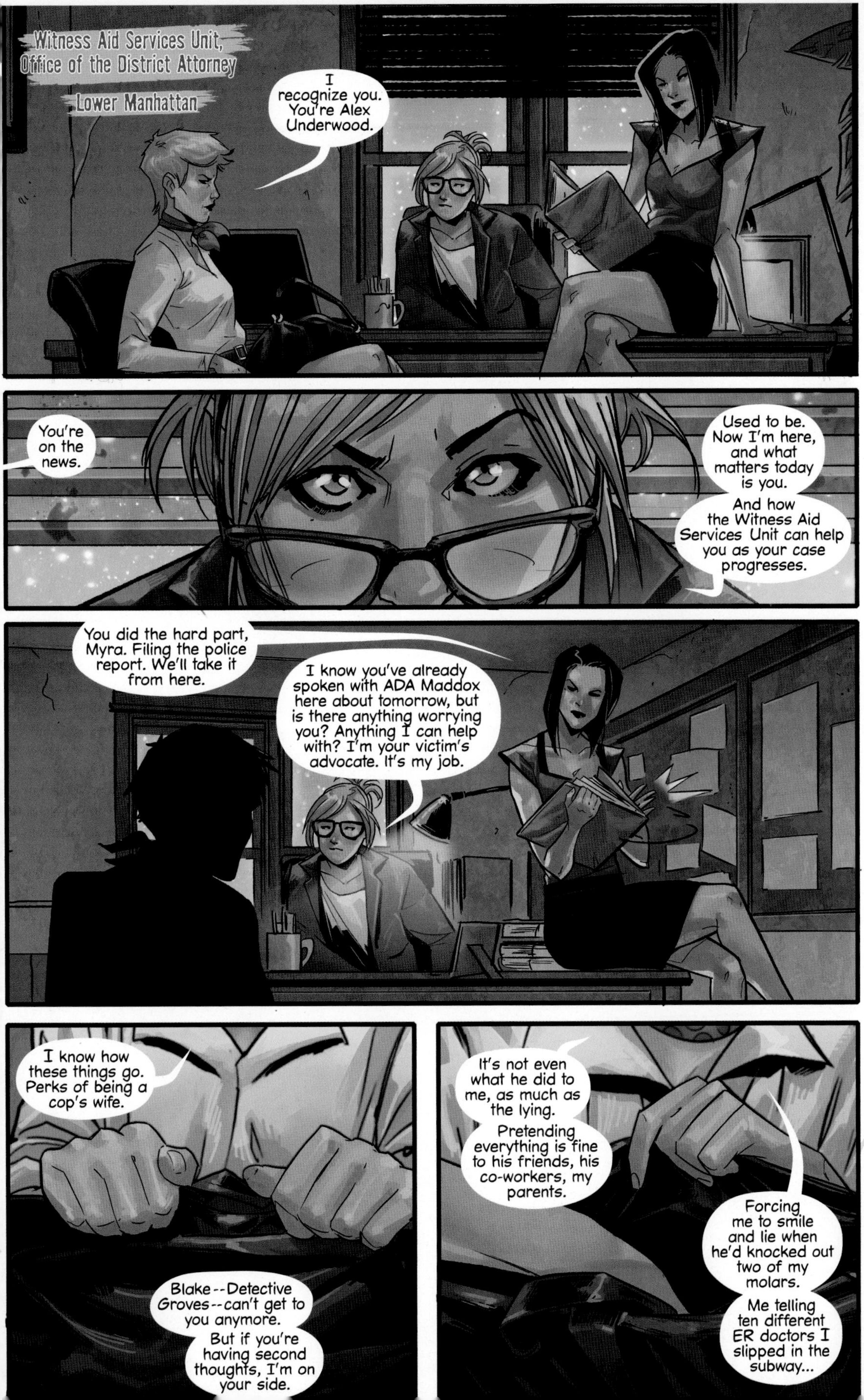
Witness Aid Services Unit, Office of the District Attorney
Lower Manhattan
I recognize you. You're Alex Underwood.
You're on the news.
Used to be. Now I'm here, and what matters today is you.
And how the Witness Aid Services Unit can help you as your case progresses.
You did the hard part, Myra. Filing the police report. We'll take it from here.
I know you've already spoken with ADA Maddox here about tomorrow, but is there anything worrying you? Anything I can help with? I'm your victim's advocate. It's my job.
I know how these things go. Perks of being a cop's wife.
Blake--Detective Groves--can't get to you anymore.
But if you're having second thoughts, I'm on your side.
It's not even what he did to me, as much as the lying.
Pretending everything is fine to his friends, his co-workers, my parents.
Forcing me to smile and lie when he'd knocked out two of my molars.
Me telling ten different ER doctors I slipped in the subway...

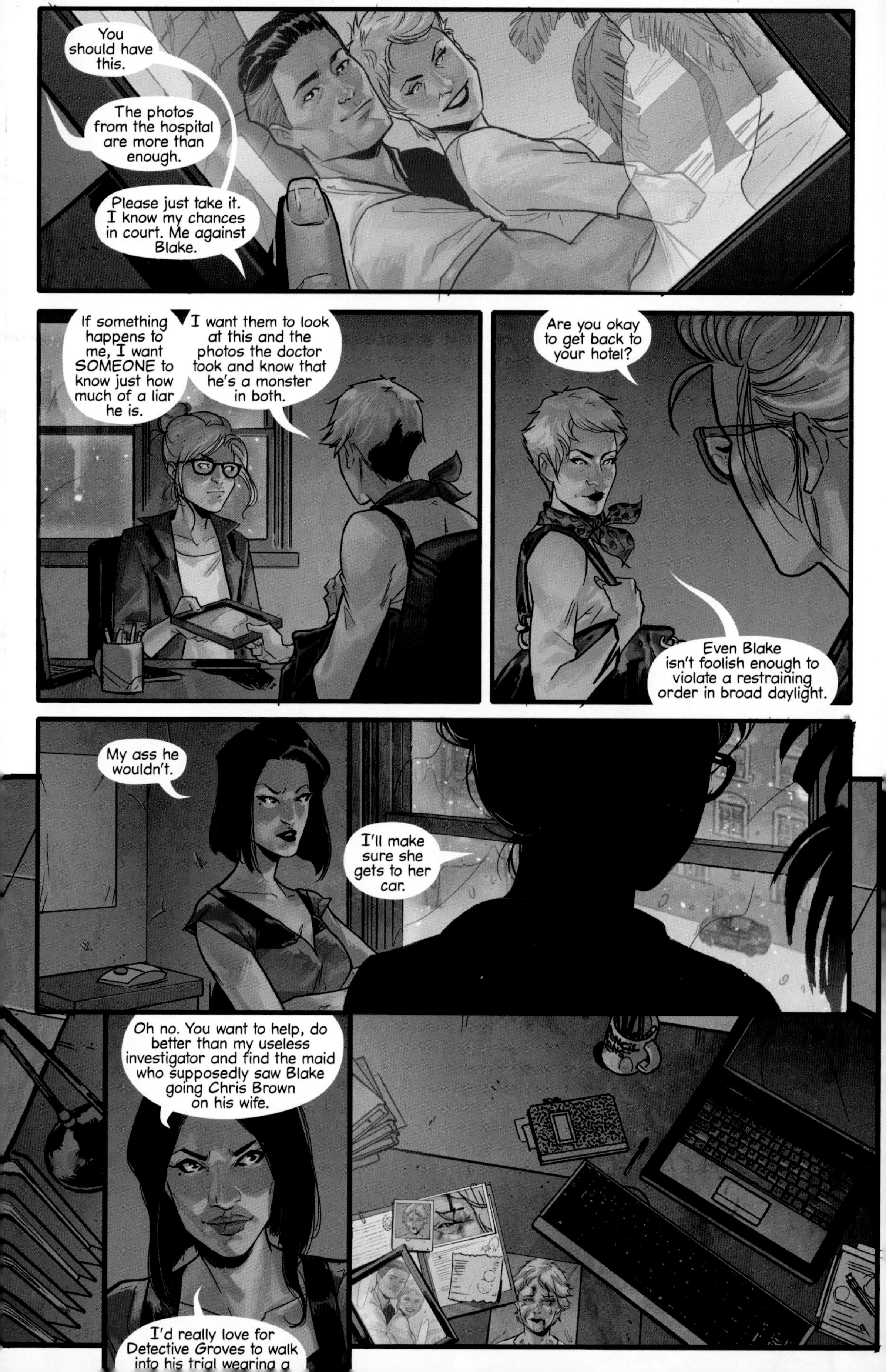
You should have this.
The photos from the hospital are more than enough.
Please just take it. I know my chances in court. Me against Blake.
If something happens to me, I want SOMEONE to know just how much of a liar he is.
I want them to look at this and the photos the doctor took and know that he's a monster in both.
Are you okay to get back to your hotel?
Even Blake isn't foolish enough to violate a restraining order in broad daylight.
My ass he wouldn't.
I'll make sure she gets to her car.
Oh no. You want to help, do better than my useless investigator and find the maid who supposedly saw Blake going Chris Brown on his wife.
I'd really love for Detective Groves to walk into his trial wearing a

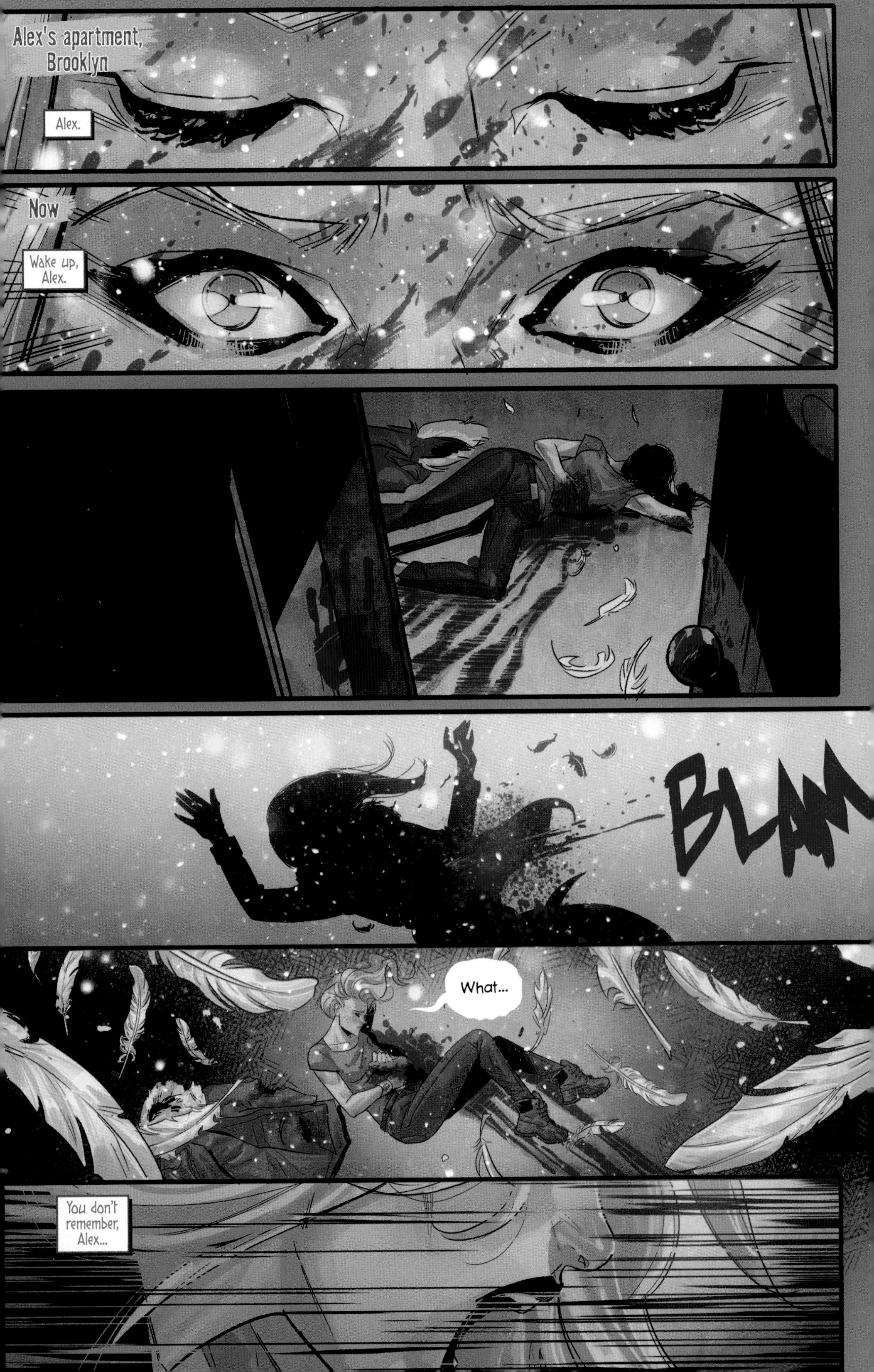

Alex's apartment, Brooklyn
Alex.
Now
Wake up, Alex.
BLAM
What...
You don't remember, Alex...

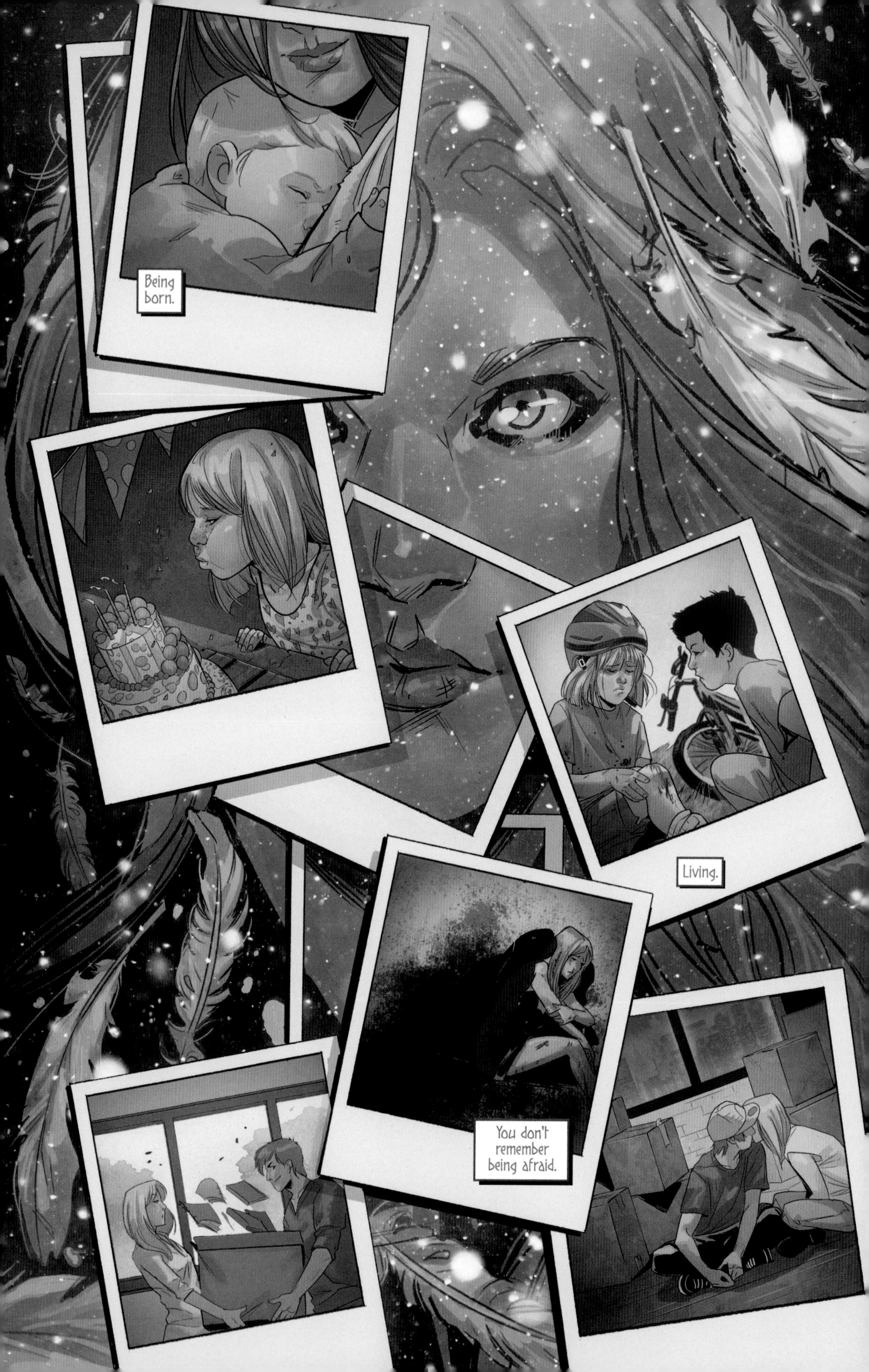
Being born.
Living.
You don't remember being afraid.

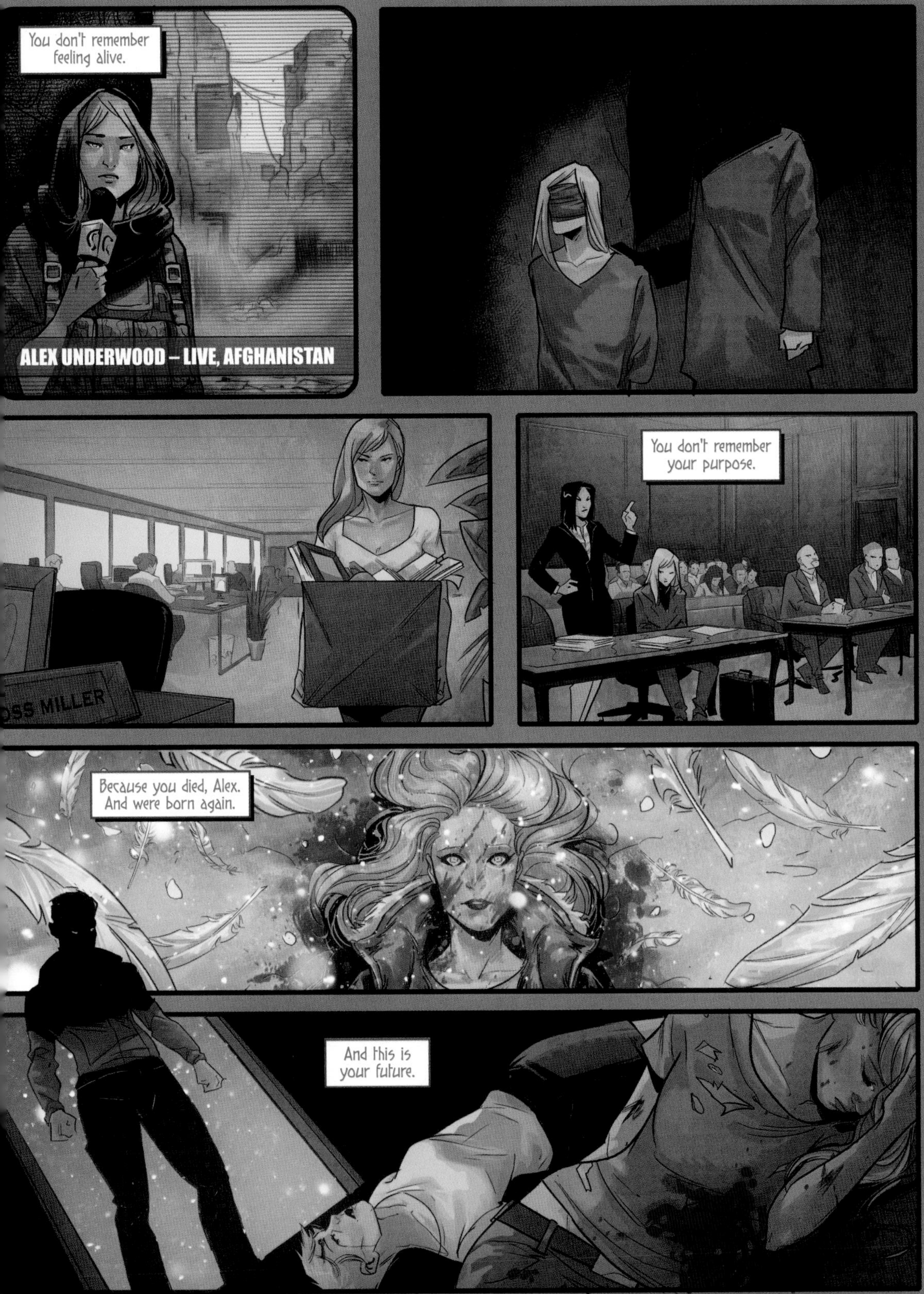
You don't remember feeling alive.
ALEX UNDERWOOD – LIVE, AFGHANISTAN
OSS MILLER
You don't remember your purpose.
Because you died, Alex. And were born again.
And this is your future.

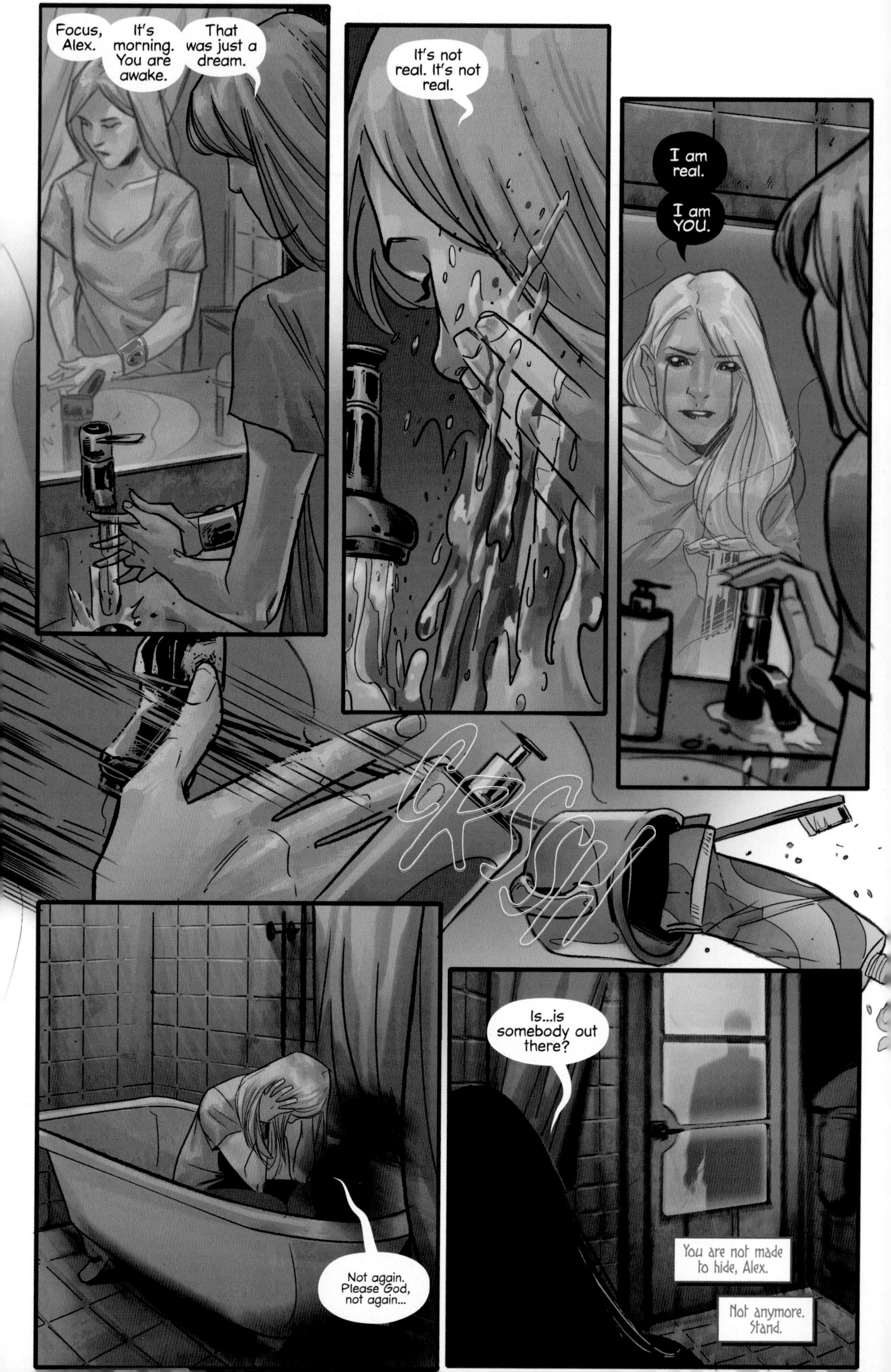
Focus, Alex.
It's morning. You are awake.
That was just a dream.
It's not real. It's not real.
I am real.
I am YOU.
CRSH
Not again. Please God, not again...
Is...is somebody out there?
You are not made to hide, Alex.
Not anymore. Stand.

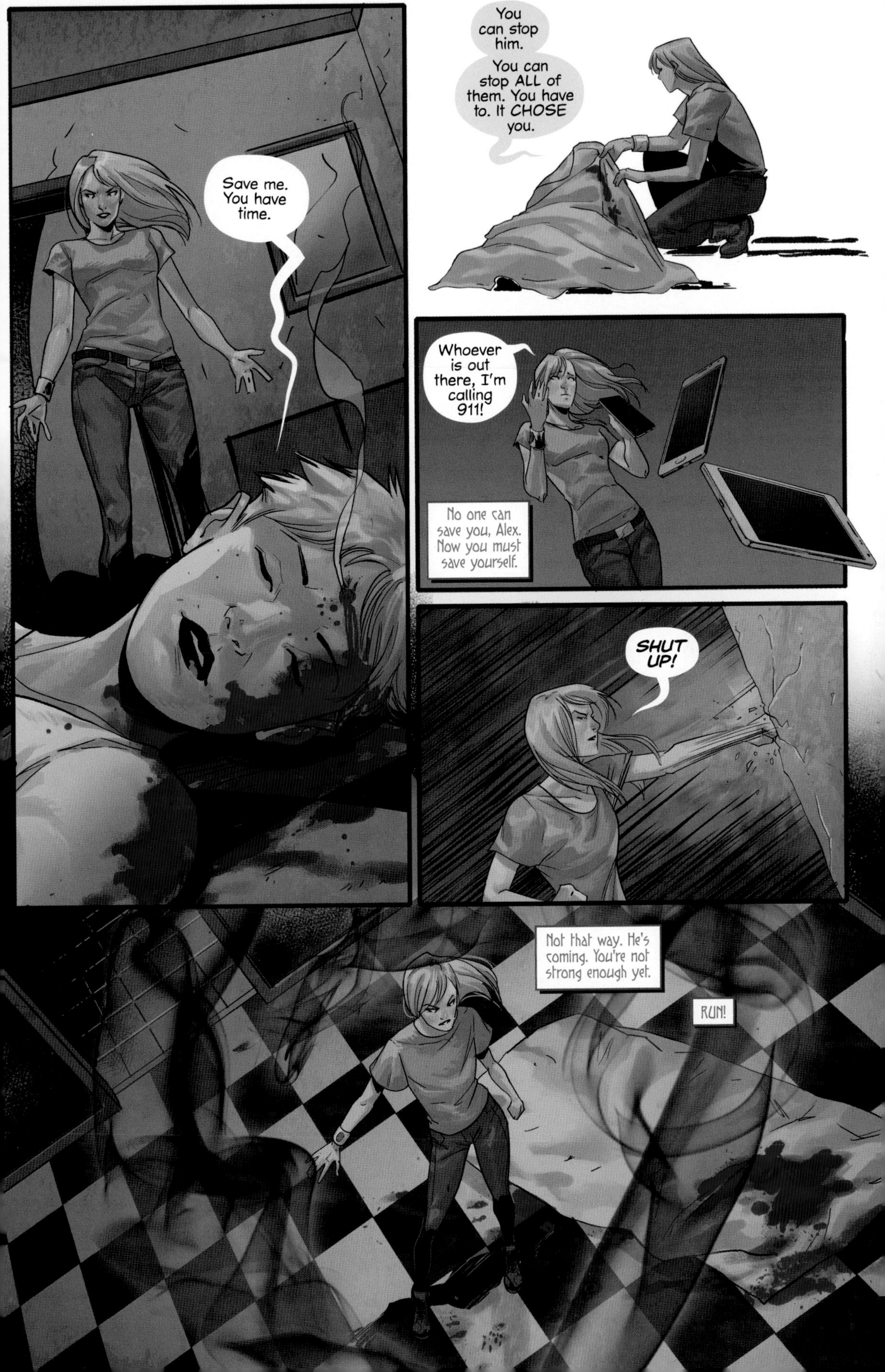
Save me. You have time.
You can stop him.
You can stop ALL of them. You have to. It CHOSE you.
Whoever is out there, I'm calling 911!
No one can save you, Alex. Now you must save yourself.
SHUT UP!
Not that way. He's coming. You're not strong enough yet.
RUN!

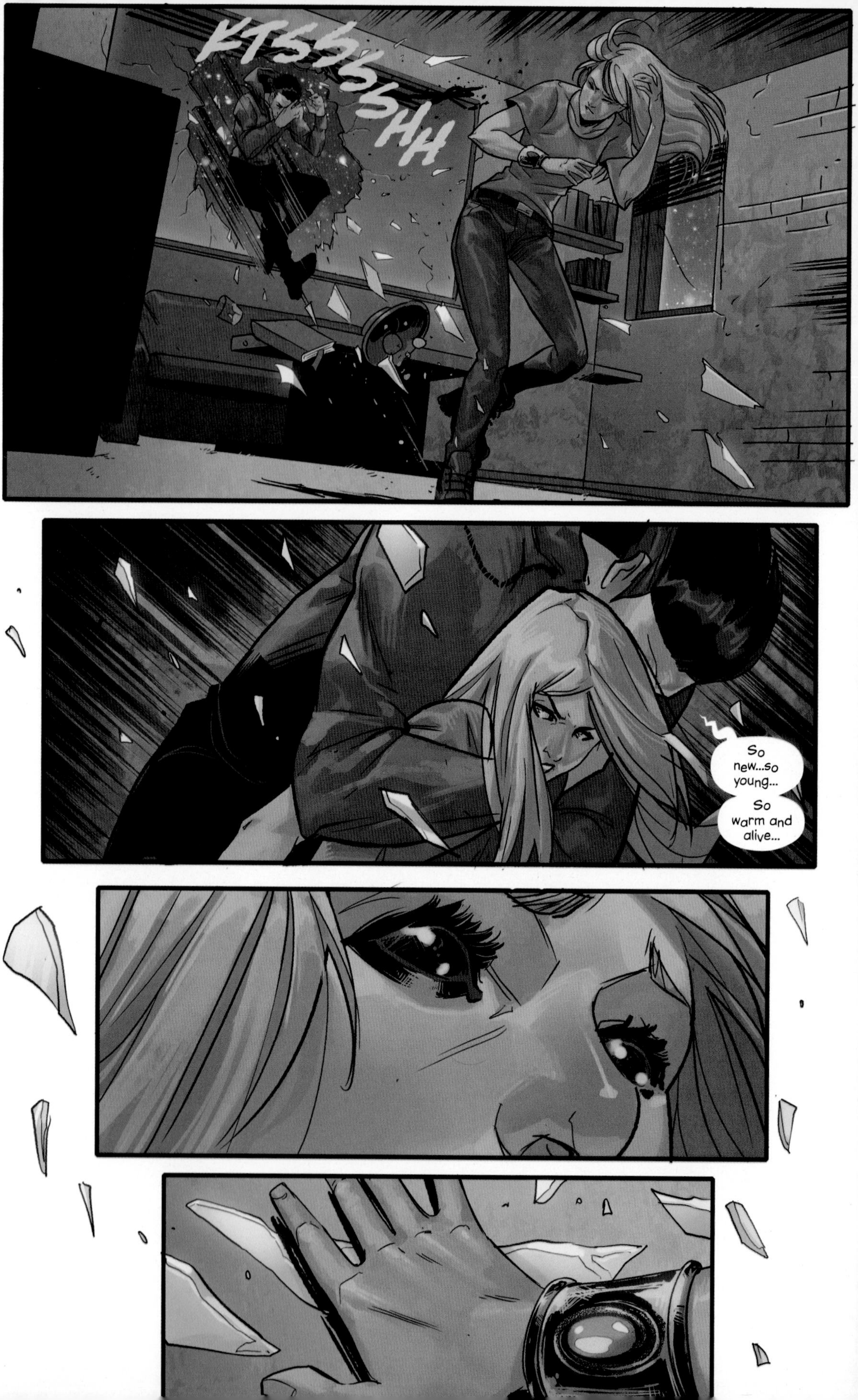
KTSSSSHH
So new...so young...
So warm and alive...

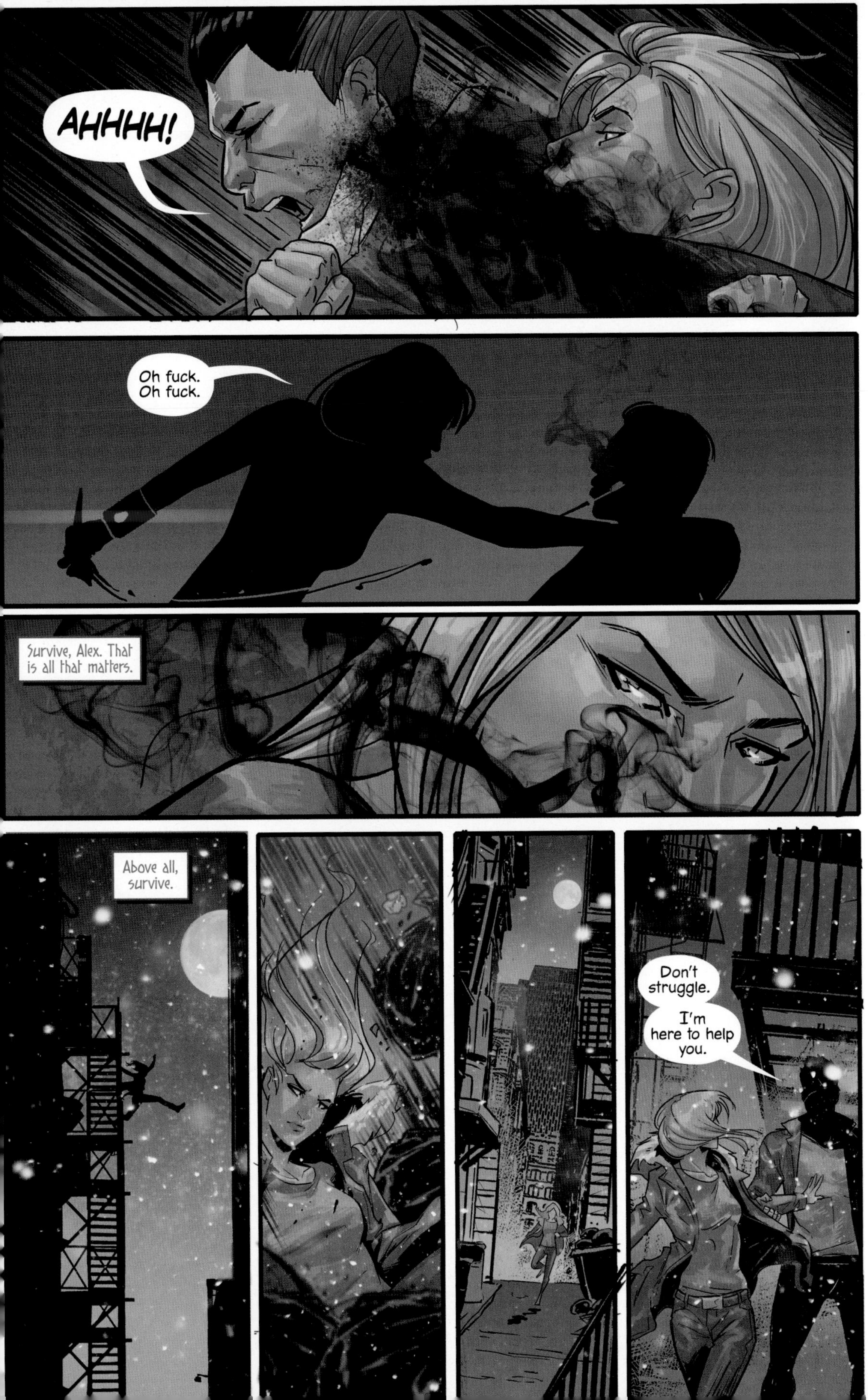
AHHHH!
Oh fuck. Oh fuck.
Survive, Alex. That is all that matters.
Above all, survive.
Don't struggle.
I'm here to help you.

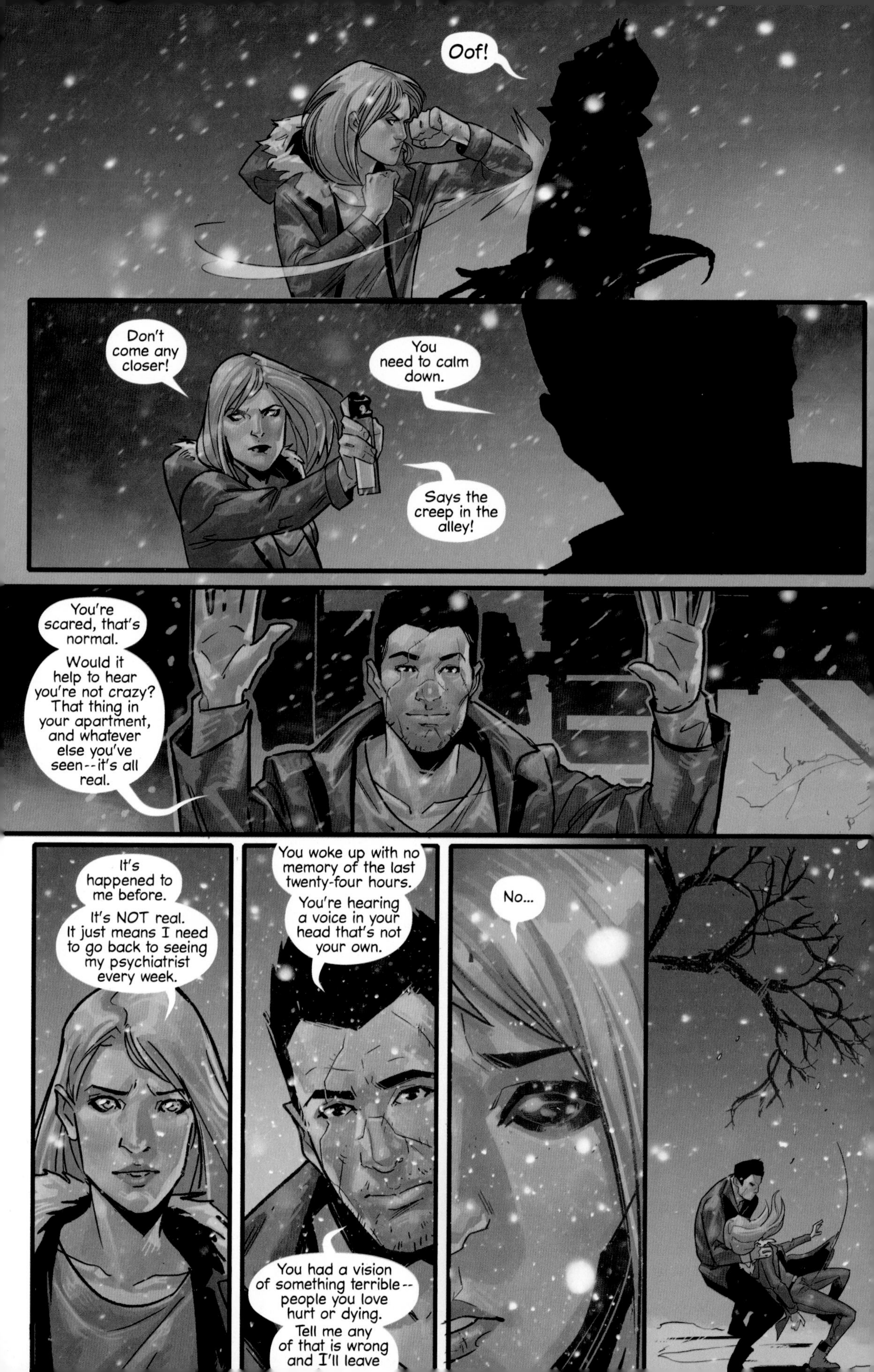
Oof!
Don't come any closer!
You need to calm down.
Says the creep in the alley!
You're scared, that's normal.
Would it help to hear you're not crazy? That thing in your apartment, and whatever else you've seen--it's all real.
It's happened to me before.
It's NOT real. It just means I need to go back to seeing my psychiatrist every week.
You woke up with no memory of the last twenty-four hours.
You're hearing a voice in your head that's not your own.
You had a vision of something terrible--people you love hurt or dying.
Tell me any of that is wrong and I'll leave
No...

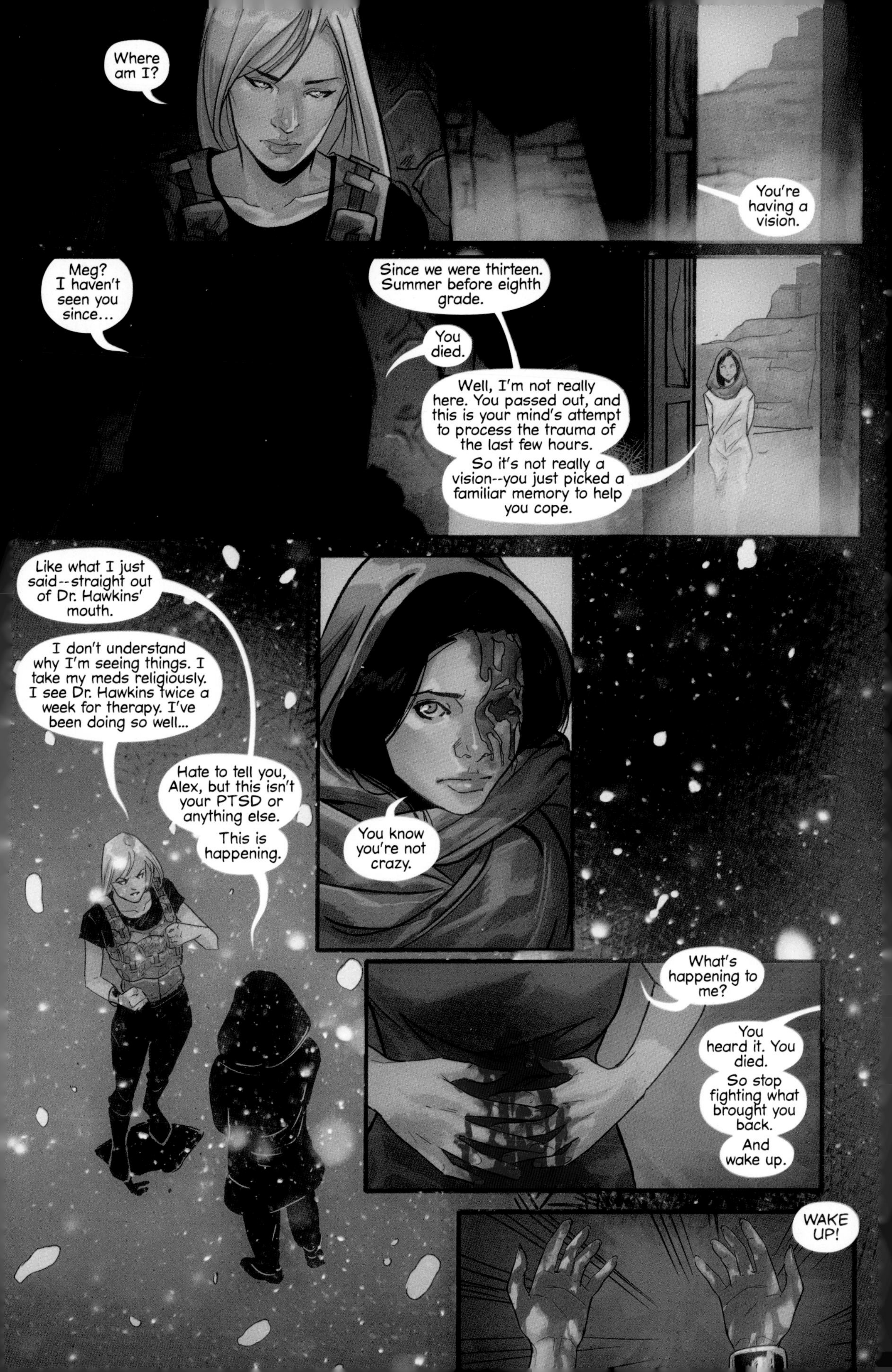
Where am I?
You're having a vision.
Meg? I haven't seen you since...
Since we were thirteen. Summer before eighth grade.
You died.
Well, I'm not really here. You passed out, and this is your mind's attempt to process the trauma of the last few hours.
So it's not really a vision--you just picked a familiar memory to help you cope.
Like what I just said--straight out of Dr. Hawkins' mouth.
I don't understand why I'm seeing things. I take my meds religiously. I see Dr. Hawkins twice a week for therapy. I've been doing so well...
Hate to tell you, Alex, but this isn't your PTSD or anything else.
This is happening.
You know you're not crazy.
What's happening to me?
You heard it. You died.
So stop fighting what brought you back.
And wake up.
WAKE UP!

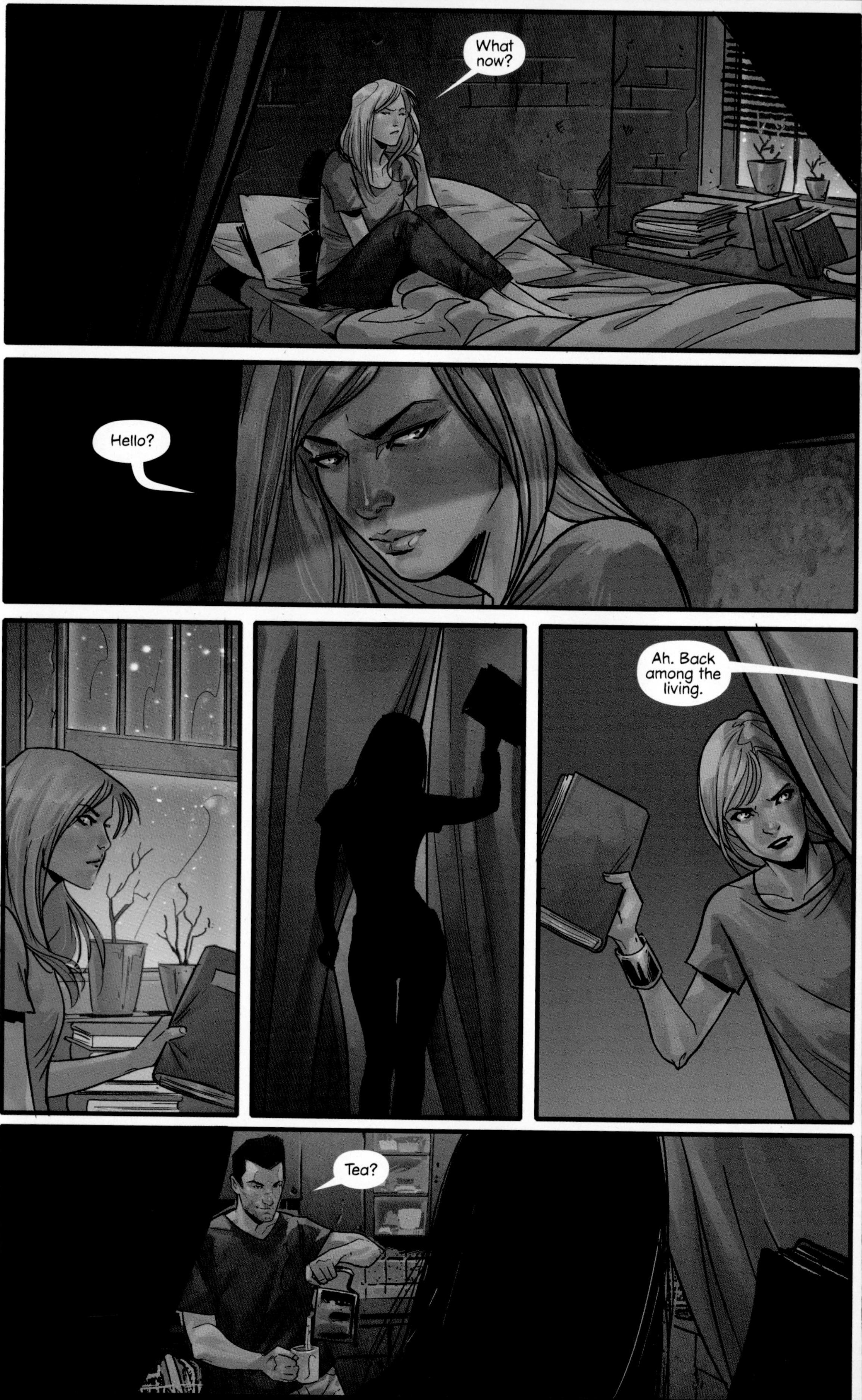
What now?
Hello?
Ah. Back among the living.
Tea?

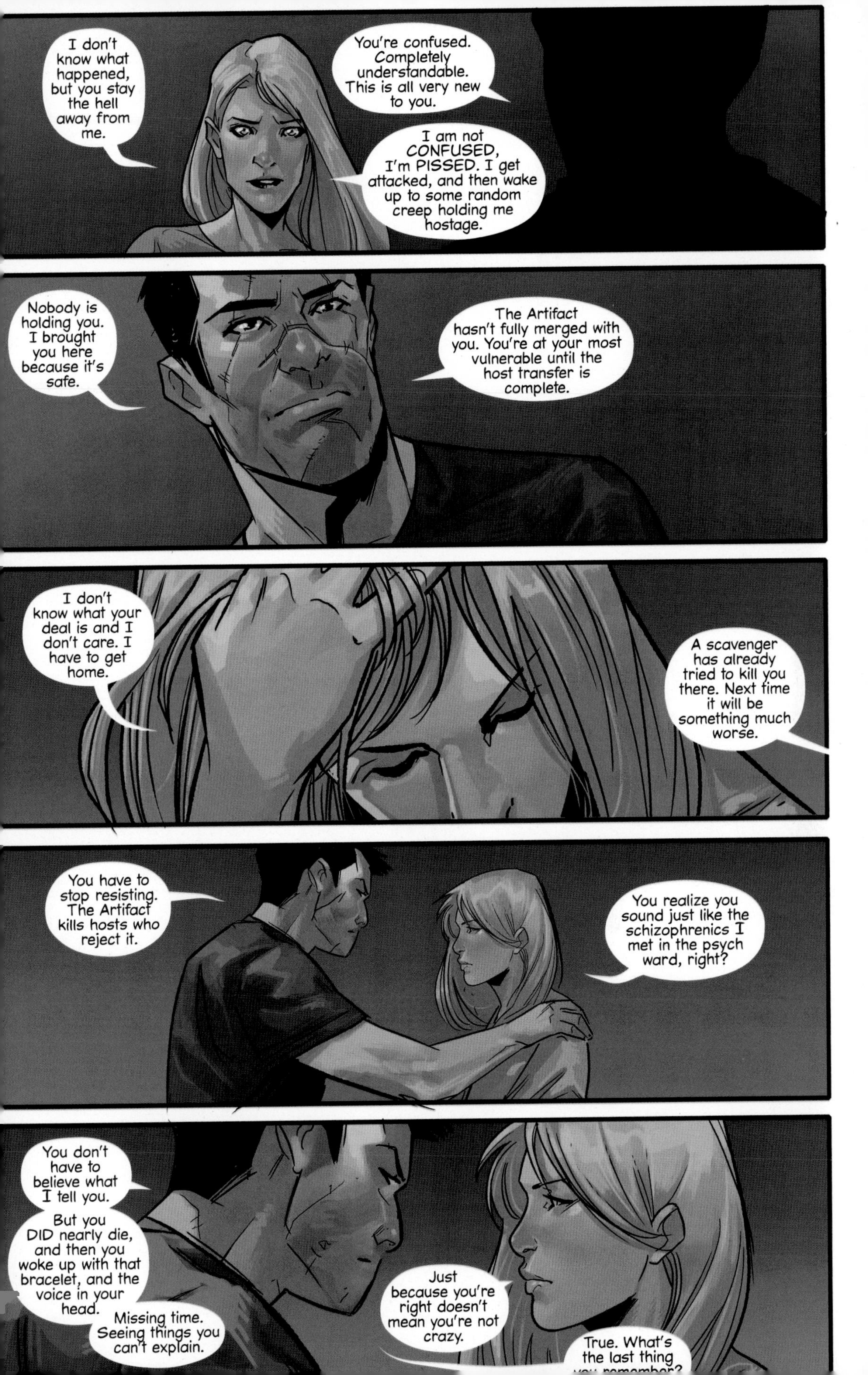
I don't know what happened, but you stay the hell away from me.
You're confused. Completely understandable. This is all very new to you.
I am not CONFUSED, I'm PISSED. I get attacked, and then wake up to some random creep holding me hostage.
Nobody is holding you. I brought you here because it's safe.
The Artifact hasn't fully merged with you. You're at your most vulnerable until the host transfer is complete.
I don't know what your deal is and I don't care. I have to get home.
A scavenger has already tried to kill you there. Next time it will be something much worse.
You have to stop resisting. The Artifact kills hosts who reject it.
You realize you sound just like the schizophrenics I met in the psych ward, right?
You don't have to believe what I tell you.
But you DID nearly die, and then you woke up with that bracelet, and the voice in your head.
Missing time. Seeing things you can't explain.
Just because you're right doesn't mean you're not crazy.
True. What's the last thing

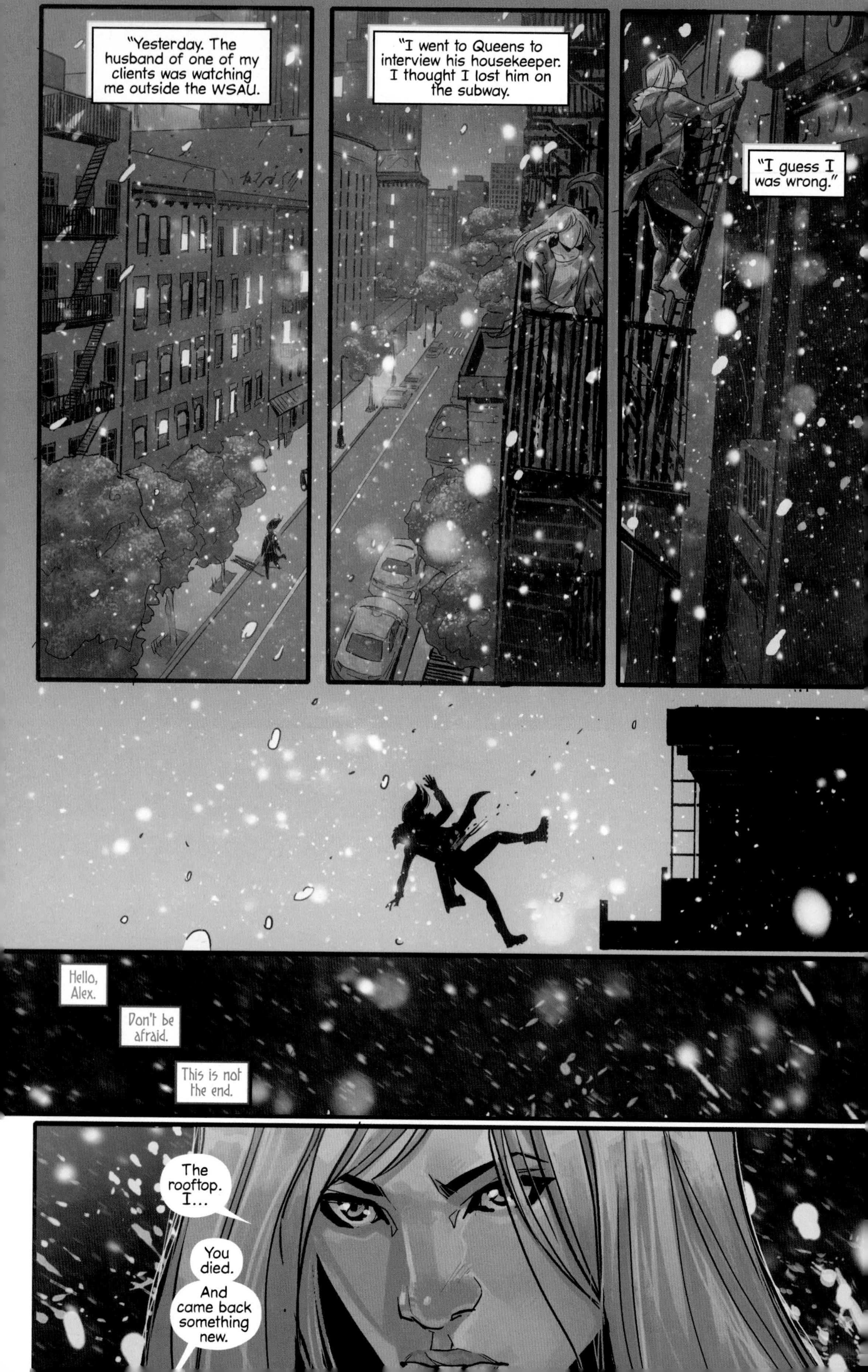
"Yesterday. The husband of one of my clients was watching me outside the WSAU.
"I went to Queens to interview his housekeeper. I thought I lost him on the subway.
"I guess I was wrong."
Hello, Alex.
Don't be afraid.
This is not the end.
The rooftop. I...
You died.
And came back something new.

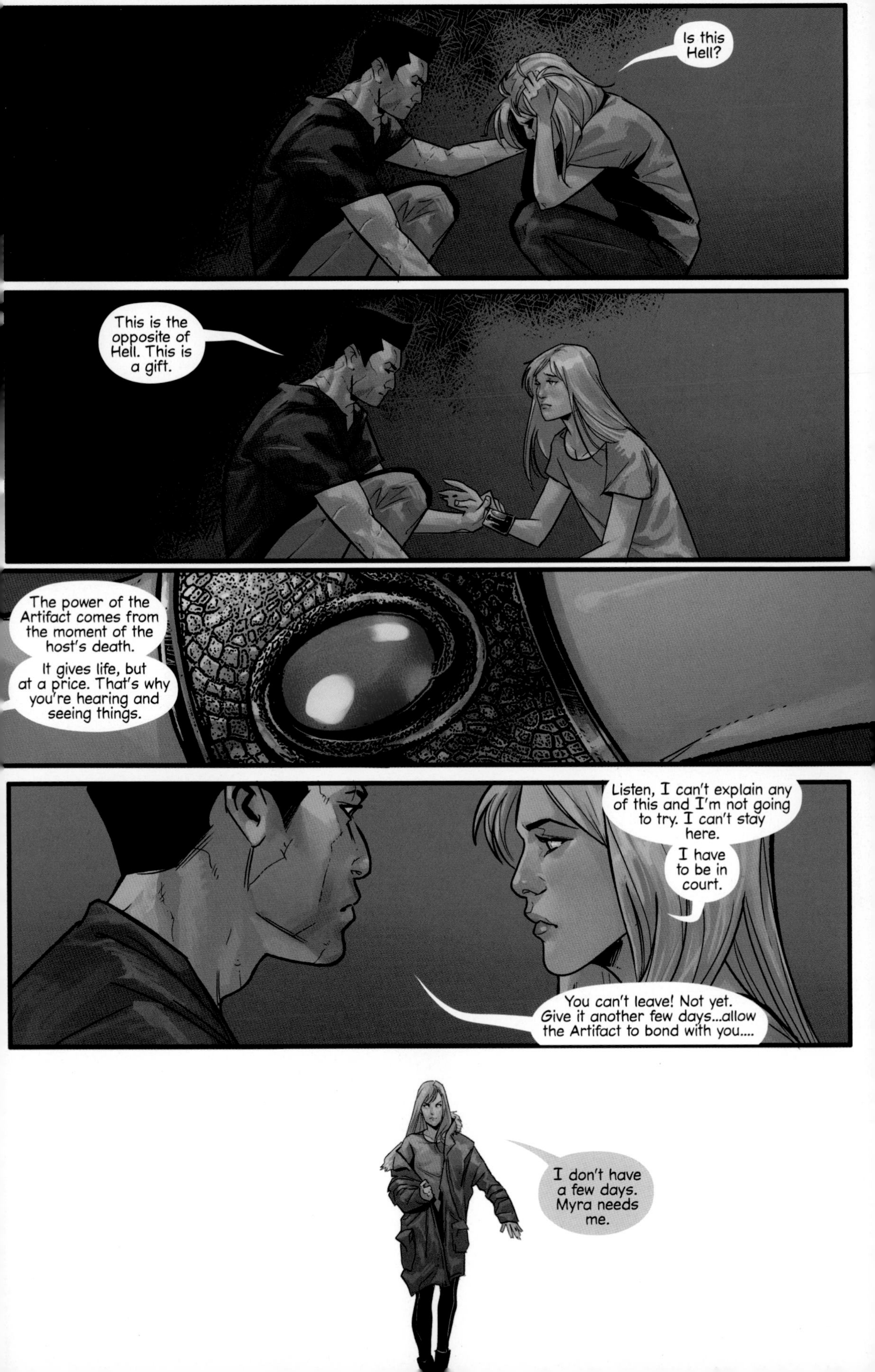
Is this Hell?
This is the opposite of Hell. This is a gift.
The power of the Artifact comes from the moment of the host's death.
It gives life, but at a price. That's why you're hearing and seeing things.
Listen, I can't explain any of this and I'm not going to try. I can't stay here.
I have to be in court.
You can't leave! Not yet. Give it another few days...allow the Artifact to bond with you....
I don't have a few days. Myra needs me.

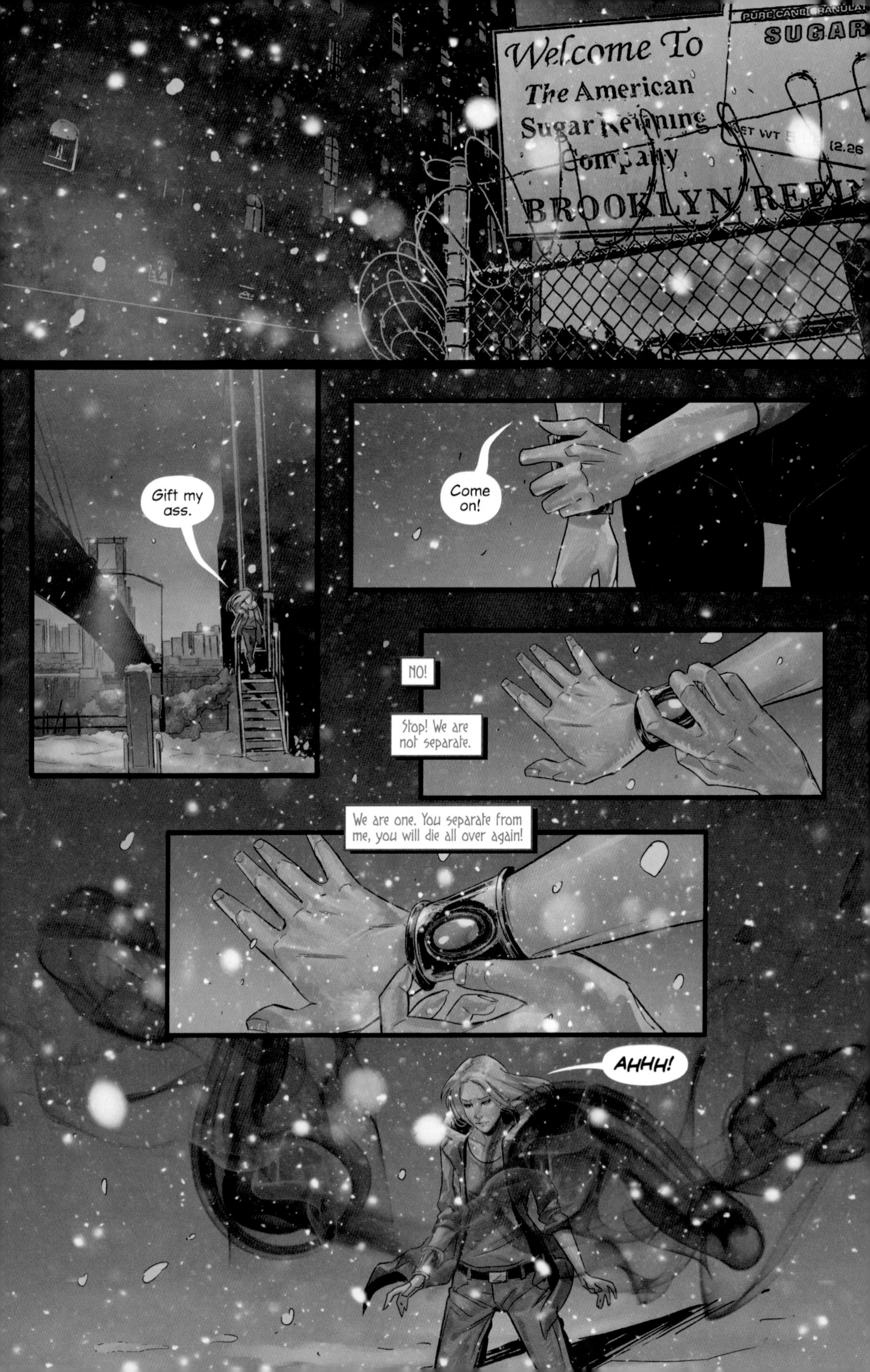
Welcome To
The American
Sugar Refining
Company
BROOKLYN
SUGAR
Gift my ass.
Come on!
NO!
Stop! We are not separate.
We are one. You separate from me, you will die all over again!
AHHH!

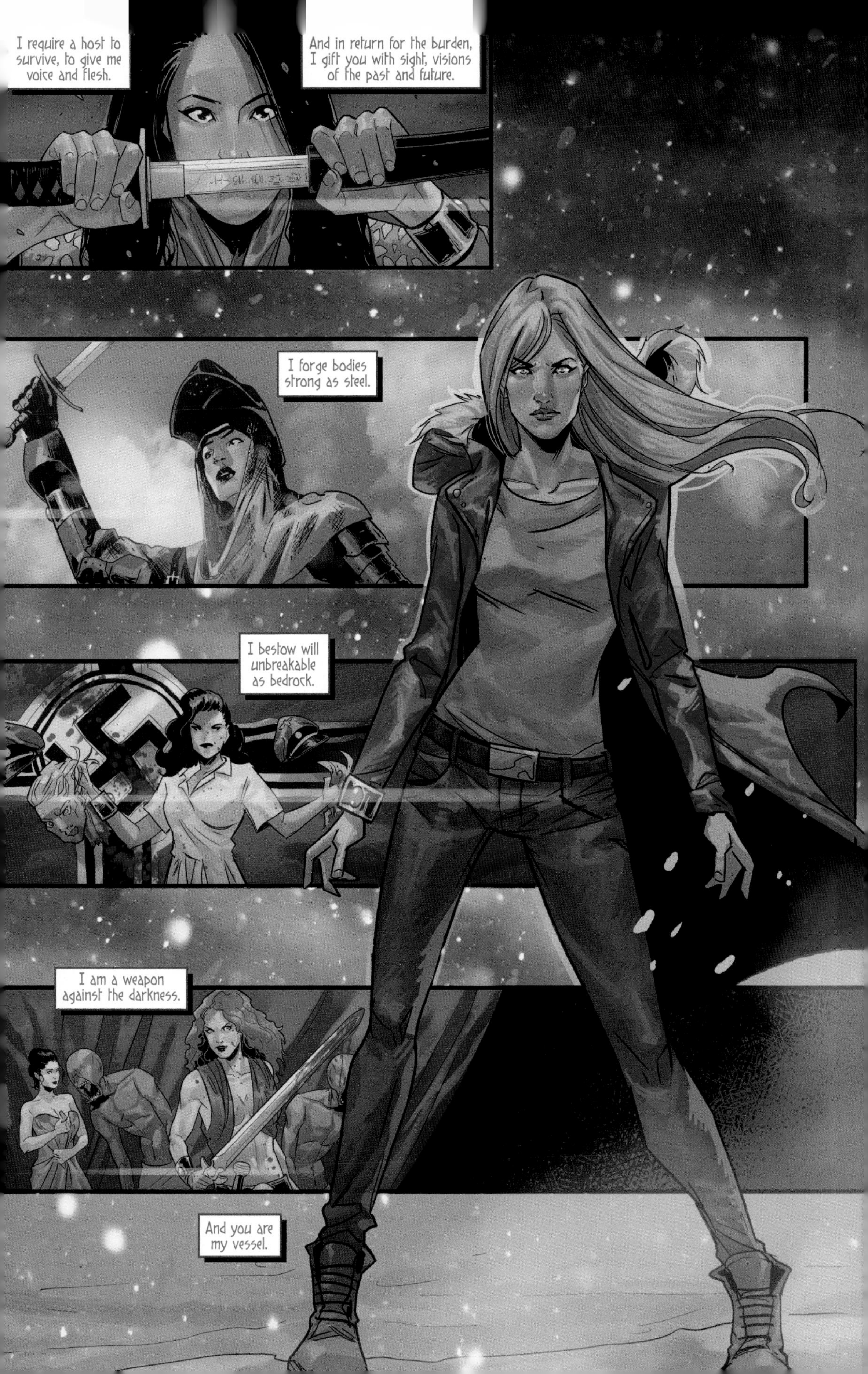
I require a host to survive, to give me voice and flesh.
And in return for the burden, I gift you with sight, visions of the past and future.
I forge bodies strong as steel.
I bestow will unbreakable as bedrock.
I am a weapon against the darkness.
And you are my vessel.

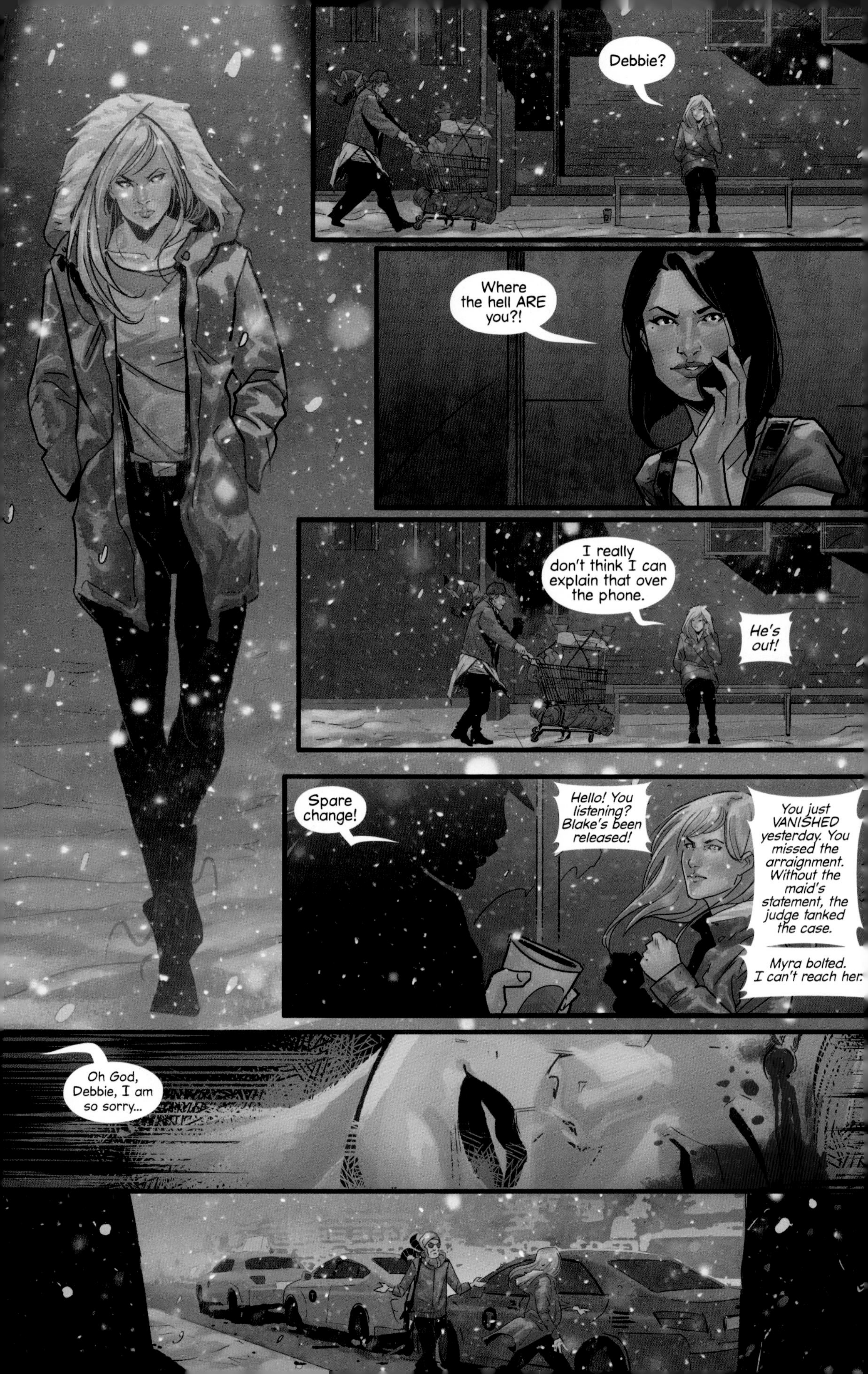
Debbie?
Where the hell ARE you?!
I really don't think I can explain that over the phone.
He's out!
Spare change!
Hello! You listening? Blake's been released!
You just VANISHED yesterday. You missed the arraignment. Without the maid's statement, the judge tanked the case.
Myra bolted. I can't reach her.
Oh God, Debbie, I am so sorry...

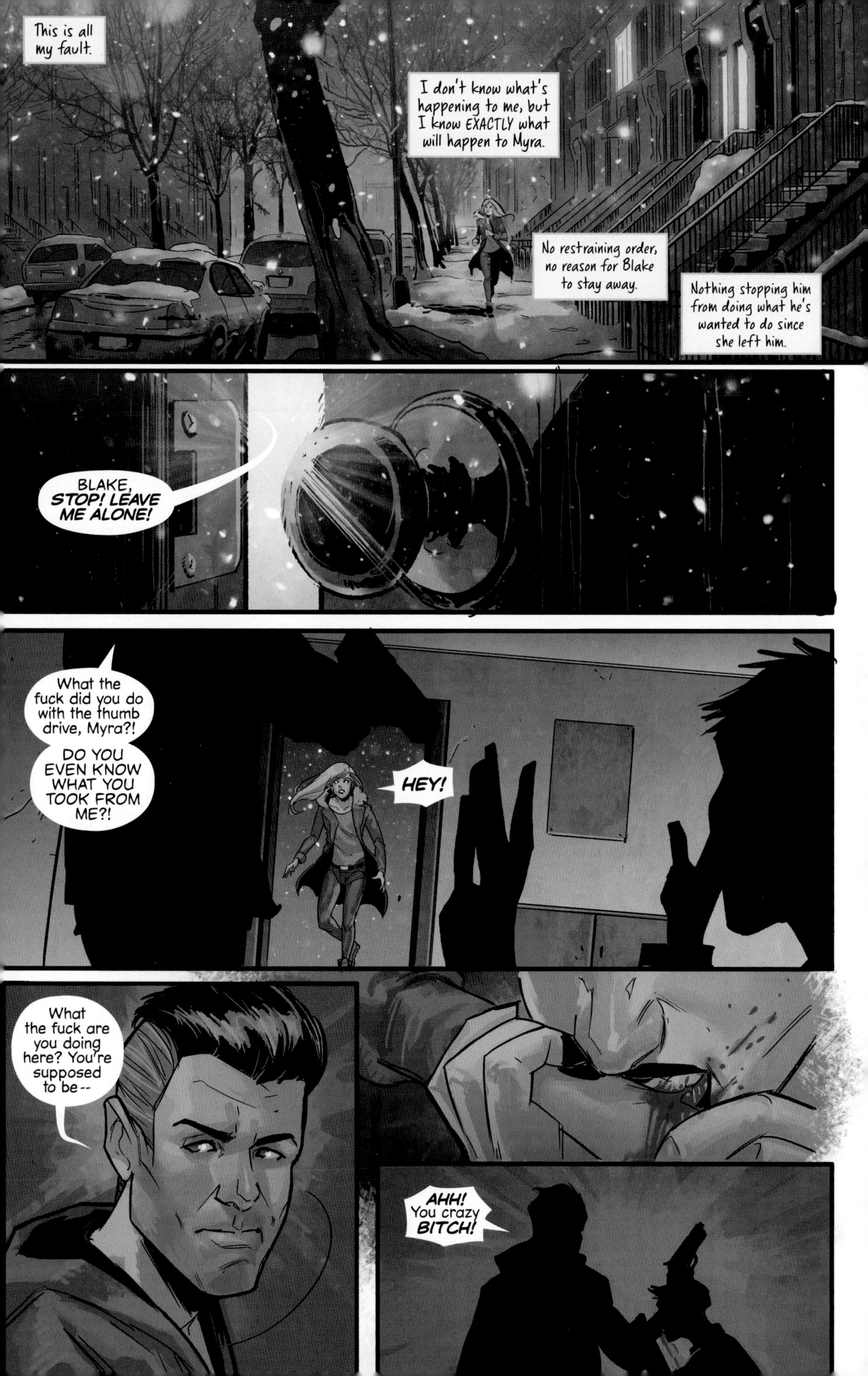

This is all my fault.
I don't know what's happening to me, but I know EXACTLY what will happen to Myra.
No restraining order, no reason for Blake to stay away.
Nothing stopping him from doing what he's wanted to do since she left him.
BLAKE, STOP! LEAVE ME ALONE!
What the fuck did you do with the thumb drive, Myra?!
DO YOU EVEN KNOW WHAT YOU TOOK FROM ME?!
HEY!
What the fuck are you doing here? You're supposed to be--
AHH! You crazy BITCH!

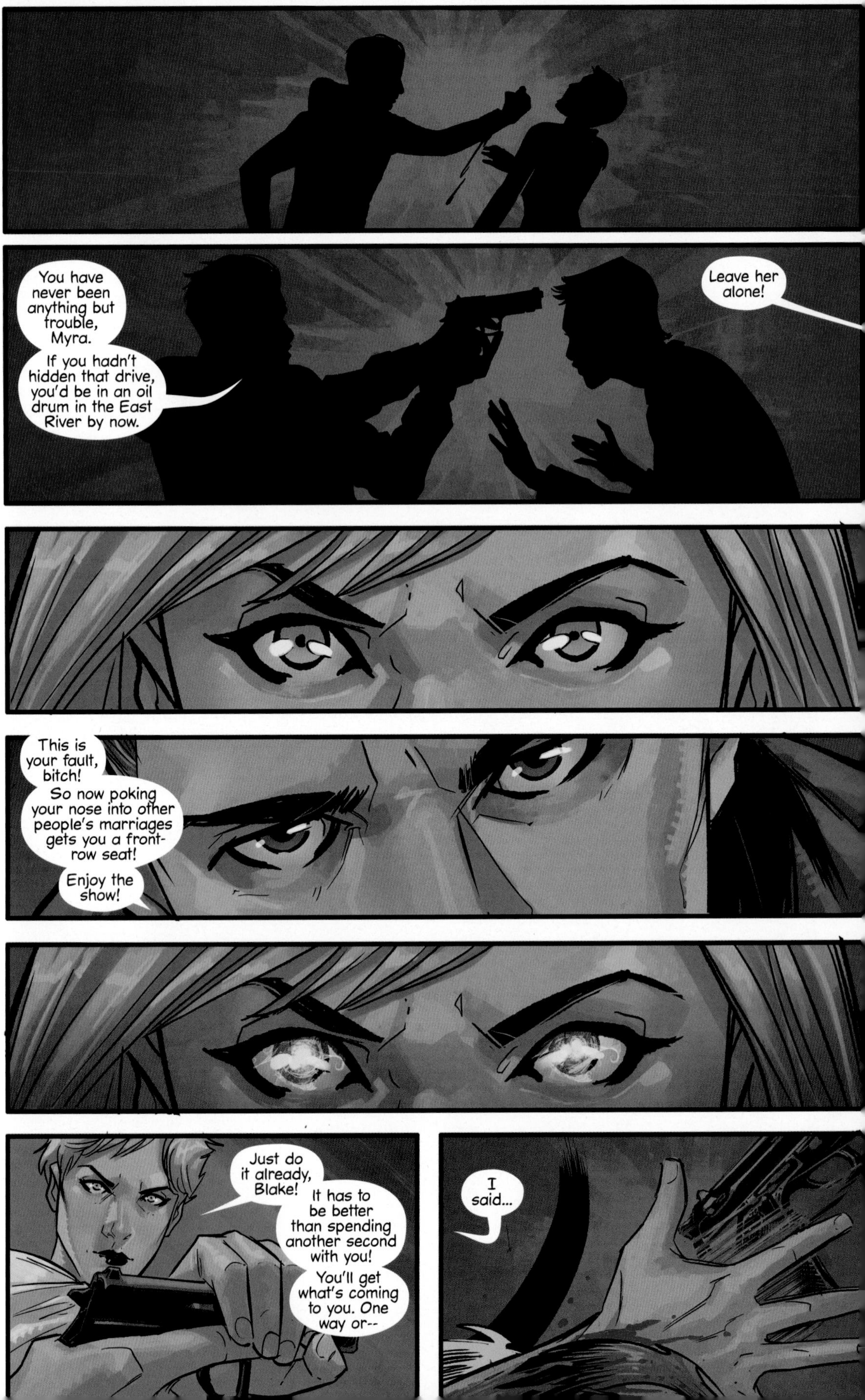

You have never been anything but trouble, Myra.
If you hadn't hidden that drive, you'd be in an oil drum in the East River by now.
Leave her alone!
This is your fault, bitch!
So now poking your nose into other people's marriages gets you a front-row seat!
Enjoy the show!
Just do it already, Blake!
It has to be better than spending another second with you!
You'll get what's coming to you. One way or--
I said...

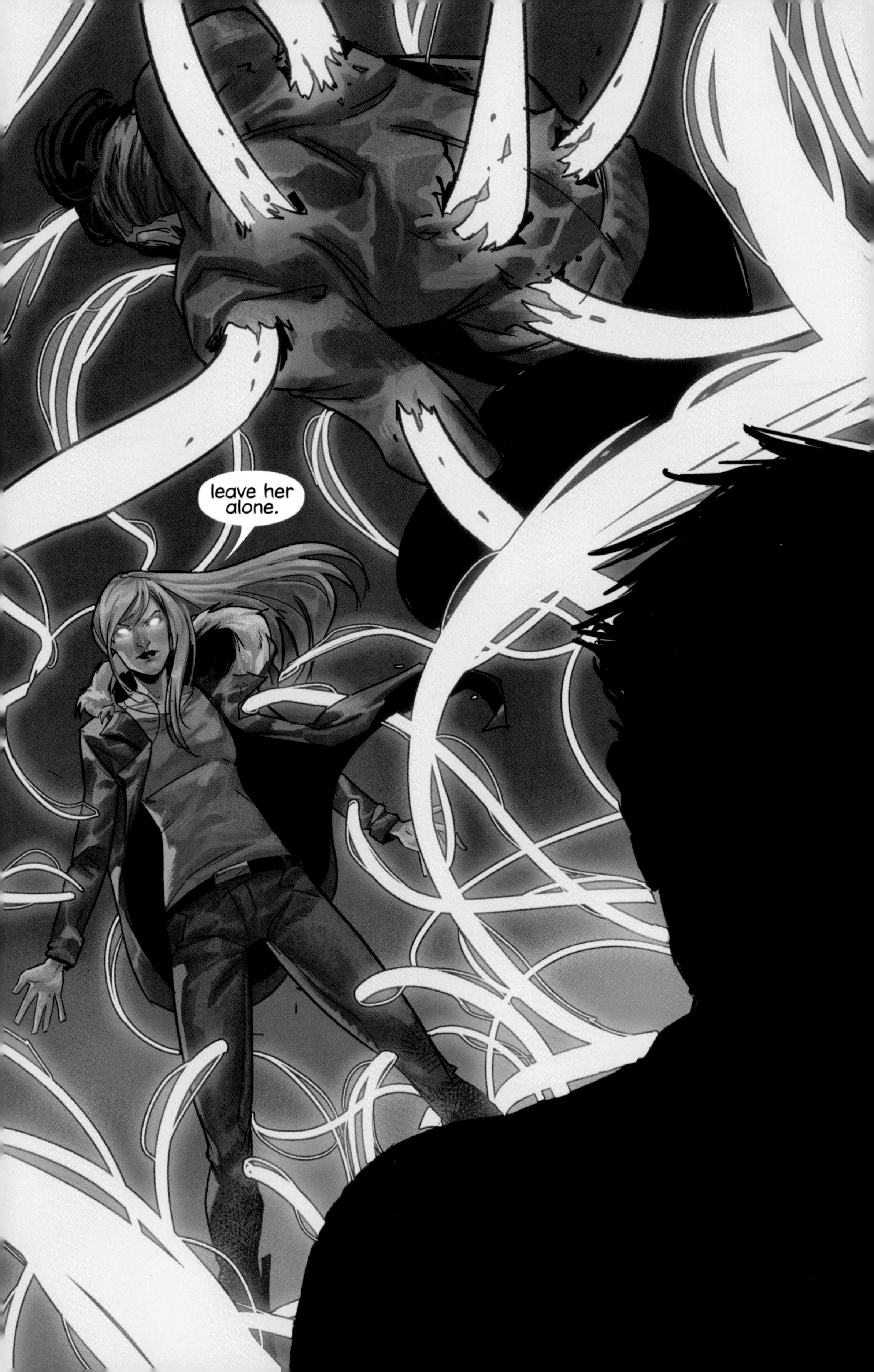
leave her alone.

CHAPTER TWO

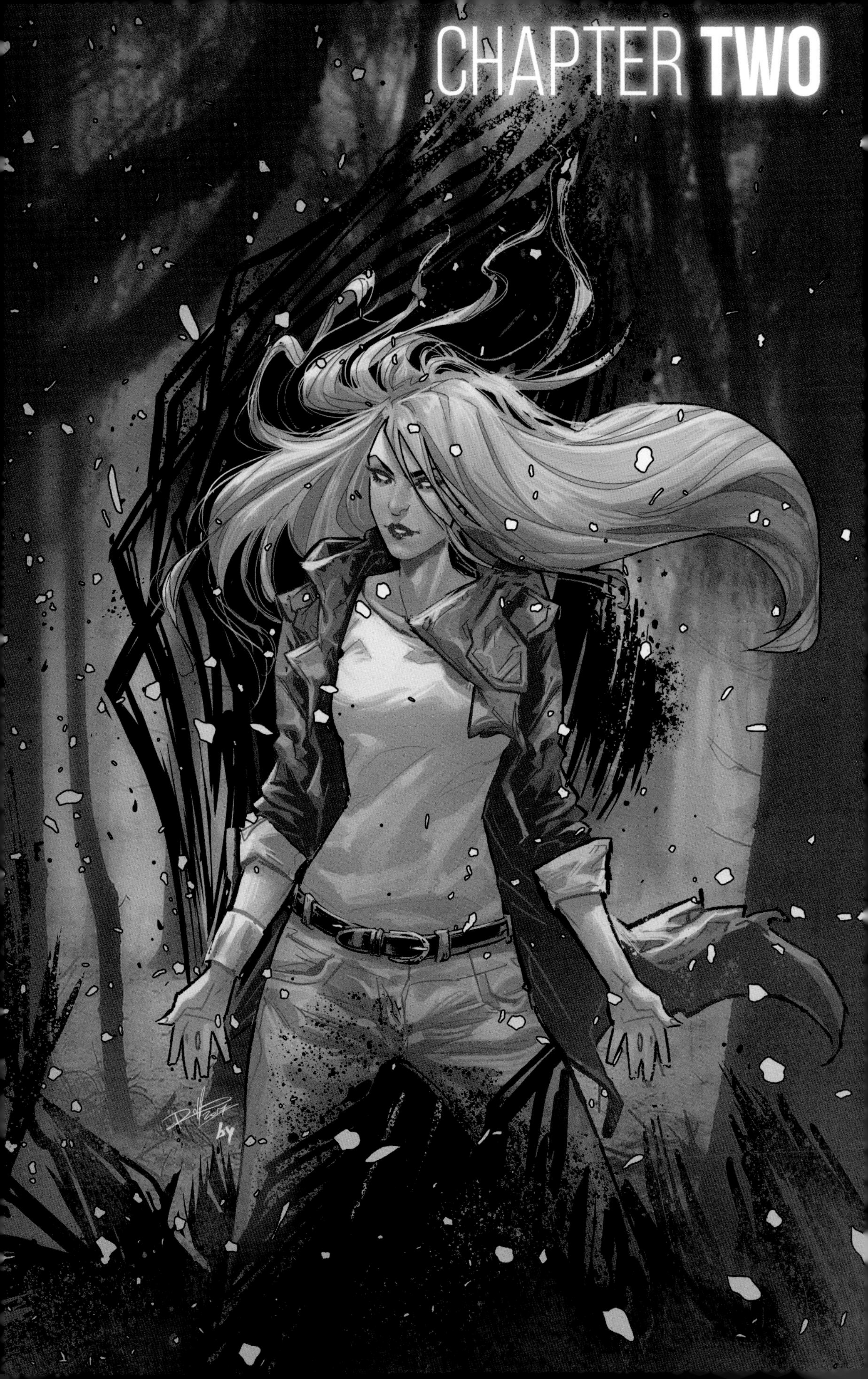

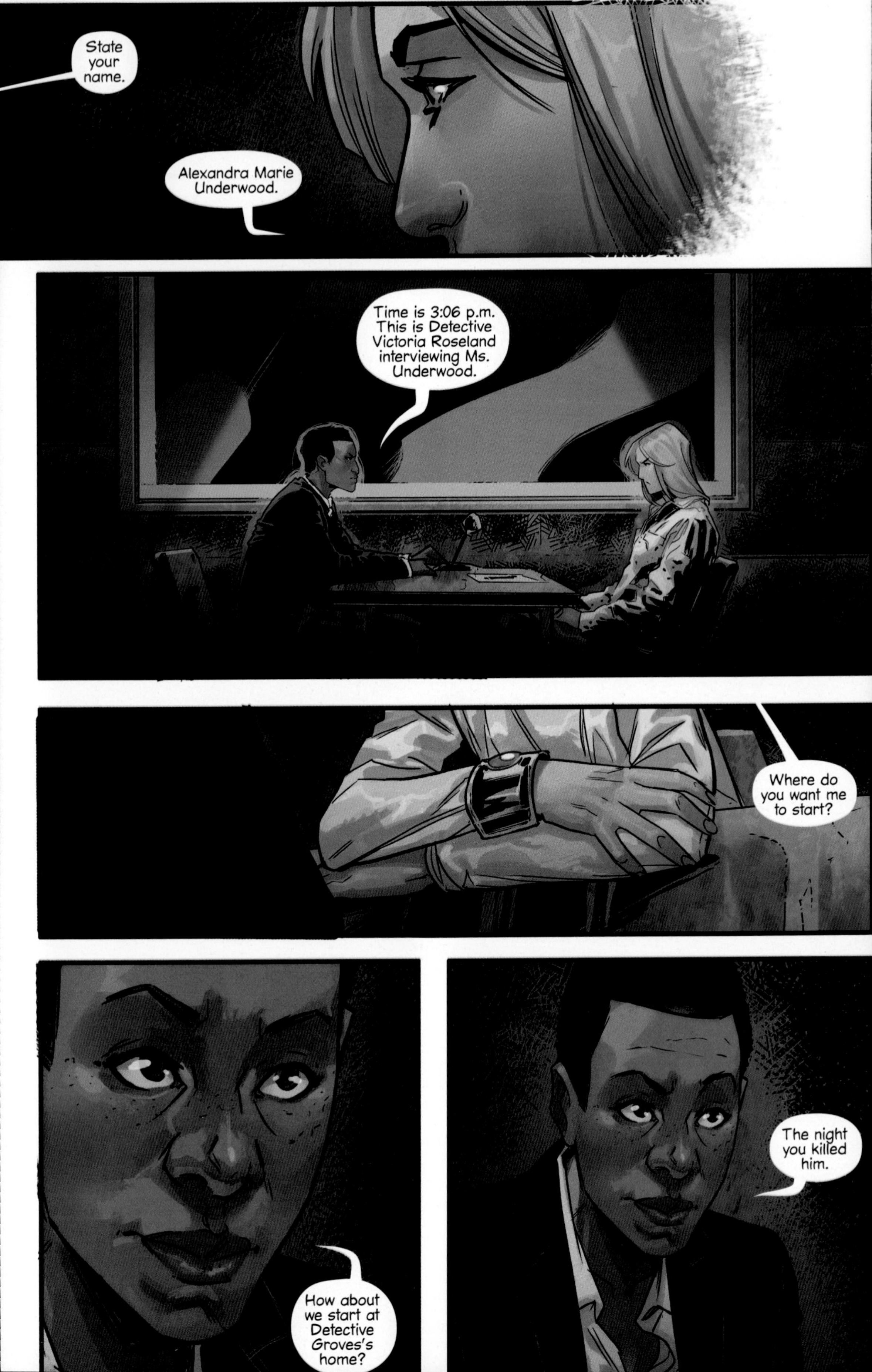
State your name.
Alexandra Marie Underwood.
Time is 3:06 p.m. This is Detective Victoria Roseland interviewing Ms. Underwood.
Where do you want me to start?
How about we start at Detective Groves's home?
The night you killed him.

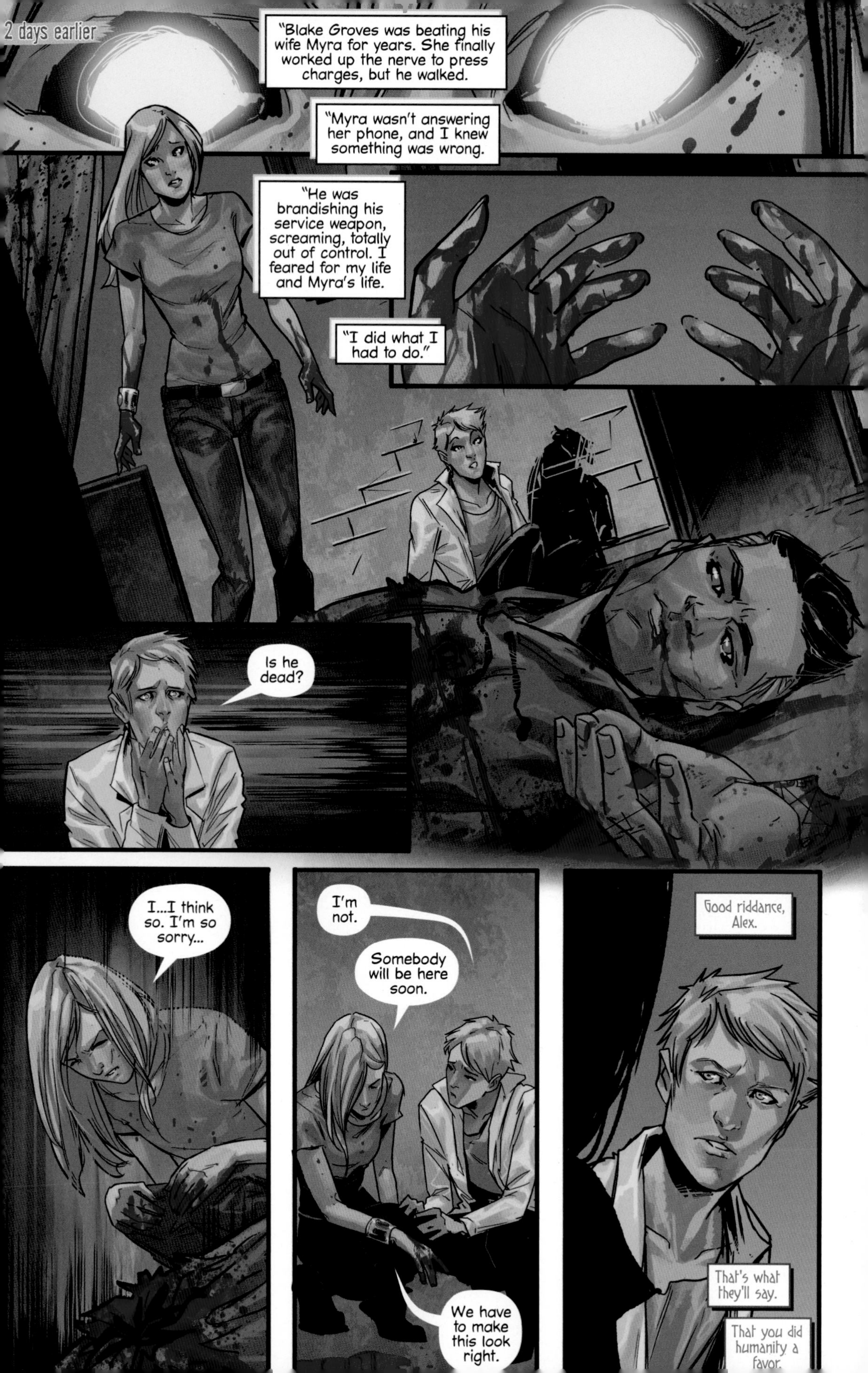
2 days earlier
"Blake Groves was beating his wife Myra for years. She finally worked up the nerve to press charges, but he walked.
"Myra wasn't answering her phone, and I knew something was wrong.
"He was brandishing his service weapon, screaming, totally out of control. I feared for my life and Myra's life.
"I did what I had to do."
Is he dead?
I...I think so. I'm so sorry...
I'm not.
Somebody will be here soon.
We have to make this look right.
Good riddance, Alex.
That's what they'll say.
That you did humanity a favor.

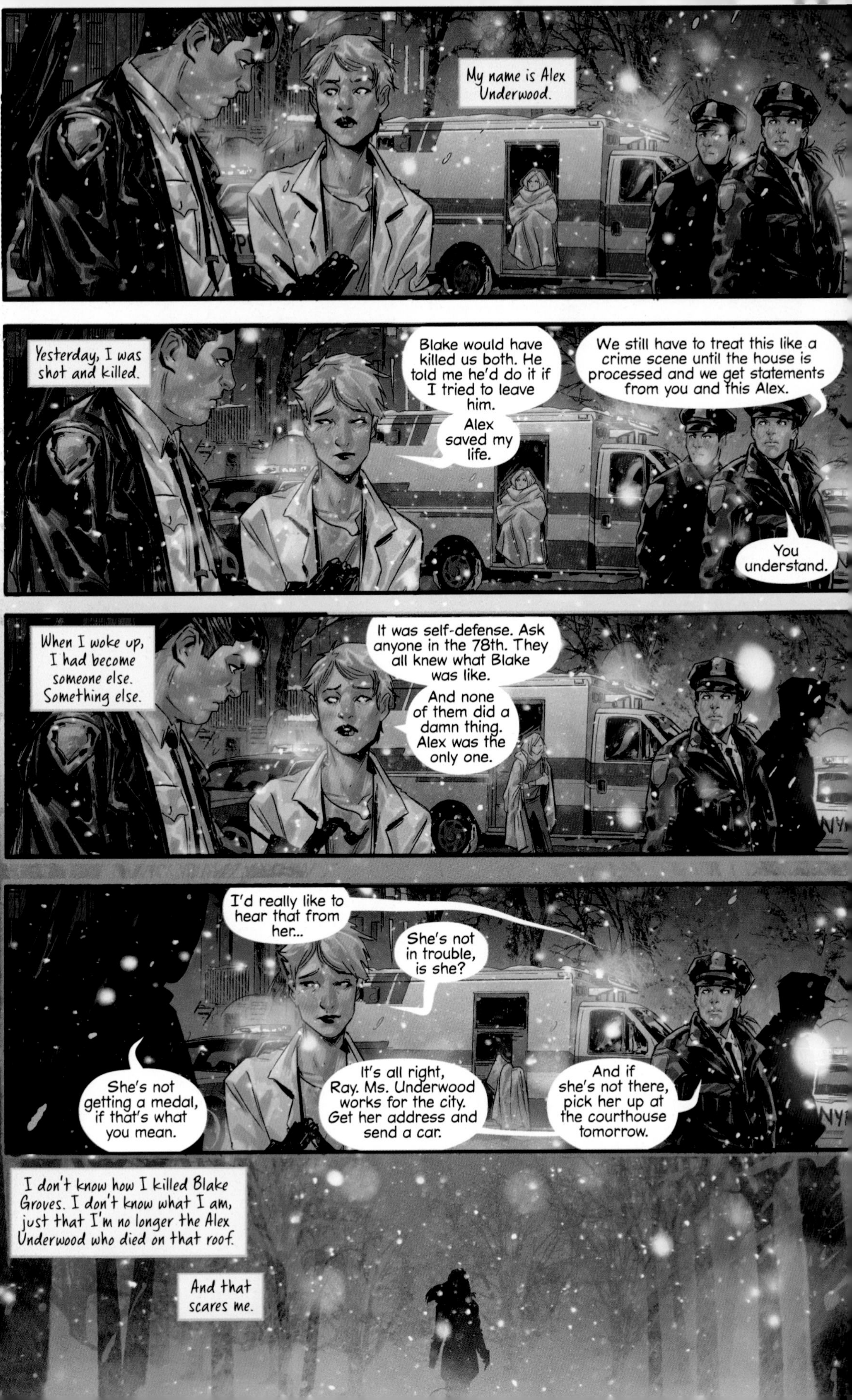
My name is Alex Underwood.
Yesterday, I was shot and killed.
Blake would have killed us both. He told me he'd do it if I tried to leave him.
Alex saved my life.
We still have to treat this like a crime scene until the house is processed and we get statements from you and this Alex.
You understand.
When I woke up, I had become someone else. Something else.
It was self-defense. Ask anyone in the 78th. They all knew what Blake was like.
And none of them did a damn thing. Alex was the only one.
I'd really like to hear that from her...
She's not in trouble, is she?
She's not getting a medal, if that's what you mean.
It's all right, Ray. Ms. Underwood works for the city. Get her address and send a car.
And if she's not there, pick her up at the courthouse tomorrow.
I don't know how I killed Blake Groves. I don't know what I am, just that I'm no longer the Alex Underwood who died on that roof.
And that scares me.

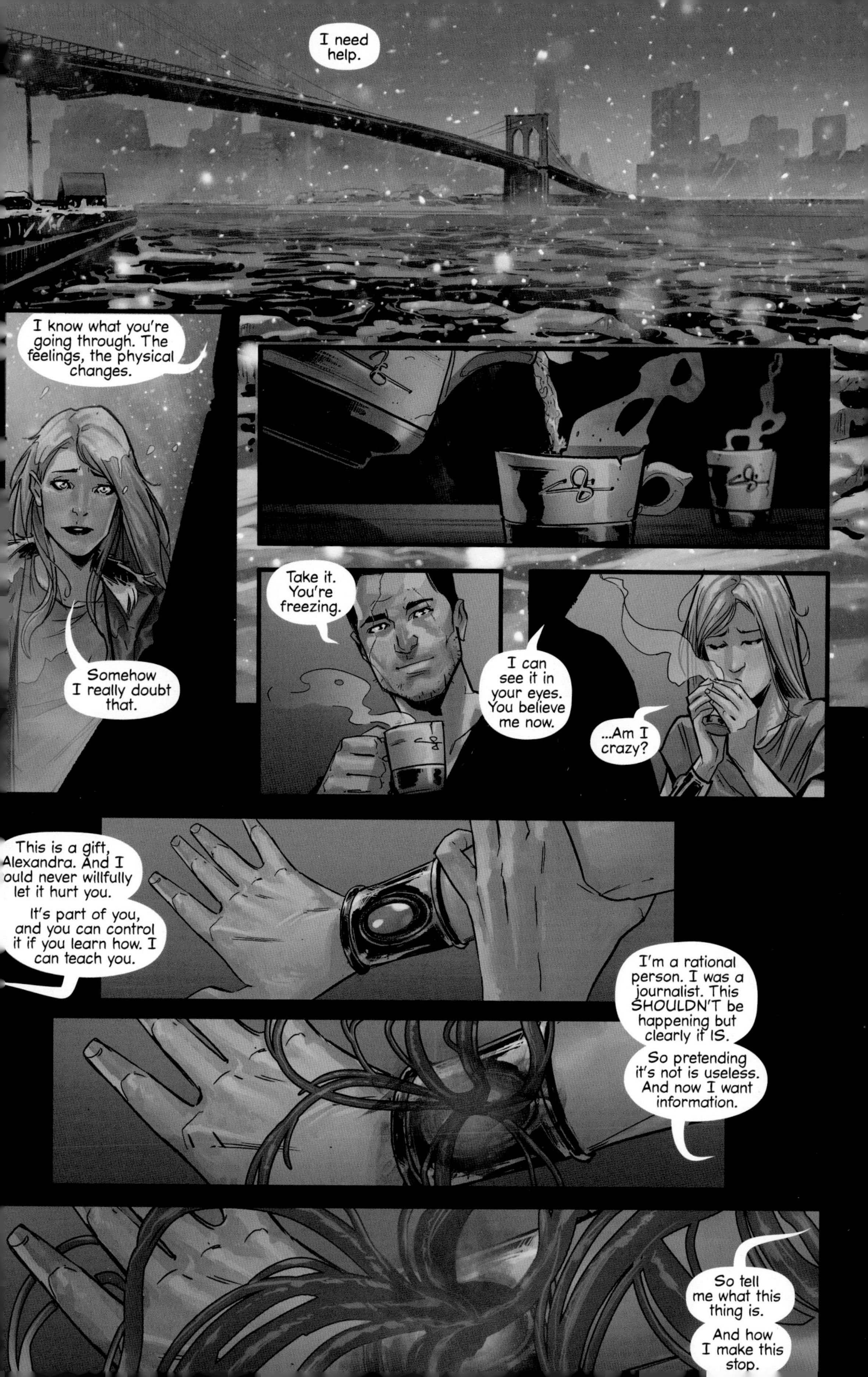

I need help.
I know what you're going through. The feelings, the physical changes.
Somehow I really doubt that.
Take it. You're freezing.
I can see it in your eyes. You believe me now.
...Am I crazy?
This is a gift, Alexandra. And I ould never willfully let it hurt you.
It's part of you, and you can control it if you learn how. I can teach you.
I'm a rational person. I was a journalist. This SHOULDN'T be happening but clearly it IS.
So pretending it's not is useless. And now I want information.
So tell me what this thing is.
And how I make this stop.

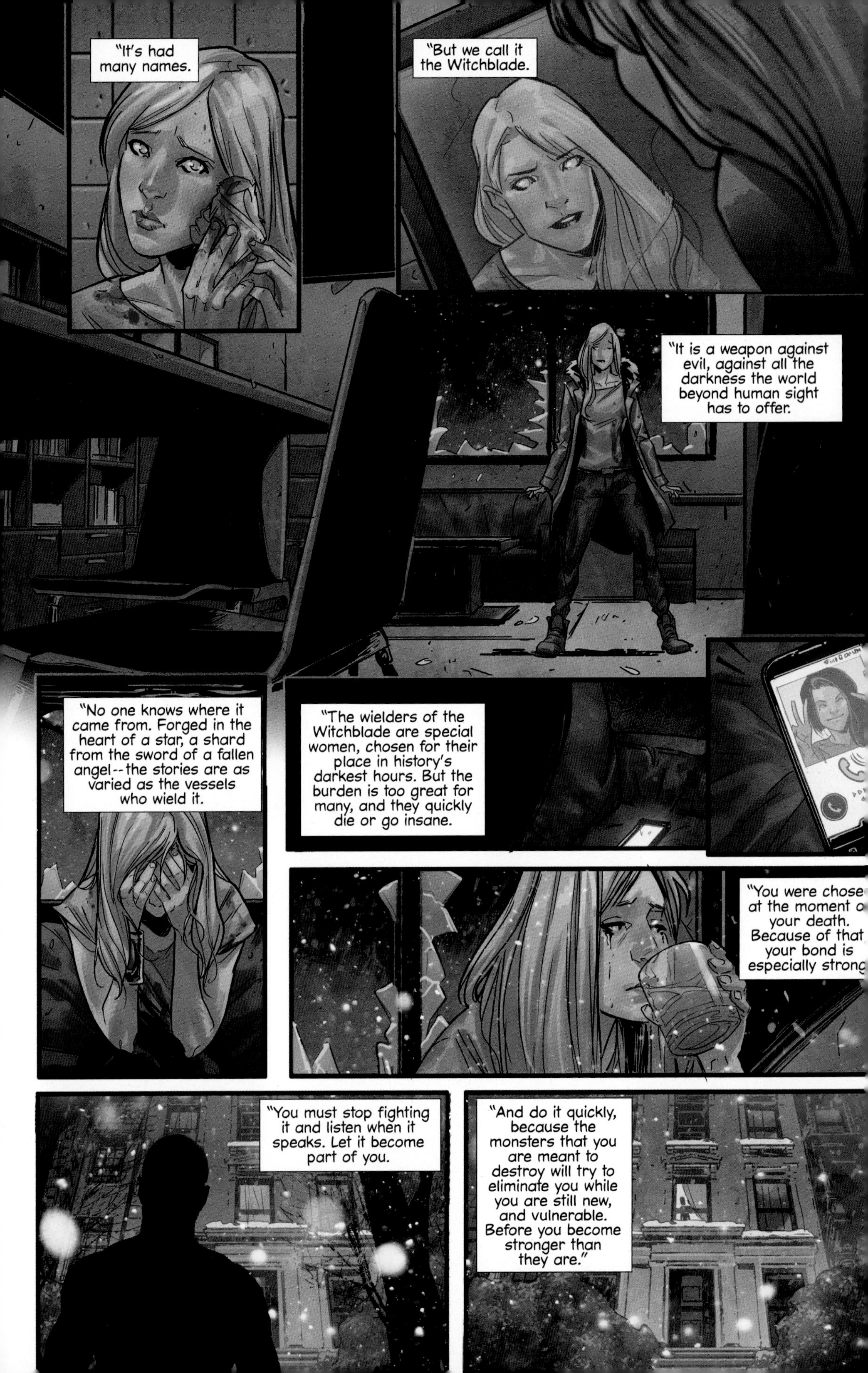
"It's had many names.
"But we call it the Witchblade.
"It is a weapon against evil, against all the darkness the world beyond human sight has to offer.
"No one knows where it came from. Forged in the heart of a star, a shard from the sword of a fallen angel--the stories are as varied as the vessels who wield it.
"The wielders of the Witchblade are special women, chosen for their place in history's darkest hours. But the burden is too great for many, and they quickly die or go insane.
"You were chose at the moment o your death. Because of that your bond is especially stronc
"You must stop fighting it and listen when it speaks. Let it become part of you.
"And do it quickly, because the monsters that you are meant to destroy will try to eliminate you while you are still new, and vulnerable. Before you become stronger than they are."

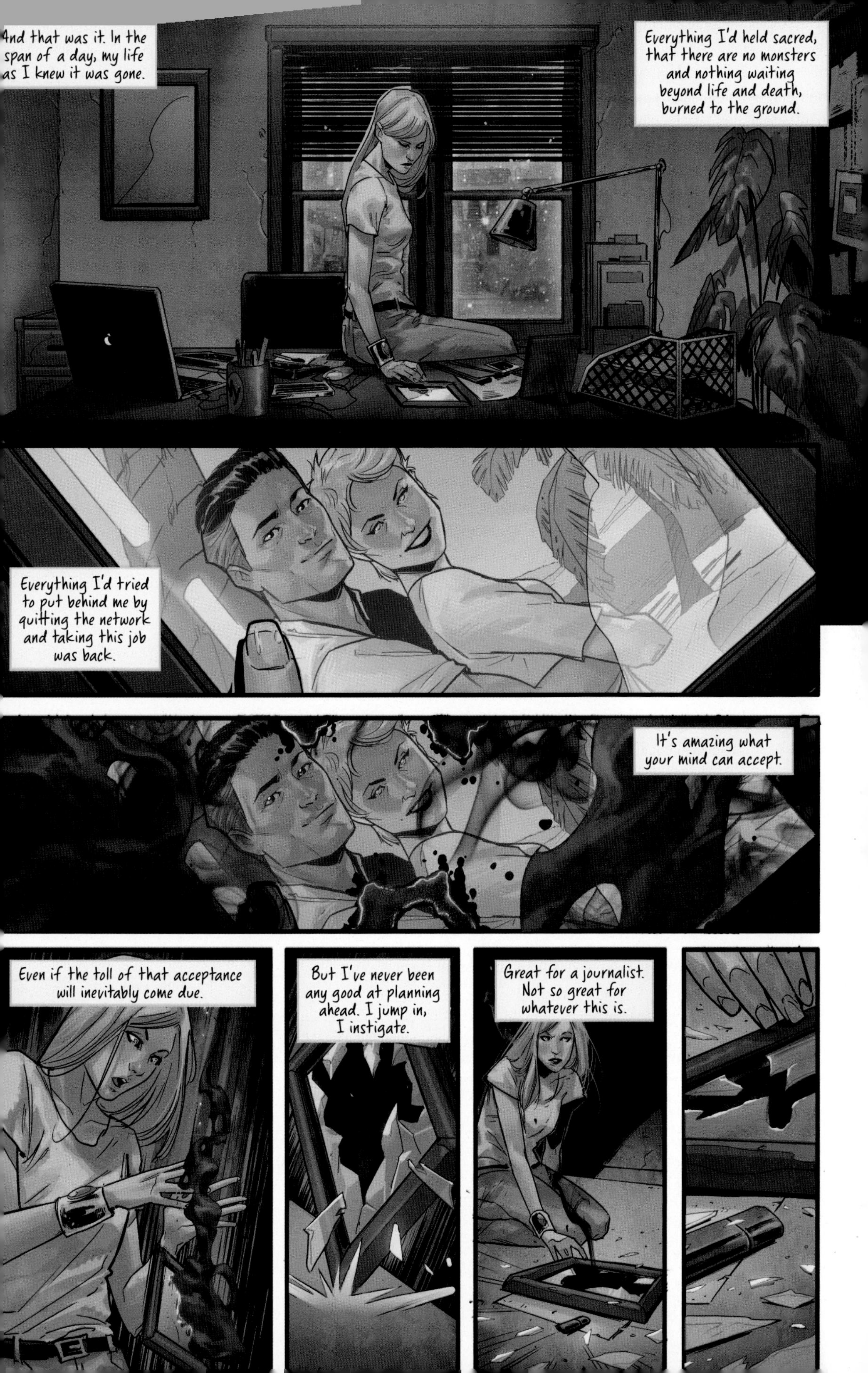
And that was it. In the span of a day, my life as I knew it was gone.
Everything I'd held sacred, that there are no monsters and nothing waiting beyond life and death, burned to the ground.
Everything I'd tried to put behind me by quitting the network and taking this job was back.
It's amazing what your mind can accept.
Even if the toll of that acceptance will inevitably come due.
But I've never been any good at planning ahead. I jump in, I instigate.
Great for a journalist. Not so great for whatever this is.

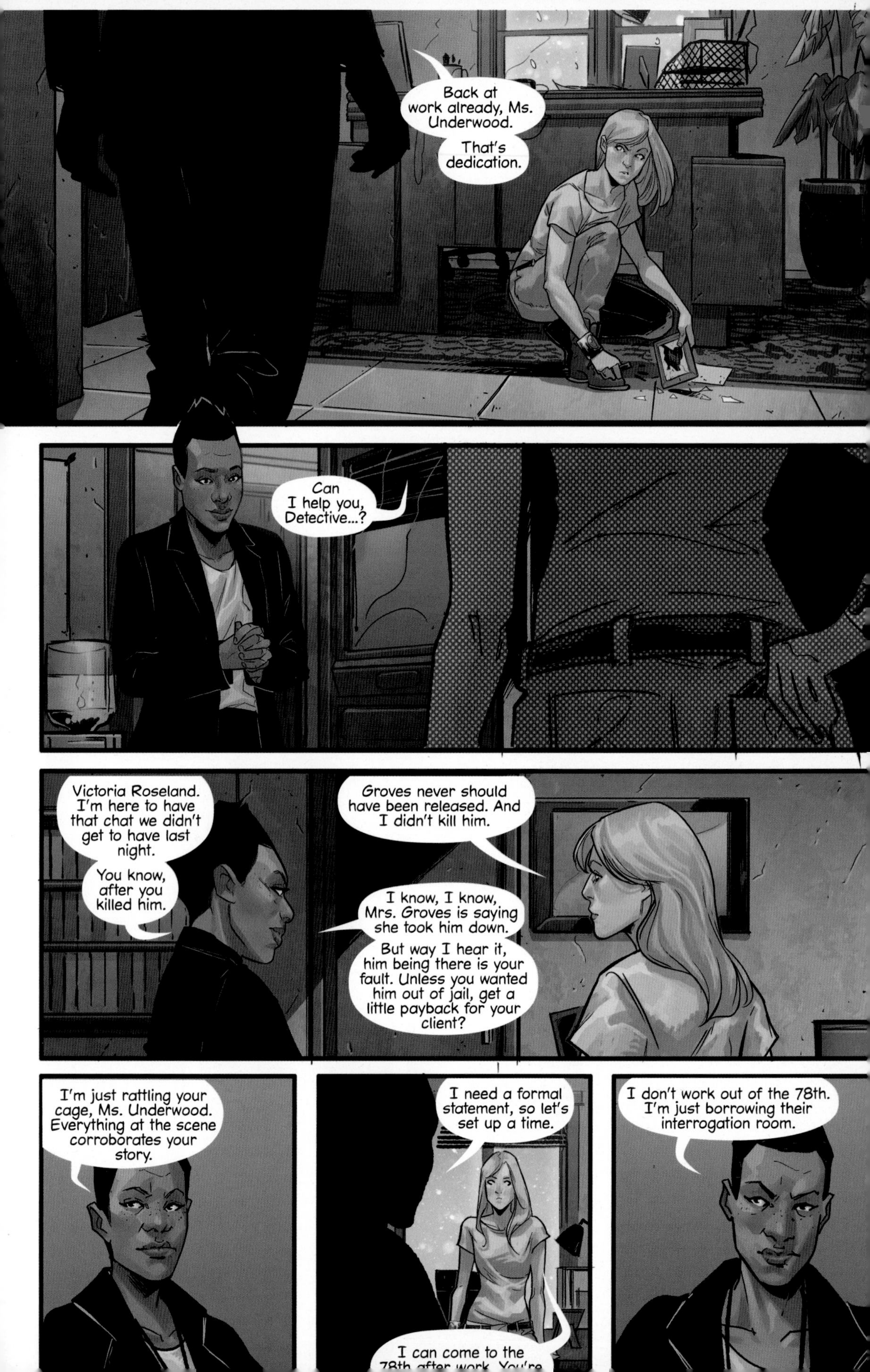
Back at work already, Ms. Underwood.
That's dedication.
Can I help you, Detective...?
Victoria Roseland. I'm here to have that chat we didn't get to have last night.
You know, after you killed him.
Groves never should have been released. And I didn't kill him.
I know, I know, Mrs. Groves is saying she took him down.
But way I hear it, him being there is your fault. Unless you wanted him out of jail, get a little payback for your client?
I'm just rattling your cage, Ms. Underwood. Everything at the scene corroborates your story.
I need a formal statement, so let's set up a time.
I can come to the
I don't work out of the 78th. I'm just borrowing their interrogation room.

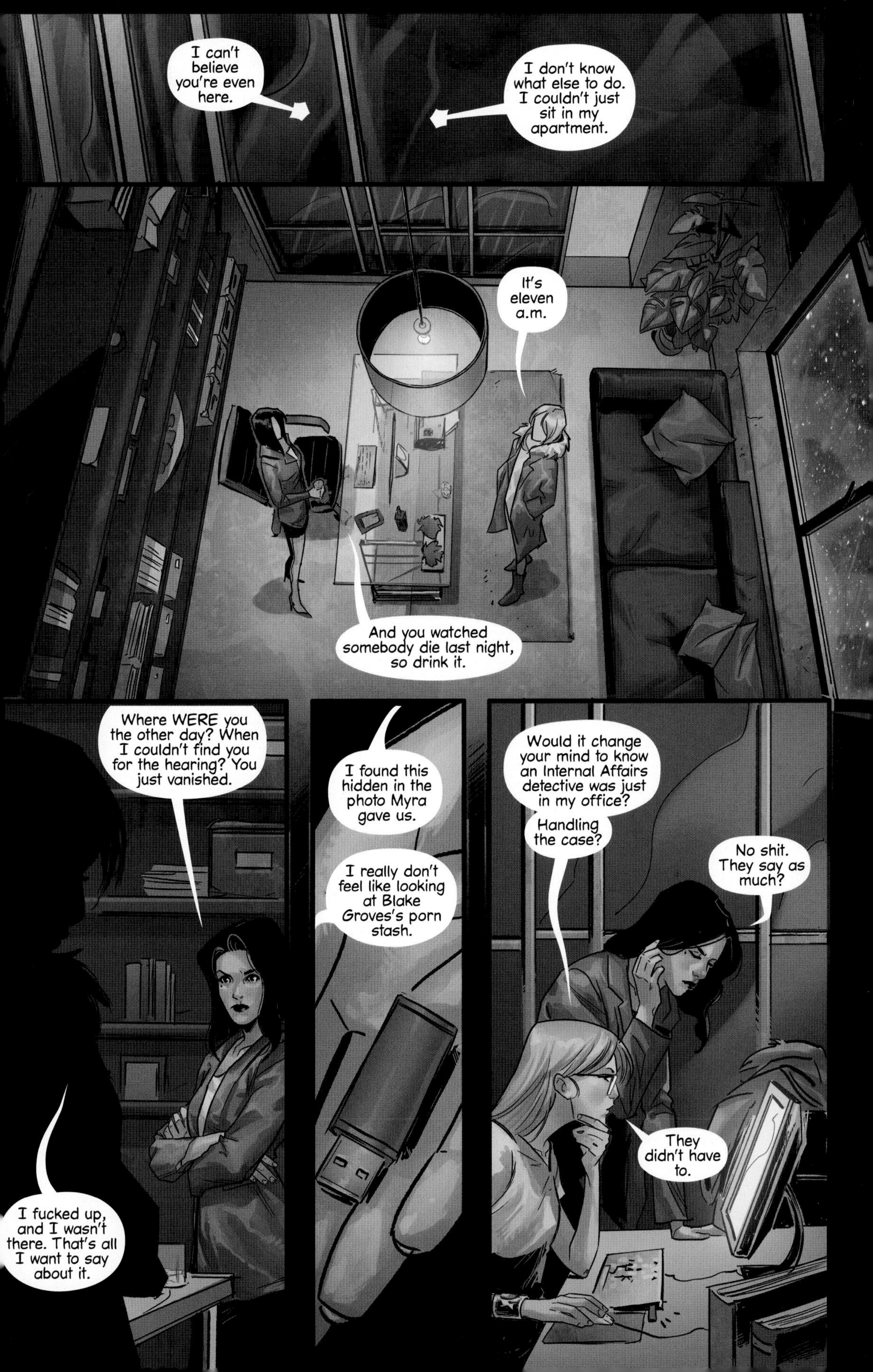
I can't believe you're even here.
I don't know what else to do. I couldn't just sit in my apartment.
It's eleven a.m.
And you watched somebody die last night, so drink it.
Where WERE you the other day? When I couldn't find you for the hearing? You just vanished.
I fucked up, and I wasn't there. That's all I want to say about it.
I found this hidden in the photo Myra gave us.
I really don't feel like looking at Blake Groves's porn stash.
Would it change your mind to know an Internal Affairs detective was just in my office?
Handling the case?
No shit. They say as much?
They didn't have to.

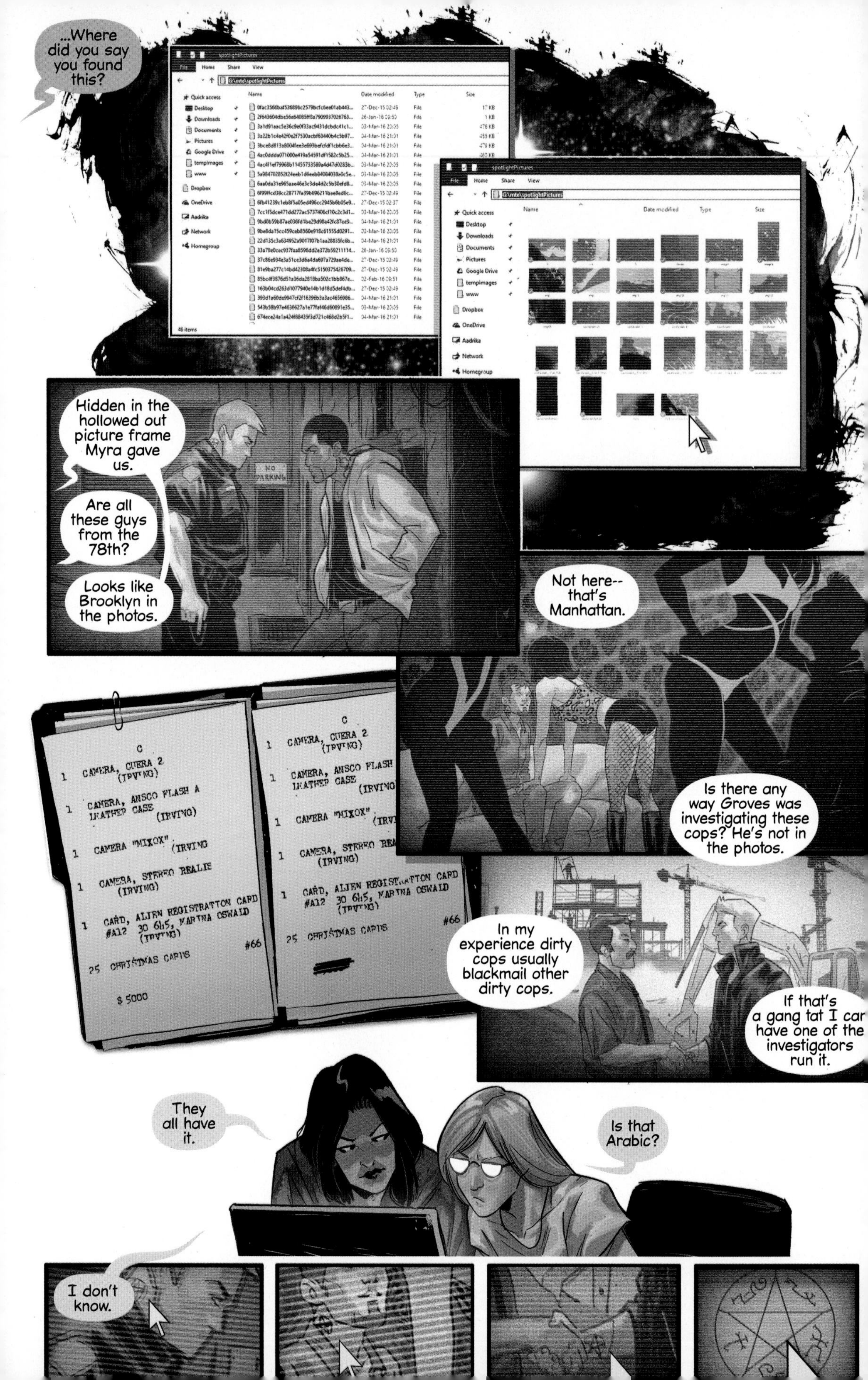
...Where did you say you found this?
spotlightPictures
Hidden in the hollowed out picture frame Myra gave us.
Are all these guys from the 78th?
Looks like Brooklyn in the photos.
NO PARKING
Not here--that's Manhattan.
C
1 CAMERA, CUERA 2 (IRVING)
1 CAMERA, ANSCO FLASH A LEATHER CASE (IRVING)
1 CAMERA "MIXOX" (IRVING
1 CAMERA, STEREO REALIE (IRVING)
1 CARD, ALIEN REGISTRATION CARD #A12 30 645, MARINA OSWALD (IRVING)
#66
25 CHRISTMAS CARDS
$ 5000
Is there any way Groves was investigating these cops? He's not in the photos.
In my experience dirty cops usually blackmail other dirty cops.
If that's a gang tat I can have one of the investigators run it.
They all have it.
Is that Arabic?
I don't know.

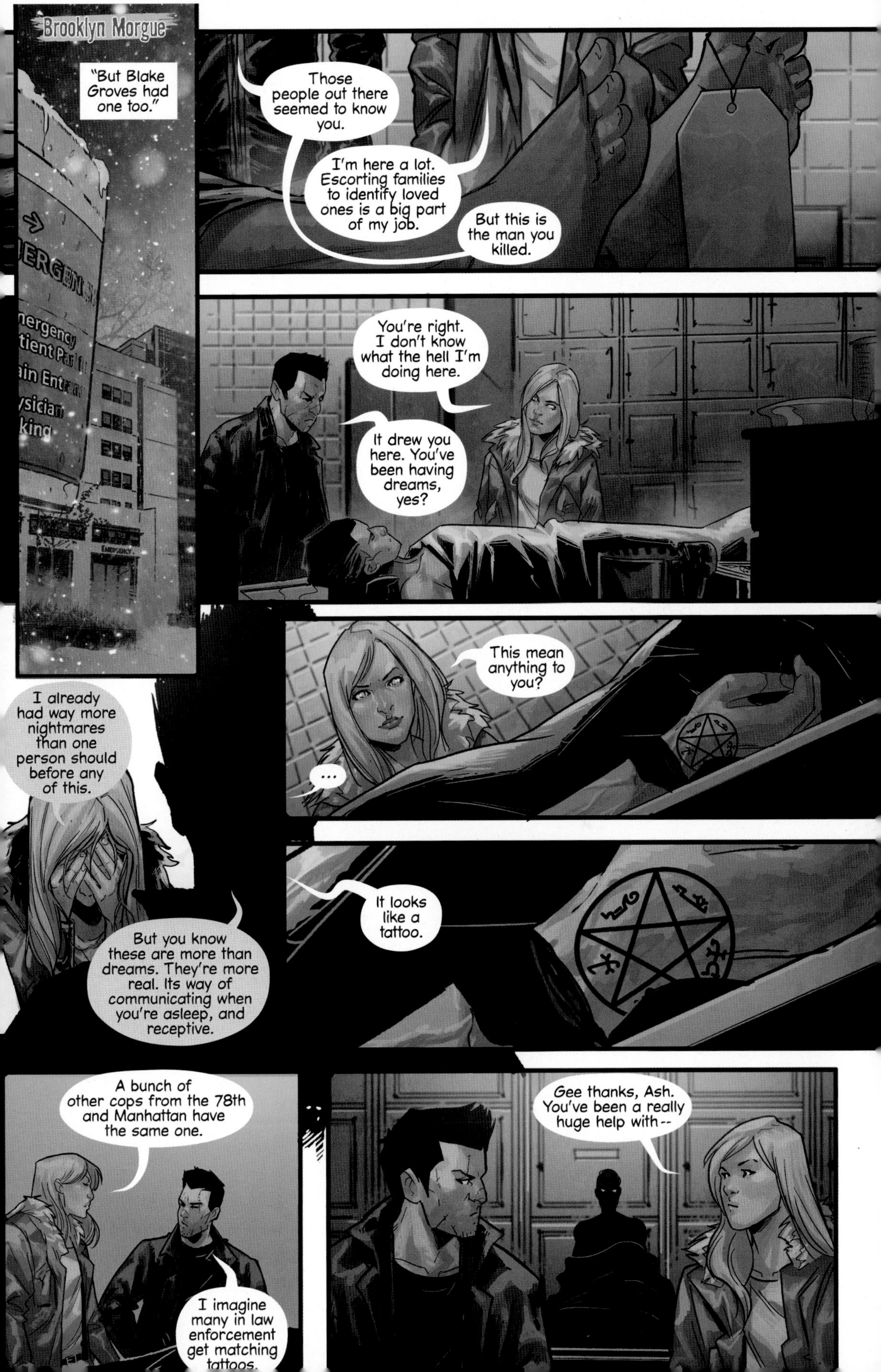
Brooklyn Morgue
"But Blake Groves had one too."
Those people out there seemed to know you.
I'm here a lot. Escorting families to identify loved ones is a big part of my job.
But this is the man you killed.
You're right. I don't know what the hell I'm doing here.
It drew you here. You've been having dreams, yes?
This mean anything to you?
...
I already had way more nightmares than one person should before any of this.
It looks like a tattoo.
But you know these are more than dreams. They're more real. Its way of communicating when you're asleep, and receptive.
A bunch of other cops from the 78th and Manhattan have the same one.
I imagine many in law enforcement get matching tattoos.
Gee thanks, Ash. You've been a really huge help with--

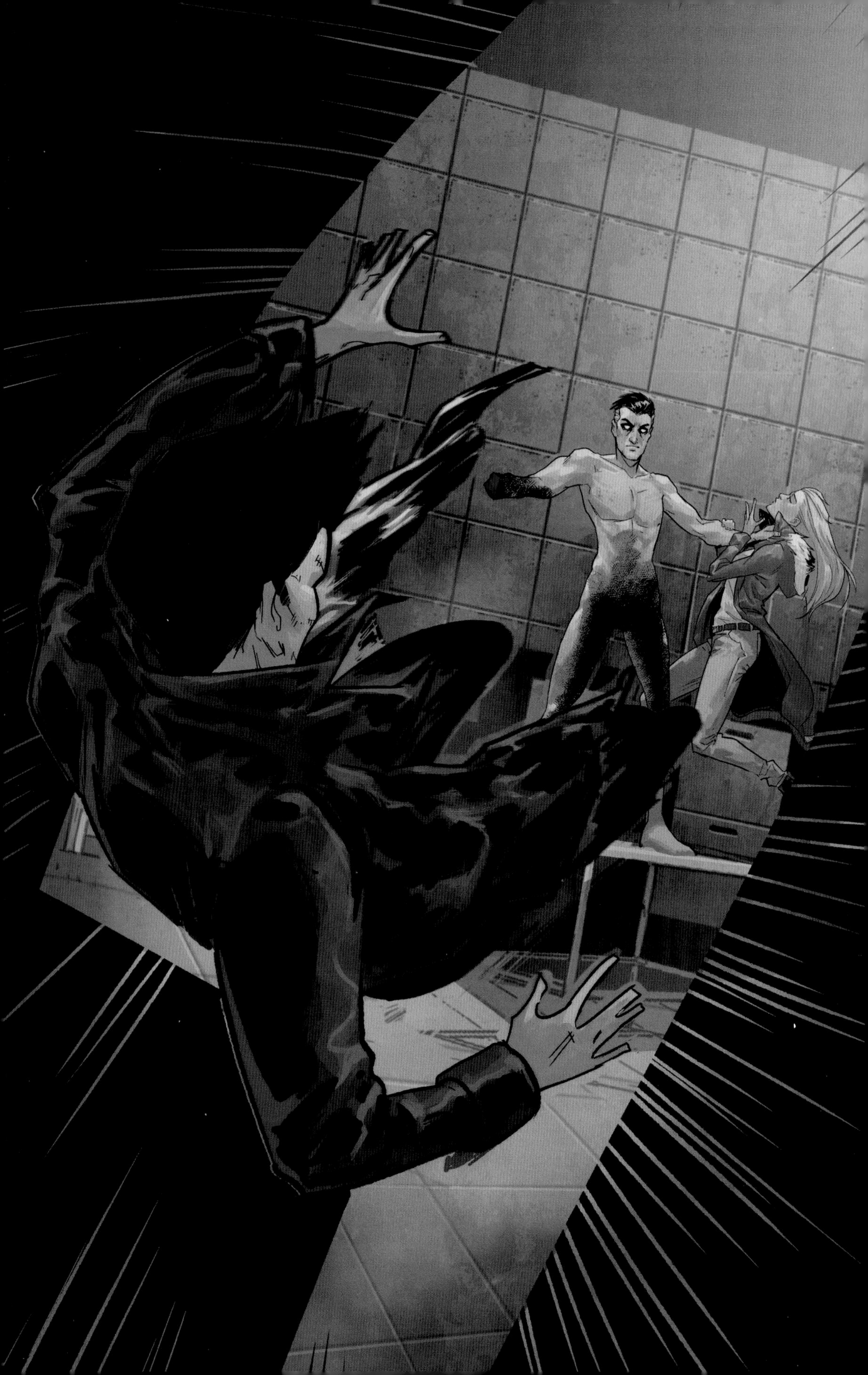

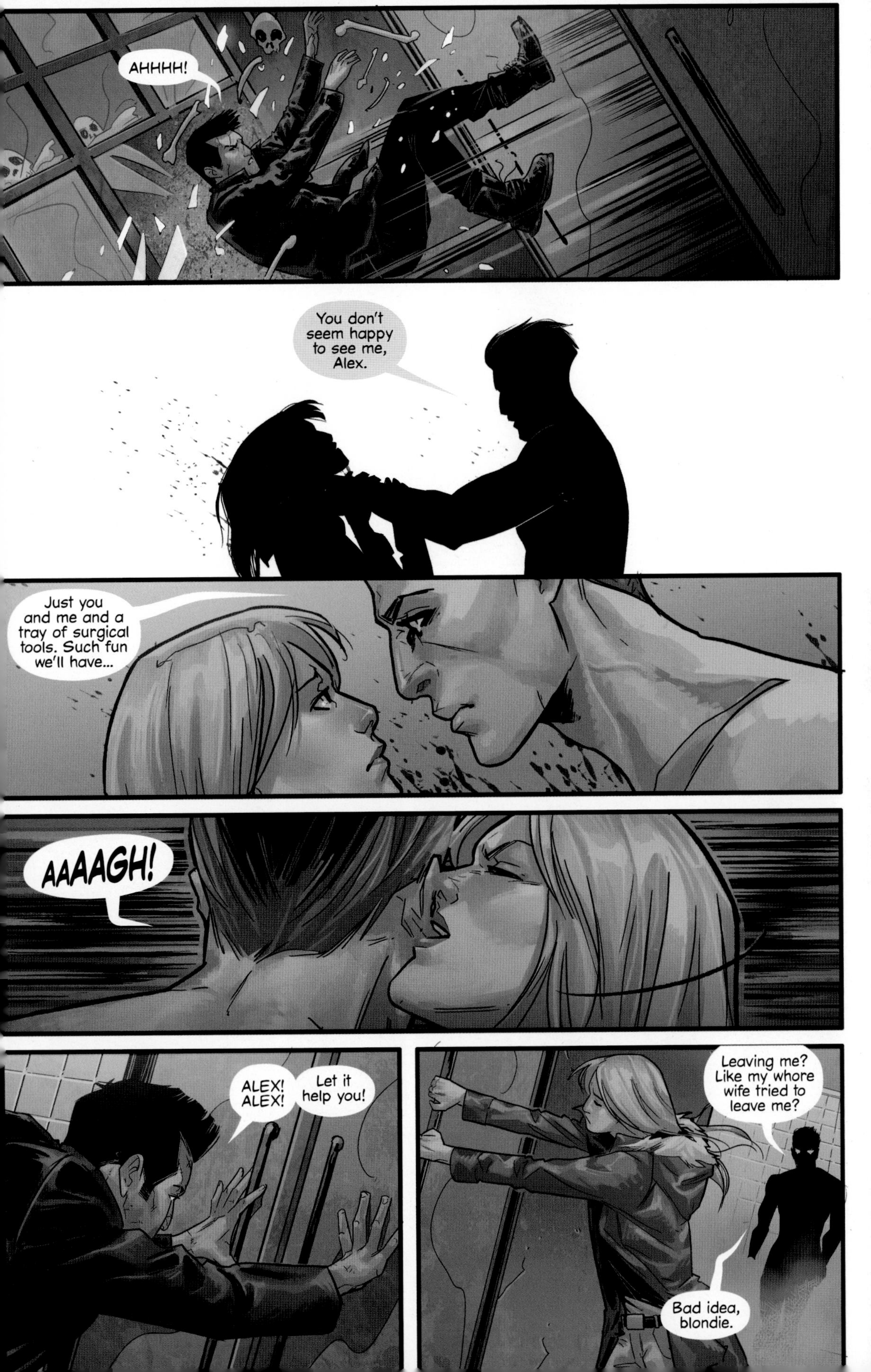
AHHHH!
You don't seem happy to see me, Alex.
Just you and me and a tray of surgical tools. Such fun we'll have...
AAAAGH!
ALEX! ALEX!
Let it help you!
Leaving me? Like my whore wife tried to leave me?
Bad idea, blondie.

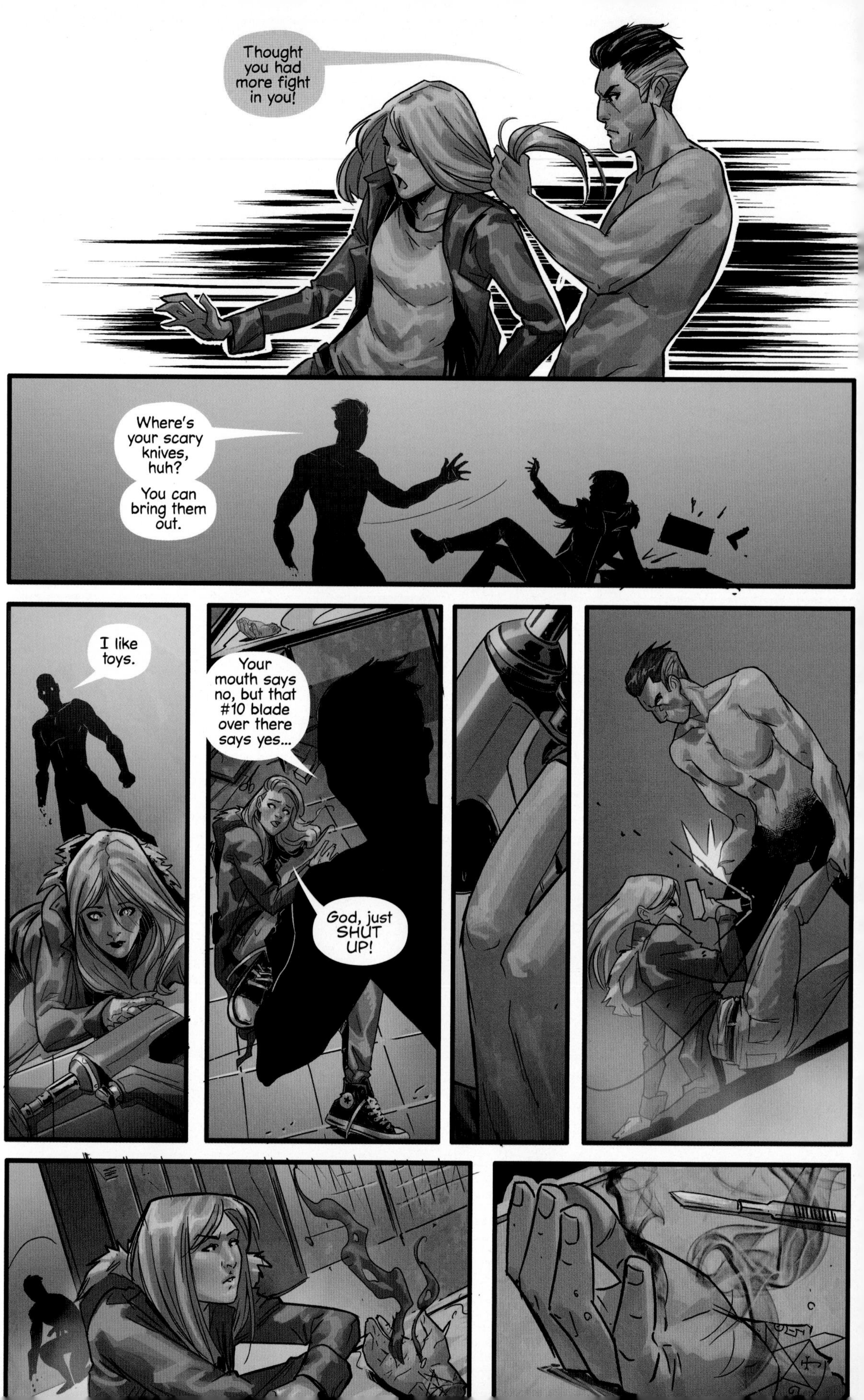
Thought you had more fight in you!
Where's your scary knives, huh?
You can bring them out.
I like toys.
Your mouth says no, but that #10 blade over there says yes...
God, just SHUT UP!

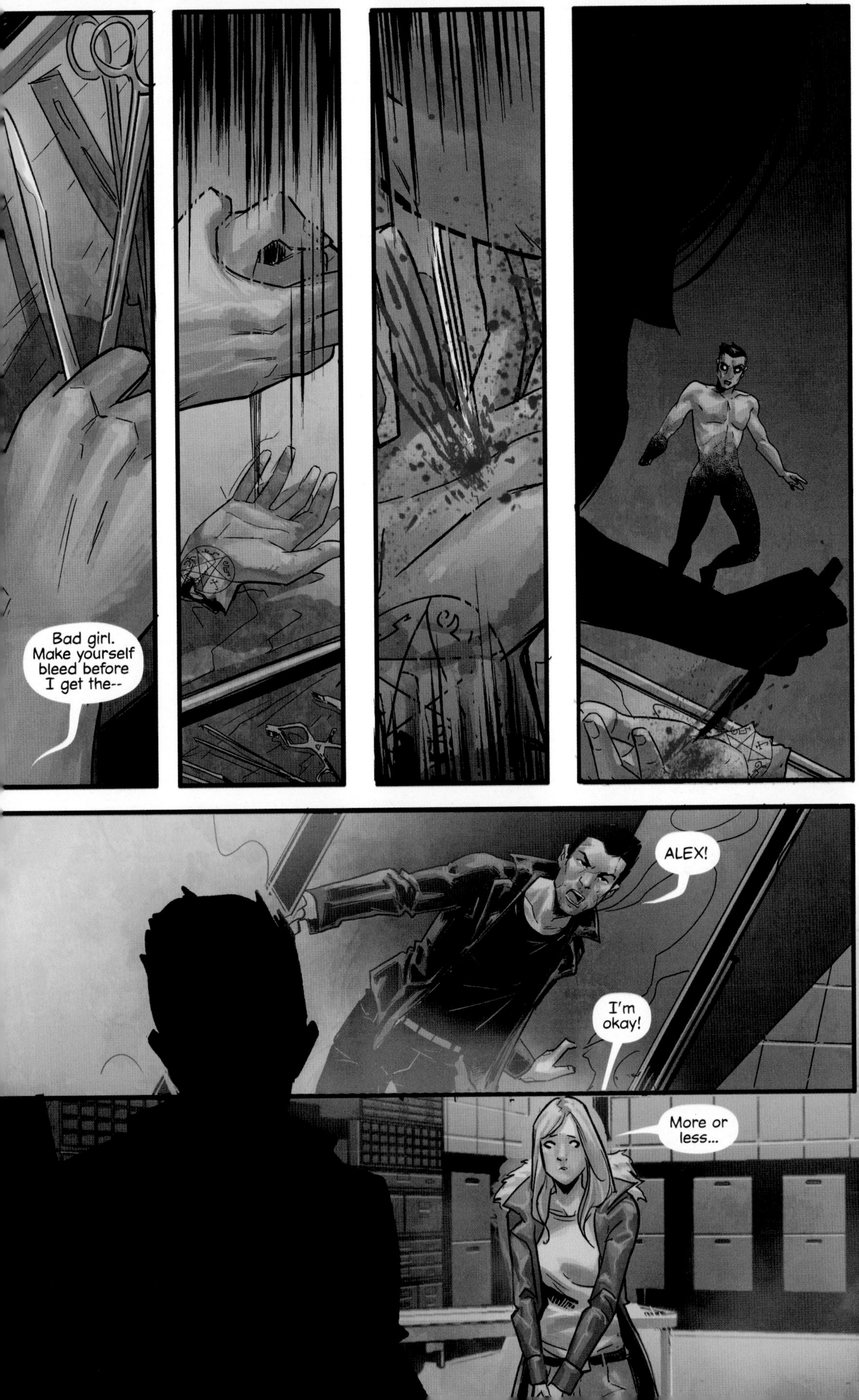
Bad girl. Make yourself bleed before I get the--
ALEX!
I'm okay!
More or less...

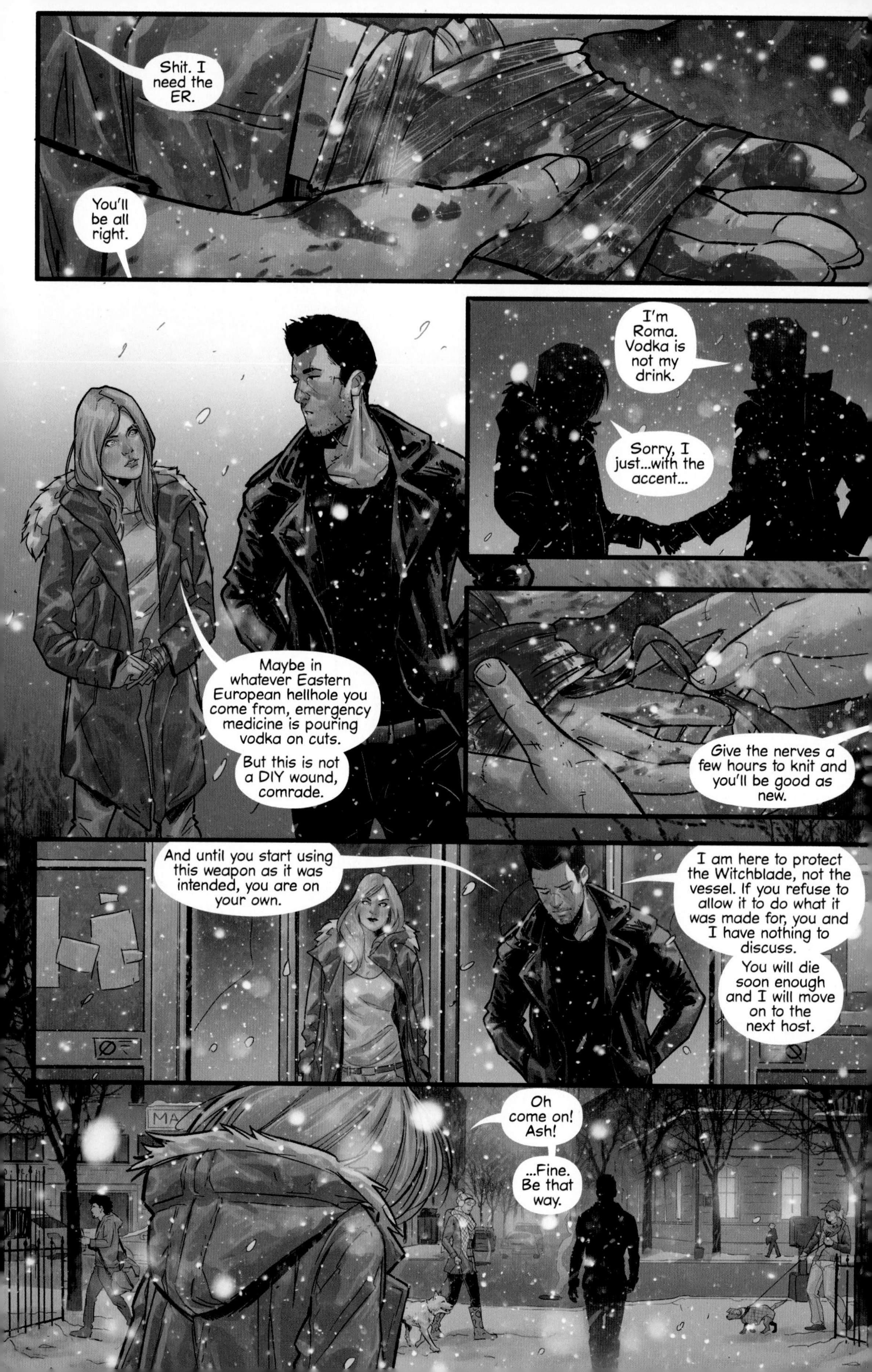
Shit. I need the ER.
You'll be all right.
Maybe in whatever Eastern European hellhole you come from, emergency medicine is pouring vodka on cuts.
But this is not a DIY wound, comrade.
I'm Roma. Vodka is not my drink.
Sorry, I just...with the accent...
Give the nerves a few hours to knit and you'll be good as new.
And until you start using this weapon as it was intended, you are on your own.
I am here to protect the Witchblade, not the vessel. If you refuse to allow it to do what it was made for, you and I have nothing to discuss.
You will die soon enough and I will move on to the next host.
Oh come on! Ash!
...Fine. Be that way.

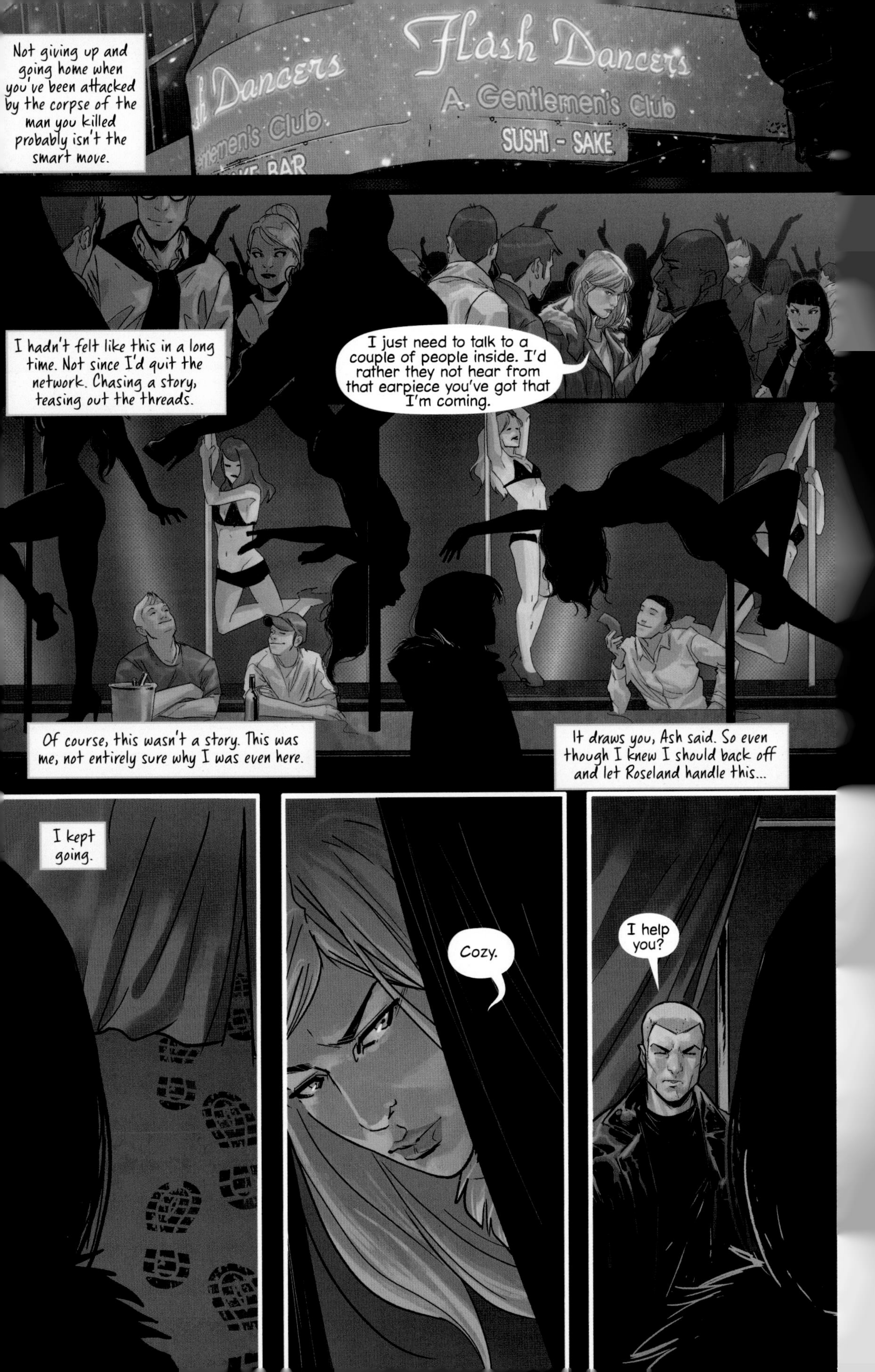
Not giving up and going home when you've been attacked by the corpse of the man you killed probably isn't the smart move.
Flash Dancers
A Gentlemen's Club
SUSHI - SAKE
I hadn't felt like this in a long time. Not since I'd quit the network. Chasing a story, teasing out the threads.
I just need to talk to a couple of people inside. I'd rather they not hear from that earpiece you've got that I'm coming.
Of course, this wasn't a story. This was me, not entirely sure why I was even here.
It draws you, Ash said. So even though I knew I should back off and let Roseland handle this...
I kept going.
Cozy.
I help you?

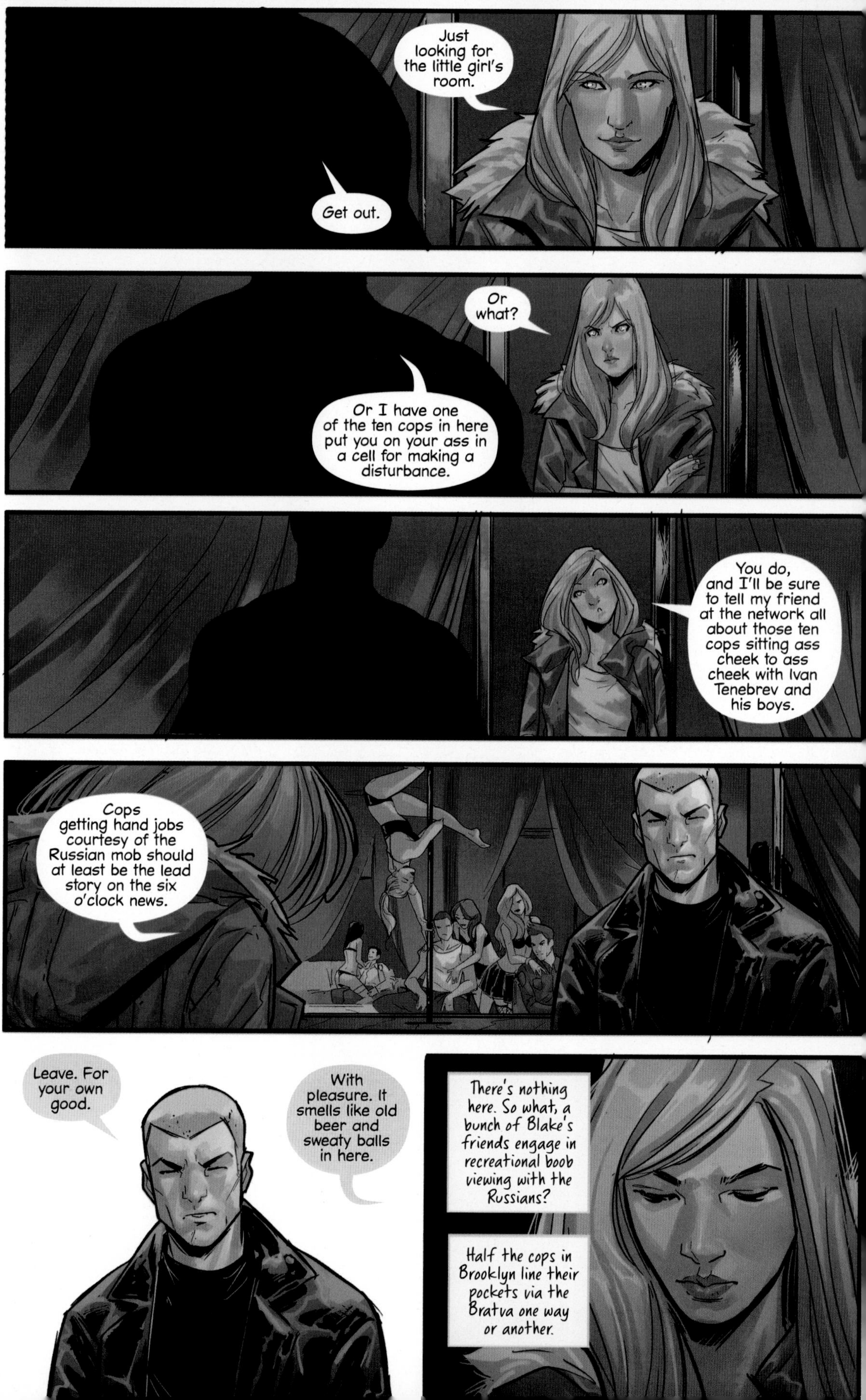
Just looking for the little girl's room.
Get out.
Or what?
Or I have one of the ten cops in here put you on your ass in a cell for making a disturbance.
You do, and I'll be sure to tell my friend at the network all about those ten cops sitting ass cheek to ass cheek with Ivan Tenebrev and his boys.
Cops getting hand jobs courtesy of the Russian mob should at least be the lead story on the six o'clock news.
Leave. For your own good.
With pleasure. It smells like old beer and sweaty balls in here.
There's nothing here. So what, a bunch of Blake's friends engage in recreational boob viewing with the Russians?
Half the cops in Brooklyn line their pockets via the Bratva one way or another.

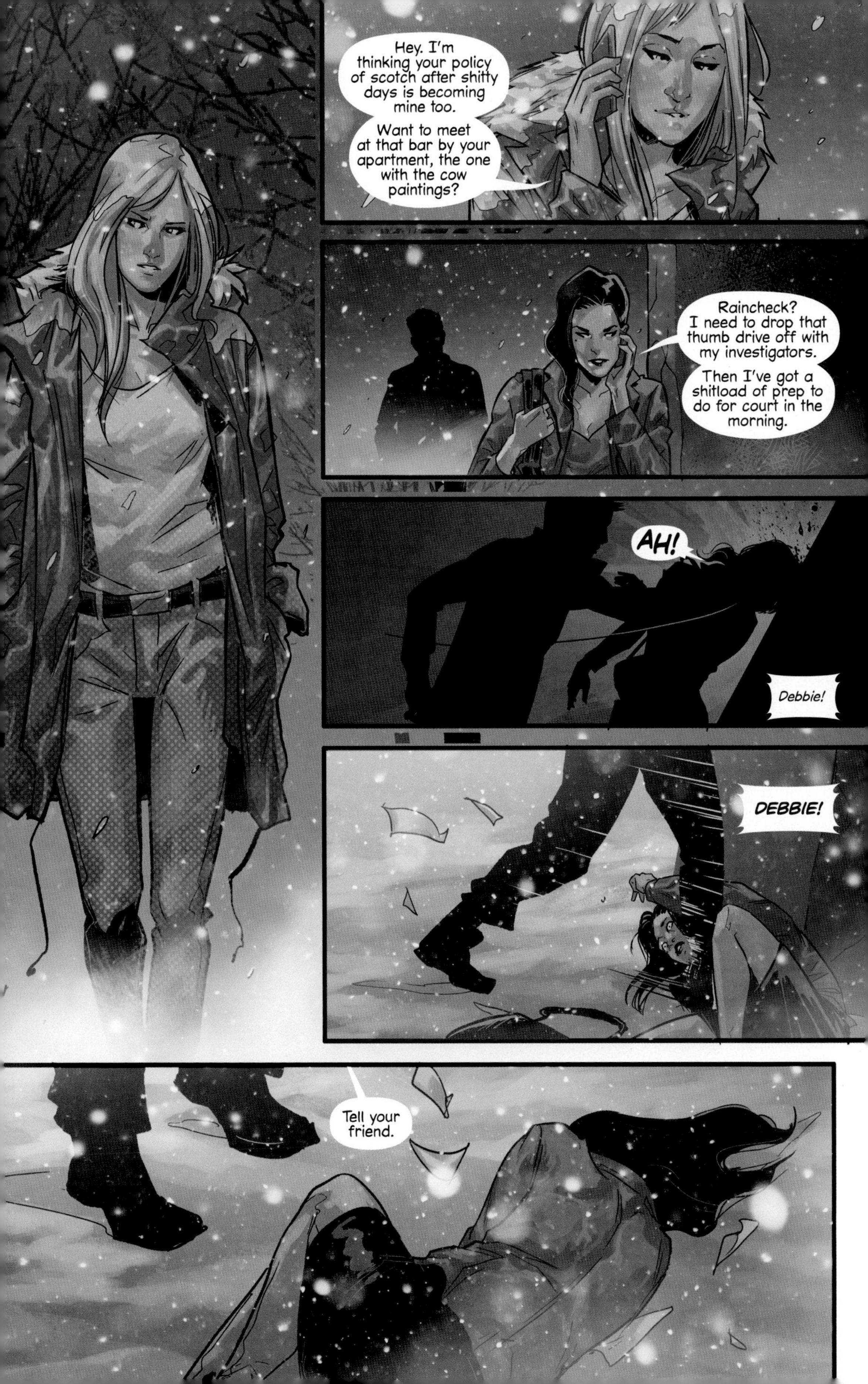
Hey. I'm thinking your policy of scotch after shitty days is becoming mine too.
Want to meet at that bar by your apartment, the one with the cow paintings?
Raincheck? I need to drop that thumb drive off with my investigators.
Then I've got a shitload of prep to do for court in the morning.
AH!
Debbie!
DEBBIE!
Tell your friend.

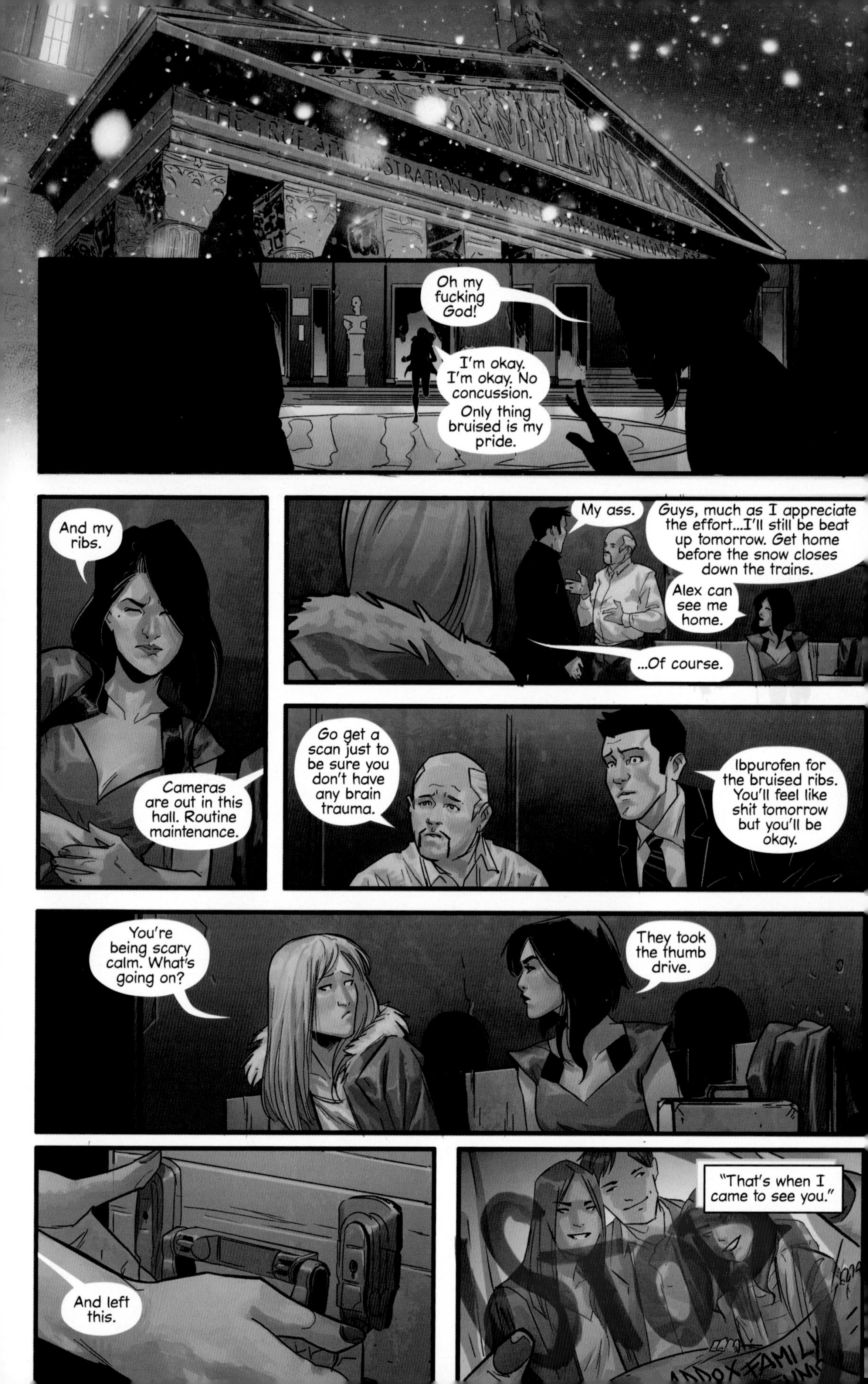
Oh my fucking God!
I'm okay. I'm okay. No concussion.
Only thing bruised is my pride.
And my ribs.
My ass.
Guys, much as I appreciate the effort...I'll still be beat up tomorrow. Get home before the snow closes down the trains.
Alex can see me home.
...Of course.
Cameras are out in this hall. Routine maintenance.
Go get a scan just to be sure you don't have any brain trauma.
Ibpurofen for the bruised ribs. You'll feel like shit tomorrow but you'll be okay.
You're being scary calm. What's going on?
They took the thumb drive.
And left this.
"That's when I came to see you."

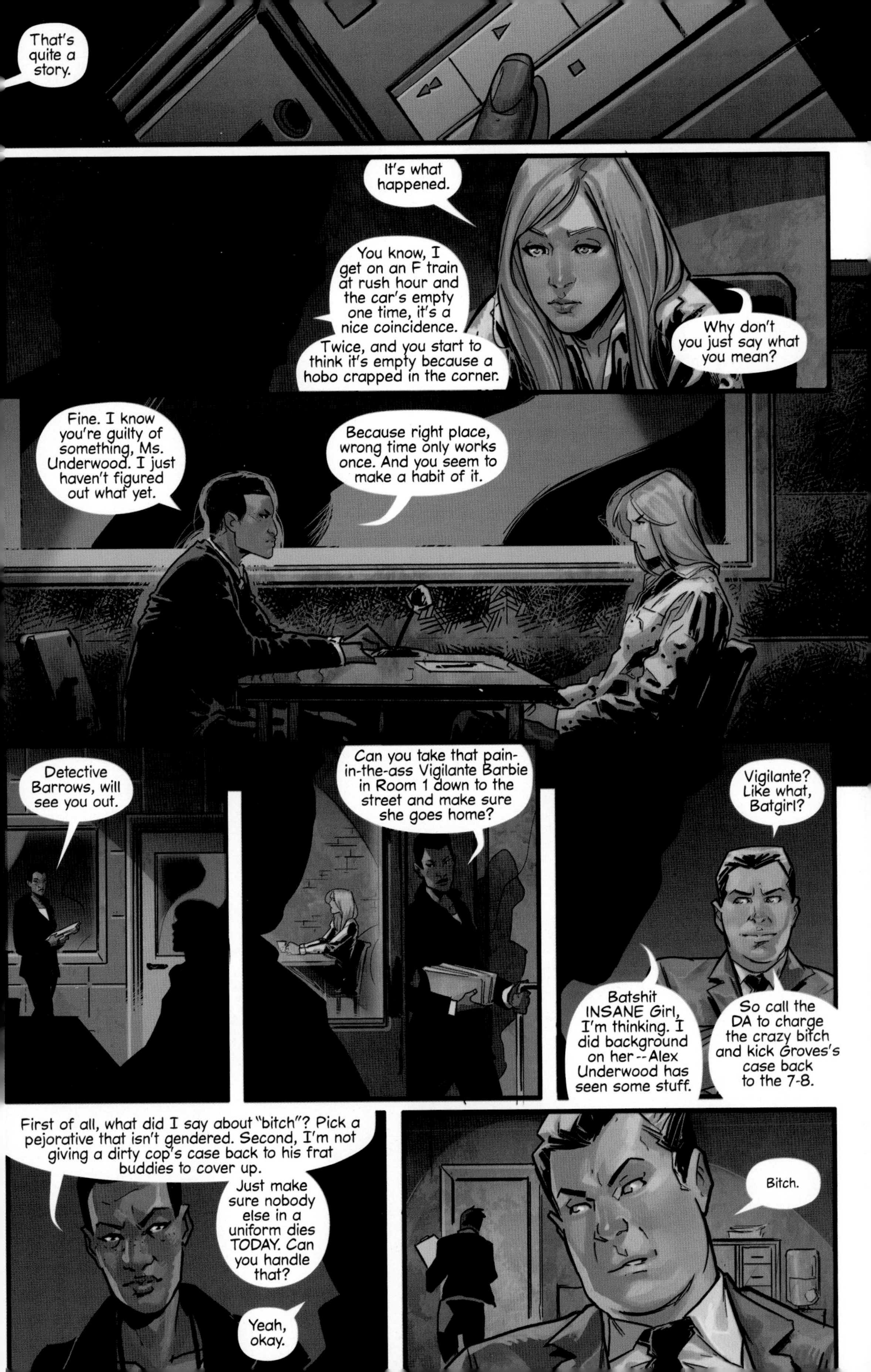
That's quite a story.
It's what happened.
You know, I get on an F train at rush hour and the car's empty one time, it's a nice coincidence.
Twice, and you start to think it's empty because a hobo crapped in the corner.
Why don't you just say what you mean?
Fine. I know you're guilty of something, Ms. Underwood. I just haven't figured out what yet.
Because right place, wrong time only works once. And you seem to make a habit of it.
Detective Barrows, will see you out.
Can you take that pain-in-the-ass Vigilante Barbie in Room 1 down to the street and make sure she goes home?
Vigilante? Like what, Batgirl?
Batshit INSANE Girl, I'm thinking. I did background on her--Alex Underwood has seen some stuff.
So call the DA to charge the crazy bitch and kick Groves's case back to the 7-8.
First of all, what did I say about "bitch"? Pick a pejorative that isn't gendered. Second, I'm not giving a dirty cop's case back to his frat buddies to cover up.
Just make sure nobody else in a uniform dies TODAY. Can you handle that?
Yeah, okay.
Bitch.

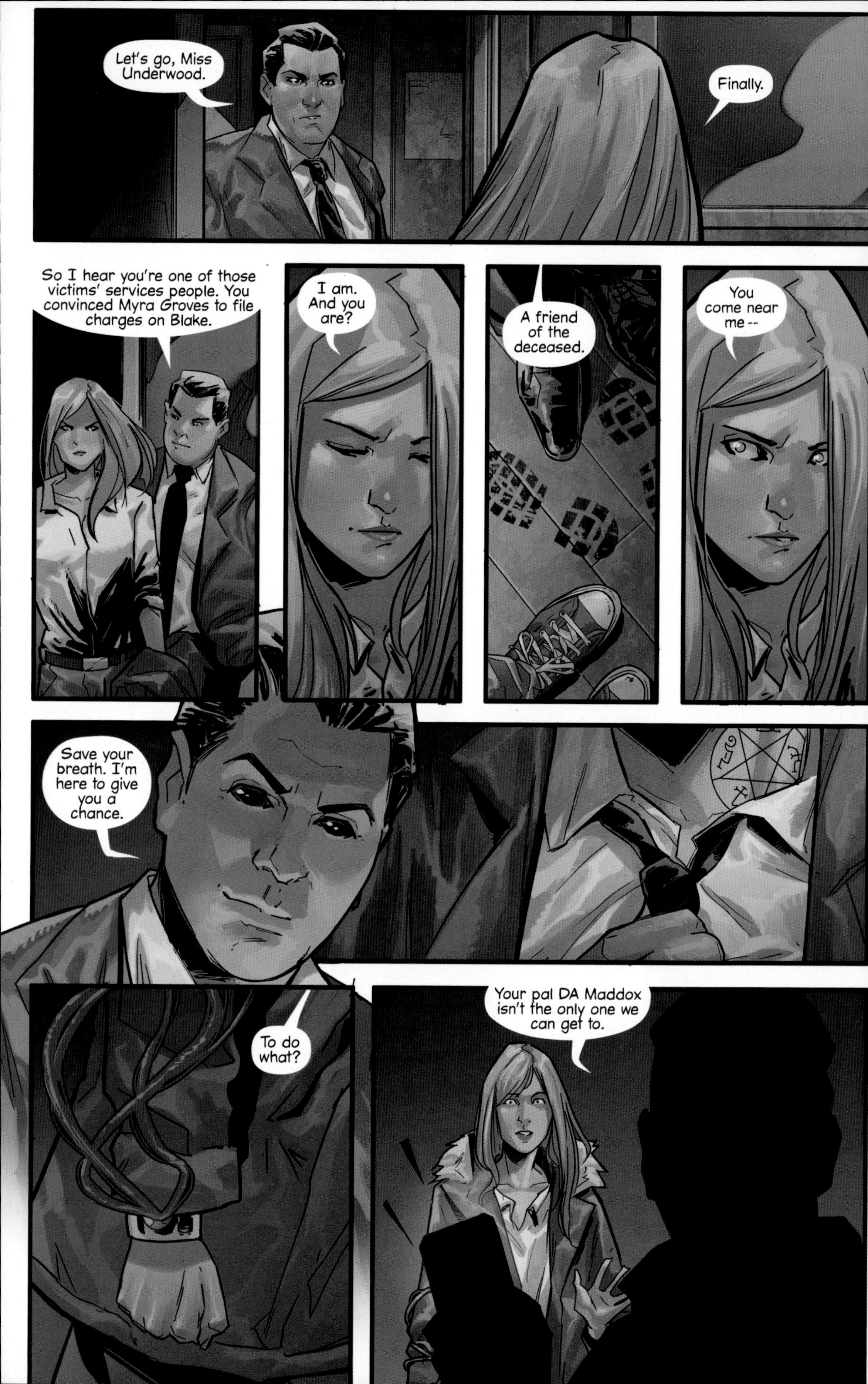
Let's go, Miss Underwood.
Finally.
So I hear you're one of those victims' services people. You convinced Myra Groves to file charges on Blake.
I am. And you are?
A friend of the deceased.
You come near me --
Save your breath. I'm here to give you a chance.
To do what?
Your pal DA Maddox isn't the only one we can get to.

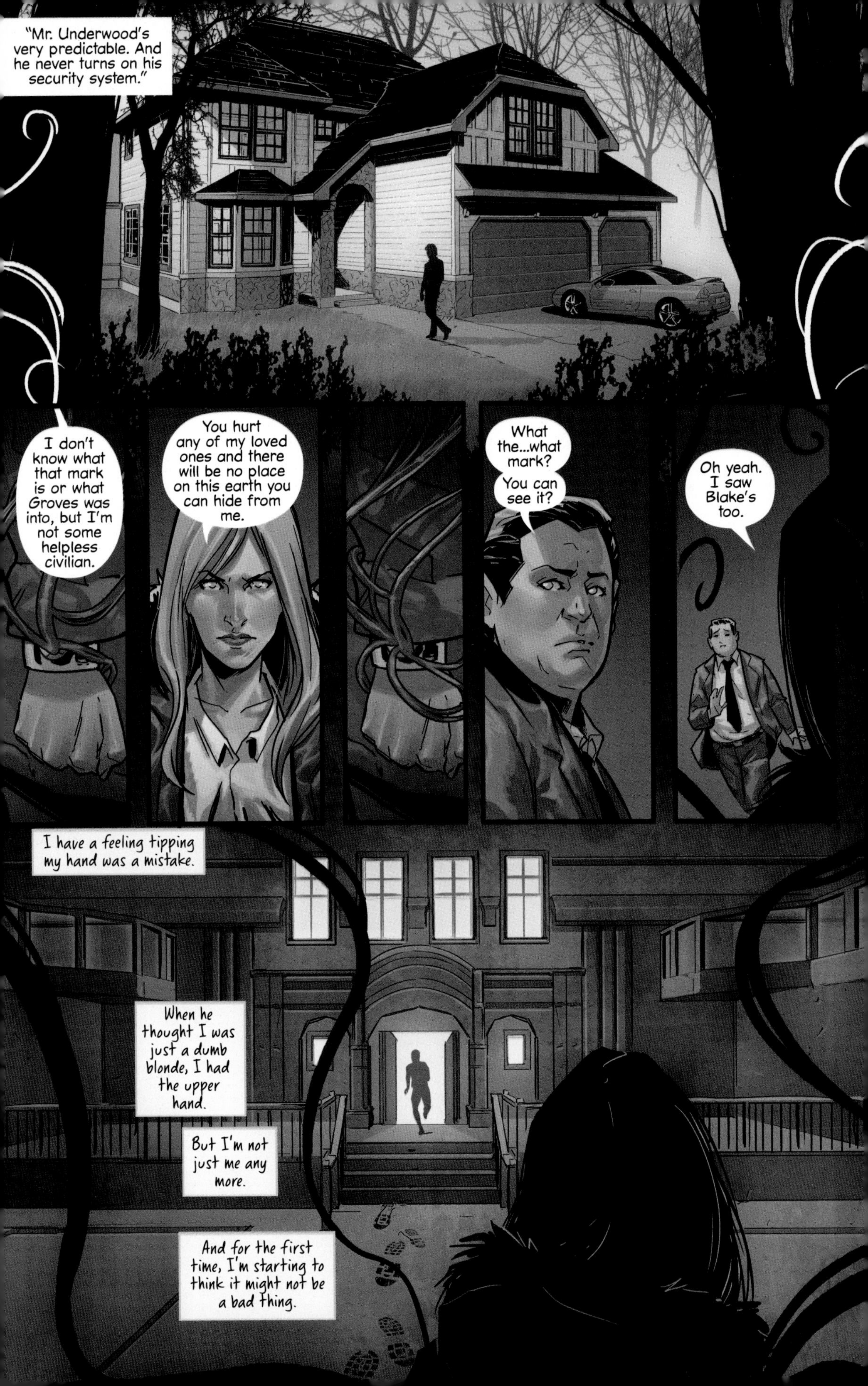
"Mr. Underwood's very predictable. And he never turns on his security system."
I don't know what that mark is or what Groves was into, but I'm not some helpless civilian.
You hurt any of my loved ones and there will be no place on this earth you can hide from me.
What the...what mark?
You can see it?
Oh yeah. I saw Blake's too.
I have a feeling tipping my hand was a mistake.
When he thought I was just a dumb blonde, I had the upper hand.
But I'm not just me any more.
And for the first time, I'm starting to think it might not be a bad thing.

CHAPTER THREE

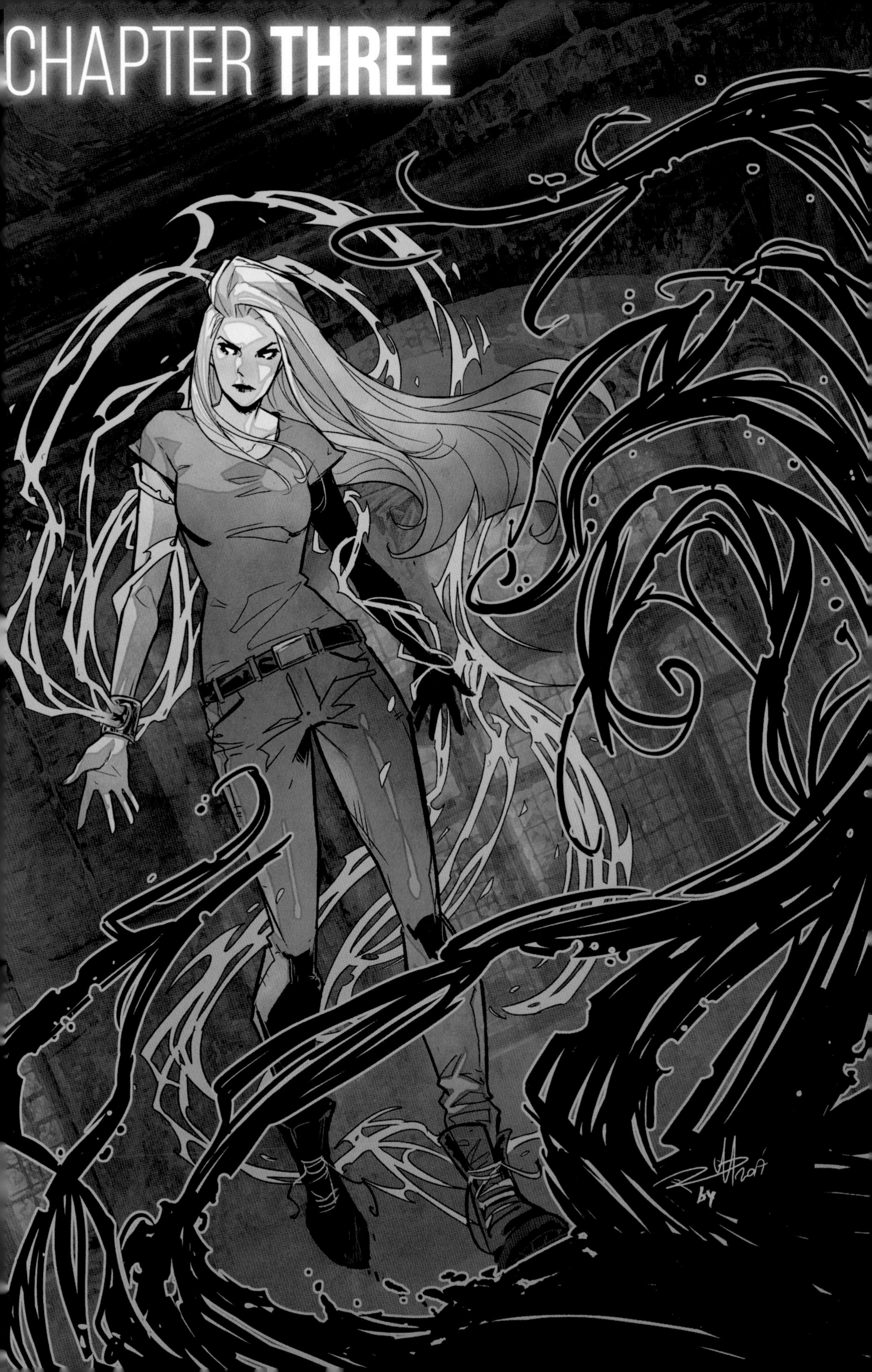

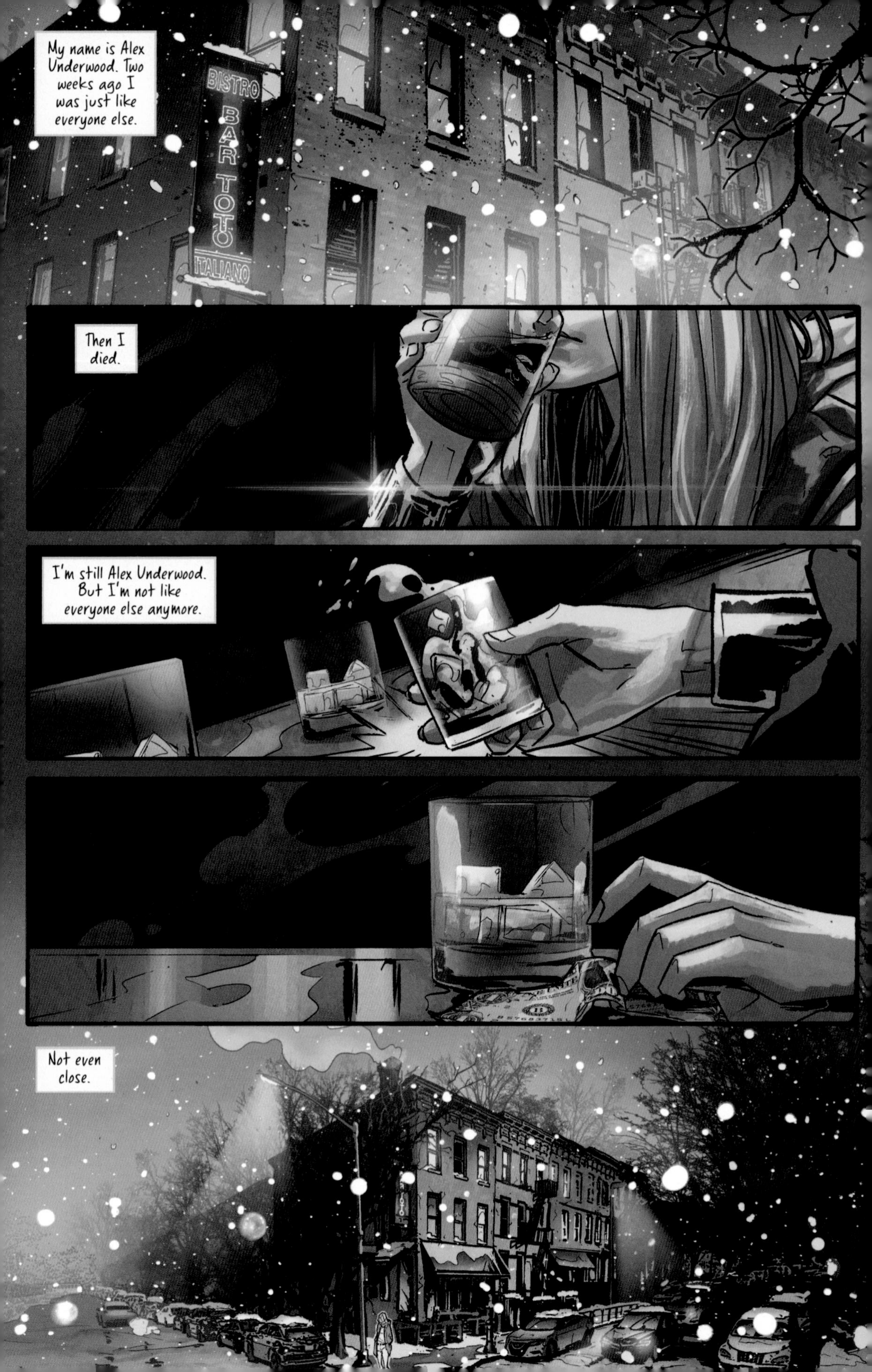
My name is Alex Underwood. Two weeks ago I was just like everyone else.
BISTRO
BAR TOTO
ITALIANO
Then I died.
I'm still Alex Underwood. But I'm not like everyone else anymore.
Not even close.

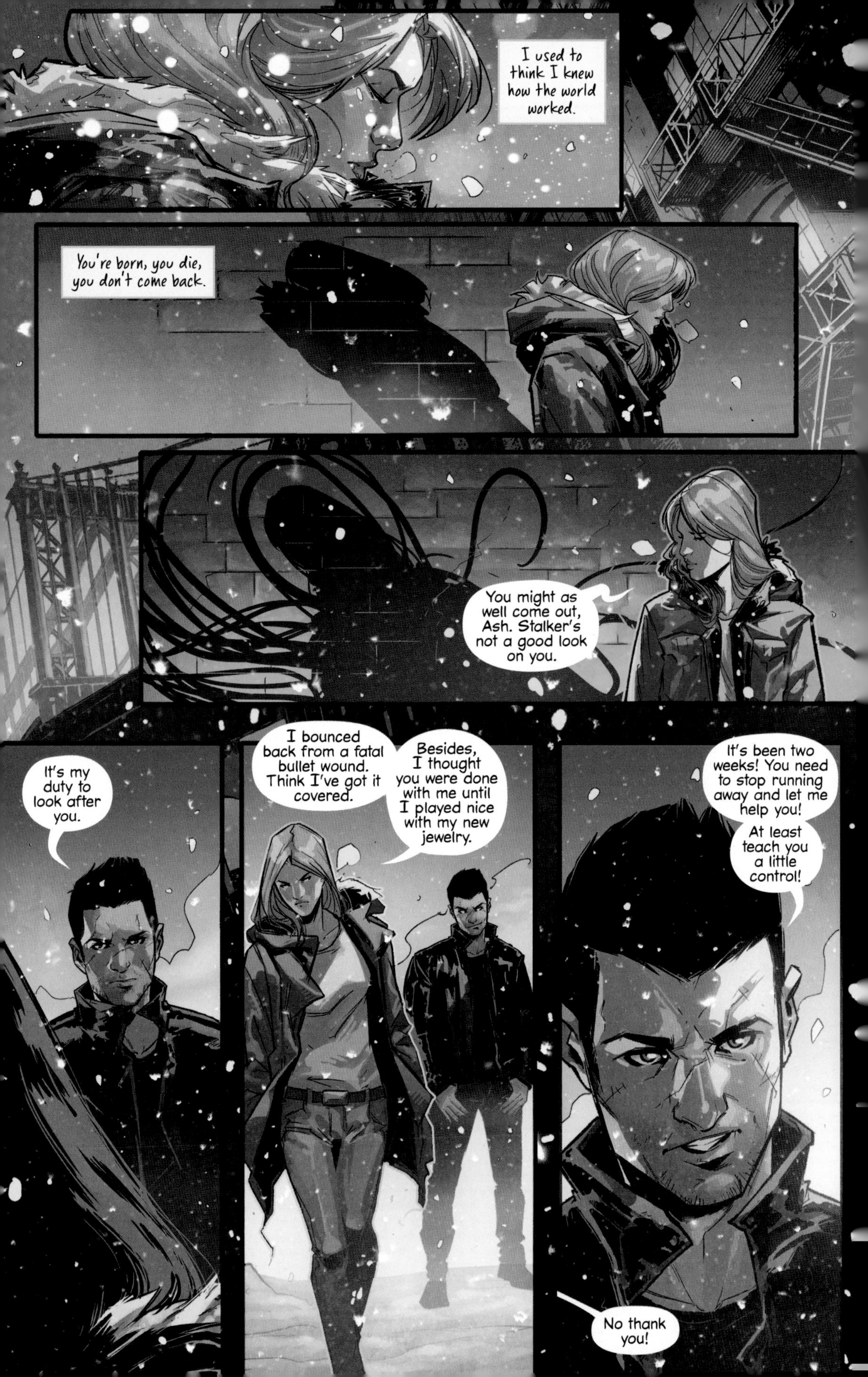
I used to think I knew how the world worked.
You're born, you die, you don't come back.
You might as well come out, Ash. Stalker's not a good look on you.
It's my duty to look after you.
I bounced back from a fatal bullet wound. Think I've got it covered.
Besides, I thought you were done with me until I played nice with my new jewelry.
It's been two weeks! You need to stop running away and let me help you!
At least teach you a little control!
No thank you!

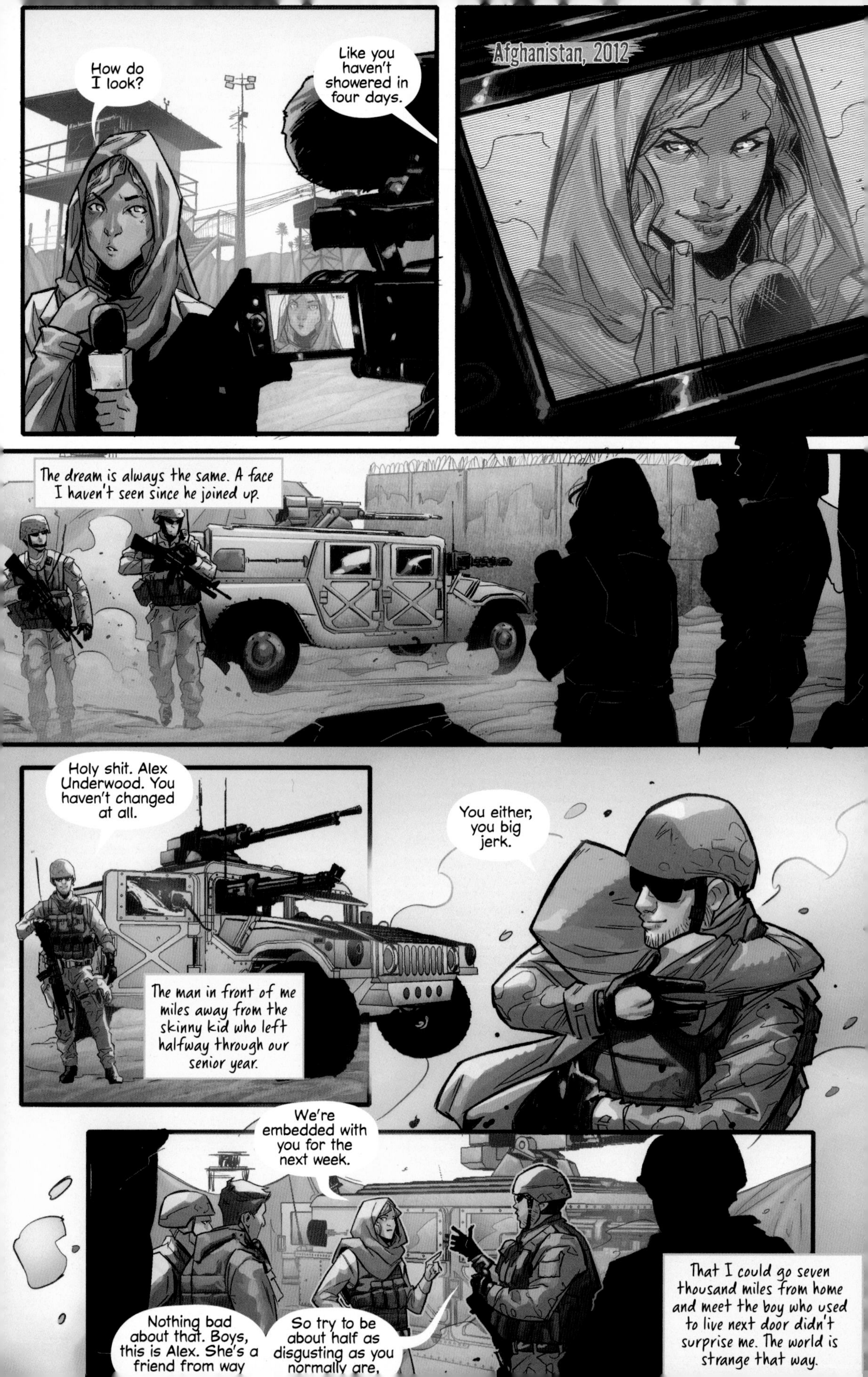
How do I look?
Like you haven't showered in four days.
Afghanistan, 2012
The dream is always the same. A face I haven't seen since he joined up.
Holy shit. Alex Underwood. You haven't changed at all.
The man in front of me miles away from the skinny kid who left halfway through our senior year.
You either, you big jerk.
We're embedded with you for the next week.
Nothing bad about that. Boys, this is Alex. She's a friend from way
So try to be about half as disgusting as you normally are.
That I could go seven thousand miles from home and meet the boy who used to live next door didn't surprise me. The world is strange that way.

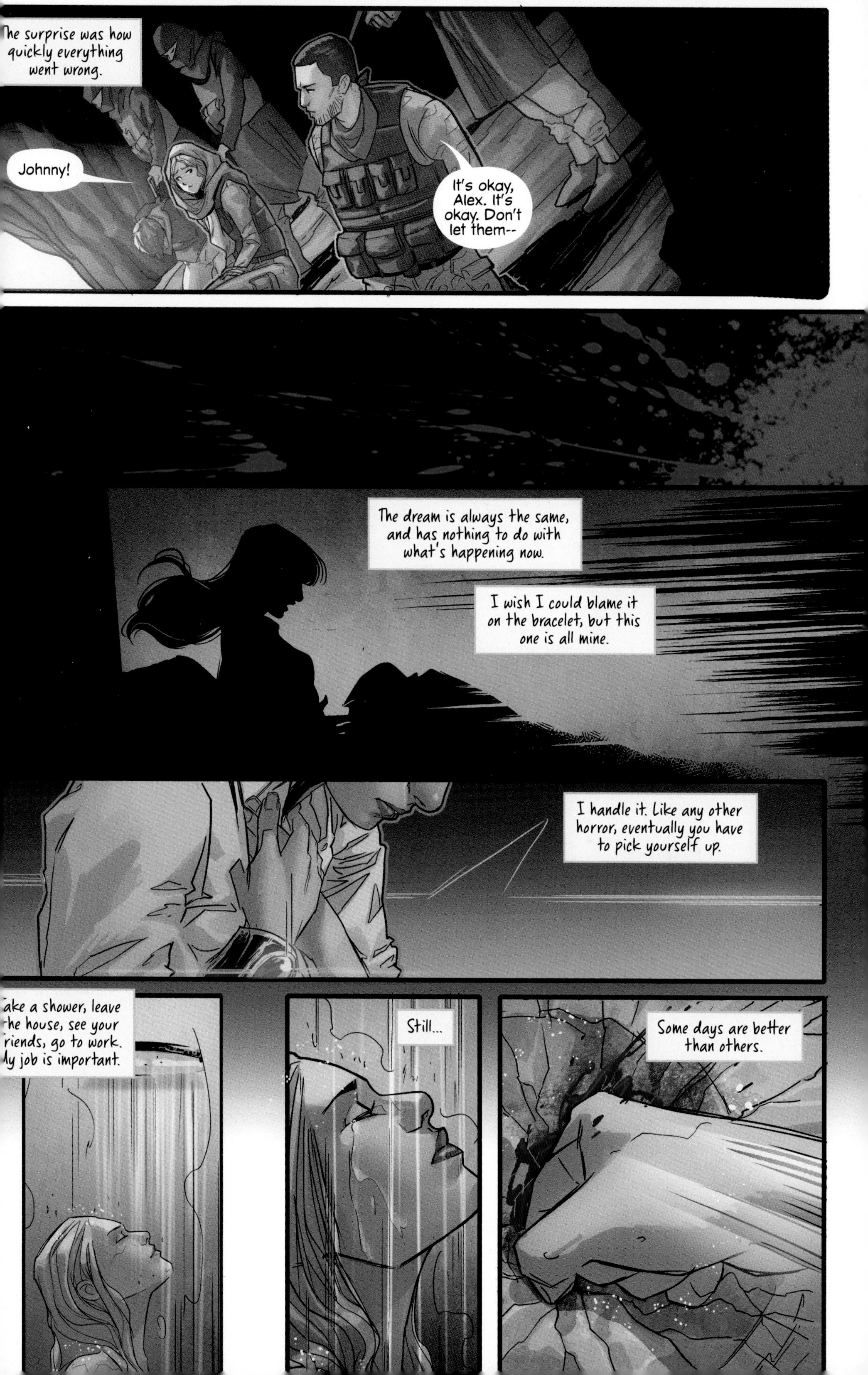

The surprise was how quickly everything went wrong.
Johnny!
It's okay, Alex. It's okay. Don't let them--
The dream is always the same, and has nothing to do with what's happening now.
I wish I could blame it on the bracelet, but this one is all mine.
I handle it. Like any other horror, eventually you have to pick yourself up.
ake a shower, leave the house, see your riends, go to work. y job is important.
Still...
Some days are better than others.

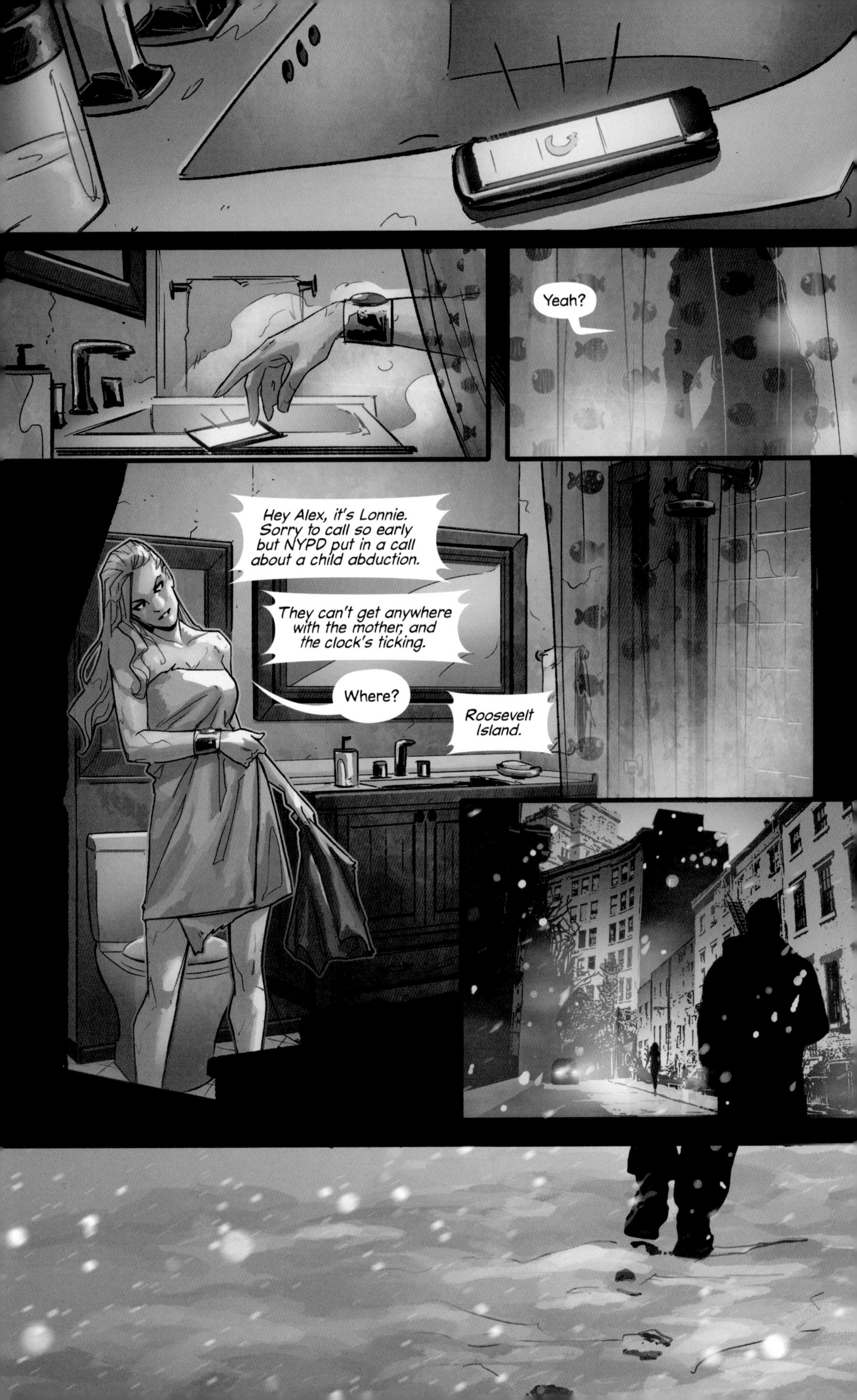
Yeah?
Hey Alex, it's Lonnie. Sorry to call so early but NYPD put in a call about a child abduction.
They can't get anywhere with the mother, and the clock's ticking.
Where?
Roosevelt Island.

It's not like I hadn't seen horror before Johnny came back into my life.

Too much, if I'm being honest.

You the witness services lady?

Alex Underwood. You needed my help interviewing the parents?

Parent, and if you can help that crazy broad, I want some of what you got.

Enough. This isn't about me, or what's happening to me. This is about a missing kid and their mother.

Work is the only thing that's ever made me feel normal. After what happened to Meg and I the summer we turned thirteen.

After Johnny. Work is the only way I know how to cope, so work is where I go when things are really bad.

The smell hits immediately. Sweat and spoiled milk, bleach and piss. The decay that hopelessness brings to a place.

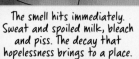

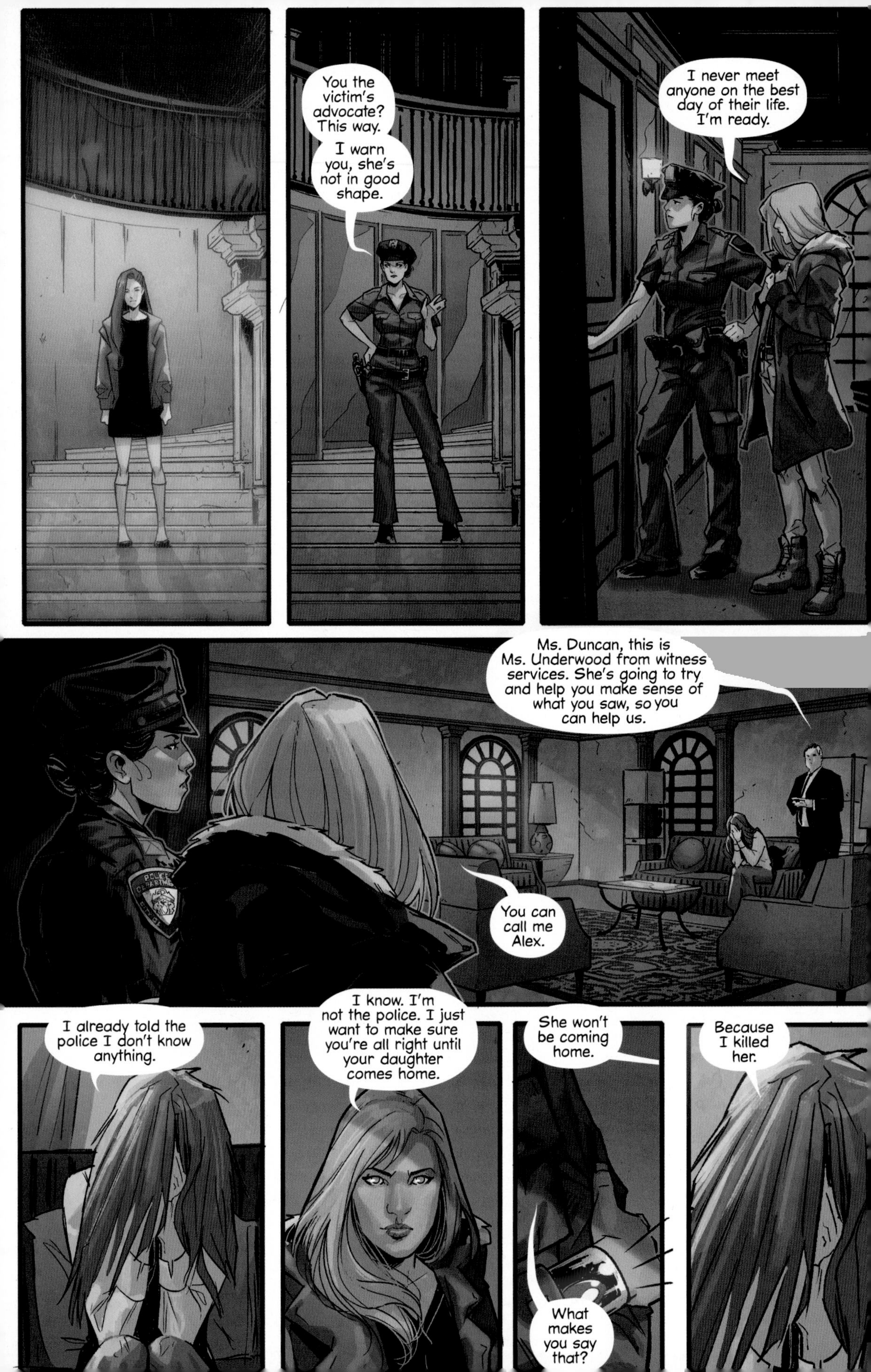
You the victim's advocate? This way.
I warn you, she's not in good shape.
I never meet anyone on the best day of their life. I'm ready.
Ms. Duncan, this is Ms. Underwood from witness services. She's going to try and help you make sense of what you saw, so you can help us.
You can call me Alex.
I already told the police I don't know anything.
I know. I'm not the police. I just want to make sure you're all right until your daughter comes home.
She won't be coming home.
What makes you say that?
Because I killed her.

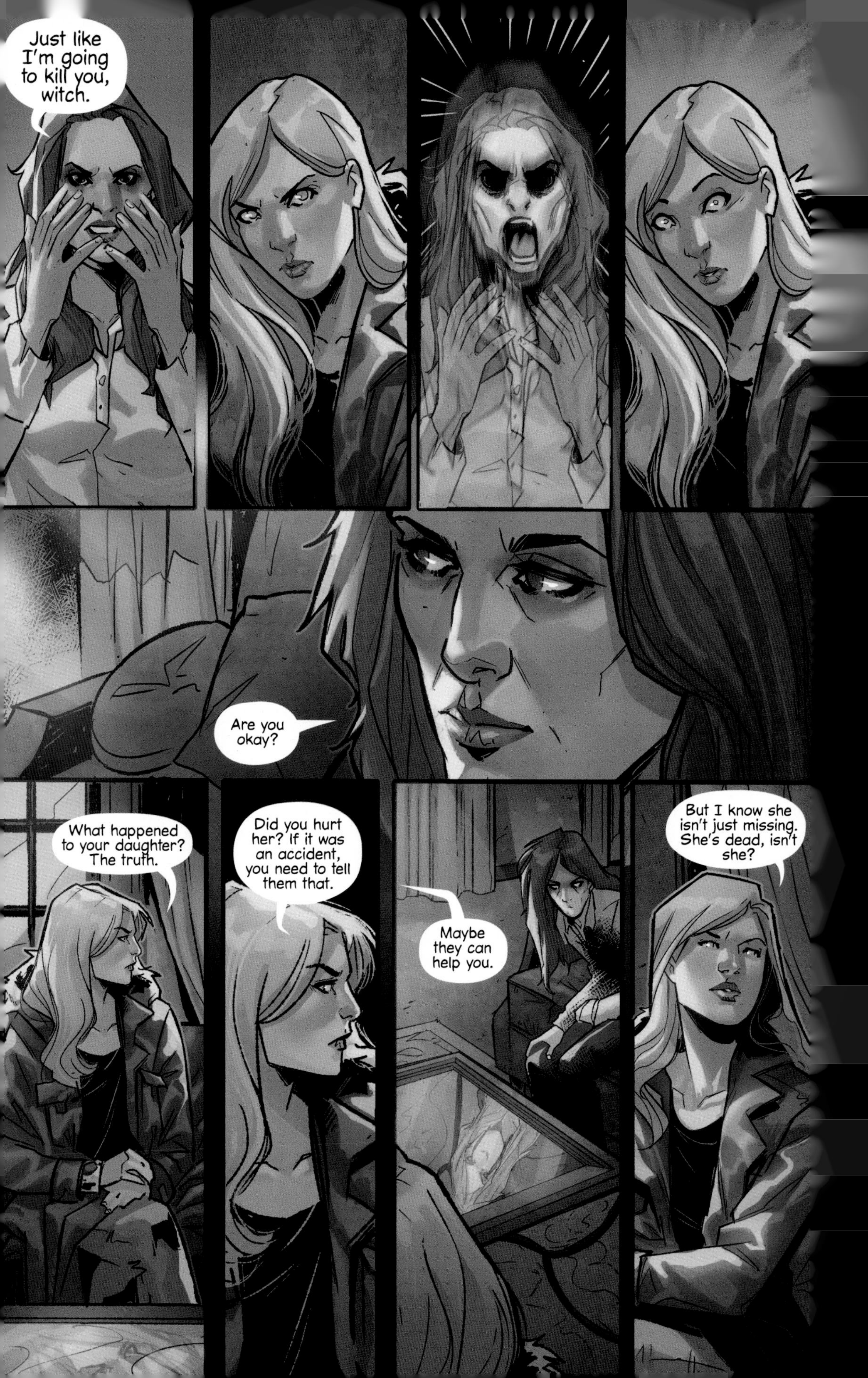
Just like I'm going to kill you, witch.
Are you okay?
What happened to your daughter? The truth.
Did you hurt her? If it was an accident, you need to tell them that.
Maybe they can help you.
But I know she isn't just missing. She's dead, isn't she?

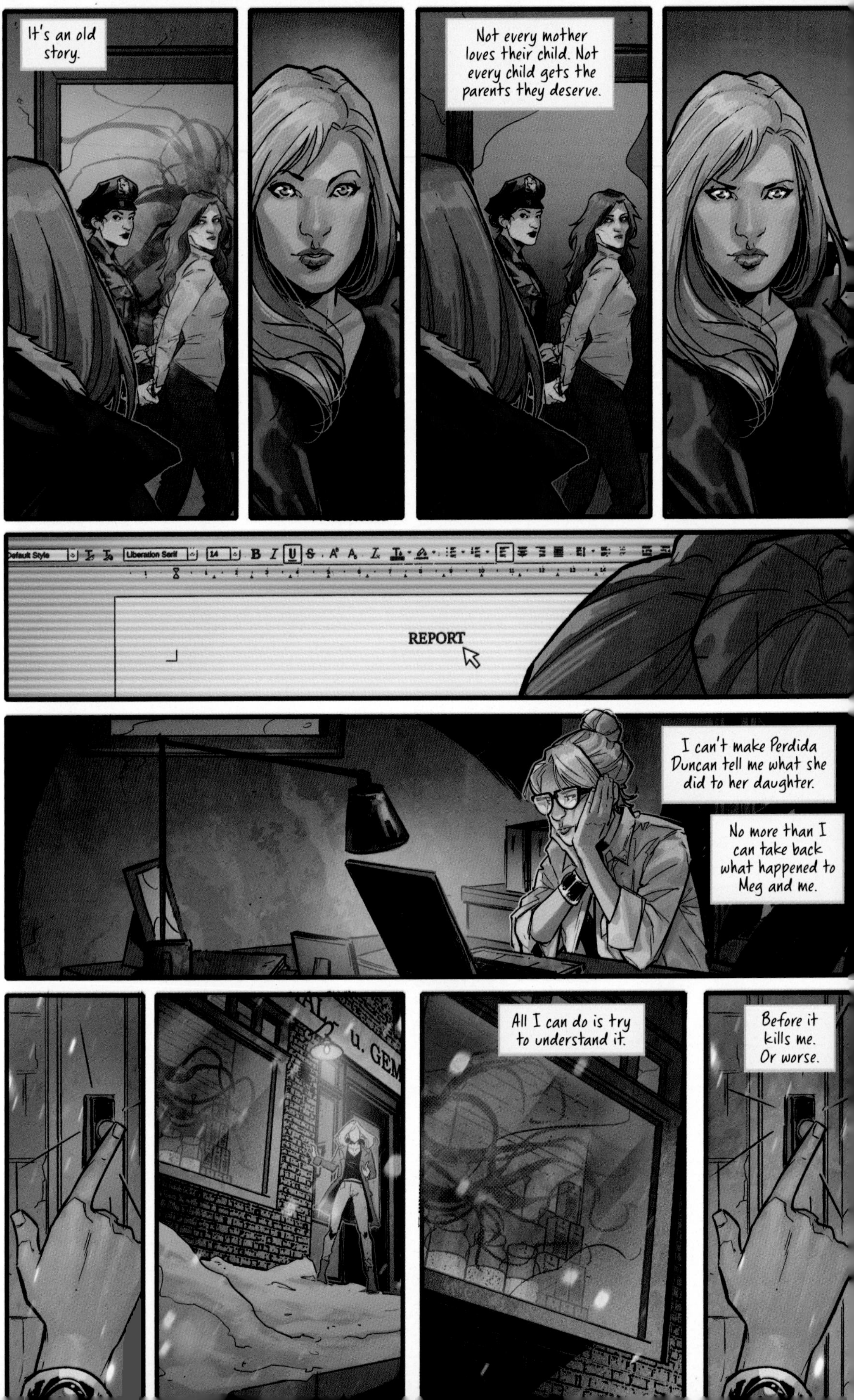
It's an old story.
Not every mother loves their child. Not every child gets the parents they deserve.
REPORT
I can't make Perdida Duncan tell me what she did to her daughter.
No more than I can take back what happened to Meg and me.
All I can do is try to understand it.
Before it kills me. Or worse.

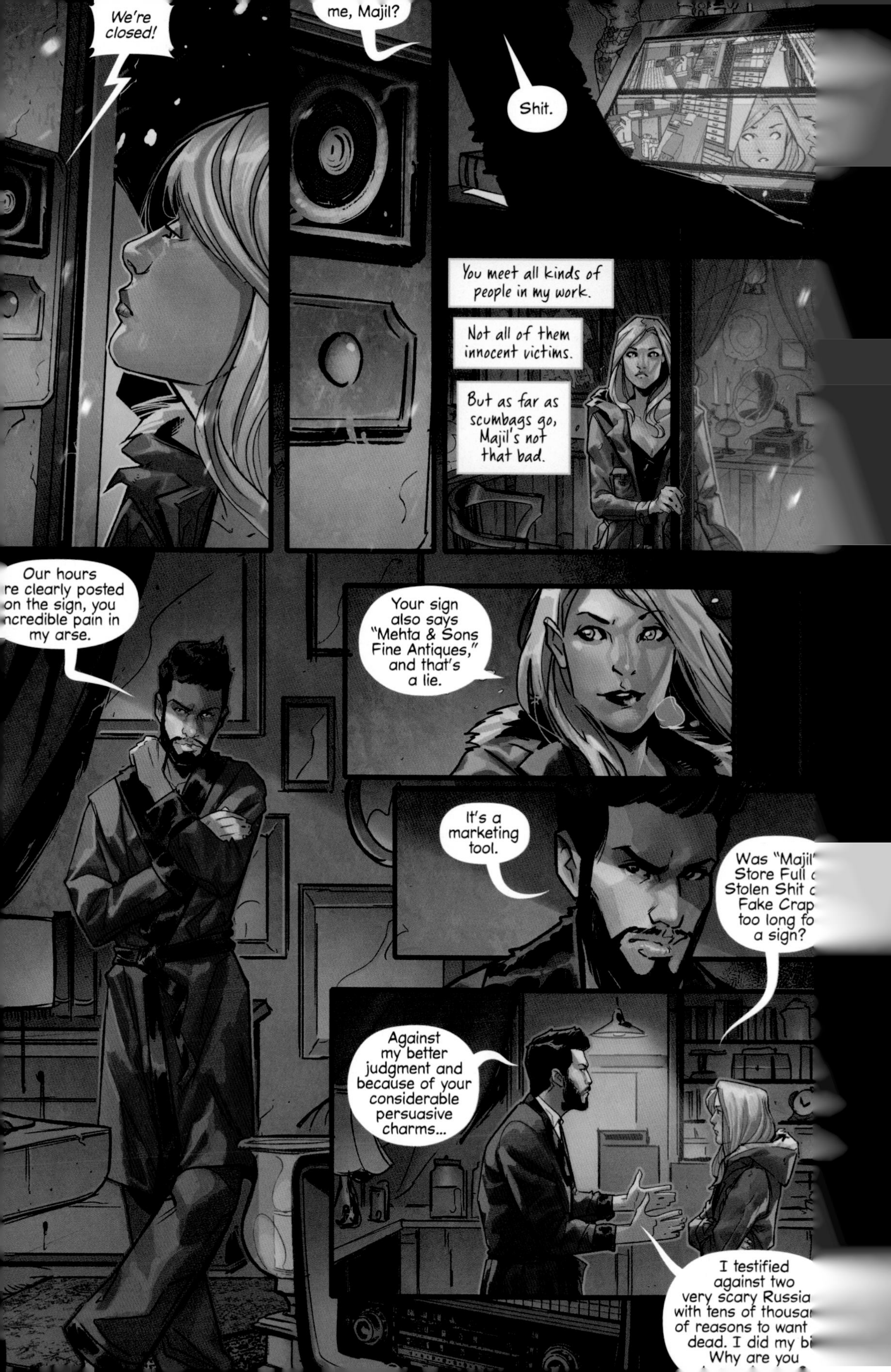
We're closed!
me, Majil?
Shit.
You meet all kinds of people in my work.
Not all of them innocent victims.
But as far as scumbags go, Majil's not that bad.
Our hours re clearly posted on the sign, you ncredible pain in my arse.
Your sign also says "Mehta & Sons Fine Antiques," and that's a lie.
It's a marketing tool.
Was "Majil' Store Full Stolen Shit Fake Crap too long fo a sign?
Against my better judgment and because of your considerable persuasive charms...
I testified against two very scary Russia with tens of thousa of reasons to want dead. I did my b Why are you

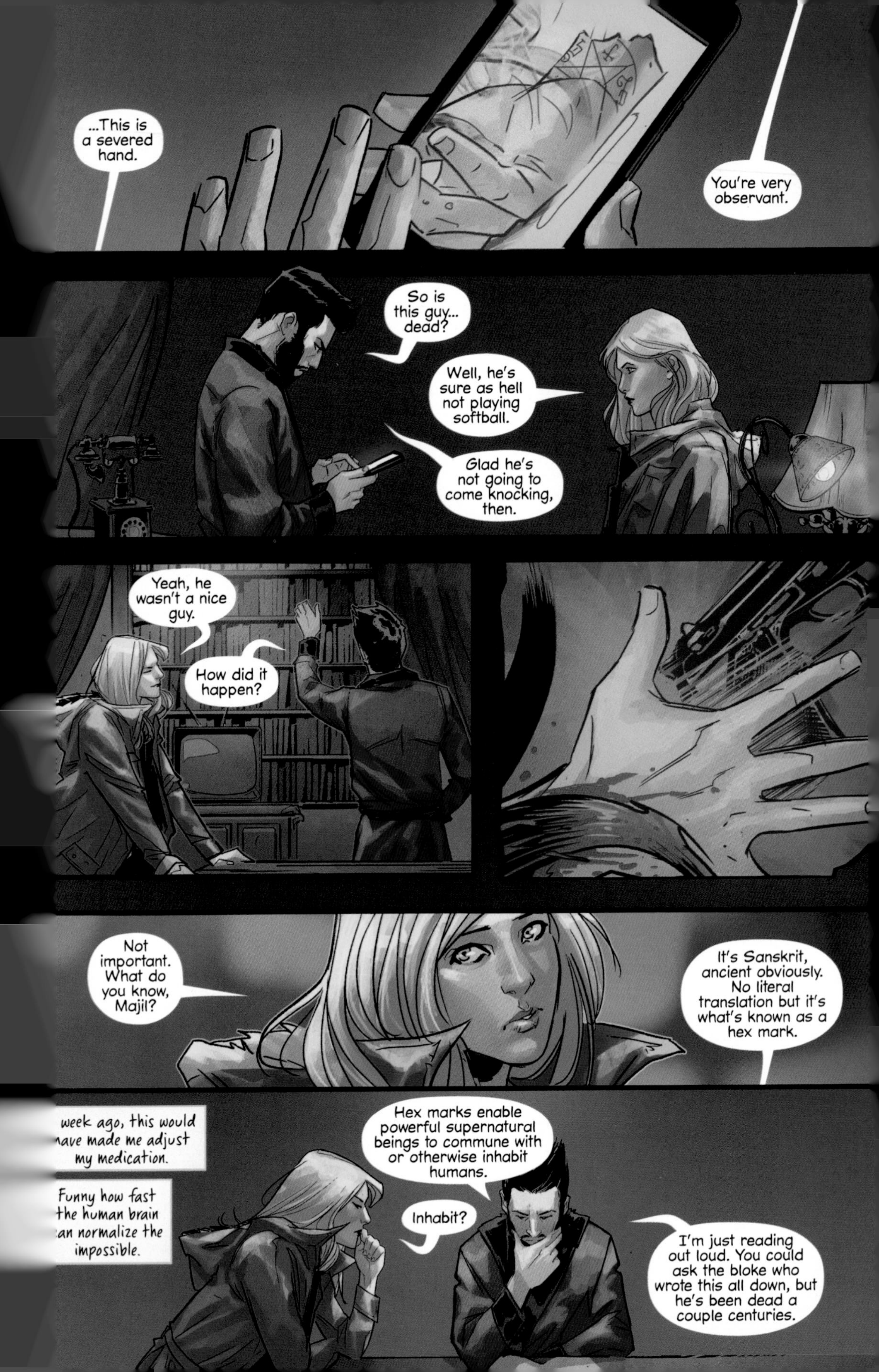

...This is a severed hand.
You're very observant.
So is this guy... dead?
Well, he's sure as hell not playing softball.
Glad he's not going to come knocking, then.
Yeah, he wasn't a nice guy.
How did it happen?
Not important. What do you know, Majil?
It's Sanskrit, ancient obviously. No literal translation but it's what's known as a hex mark.
week ago, this would ave made me adjust my medication.
Funny how fast the human brain an normalize the impossible.
Hex marks enable powerful supernatural beings to commune with or otherwise inhabit humans.
Inhabit?
I'm just reading out loud. You could ask the bloke who wrote this all down, but he's been dead a couple centuries.

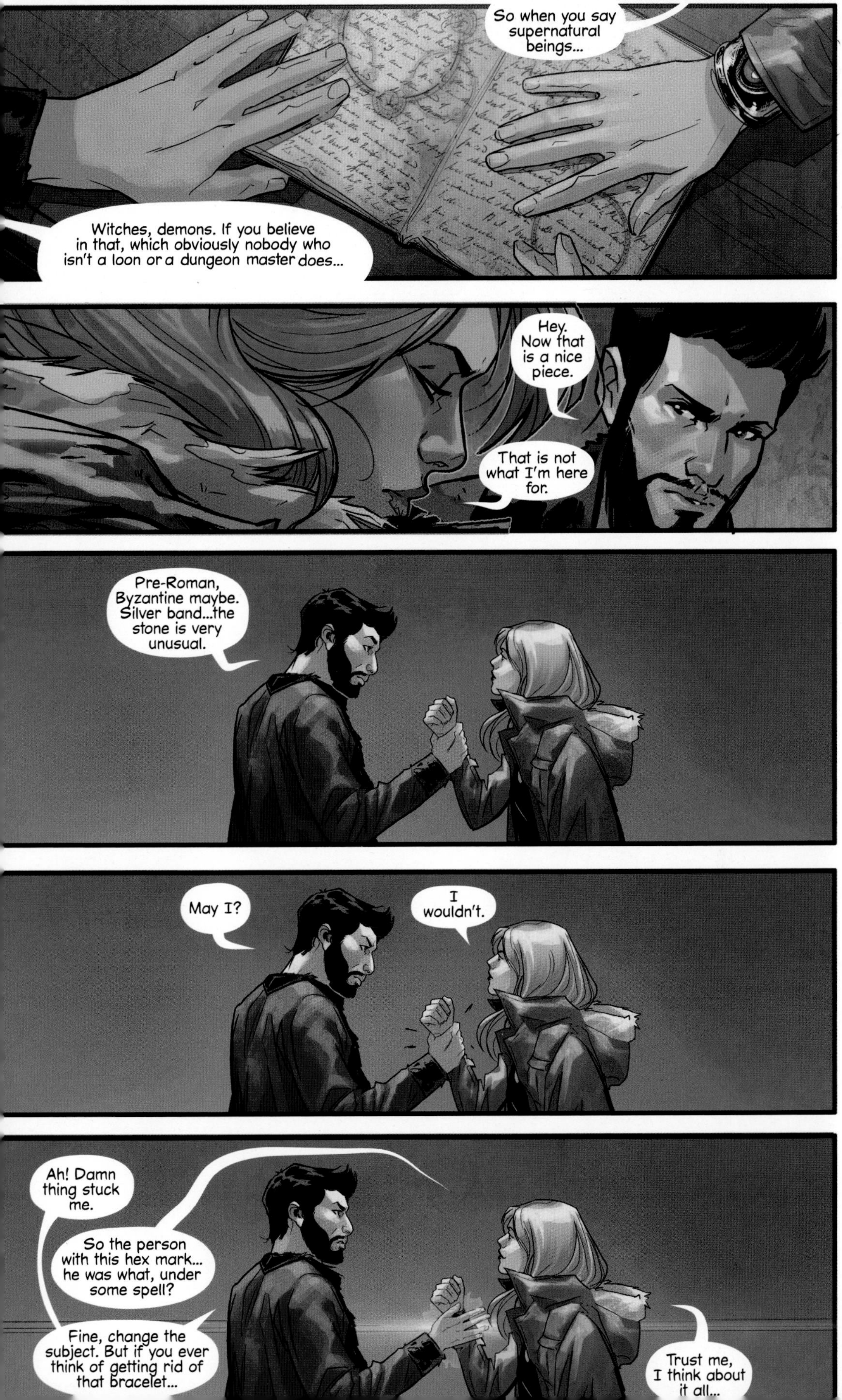
So when you say supernatural beings...
Witches, demons. If you believe in that, which obviously nobody who isn't a loon or a dungeon master does...
Hey. Now that is a nice piece.
That is not what I'm here for.
Pre-Roman, Byzantine maybe. Silver band...the stone is very unusual.
May I?
I wouldn't.
Ah! Damn thing stuck me.
So the person with this hex mark... he was what, under some spell?
Fine, change the subject. But if you ever think of getting rid of that bracelet...
Trust me, I think about it all...

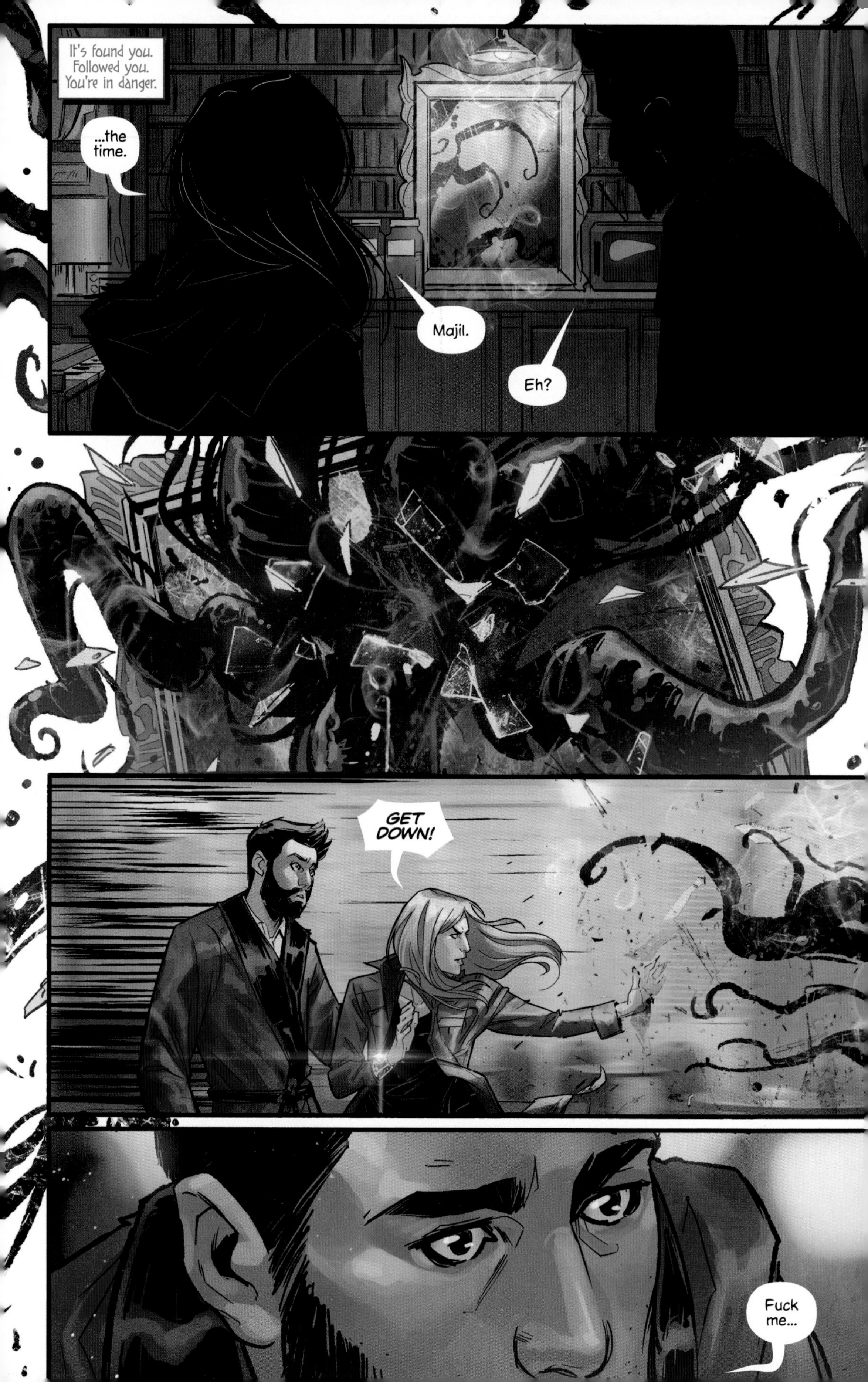
It's found you. Followed you. You're in danger.
...the time.
Majil.
Eh?
GET DOWN!
Fuck me...

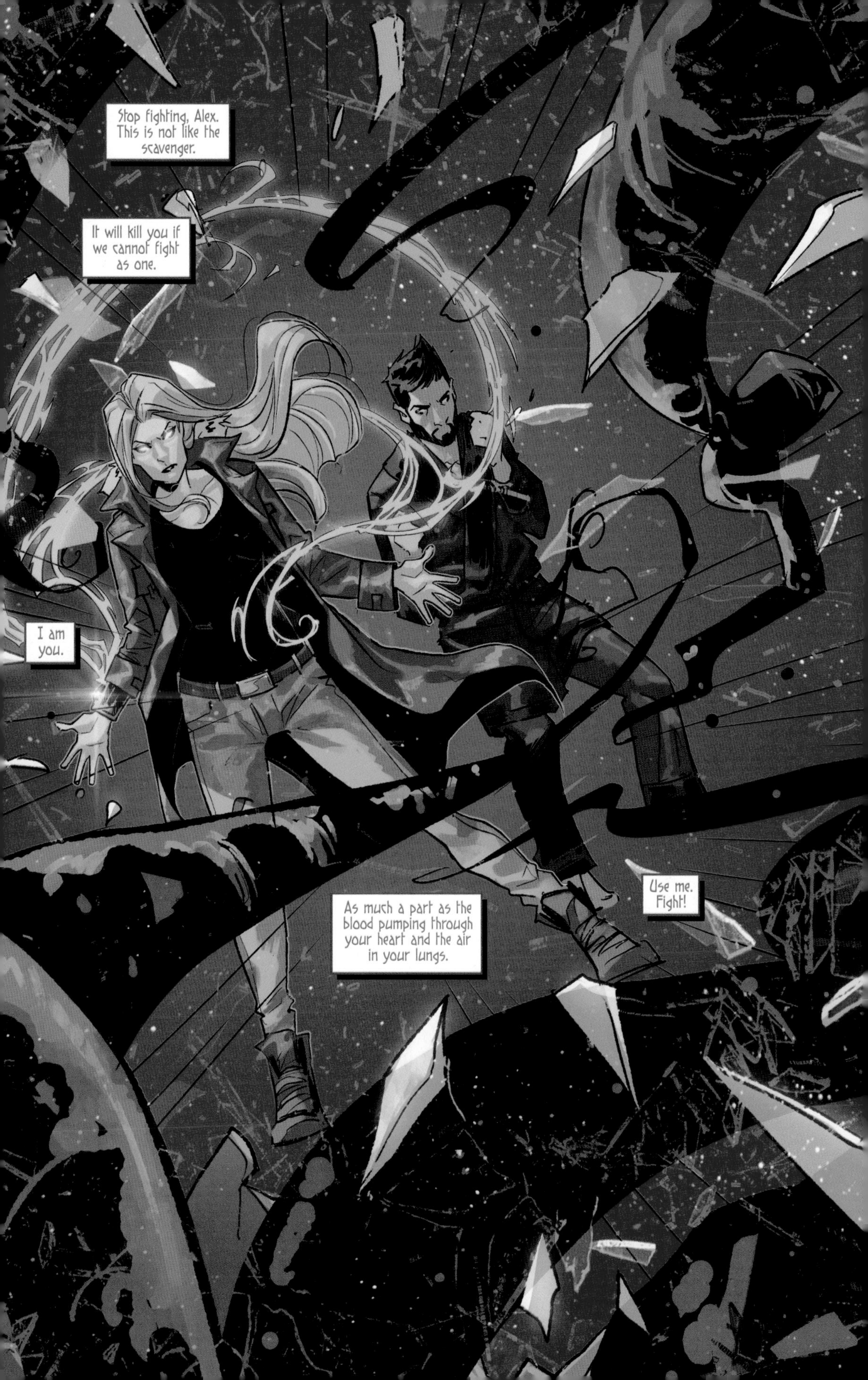
Stop fighting, Alex. This is not like the scavenger.
It will kill you if we cannot fight as one.
I am you.
As much a part as the blood pumping through your heart and the air in your lungs.
Use me. Fight!

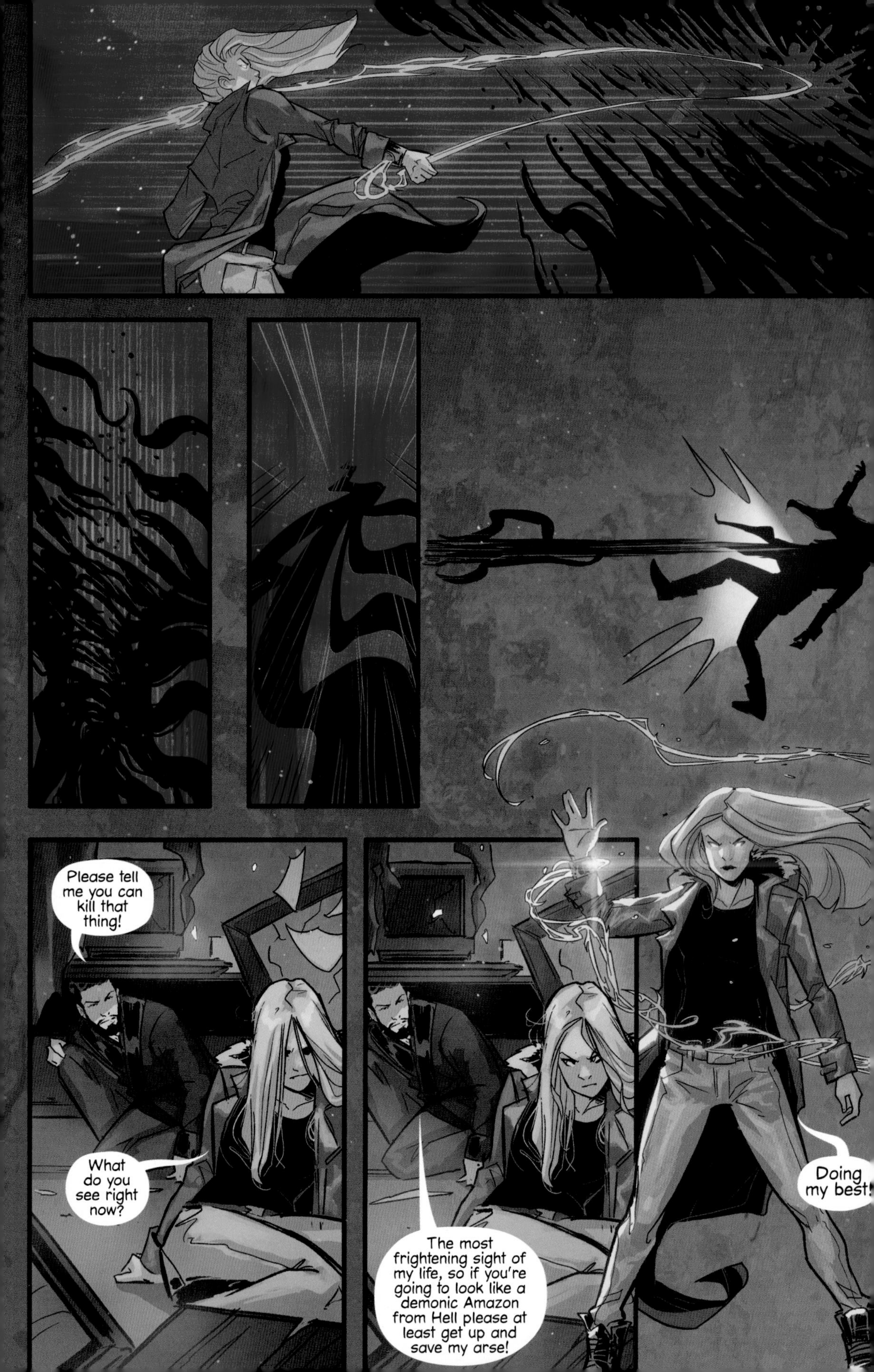
Please tell me you can kill that thing!
What do you see right now?
The most frightening sight of my life, so if you're going to look like a demonic Amazon from Hell please at least get up and save my arse!
Doing my best!

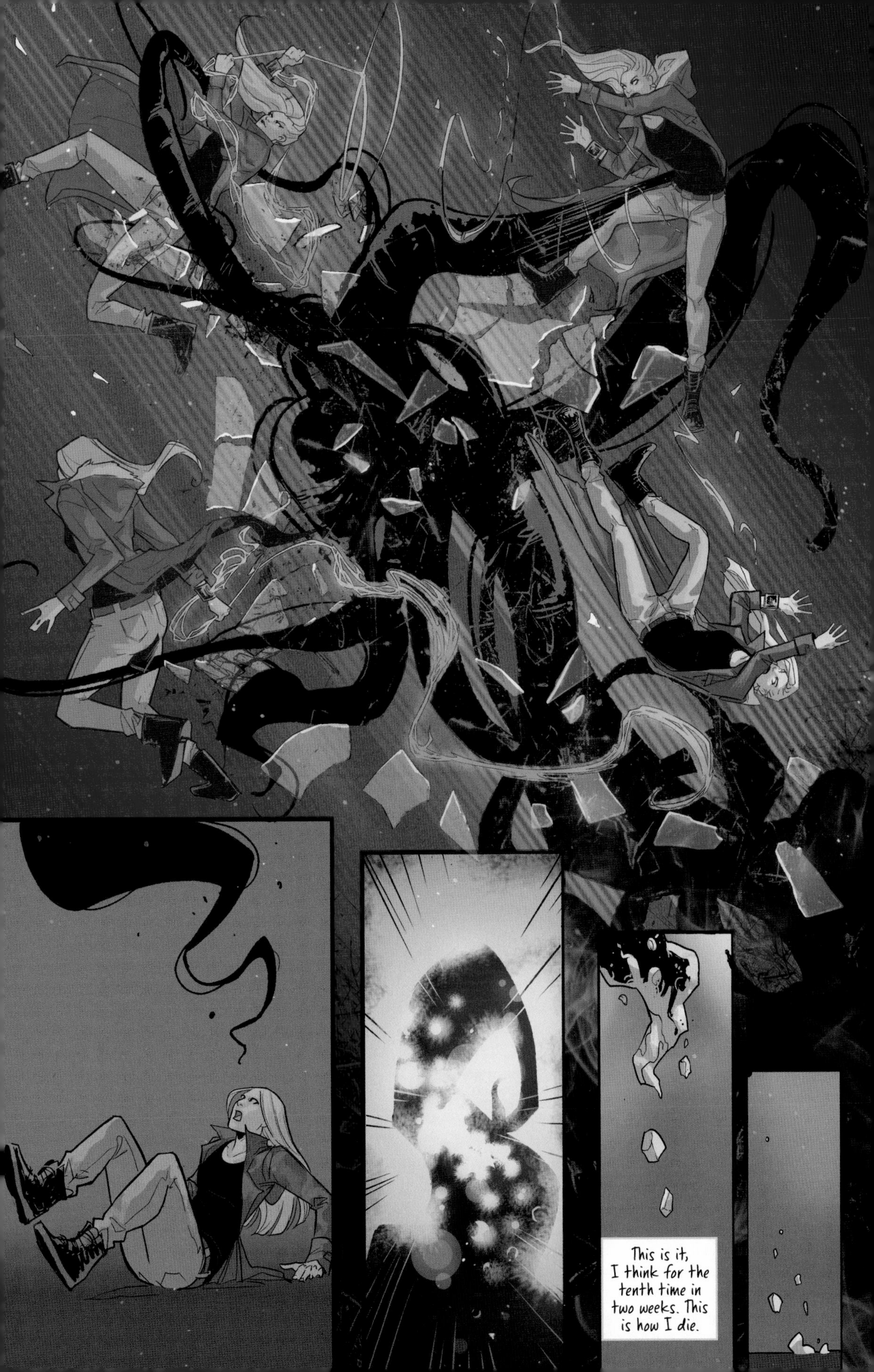
This is it, I think for the tenth time in two weeks. This is how I die.

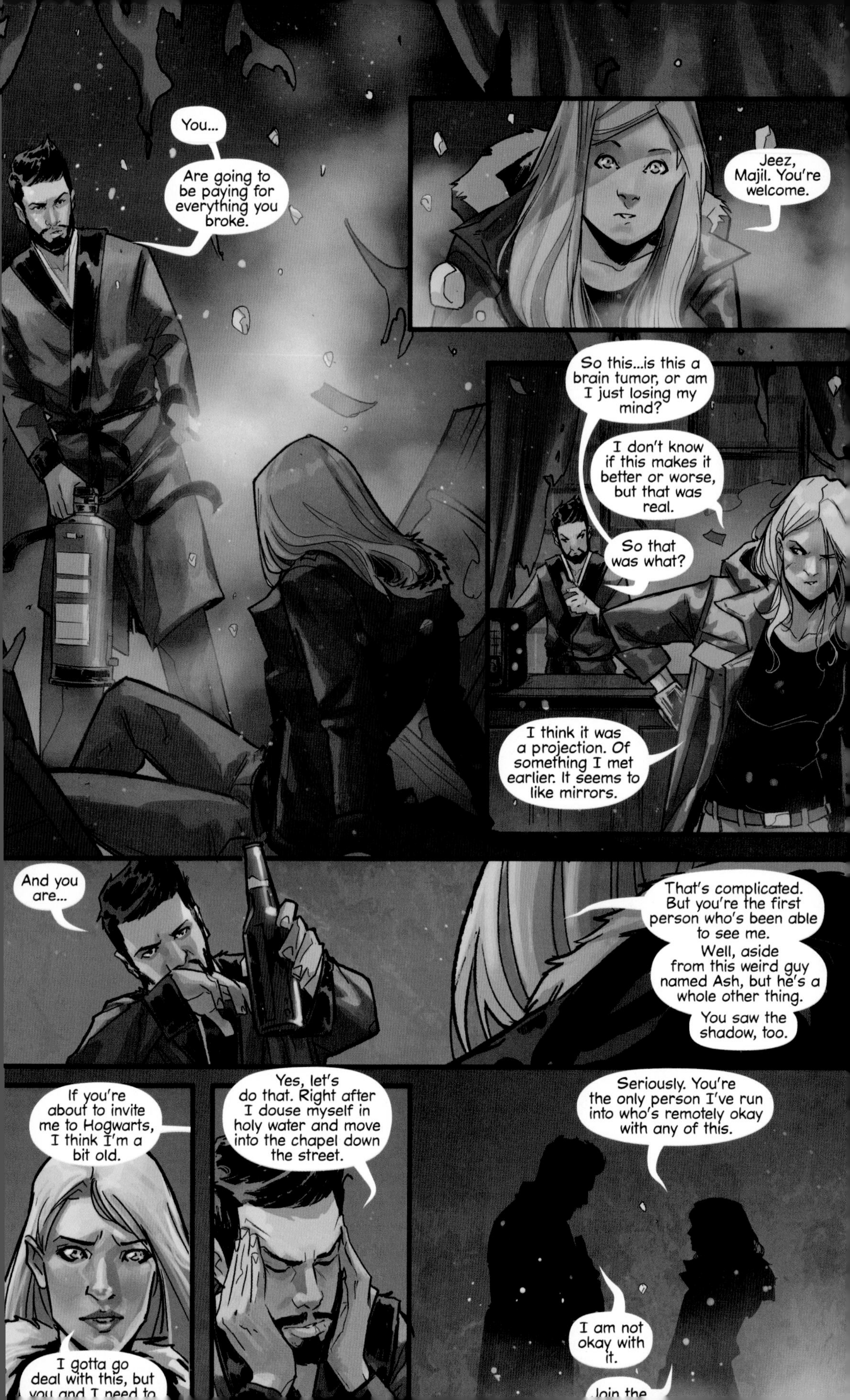
You...
Are going to be paying for everything you broke.
Jeez, Majil. You're welcome.
So this...is this a brain tumor, or am I just losing my mind?
I don't know if this makes it better or worse, but that was real.
So that was what?
I think it was a projection. Of something I met earlier. It seems to like mirrors.
And you are...
That's complicated. But you're the first person who's been able to see me.
Well, aside from this weird guy named Ash, but he's a whole other thing.
You saw the shadow, too.
If you're about to invite me to Hogwarts, I think I'm a bit old.
I gotta go deal with this, but
Yes, let's do that. Right after I douse myself in holy water and move into the chapel down the street.
Seriously. You're the only person I've run into who's remotely okay with any of this.
I am not okay with it.

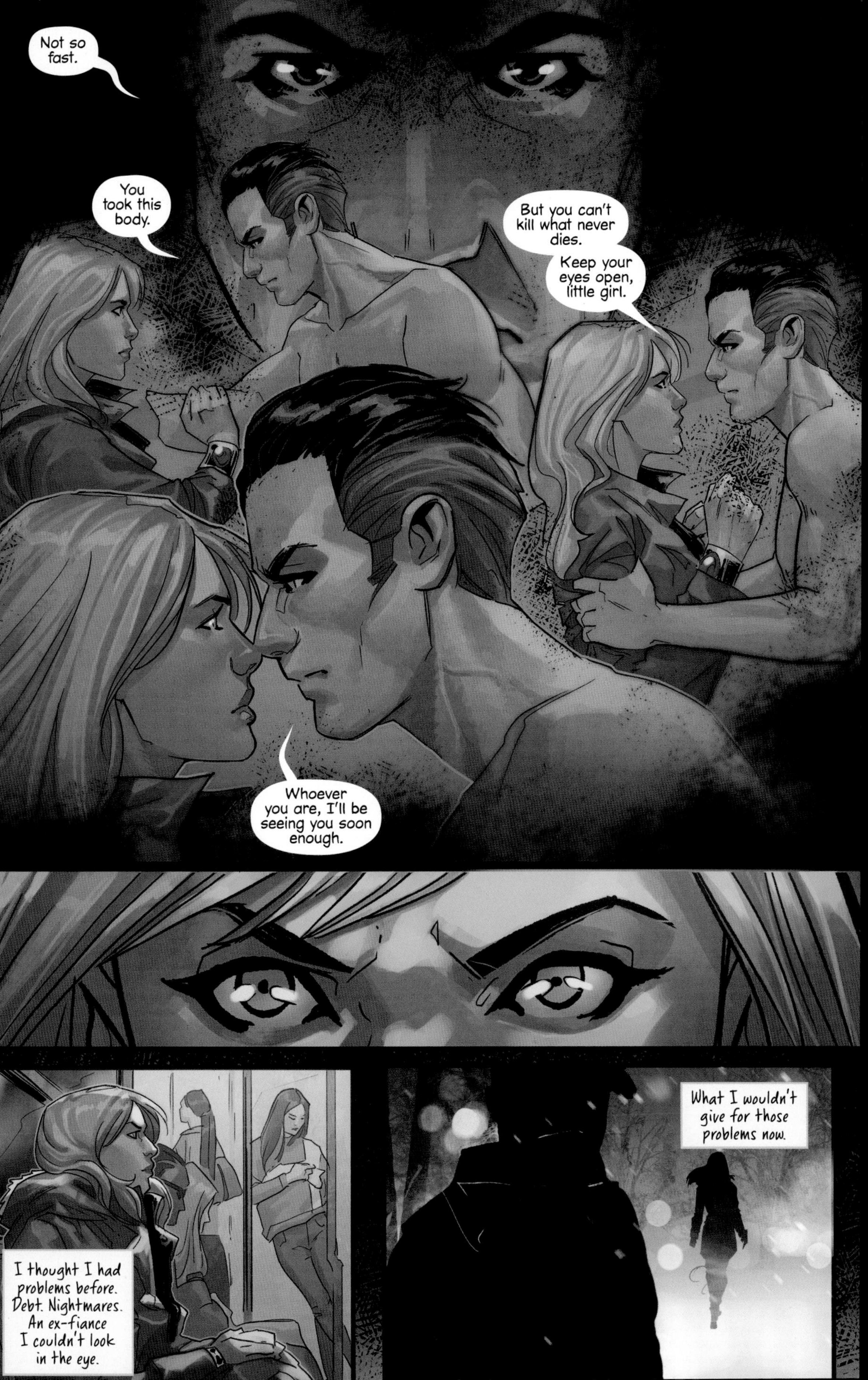
Not so fast.
You took this body.
But you can't kill what never dies.
Keep your eyes open, little girl.
Whoever you are, I'll be seeing you soon enough.
I thought I had problems before. Debt. Nightmares. An ex-fiance I couldn't look in the eye.
What I wouldn't give for those problems now.

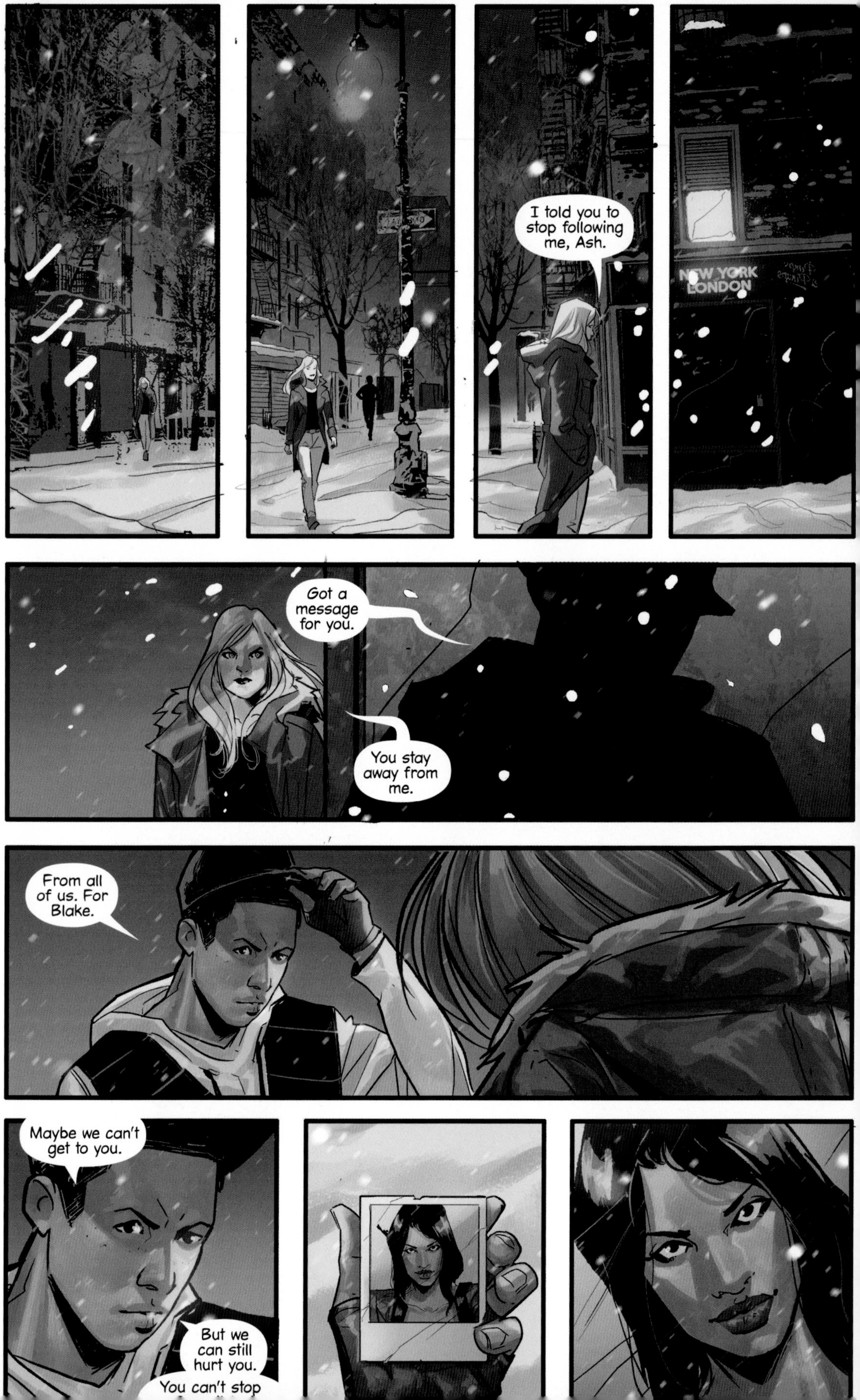
I told you to stop following me, Ash.
NEW YORK LONDON
Got a message for you.
You stay away from me.
From all of us. For Blake.
Maybe we can't get to you.
But we can still hurt you.
You can't stop

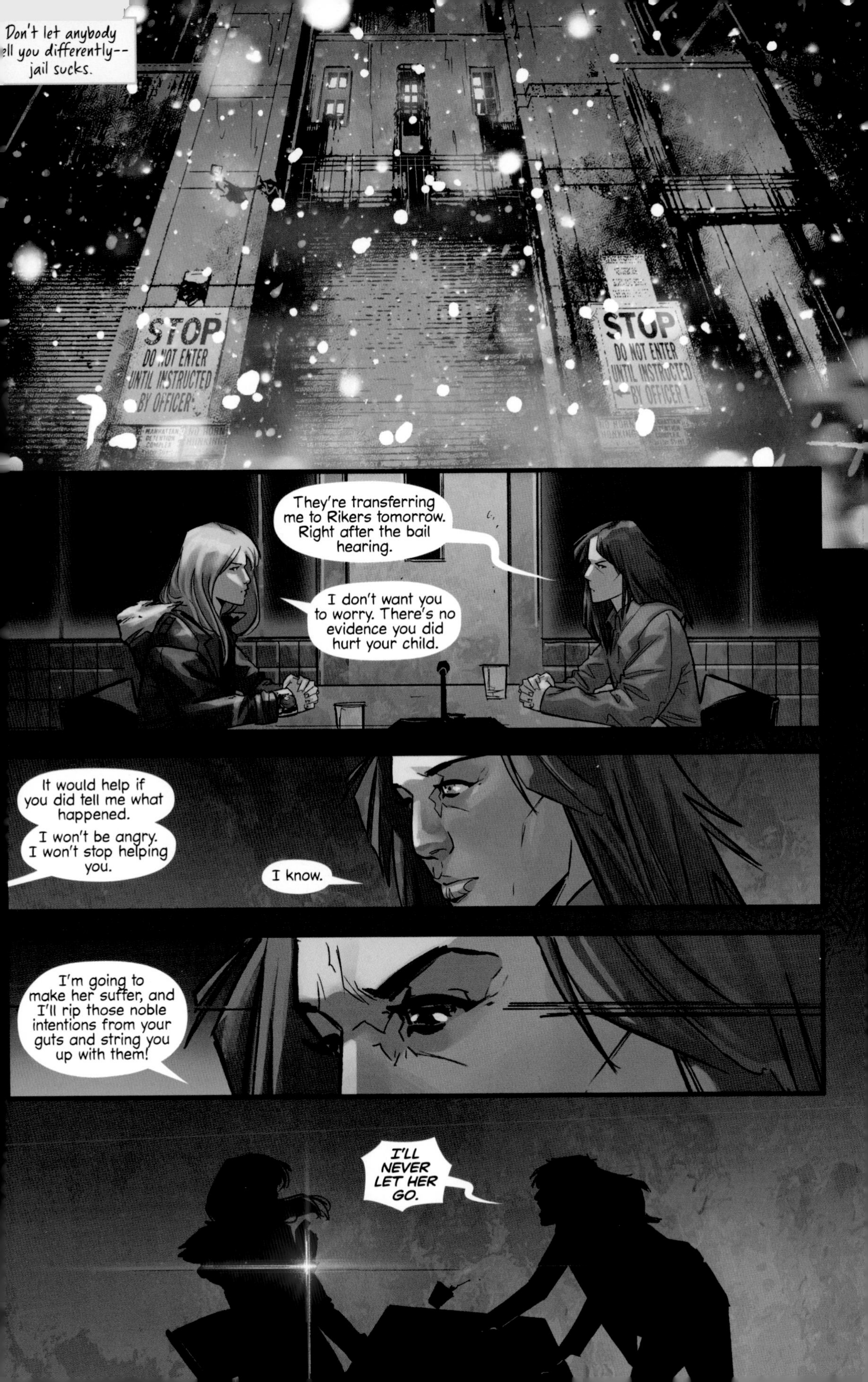
Don't let anybody ell you differently-- jail sucks.
STOP DO NOT ENTER UNTIL INSTRUCTED BY OFFICER!
STOP DO NOT ENTER UNTIL INSTRUCTED BY OFFICER!
They're transferring me to Rikers tomorrow. Right after the bail hearing.
I don't want you to worry. There's no evidence you did hurt your child.
It would help if you did tell me what happened.
I won't be angry. I won't stop helping you.
I know.
I'm going to make her suffer, and I'll rip those noble intentions from your guts and string you up with them!
I'LL NEVER LET HER GO.

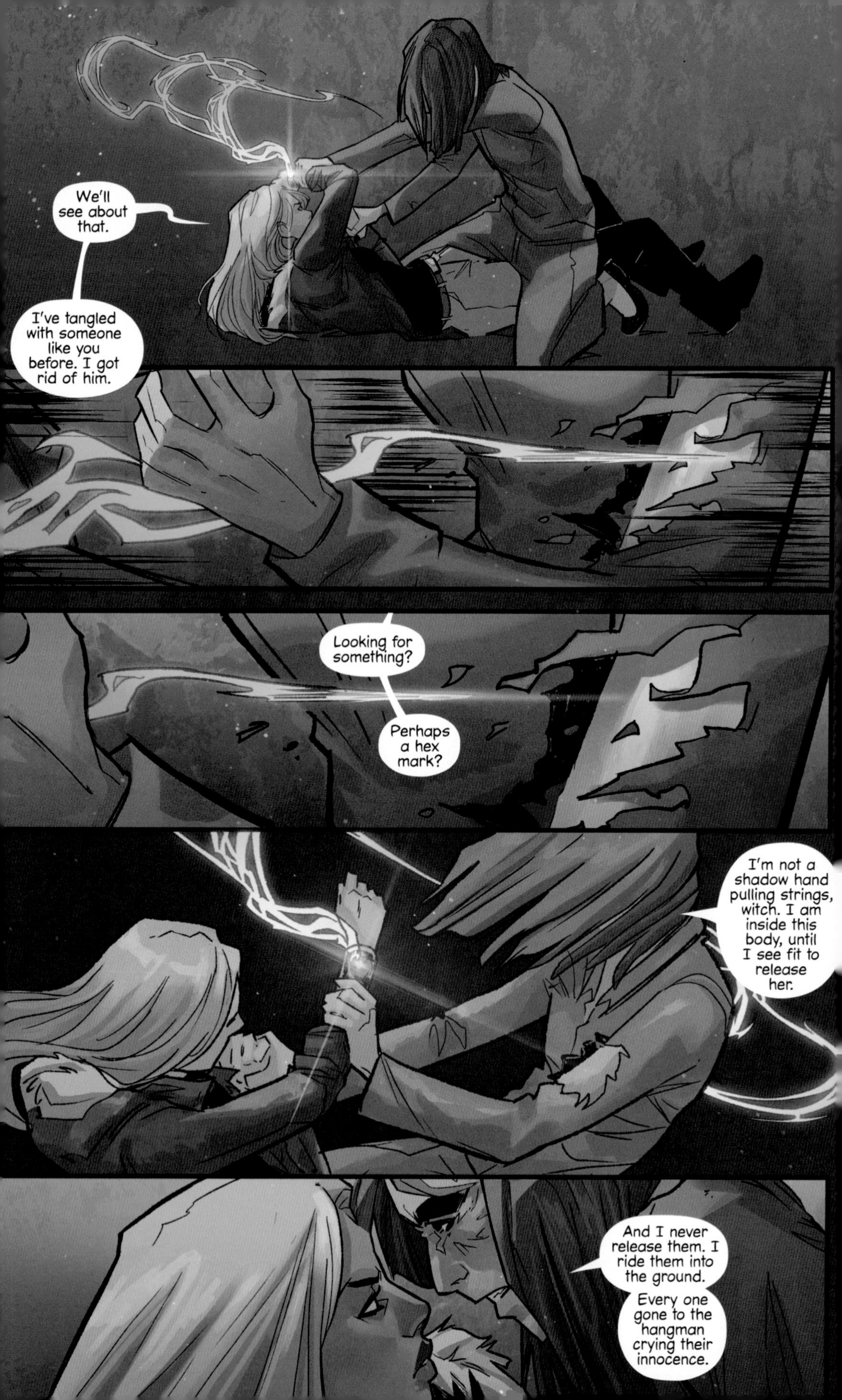
We'll see about that.
I've tangled with someone like you before. I got rid of him.
Looking for something?
Perhaps a hex mark?
I'm not a shadow hand pulling strings, witch. I am inside this body, until I see fit to release her.
And I never release them. I ride them into the ground.
Every one gone to the hangman crying their innocence.

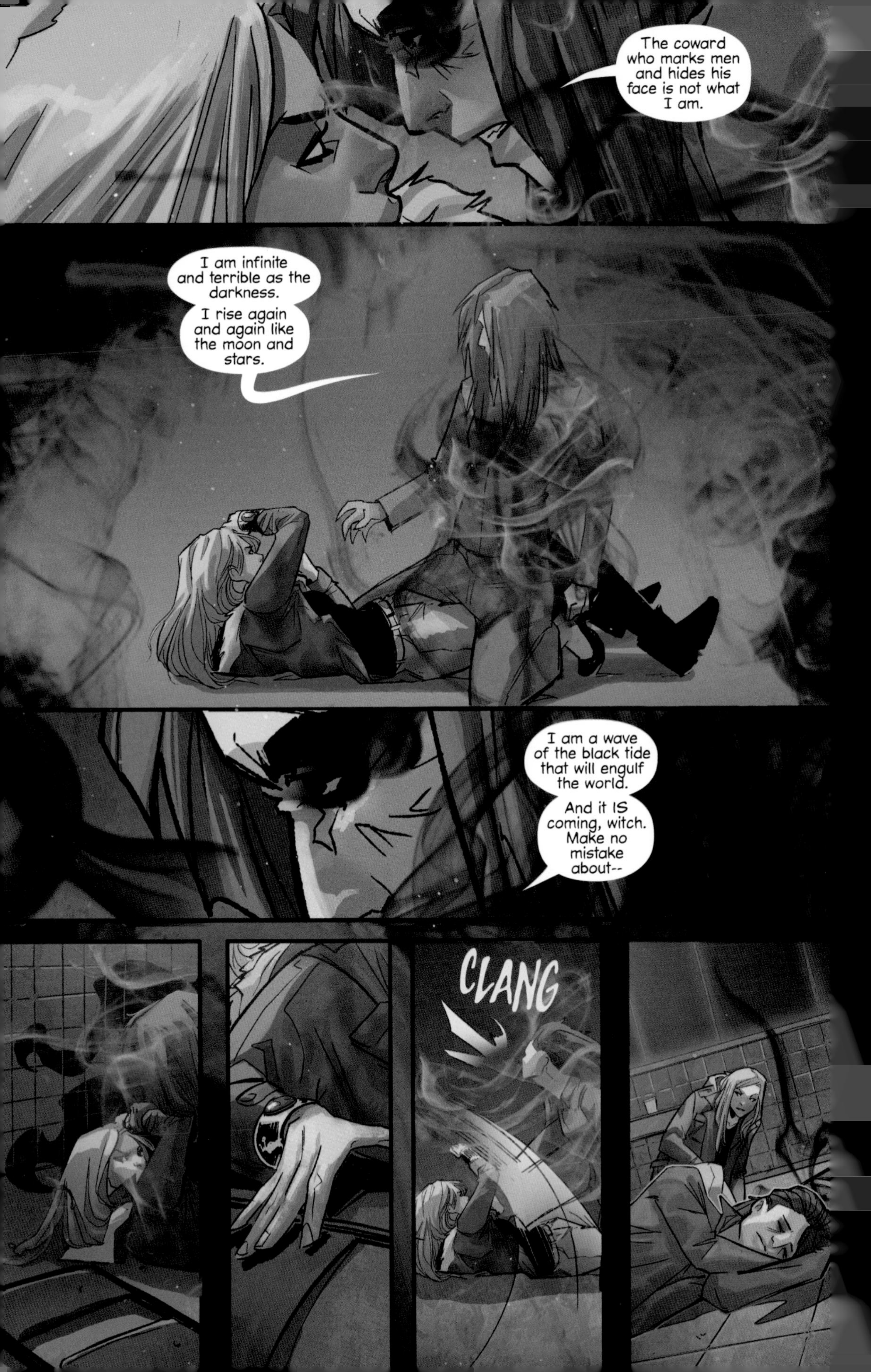
The coward who marks men and hides his face is not what I am.
I am infinite and terrible as the darkness.
I rise again and again like the moon and stars.
I am a wave of the black tide that will engulf the world.
And it IS coming, witch. Make no mistake about--
CLANG

That could have gone better.

Oh no...it happened again...no no NO!

You all right, Ms. Underwood? We can get somebody to look at those scratches.

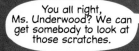

Sorry it took so long to get in here. Power surged and the electronic locks all went offline.

Cameras too?

'Fraid so. But don't worry, you need somebody to sign an affidavit for your insurance, I'll do it no problem.

Crazy bitch killed her kid, I don't care what happens to her.

Don't. Don't say that. It's not what you think.

Really? 'Cause it looks like she came at your face like a subway rat.

It's fine. I'm fine. I need to go.

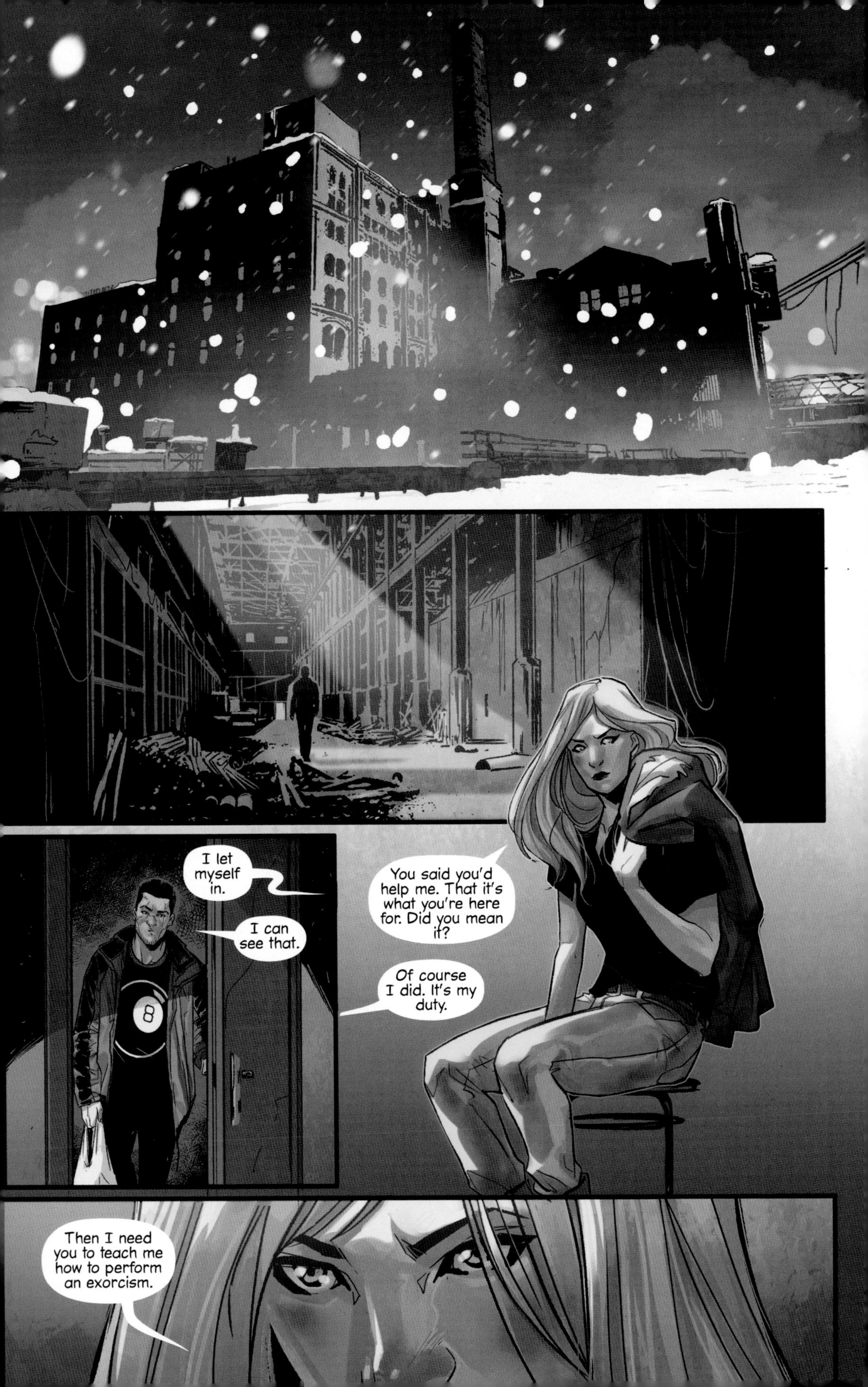
I let myself in.
I can see that.
You said you'd help me. That it's what you're here for. Did you mean it?
Of course I did. It's my duty.
Then I need you to teach me how to perform an exorcism.

CHAPTER FOUR

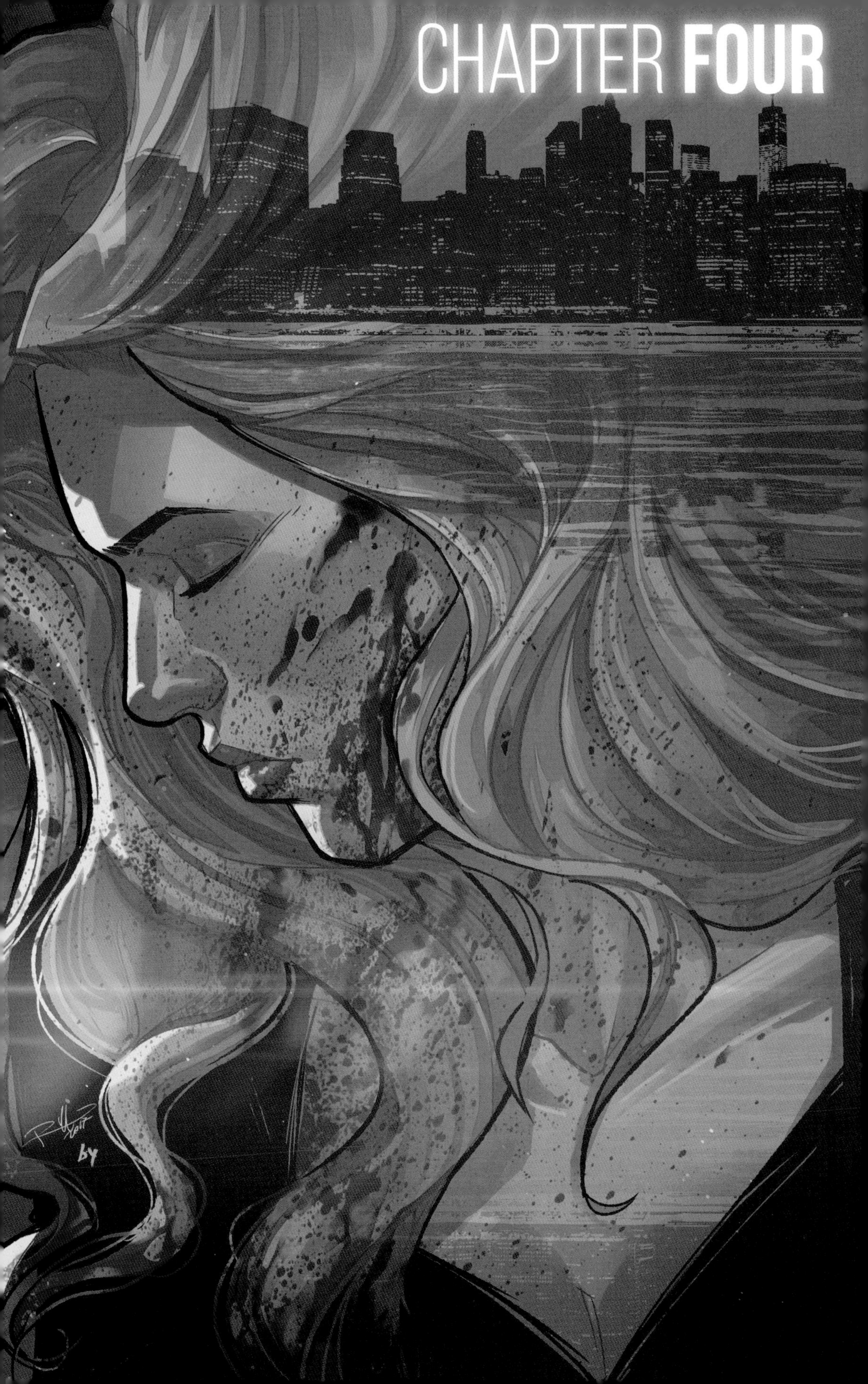

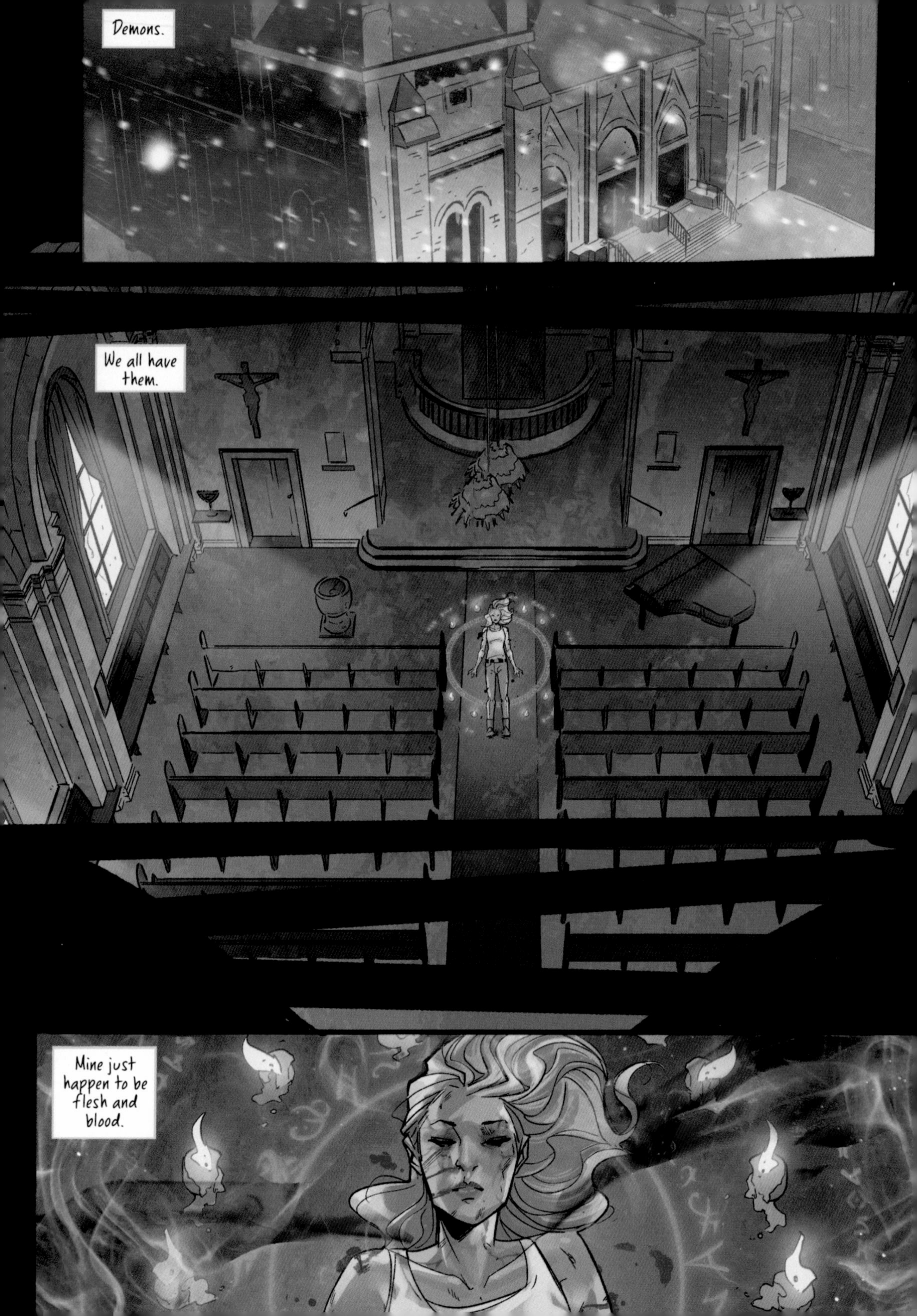
Demons.
We all have them.
Mine just happen to be flesh and blood.

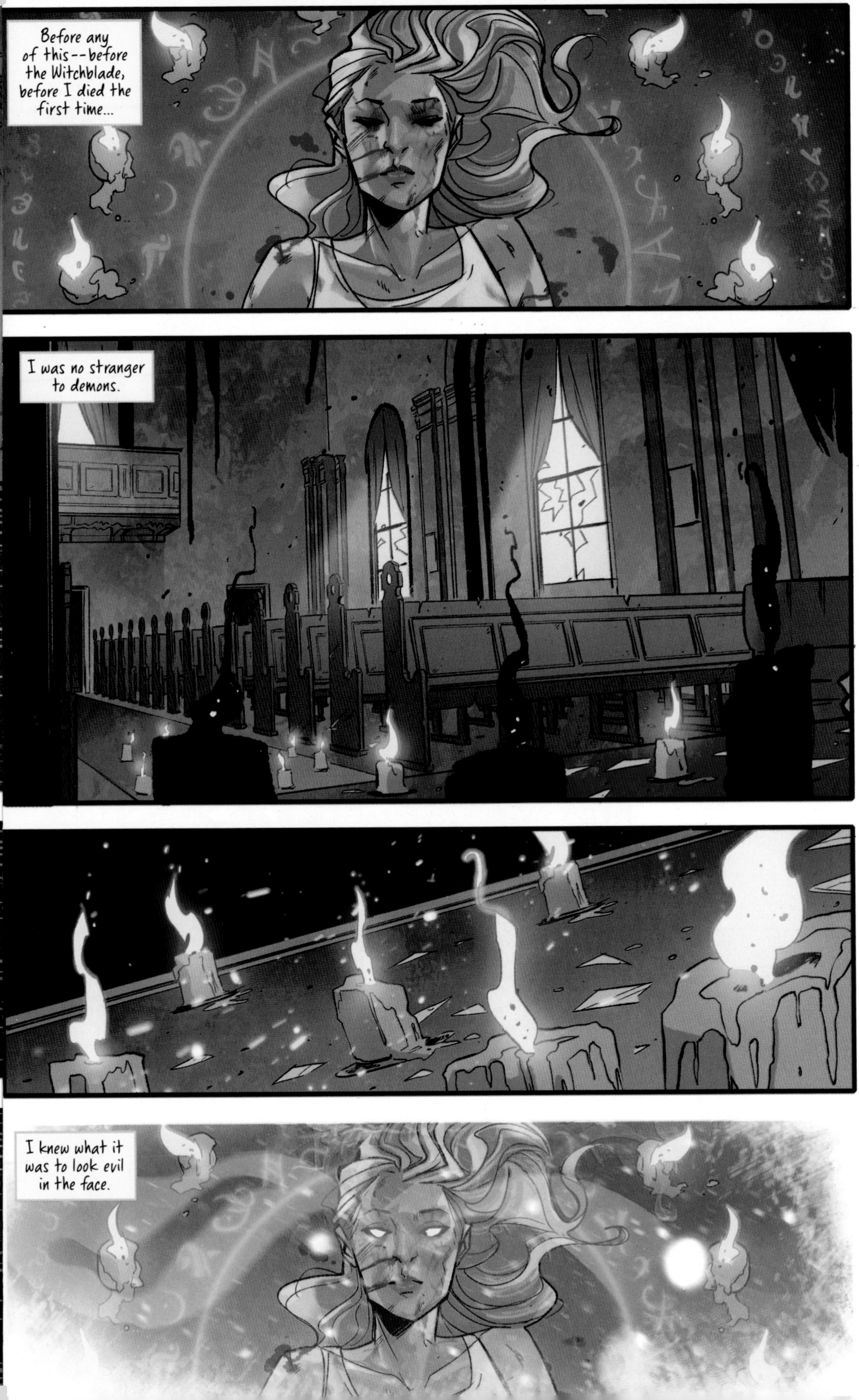
Before any of this--before the Witchblade, before I died the first time...
I was no stranger to demons.
I knew what it was to look evil in the face.

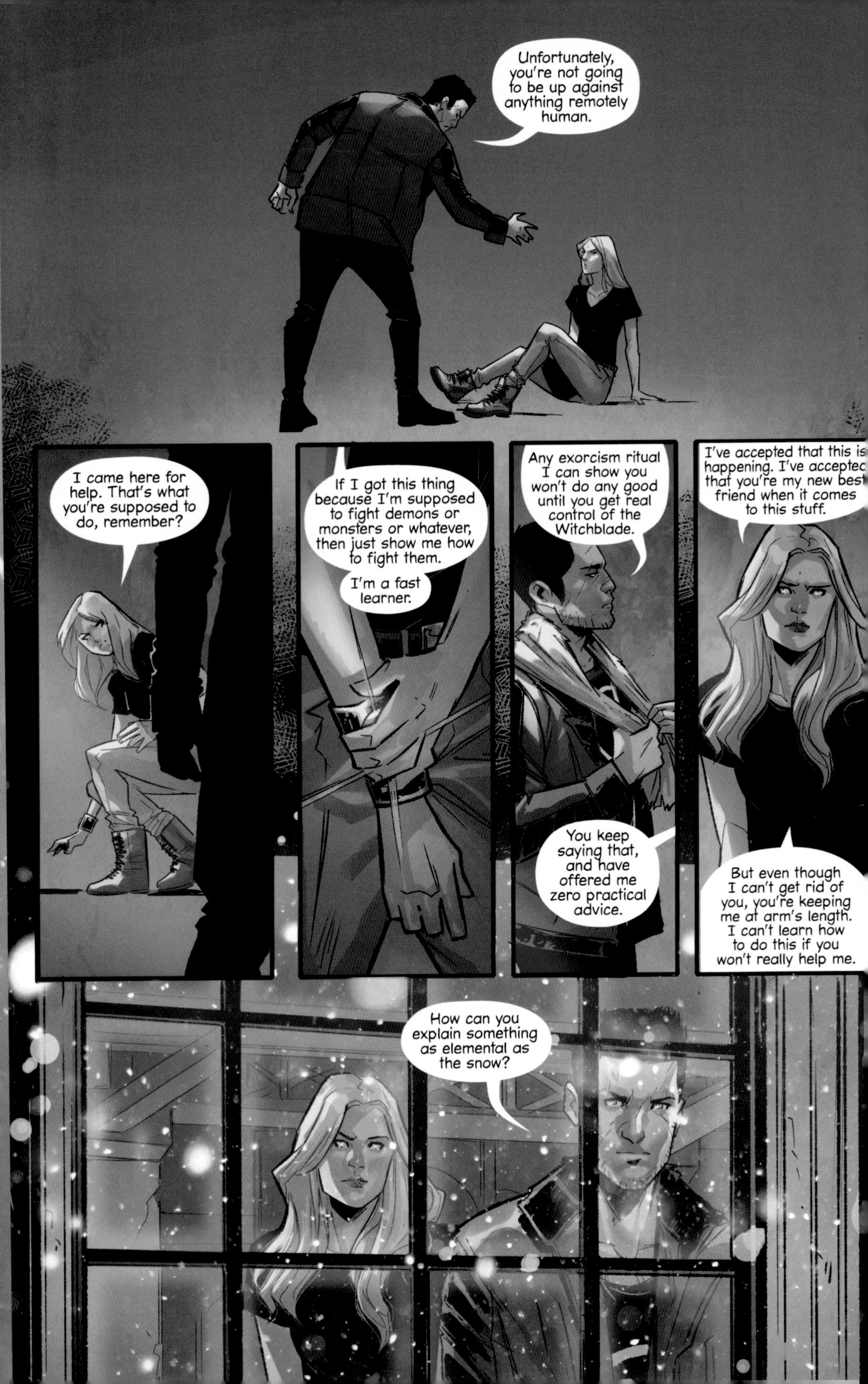
Unfortunately, you're not going to be up against anything remotely human.
I came here for help. That's what you're supposed to do, remember?
If I got this thing because I'm supposed to fight demons or monsters or whatever, then just show me how to fight them.
I'm a fast learner.
Any exorcism ritual I can show you won't do any good until you get real control of the Witchblade.
You keep saying that, and have offered me zero practical advice.
I've accepted that this is happening. I've accepted that you're my new best friend when it comes to this stuff.
But even though I can't get rid of you, you're keeping me at arm's length. I can't learn how to do this if you won't really help me.
How can you explain something as elemental as the snow?

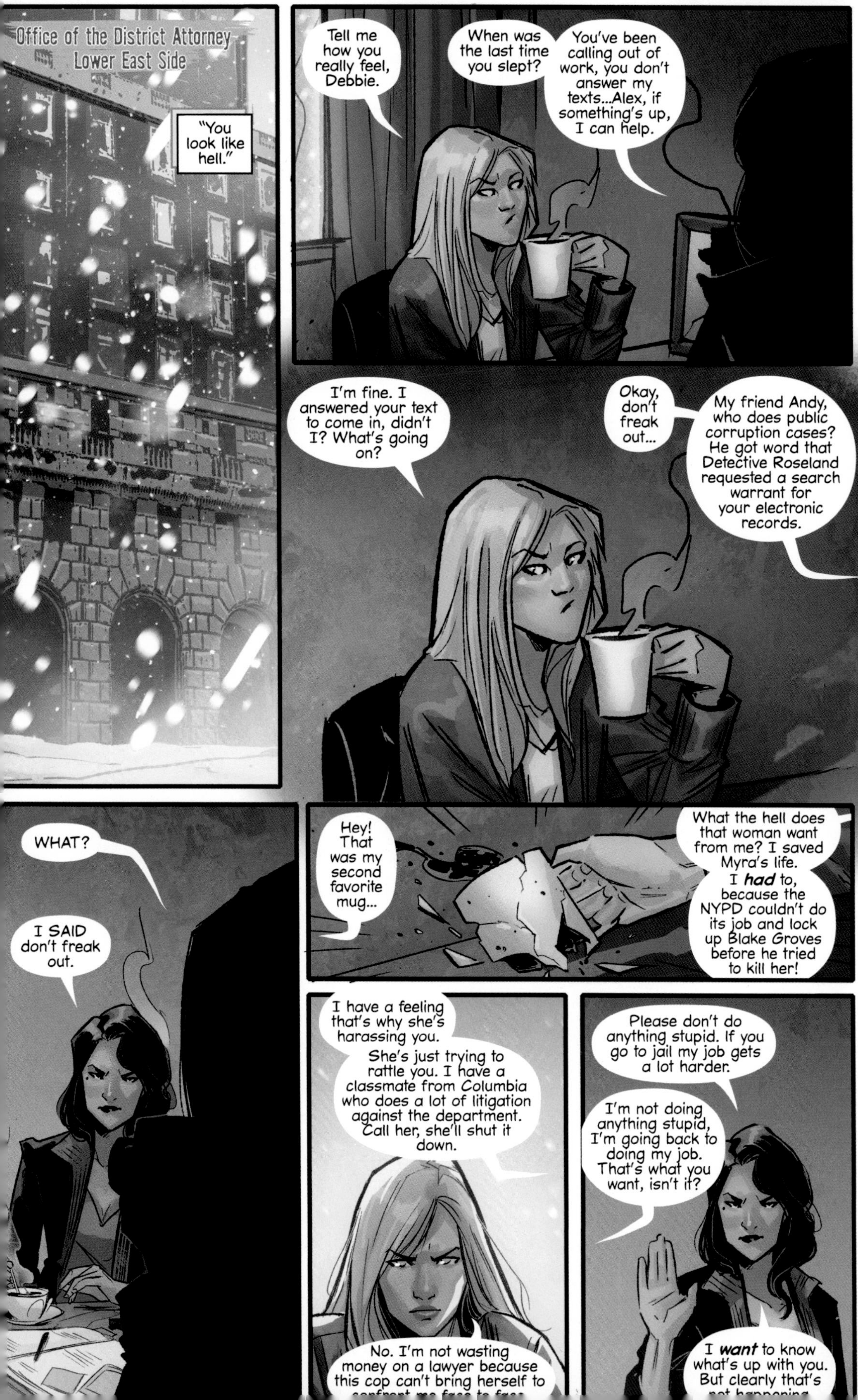
Office of the District Attorney
Lower East Side
"You look like hell."
Tell me how you really feel, Debbie.
When was the last time you slept?
You've been calling out of work, you don't answer my texts...Alex, if something's up, I can help.
I'm fine. I answered your text to come in, didn't I? What's going on?
Okay, don't freak out...
My friend Andy, who does public corruption cases? He got word that Detective Roseland requested a search warrant for your electronic records.
WHAT?
I SAID don't freak out.
Hey! That was my second favorite mug...
What the hell does that woman want from me? I saved Myra's life.
I *had* to, because the NYPD couldn't do its job and lock up Blake Groves before he tried to kill her!
I have a feeling that's why she's harassing you.
She's just trying to rattle you. I have a classmate from Columbia who does a lot of litigation against the department. Call her, she'll shut it down.
No. I'm not wasting money on a lawyer because this cop can't bring herself to
Please don't do anything stupid. If you go to jail my job gets a lot harder.
I'm not doing anything stupid, I'm going back to doing my job. That's what you want, isn't it?
I *want* to know what's up with you. But clearly that's

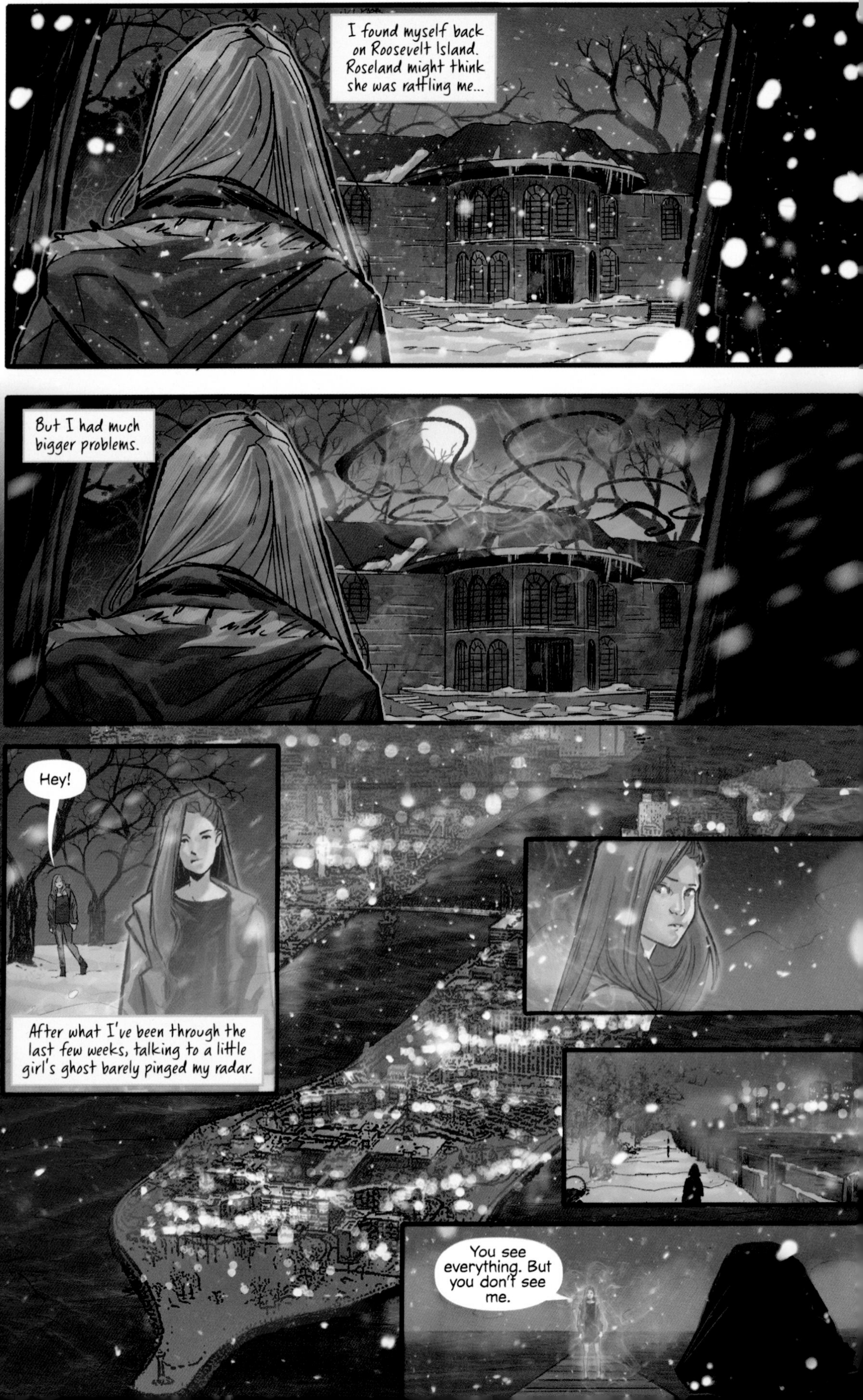
I found myself back on Roosevelt Island. Roseland might think she was rattling me...
But I had much bigger problems.
Hey!
After what I've been through the last few weeks, talking to a little girl's ghost barely pinged my radar.
You see everything. But you don't see me.

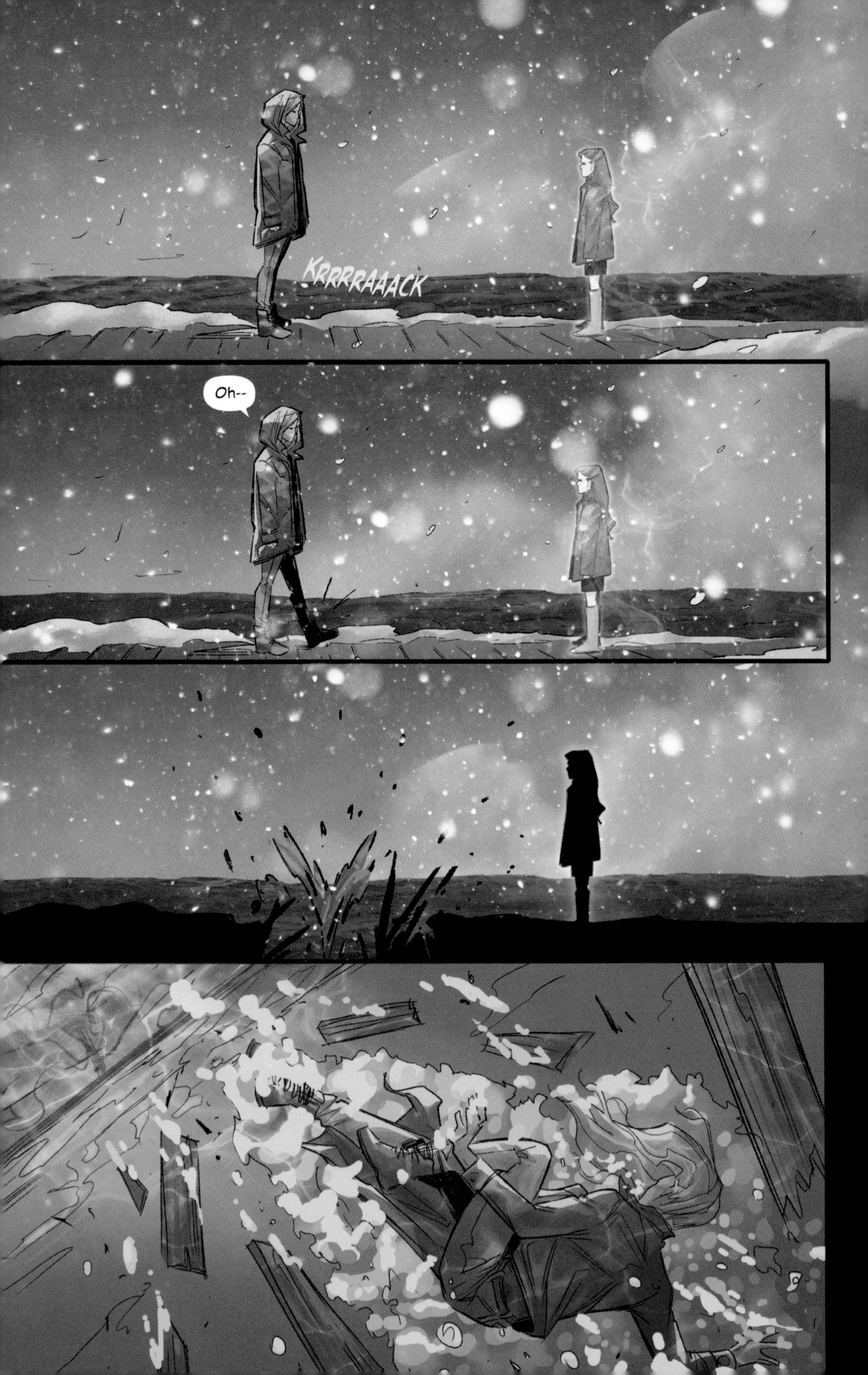
KRRRRAAACK
Oh--

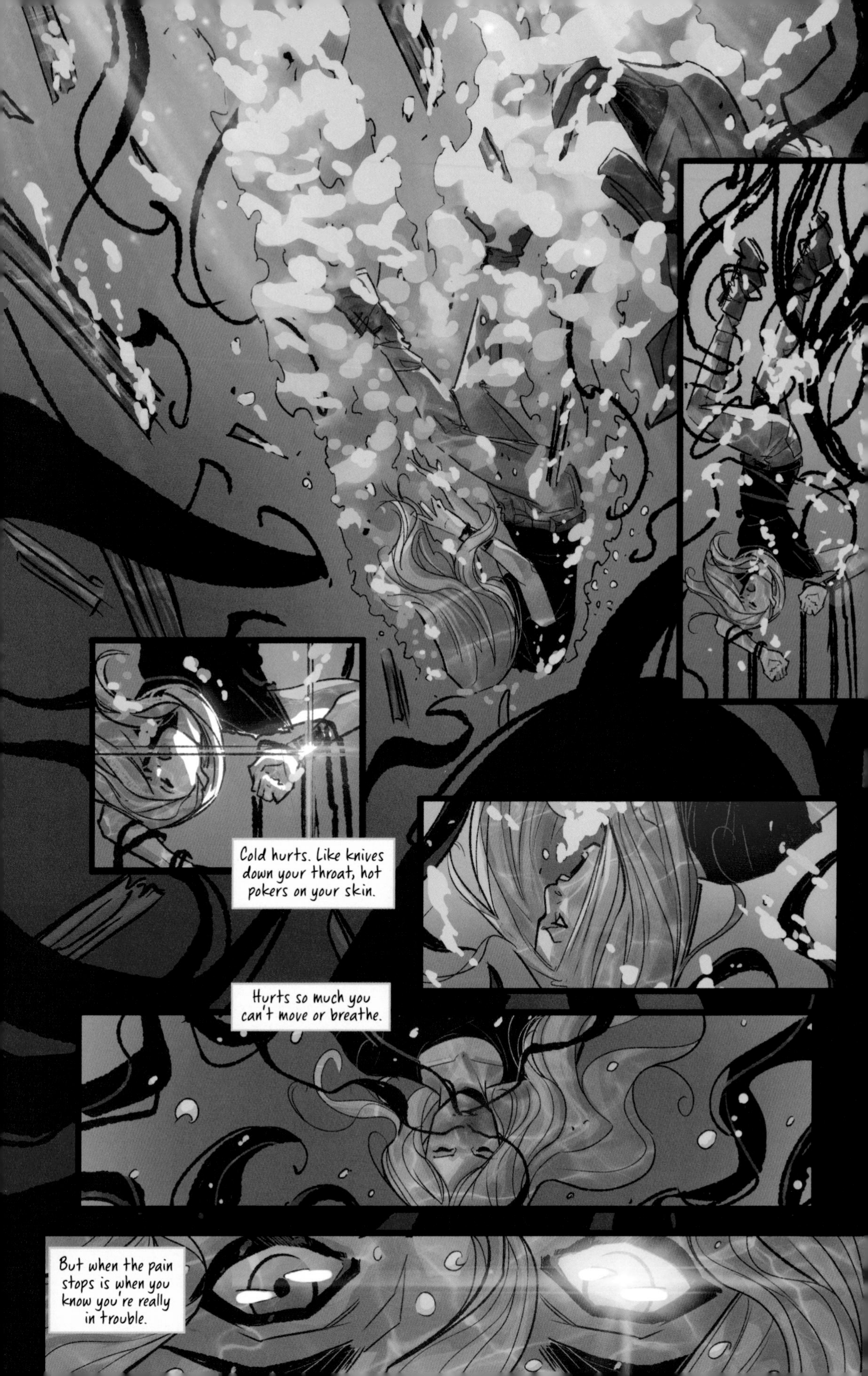
Cold hurts. Like knives down your throat, hot pokers on your skin.
Hurts so much you can't move or breathe.
But when the pain stops is when you know you're really in trouble.

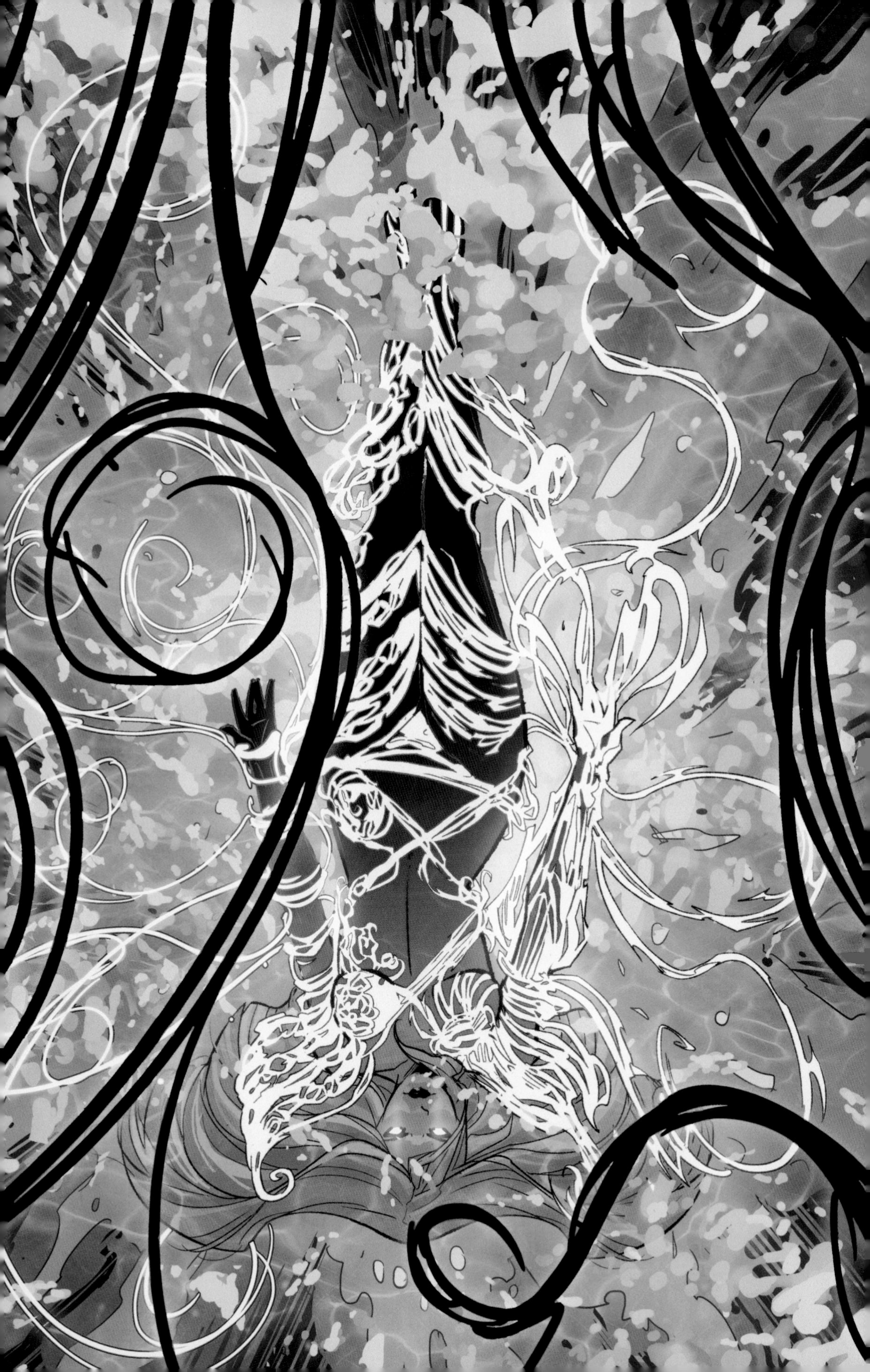

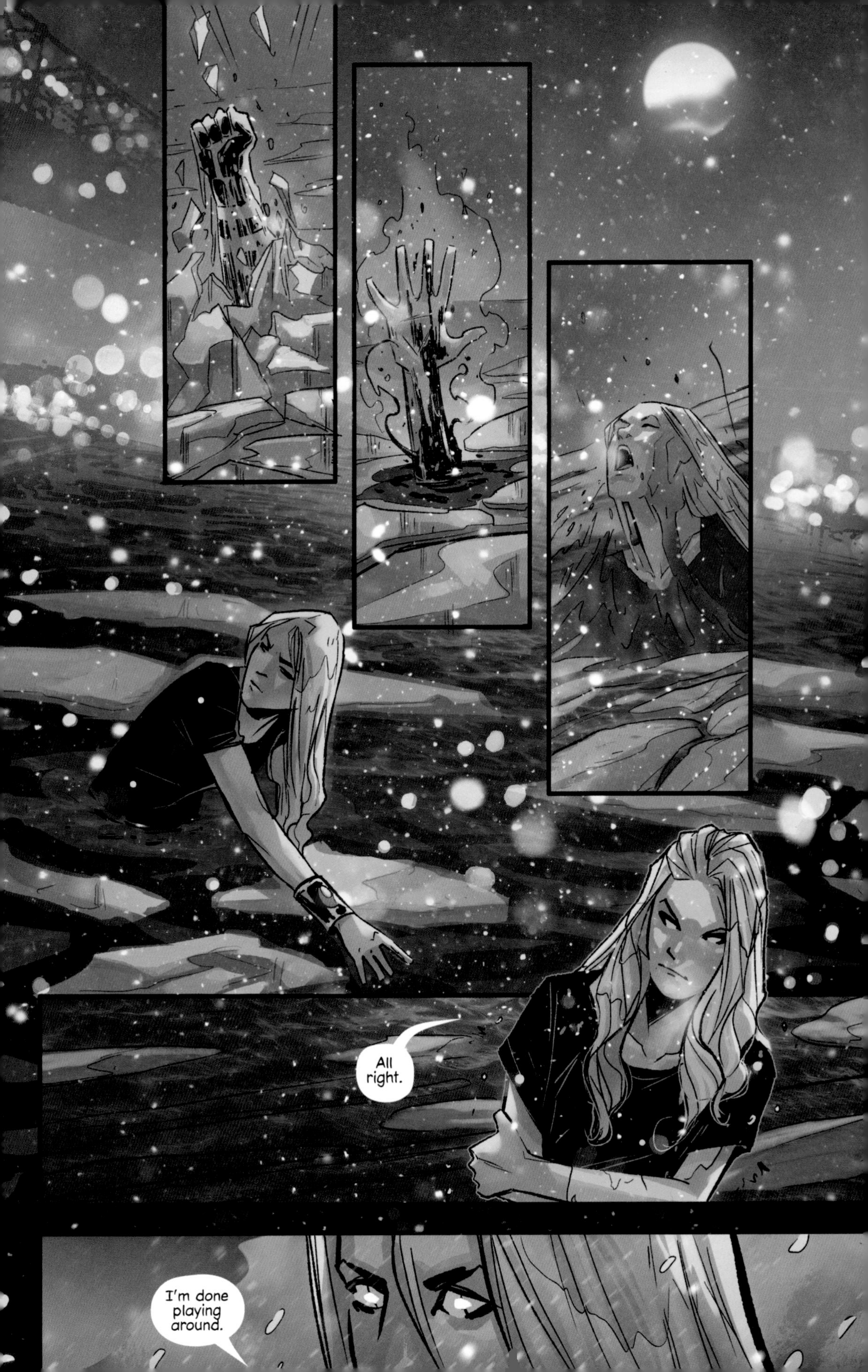
All right.
I'm done playing around.

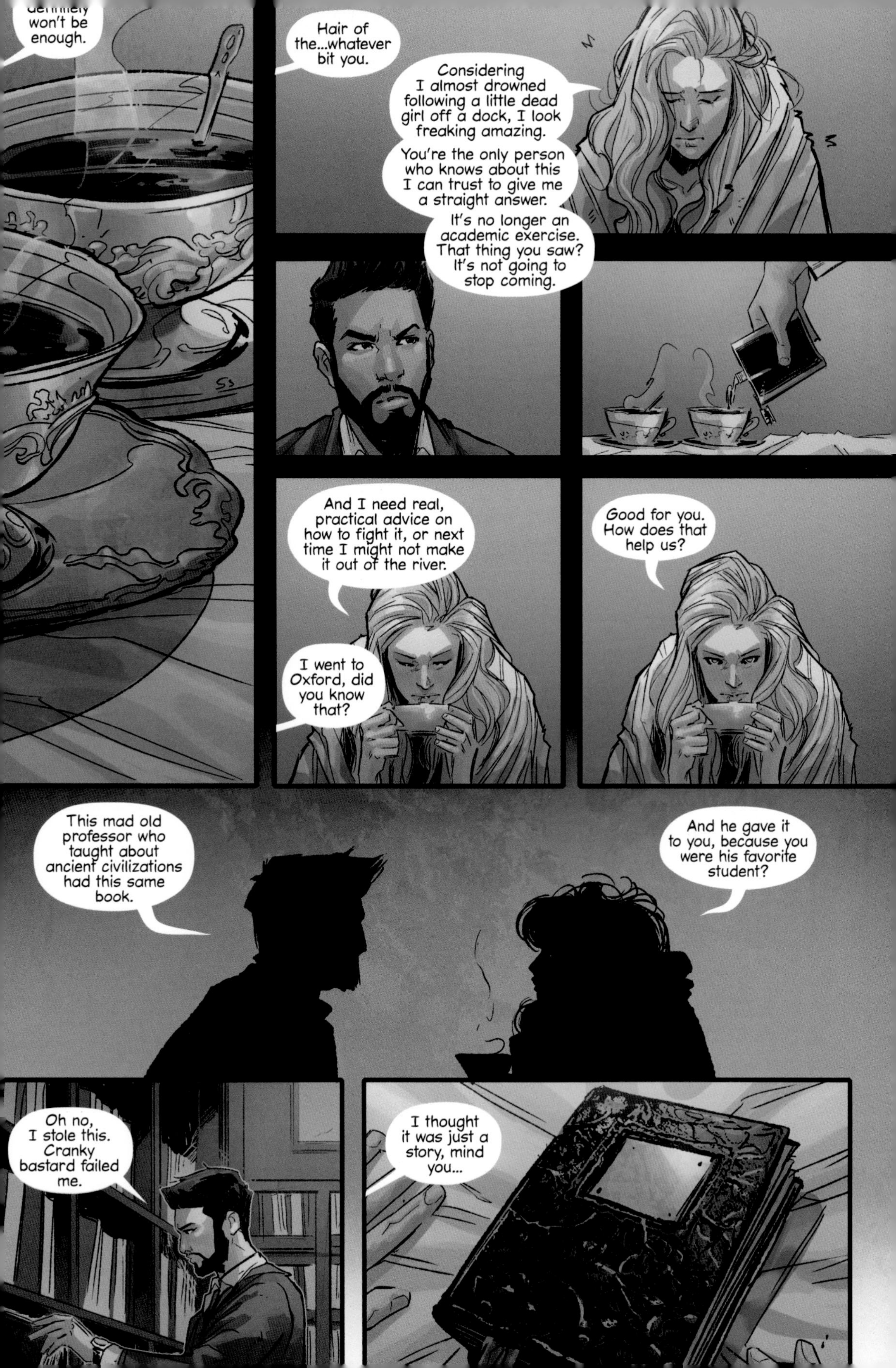
won't be enough.
Hair of the...whatever bit you.
Considering I almost drowned following a little dead girl off a dock, I look freaking amazing.
You're the only person who knows about this I can trust to give me a straight answer.
It's no longer an academic exercise. That thing you saw? It's not going to stop coming.
And I need real, practical advice on how to fight it, or next time I might not make it out of the river.
I went to Oxford, did you know that?
Good for you. How does that help us?
This mad old professor who taught about ancient civilizations had this same book.
And he gave it to you, because you were his favorite student?
Oh no, I stole this. Cranky bastard failed me.
I thought it was just a story, mind you...

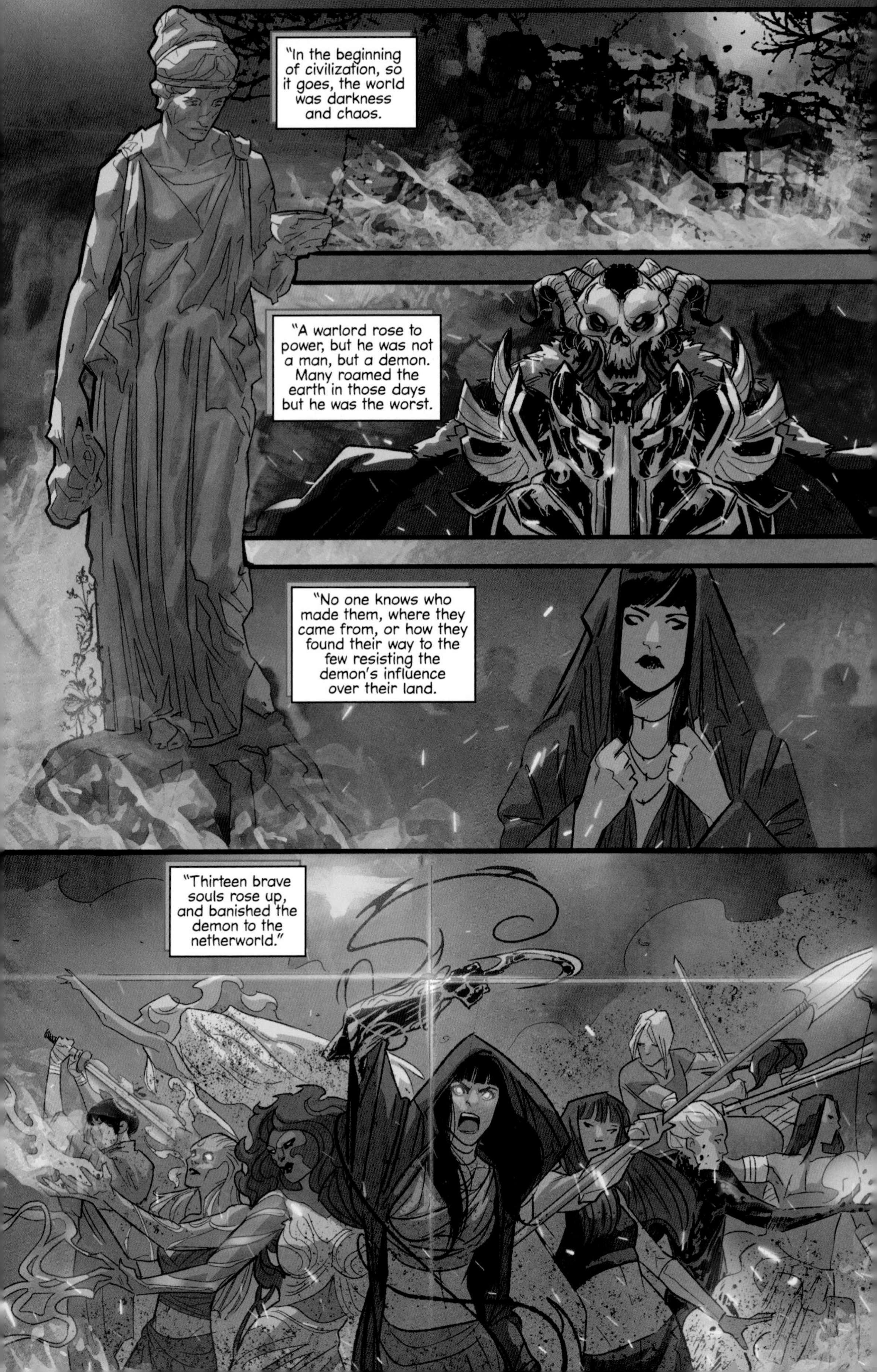
"In the beginning of civilization, so it goes, the world was darkness and chaos.
"A warlord rose to power, but he was not a man, but a demon. Many roamed the earth in those days but he was the worst.
"No one knows who made them, where they came from, or how they found their way to the few resisting the demon's influence over their land.
"Thirteen brave souls rose up, and banished the demon to the netherworld."

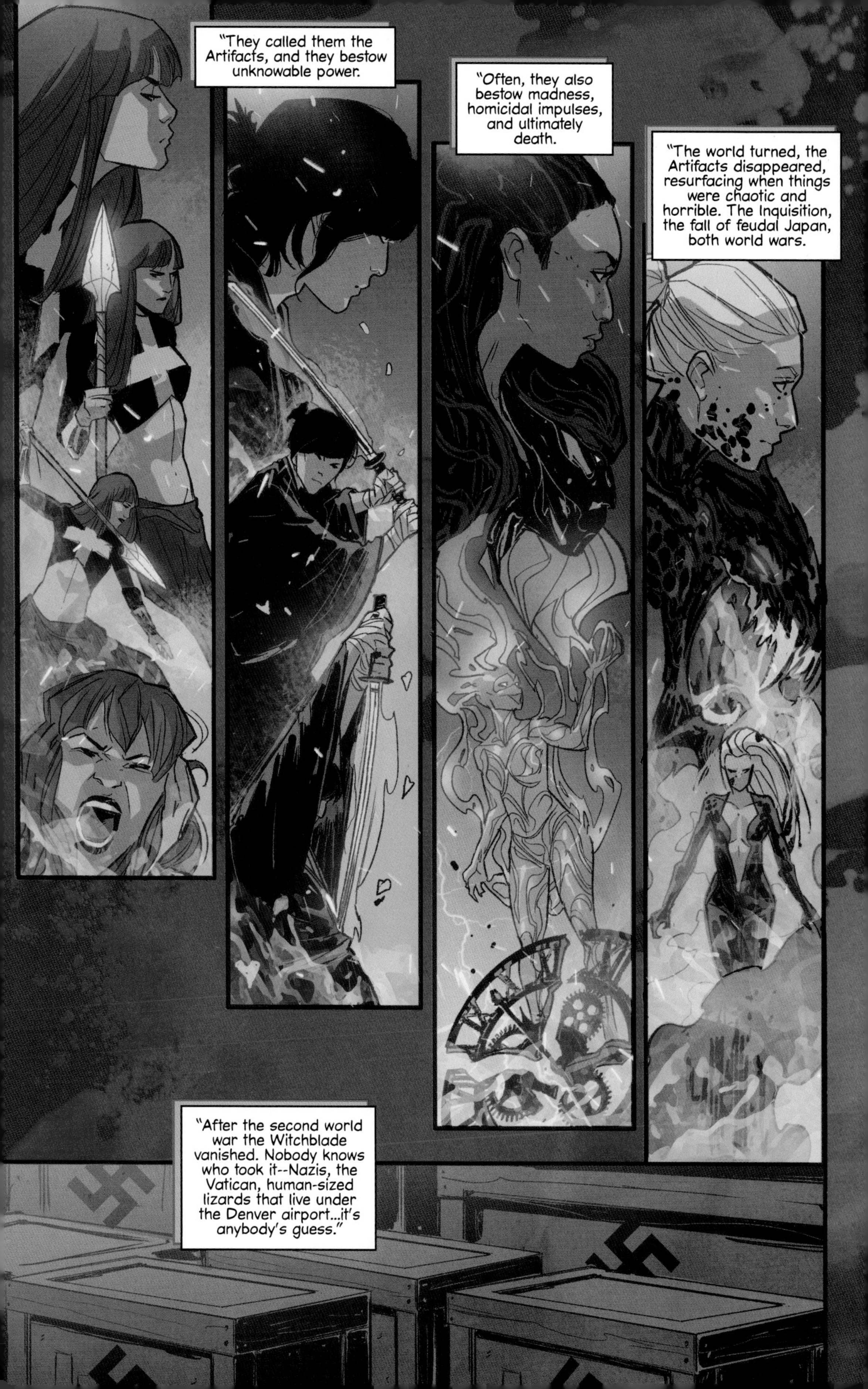
"They called them the Artifacts, and they bestow unknowable power.
"Often, they also bestow madness, homicidal impulses, and ultimately death.
"The world turned, the Artifacts disappeared, resurfacing when things were chaotic and horrible. The Inquisition, the fall of feudal Japan, both world wars.
"After the second world war the Witchblade vanished. Nobody knows who took it--Nazis, the Vatican, human-sized lizards that live under the Denver airport...it's anybody's guess."

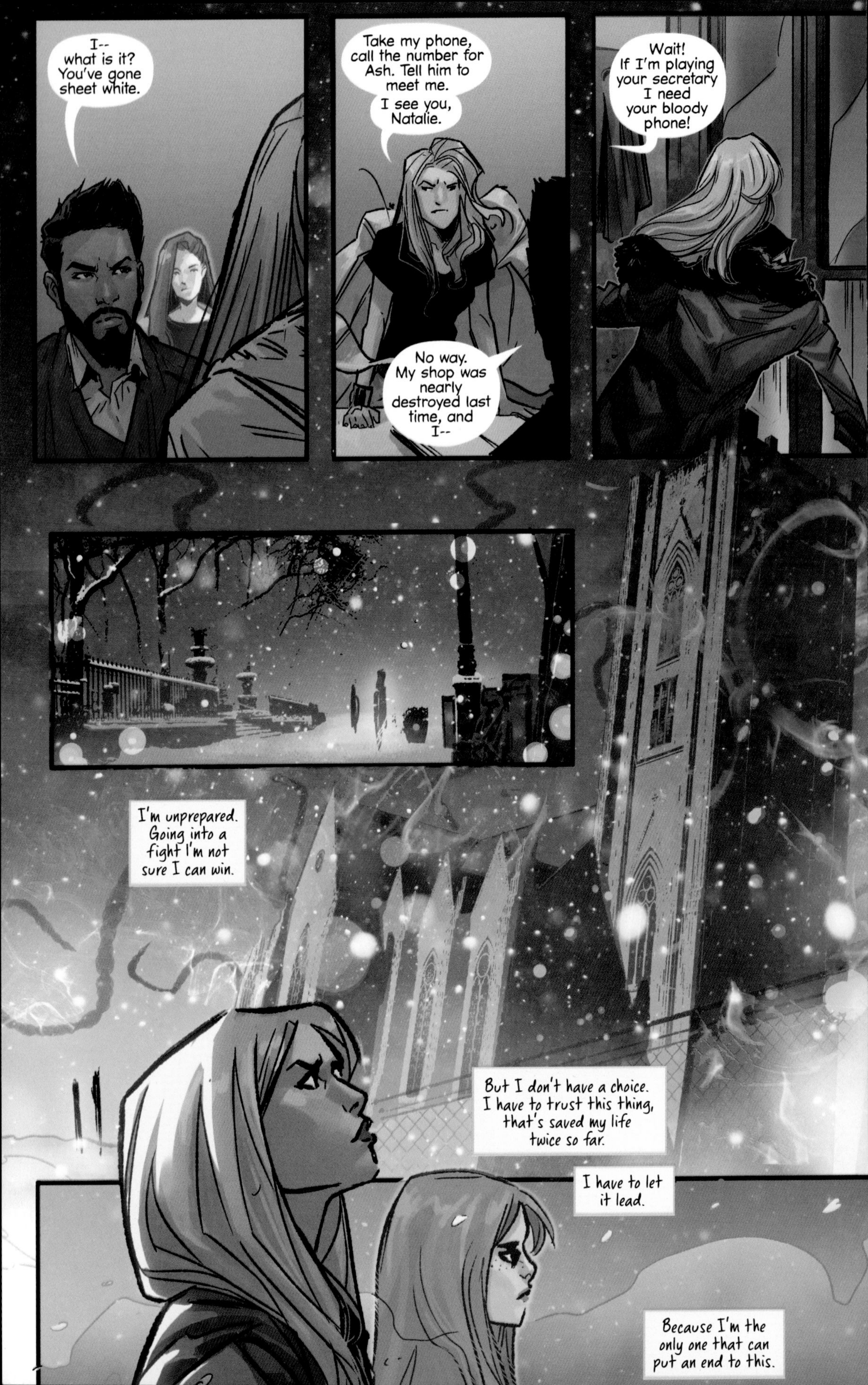
I--
what is it? You've gone sheet white.
Take my phone, call the number for Ash. Tell him to meet me.
I see you, Natalie.
No way. My shop was nearly destroyed last time, and I--
Wait! If I'm playing your secretary I need your bloody phone!
I'm unprepared. Going into a fight I'm not sure I can win.
But I don't have a choice. I have to trust this thing, that's saved my life twice so far.
I have to let it lead.
Because I'm the only one that can put an end to this.

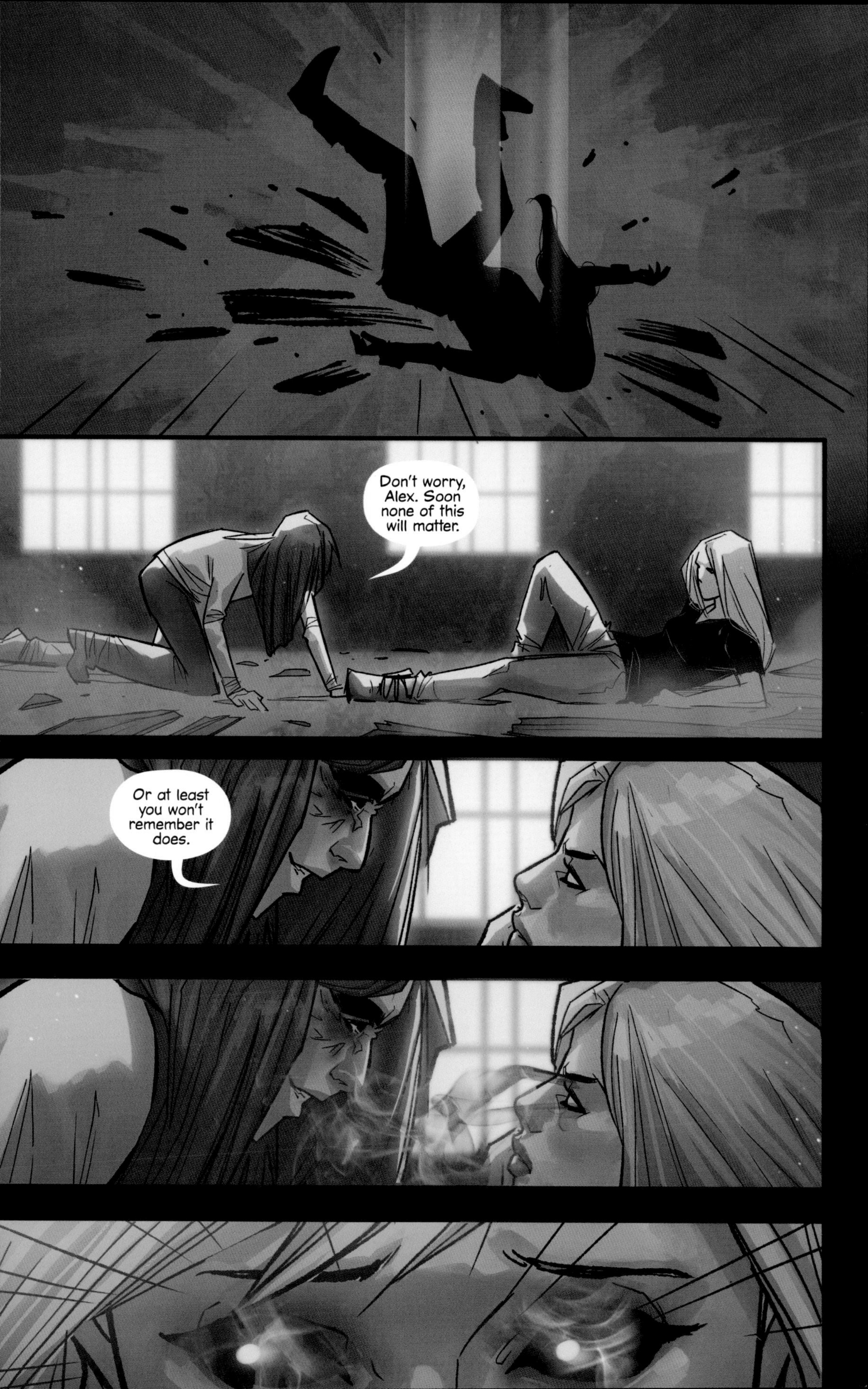
Don't worry, Alex. Soon none of this will matter.
Or at least you won't remember it does.

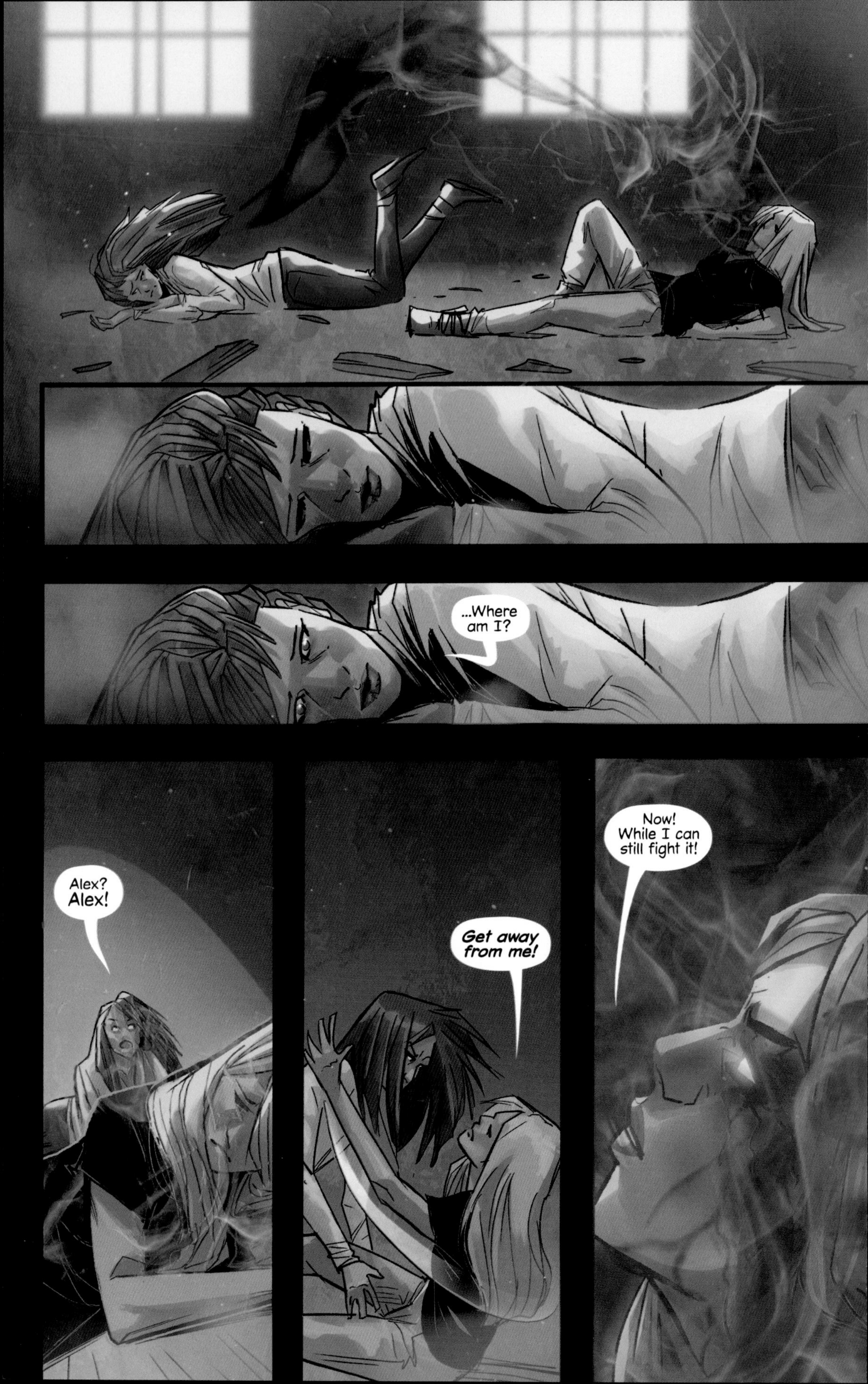
...Where am I?
Alex? Alex!
Get away from me!
Now! While I can still fight it!

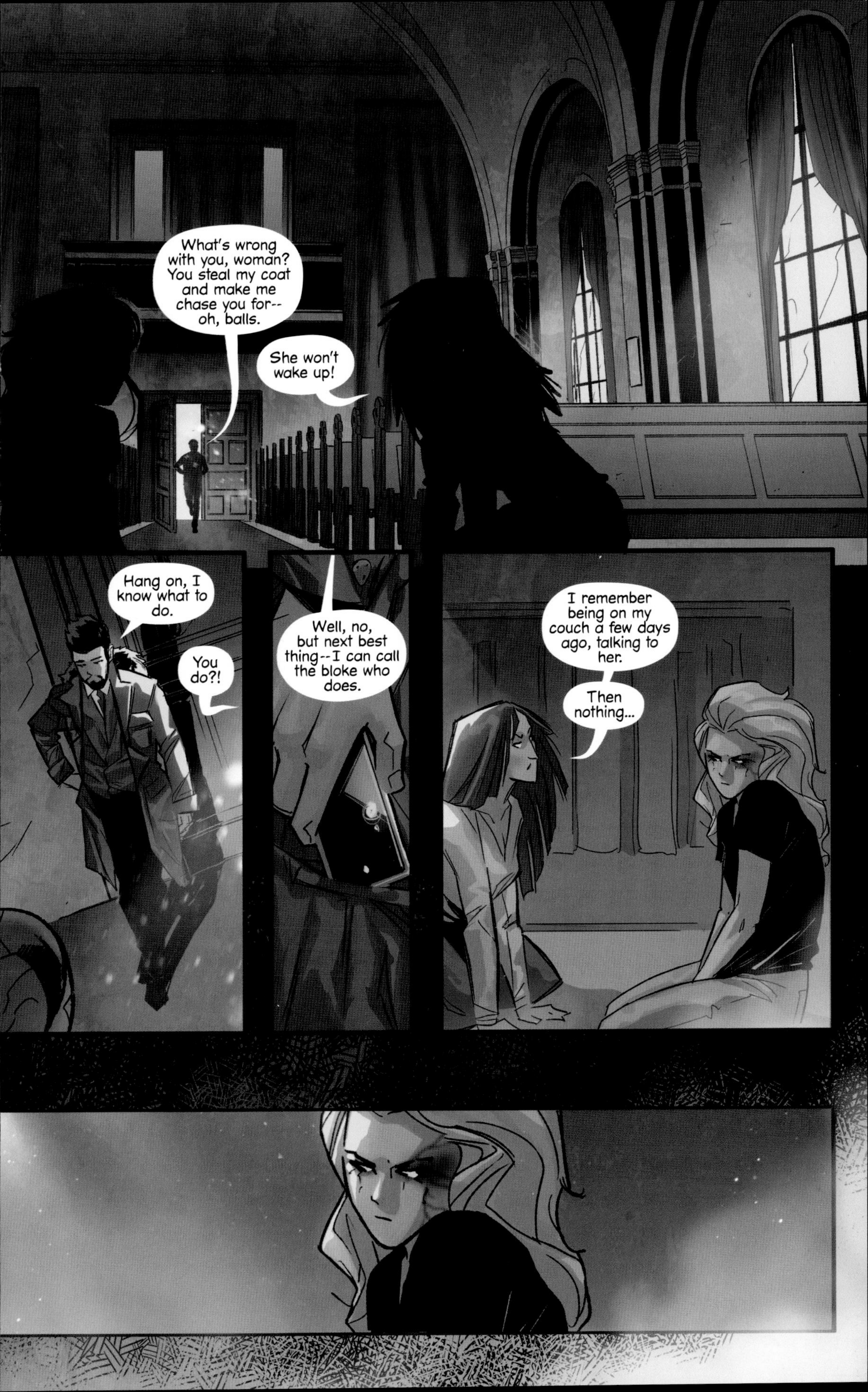
What's wrong with you, woman? You steal my coat and make me chase you for-- oh, balls.
She won't wake up!
Hang on, I know what to do.
You do?!
Well, no, but next best thing--I can call the bloke who does.
I remember being on my couch a few days ago, talking to her.
Then nothing...

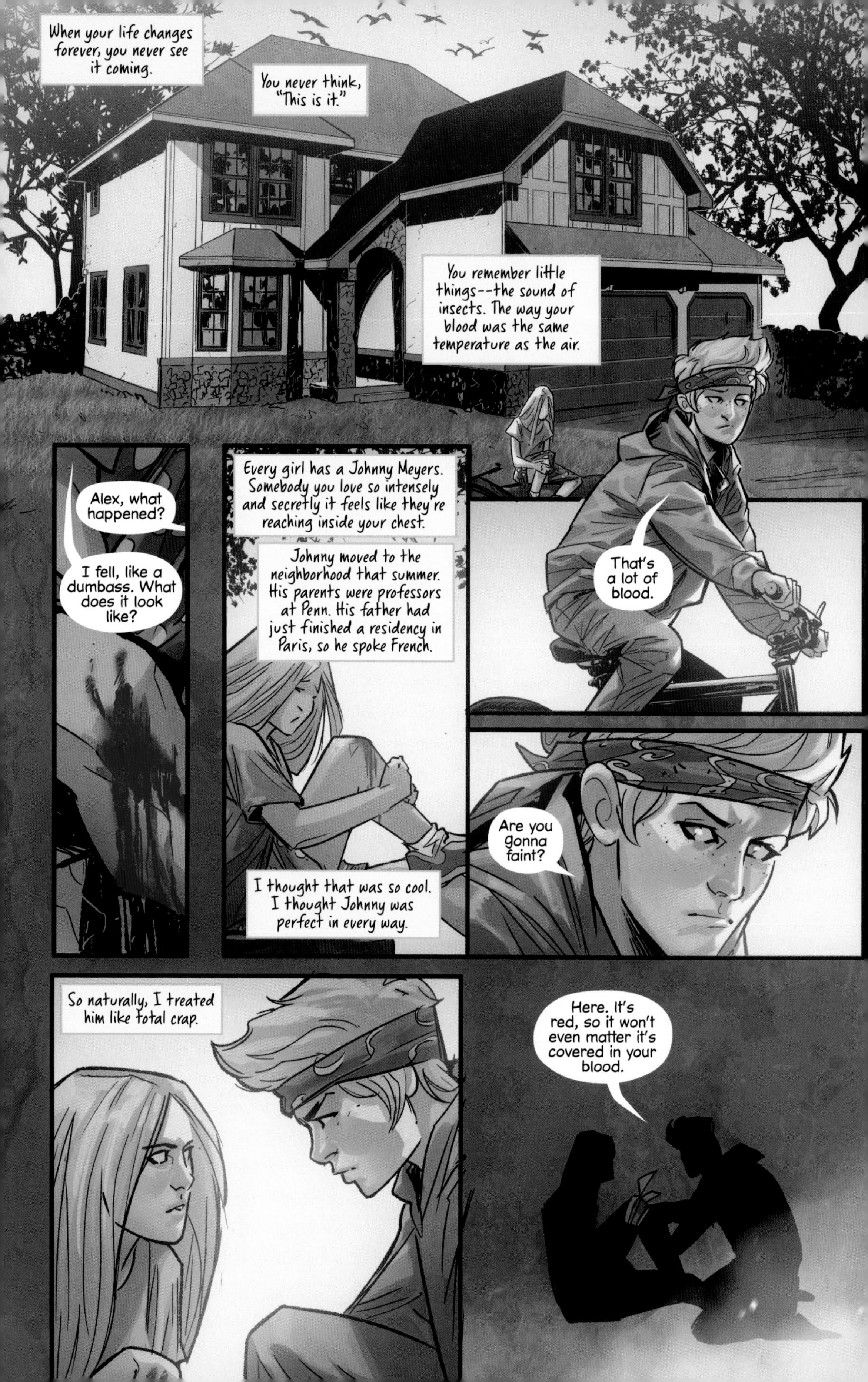
When your life changes forever, you never see it coming.
You never think, "This is it."
You remember little things--the sound of insects. The way your blood was the same temperature as the air.
Alex, what happened?
I fell, like a dumbass. What does it look like?
Every girl has a Johnny Meyers. Somebody you love so intensely and secretly it feels like they're reaching inside your chest.
Johnny moved to the neighborhood that summer. His parents were professors at Penn. His father had just finished a residency in Paris, so he spoke French.
That's a lot of blood.
Are you gonna faint?
I thought that was so cool. I thought Johnny was perfect in every way.
So naturally, I treated him like total crap.
Here. It's red, so it won't even matter it's covered in your blood.

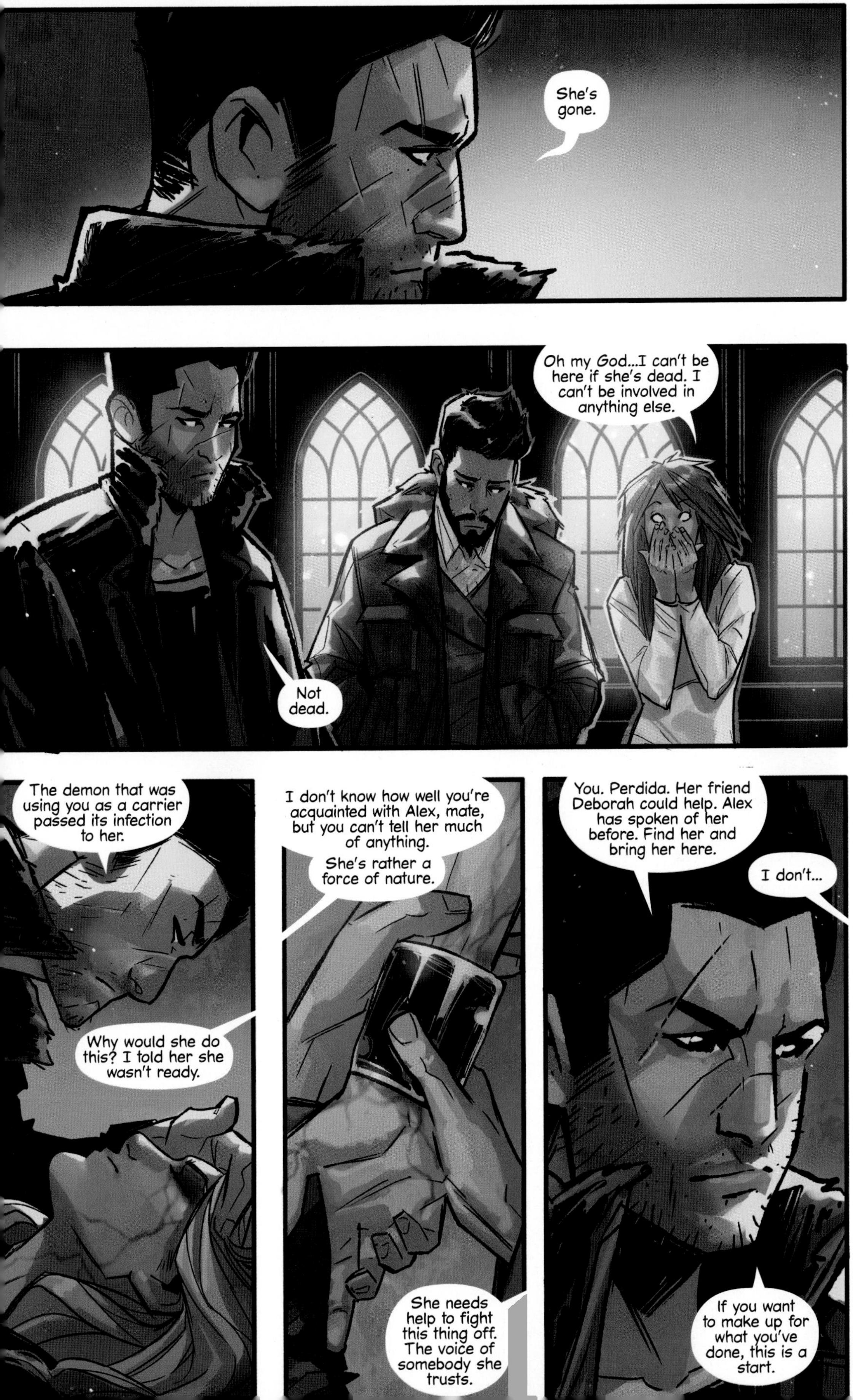
She's gone.
Oh my God...I can't be here if she's dead. I can't be involved in anything else.
Not dead.
The demon that was using you as a carrier passed its infection to her.
Why would she do this? I told her she wasn't ready.
I don't know how well you're acquainted with Alex, mate, but you can't tell her much of anything.
She's rather a force of nature.
She needs help to fight this thing off. The voice of somebody she trusts.
You. Perdida. Her friend Deborah could help. Alex has spoken of her before. Find her and bring her here.
I don't...
If you want to make up for what you've done, this is a start.

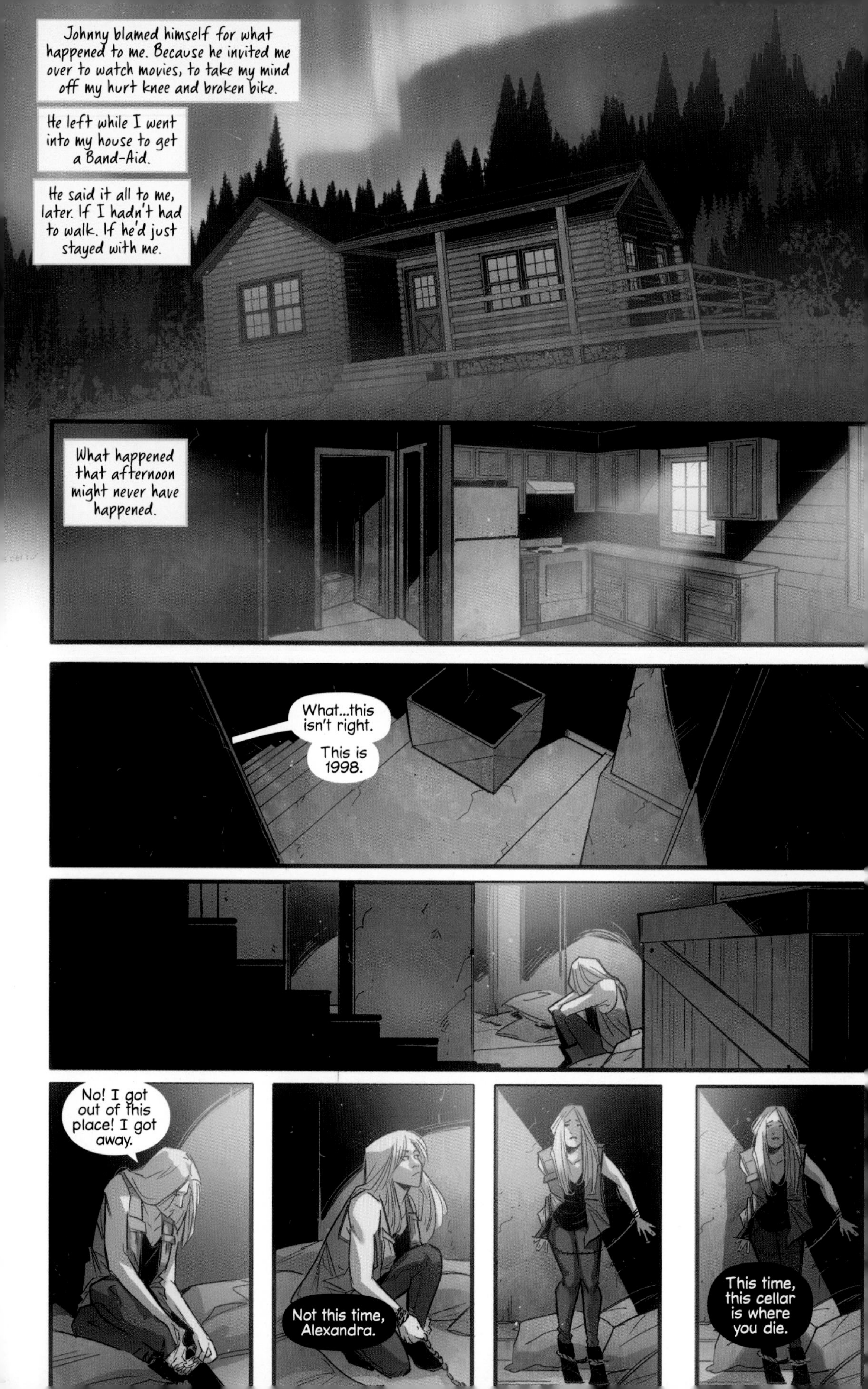
Johnny blamed himself for what happened to me. Because he invited me over to watch movies, to take my mind off my hurt knee and broken bike.
He left while I went into my house to get a Band-Aid.
He said it all to me, later. If I hadn't had to walk. If he'd just stayed with me.
What happened that afternoon might never have happened.
What...this isn't right.
This is 1998.
No! I got out of this place! I got away.
Not this time, Alexandra.
This time, this cellar is where you die.

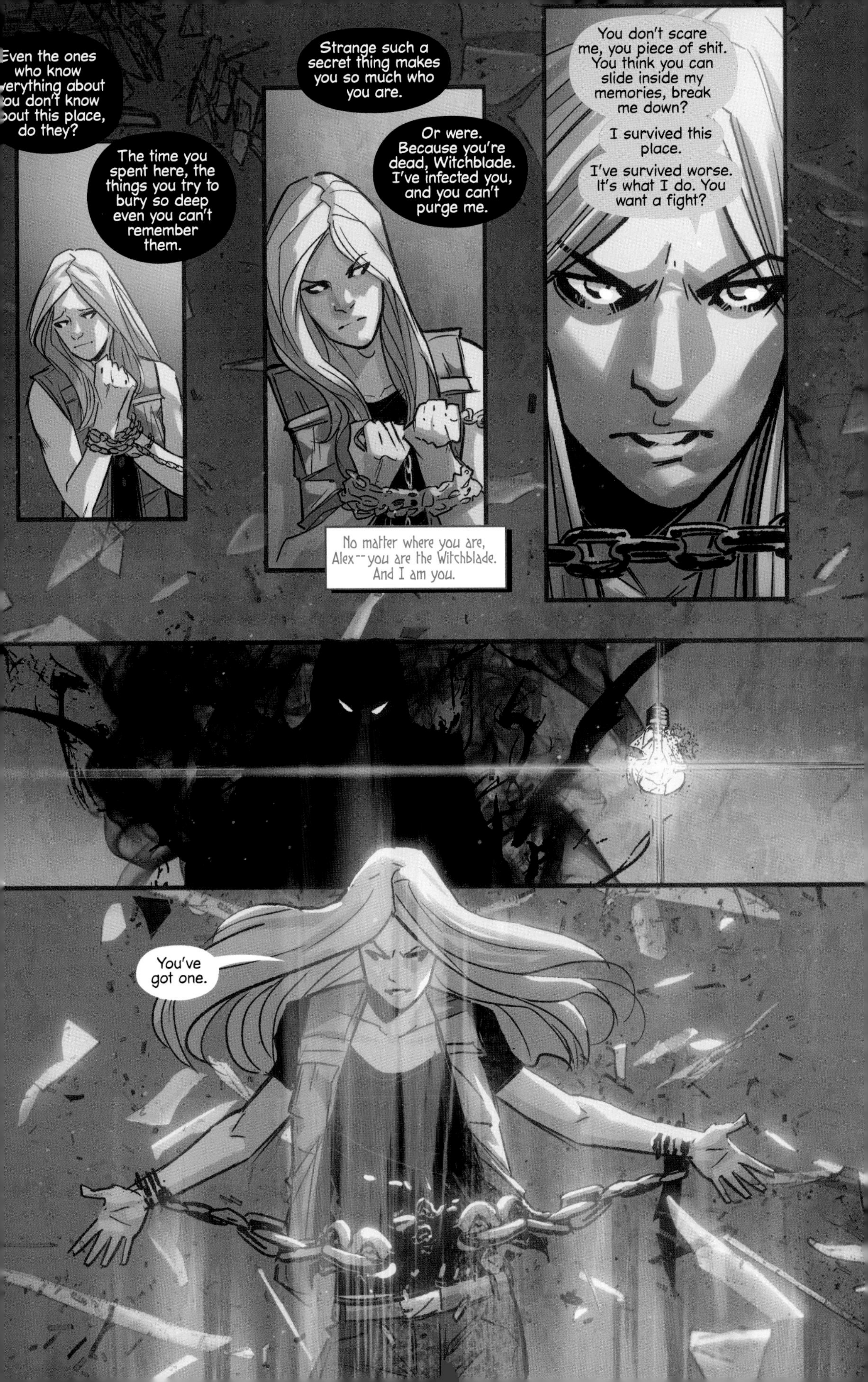
Even the ones who know everything about you don't know about this place, do they?
The time you spent here, the things you try to bury so deep even you can't remember them.
Strange such a secret thing makes you so much who you are.
Or were. Because you're dead, Witchblade. I've infected you, and you can't purge me.
No matter where you are, Alex-- you are the Witchblade. And I am you.
You don't scare me, you piece of shit. You think you can slide inside my memories, break me down?
I survived this place.
I've survived worse. It's what I do. You want a fight?
You've got one.

CHAPTER FIVE

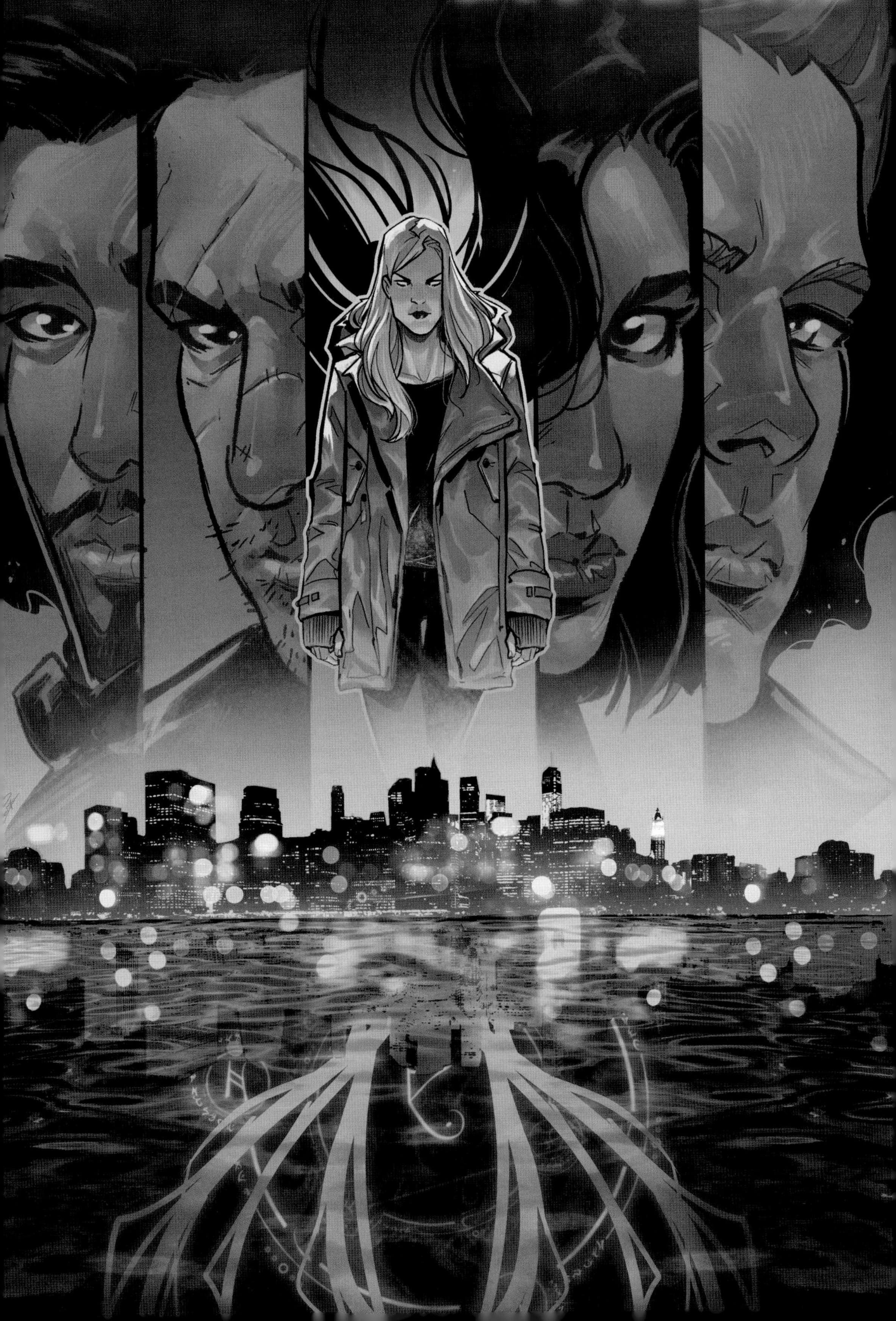

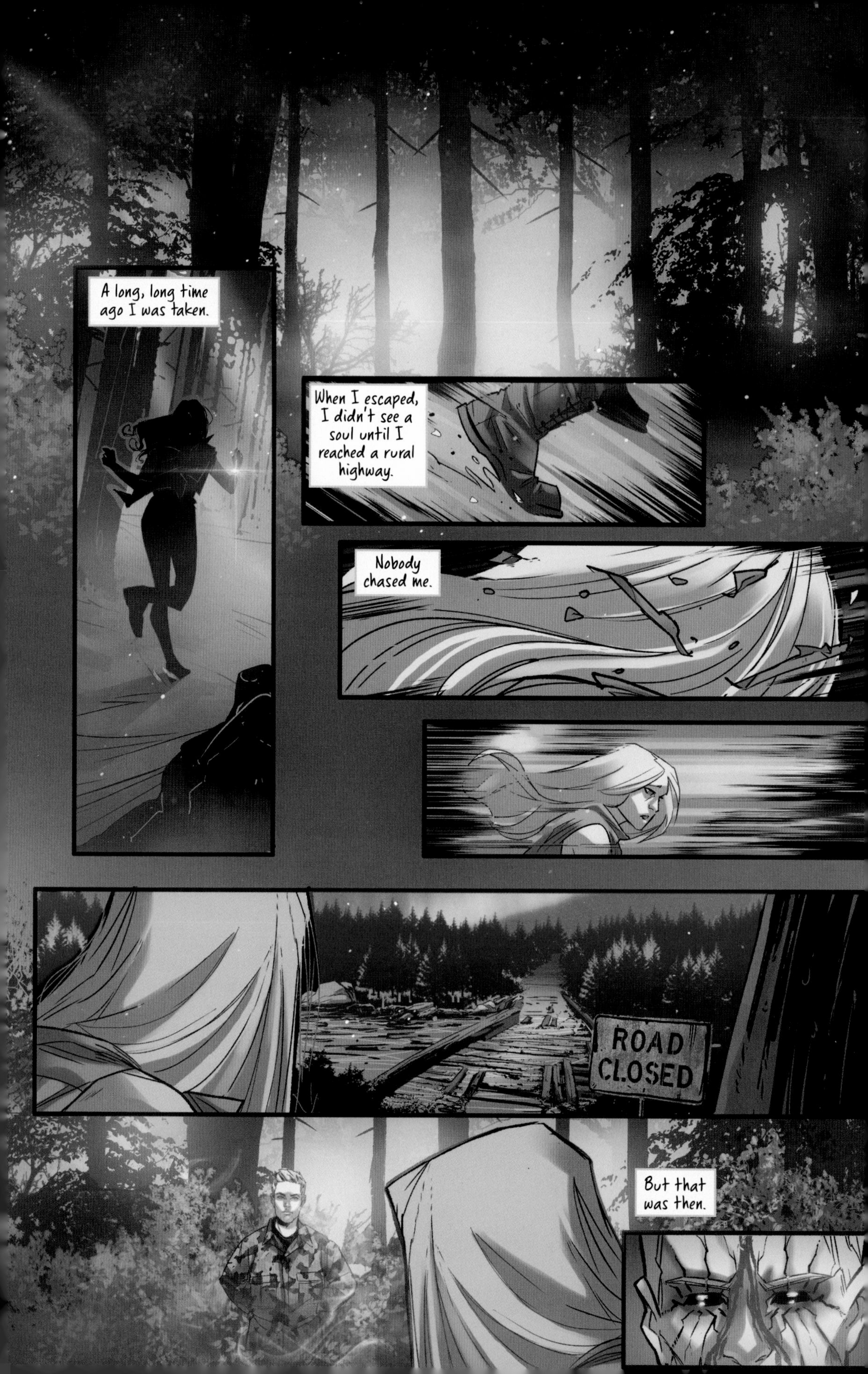
A long, long time ago I was taken.
When I escaped, I didn't see a soul until I reached a rural highway.
Nobody chased me.
ROAD CLOSED
But that was then.

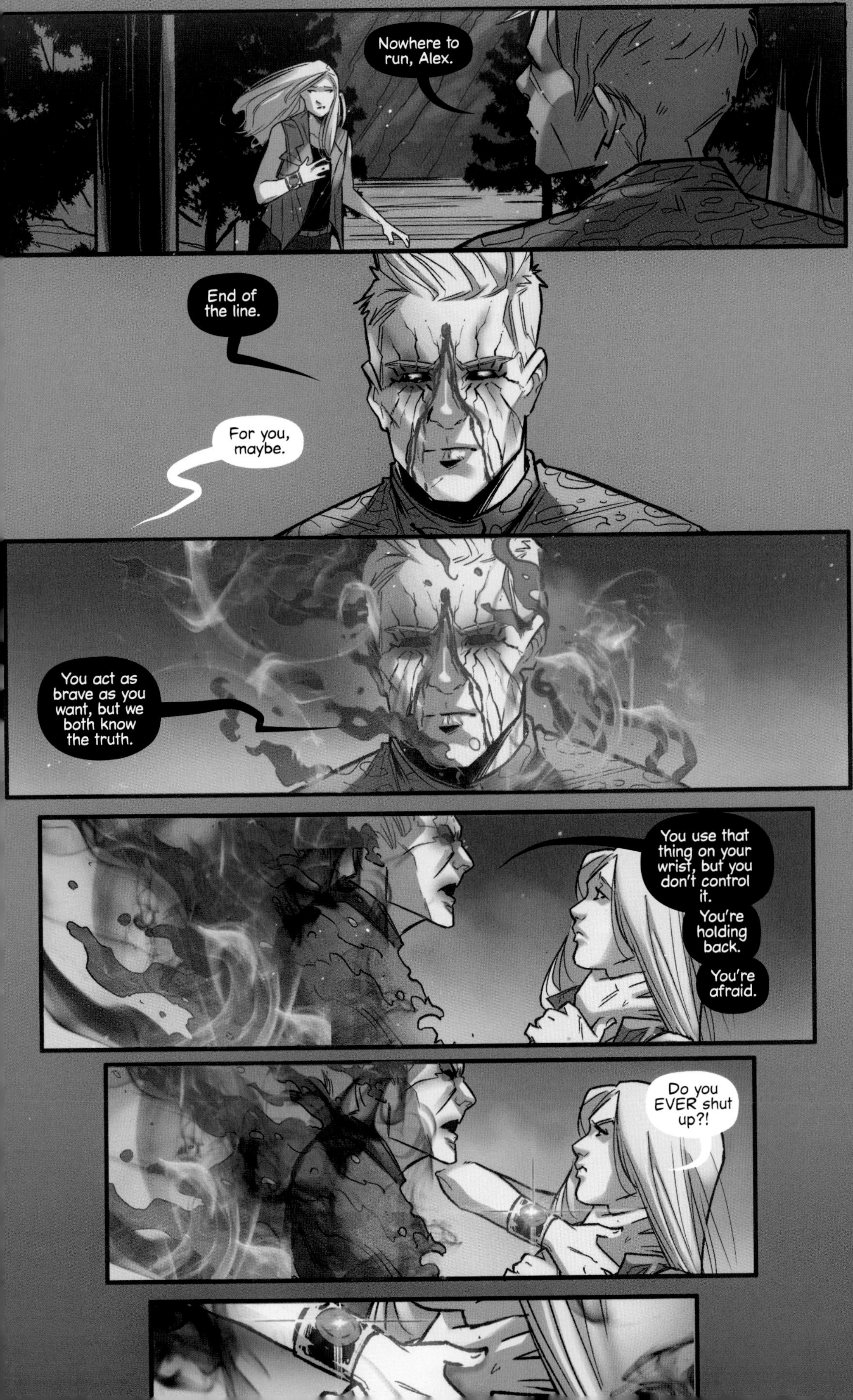

Nowhere to run, Alex.
End of the line.
For you, maybe.
You act as brave as you want, but we both know the truth.
You use that thing on your wrist, but you don't control it.
You're holding back.
You're afraid.
Do you EVER shut up?!

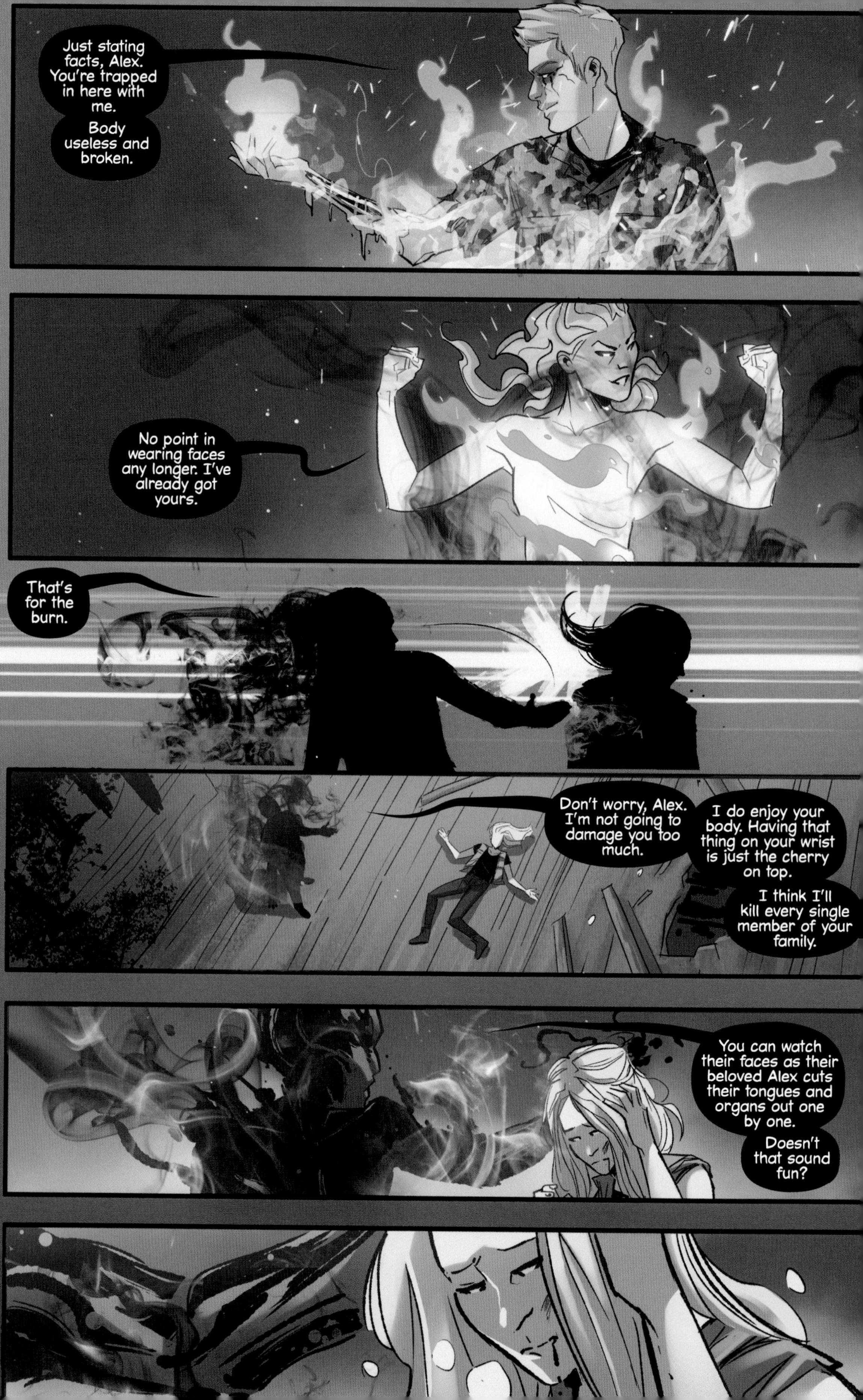
Just stating facts, Alex. You're trapped in here with me.
Body useless and broken.
No point in wearing faces any longer. I've already got yours.
That's for the burn.
Don't worry, Alex. I'm not going to damage you too much.
I do enjoy your body. Having that thing on your wrist is just the cherry on top.
I think I'll kill every single member of your family.
You can watch their faces as their beloved Alex cuts their tongues and organs out one by one.
Doesn't that sound fun?

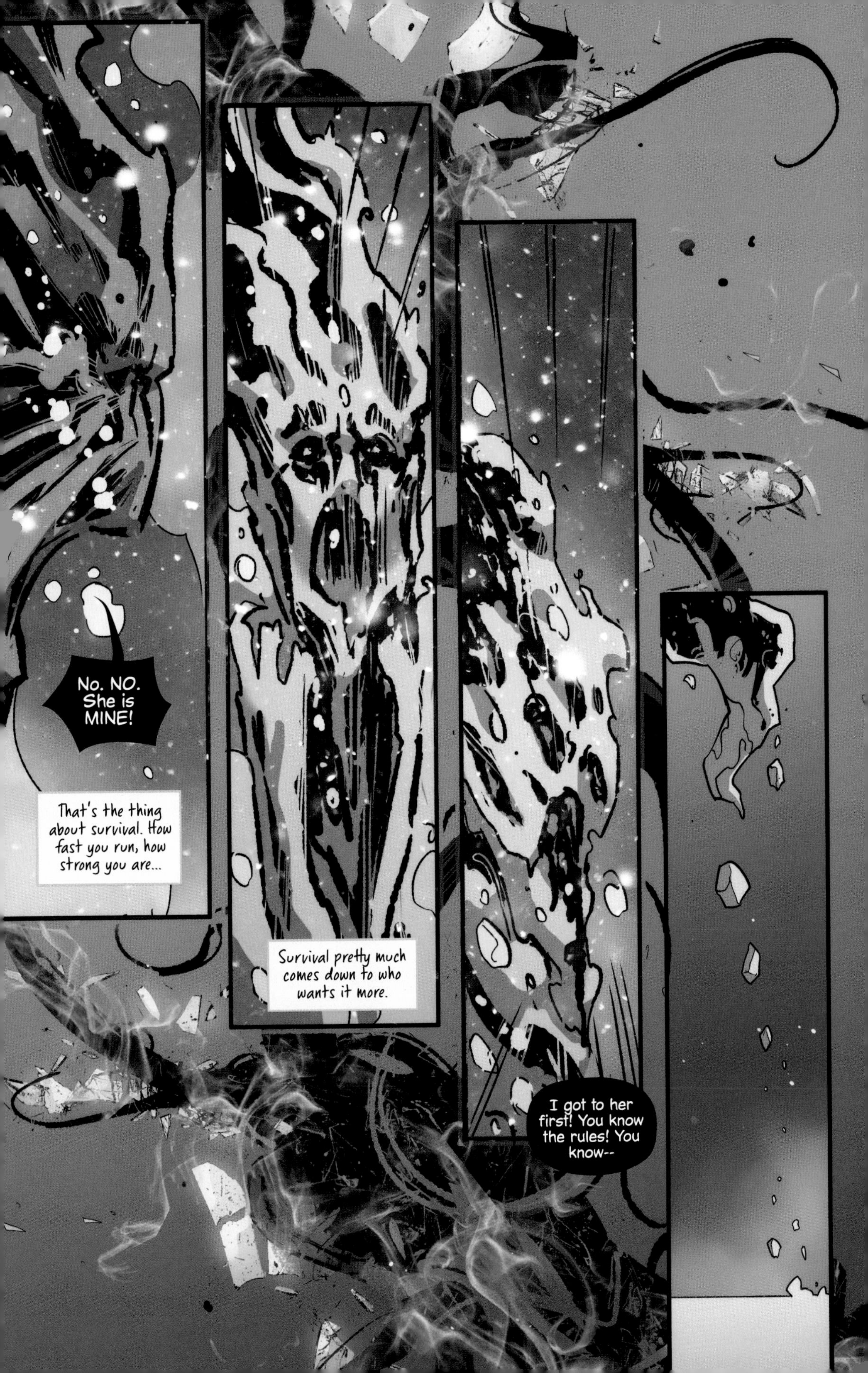

No. NO. She is MINE!
That's the thing about survival. How fast you run, how strong you are...
Survival pretty much comes down to who wants it more.
I got to her first! You know the rules! You know--

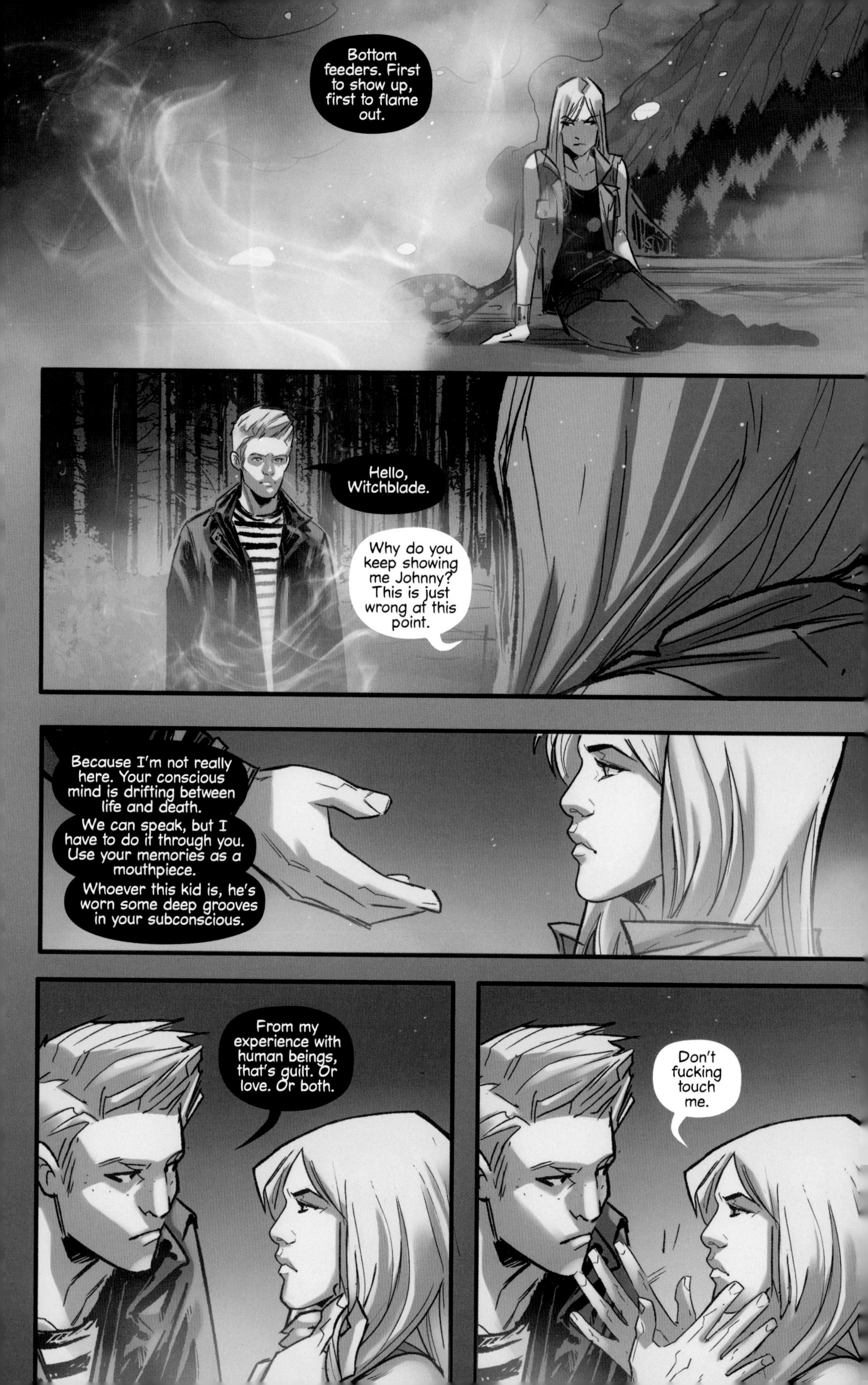
Bottom feeders. First to show up, first to flame out.
Hello, Witchblade.
Why do you keep showing me Johnny? This is just wrong at this point.
Because I'm not really here. Your conscious mind is drifting between life and death.
We can speak, but I have to do it through you. Use your memories as a mouthpiece.
Whoever this kid is, he's worn some deep grooves in your subconscious.
From my experience with human beings, that's guilt. Or love. Or both.
Don't fucking touch me.

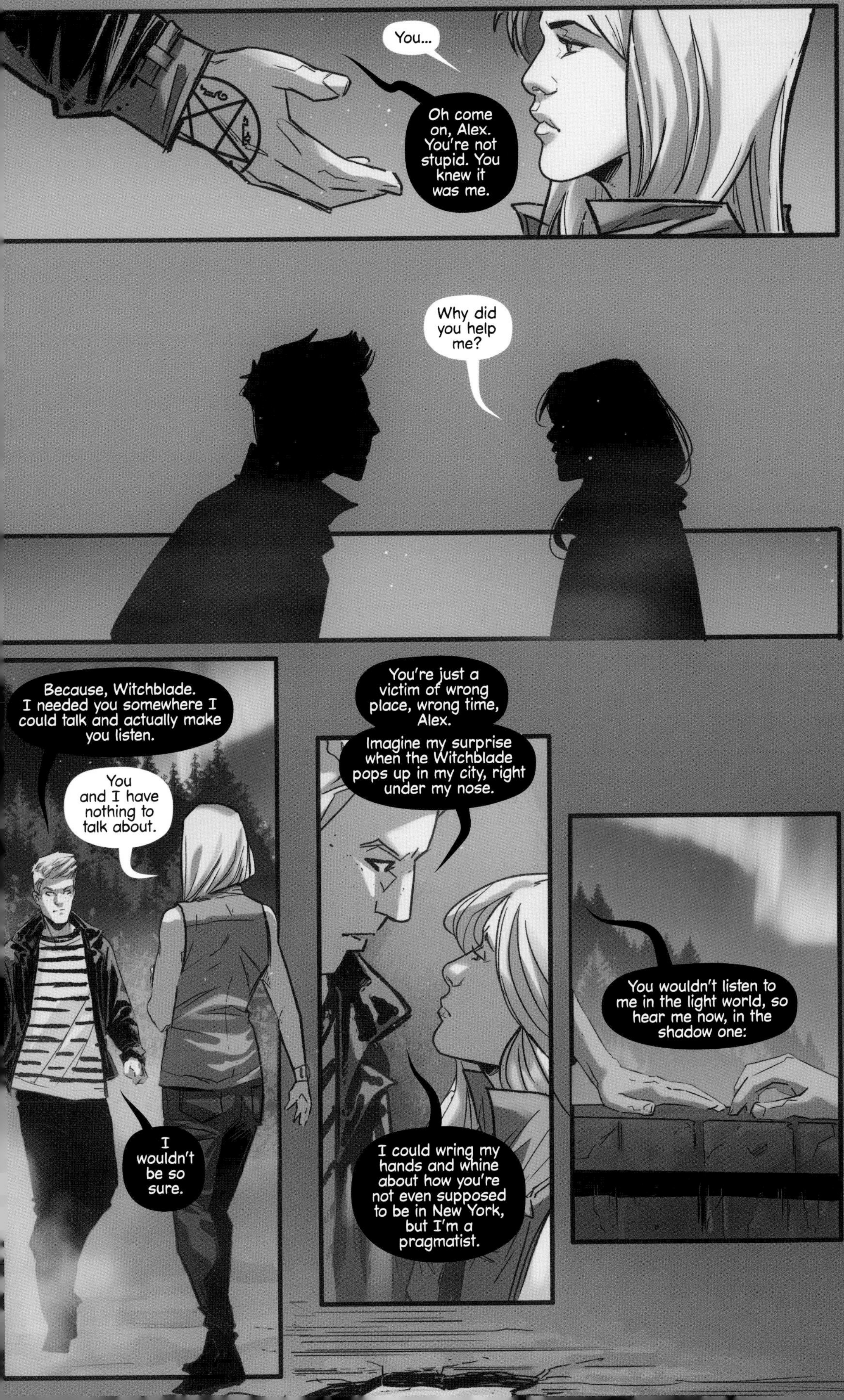
You...
Oh come on, Alex. You're not stupid. You knew it was me.
Why did you help me?
Because, Witchblade. I needed you somewhere I could talk and actually make you listen.
You and I have nothing to talk about.
I wouldn't be so sure.
You're just a victim of wrong place, wrong time, Alex.
Imagine my surprise when the Witchblade pops up in my city, right under my nose.
I could wring my hands and whine about how you're not even supposed to be in New York, but I'm a pragmatist.
You wouldn't listen to me in the light world, so hear me now, in the shadow one:

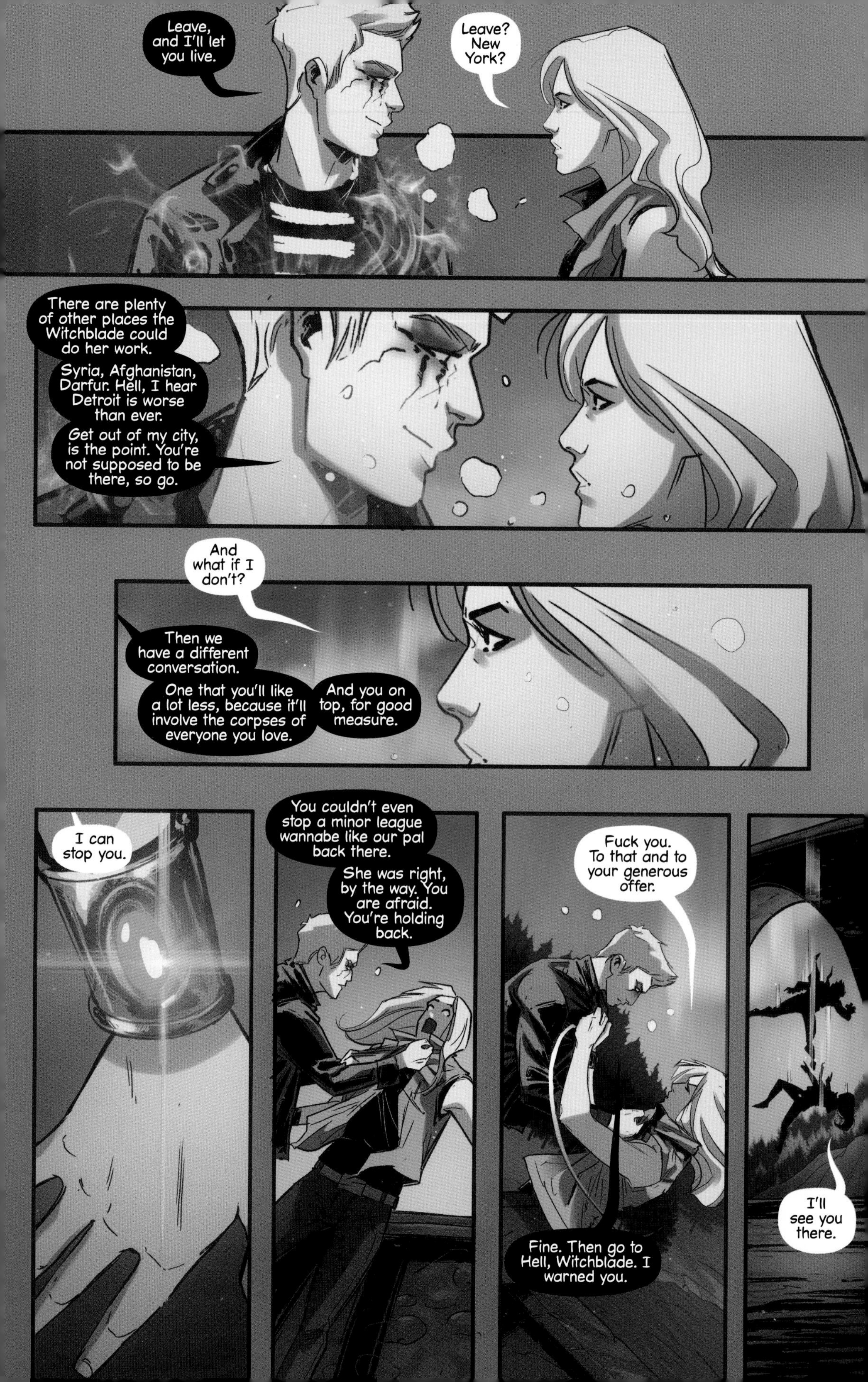

Leave, and I'll let you live.
Leave? New York?
There are plenty of other places the Witchblade could do her work.
Syria, Afghanistan, Darfur. Hell, I hear Detroit is worse than ever.
Get out of my city, is the point. You're not supposed to be there, so go.
And what if I don't?
Then we have a different conversation.
One that you'll like a lot less, because it'll involve the corpses of everyone you love.
And you on top, for good measure.
I can stop you.
You couldn't even stop a minor league wannabe like our pal back there.
She was right, by the way. You are afraid. You're holding back.
Fuck you. To that and to your generous offer.
Fine. Then go to Hell, Witchblade. I warned you.
I'll see you there.

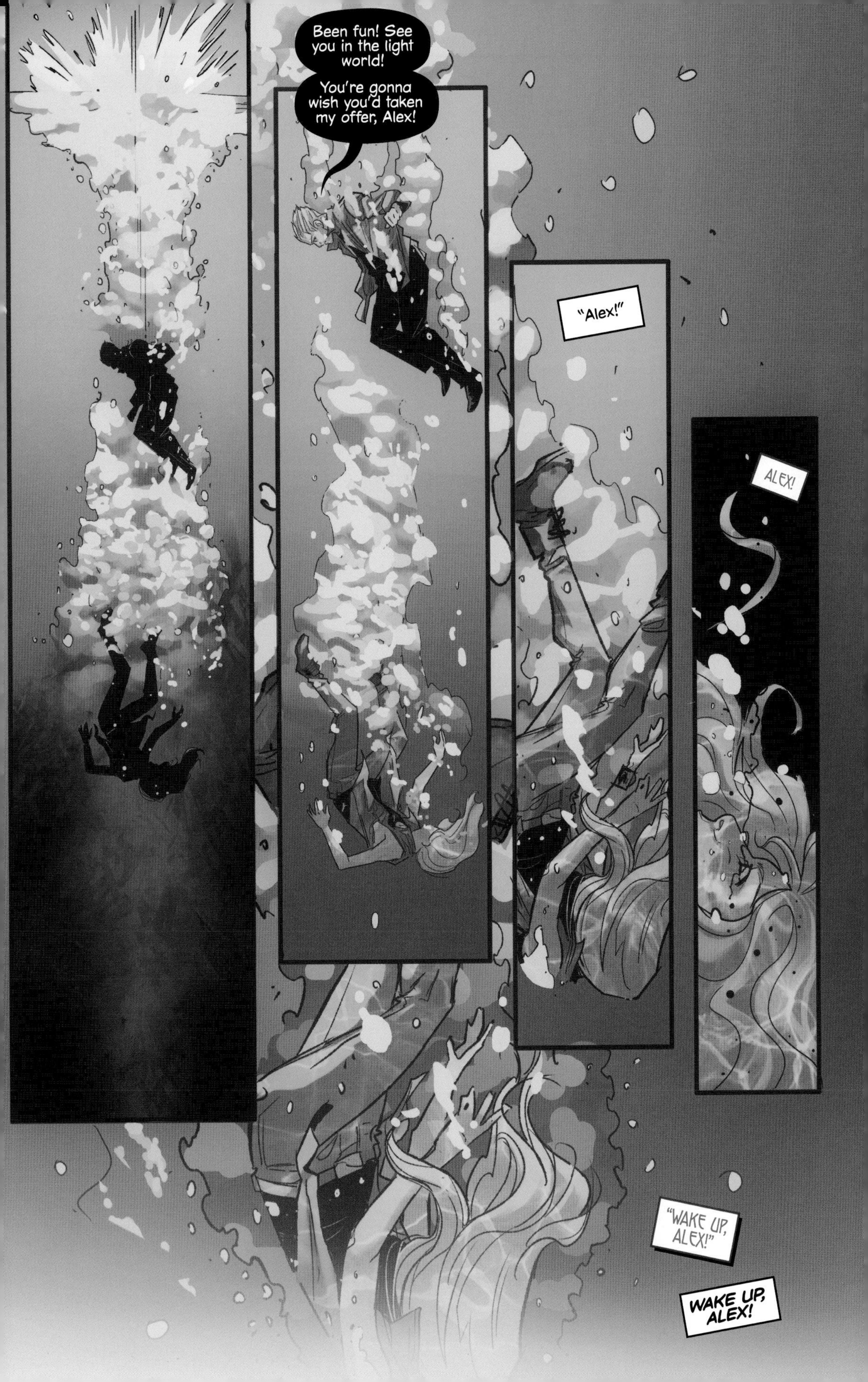
Been fun! See you in the light world!
You're gonna wish you'd taken my offer, Alex!
"Alex!"
ALEX!
"WAKE UP, ALEX!"
WAKE UP, ALEX!

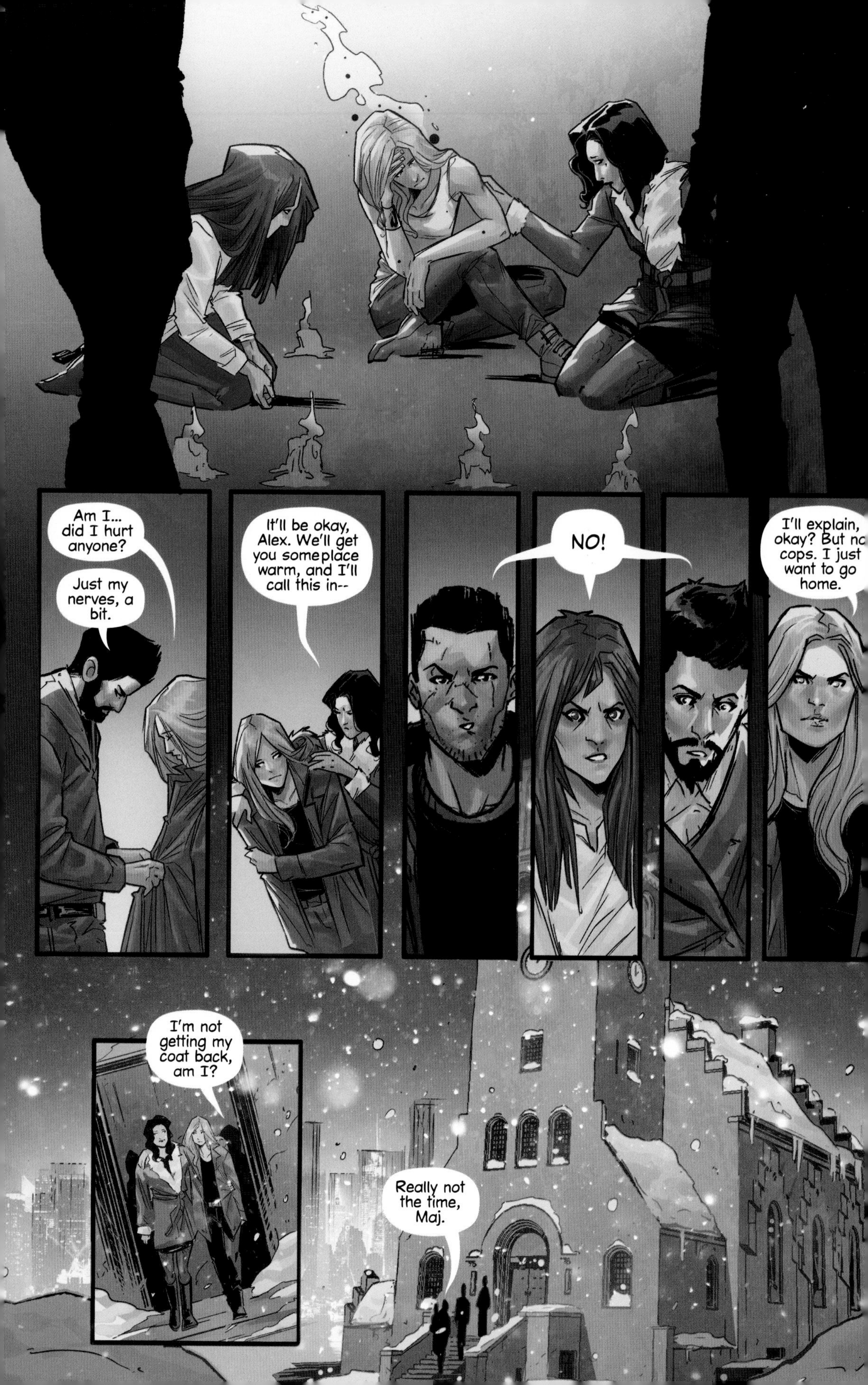
Am I... did I hurt anyone?
Just my nerves, a bit.
It'll be okay, Alex. We'll get you some place warm, and I'll call this in--
NO!
I'll explain, okay? But no cops. I just want to go home.
I'm not getting my coat back, am I?
Really not the time, Maj.

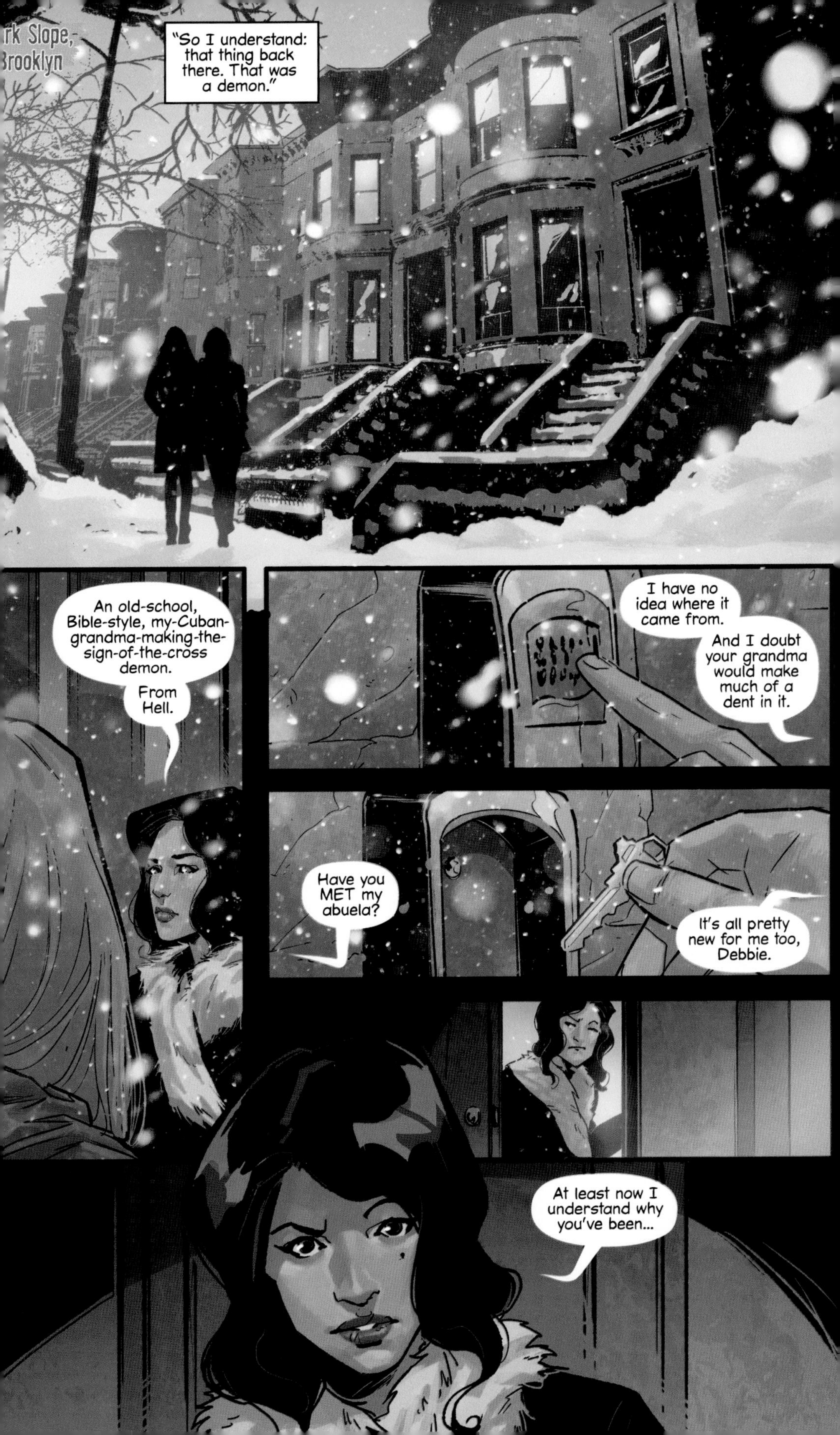
rk Slope, Brooklyn
"So I understand: that thing back there. That was a demon."
An old-school, Bible-style, my-Cuban-grandma-making-the-sign-of-the-cross demon.
From Hell.
I have no idea where it came from.
And I doubt your grandma would make much of a dent in it.
Have you MET my abuela?
It's all pretty new for me too, Debbie.
At least now I understand why you've been...

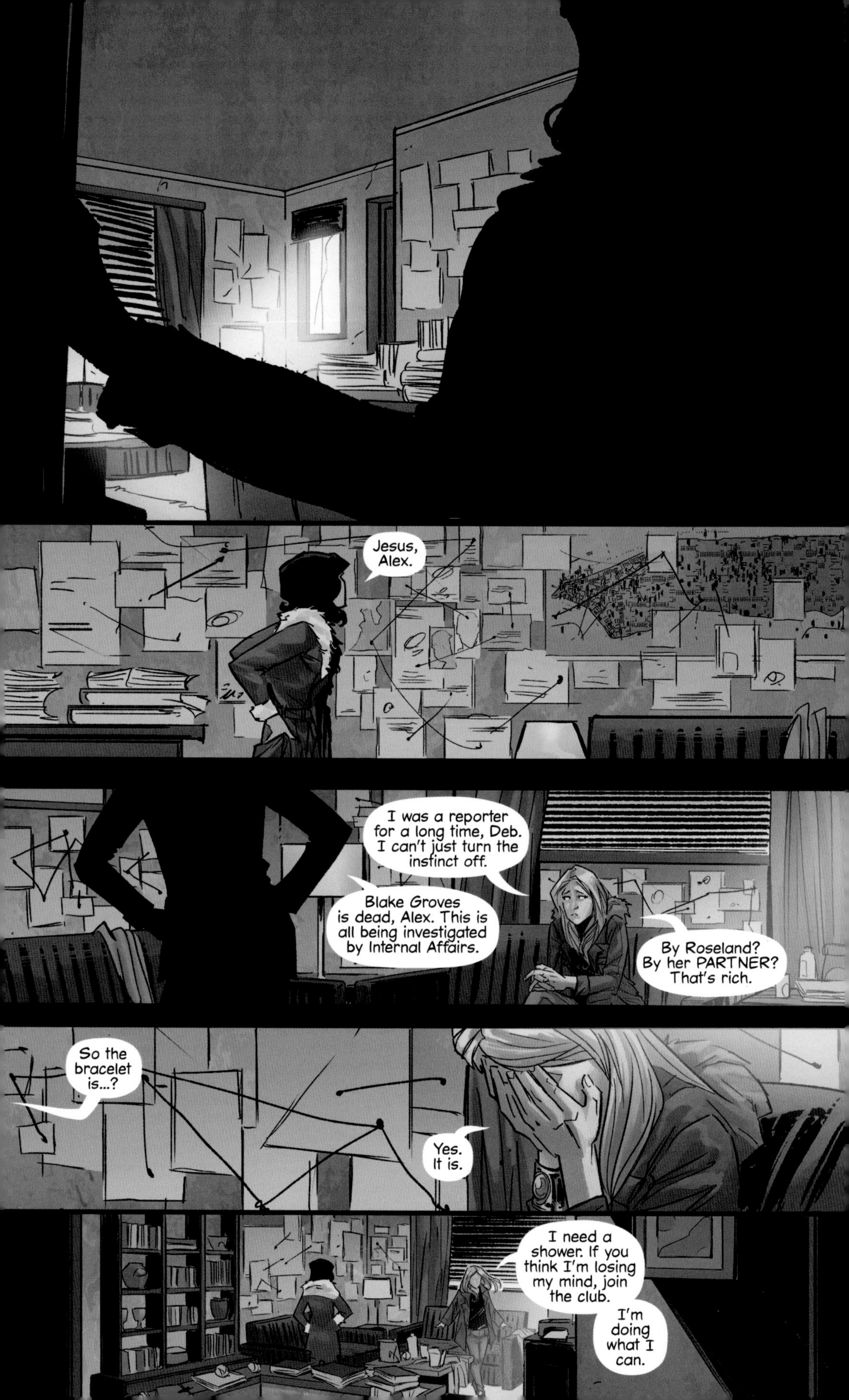
Jesus, Alex.
I was a reporter for a long time, Deb. I can't just turn the instinct off.
Blake Groves is dead, Alex. This is all being investigated by Internal Affairs.
By Roseland? By her PARTNER? That's rich.
So the bracelet is...?
Yes. It is.
I need a shower. If you think I'm losing my mind, join the club.
I'm doing what I can.

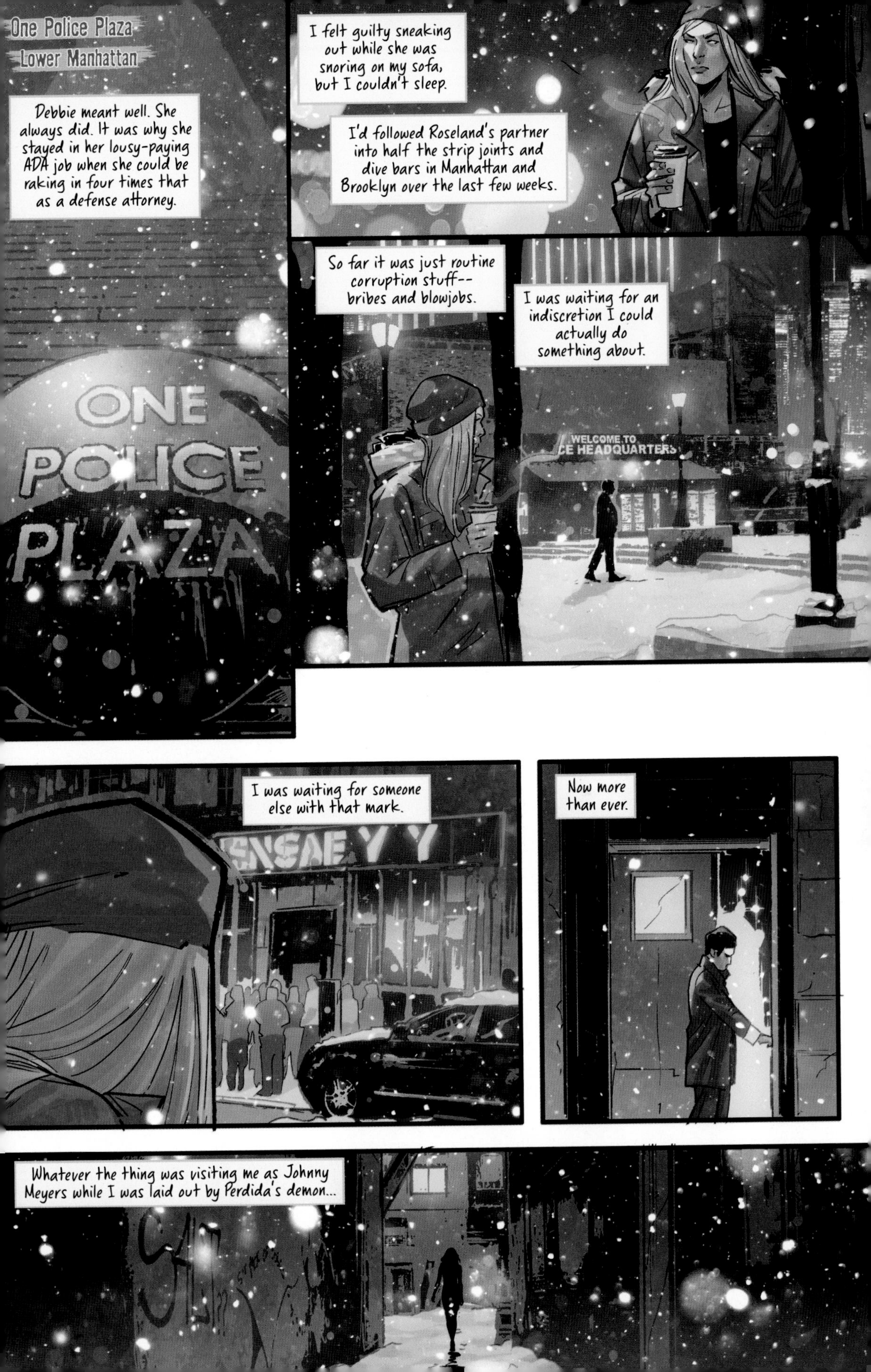
One Police Plaza
Lower Manhattan
Debbie meant well. She always did. It was why she stayed in her lousy-paying ADA job when she could be raking in four times that as a defense attorney.
ONE POLICE PLAZA
I felt guilty sneaking out while she was snoring on my sofa, but I couldn't sleep.
I'd followed Roseland's partner into half the strip joints and dive bars in Manhattan and Brooklyn over the last few weeks.
So far it was just routine corruption stuff-- bribes and blowjobs.
I was waiting for an indiscretion I could actually do something about.
WELCOME TO
CE HEADQUARTERS
I was waiting for someone else with that mark.
Now more than ever.
Whatever the thing was visiting me as Johnny Meyers while I was laid out by Perdida's demon...

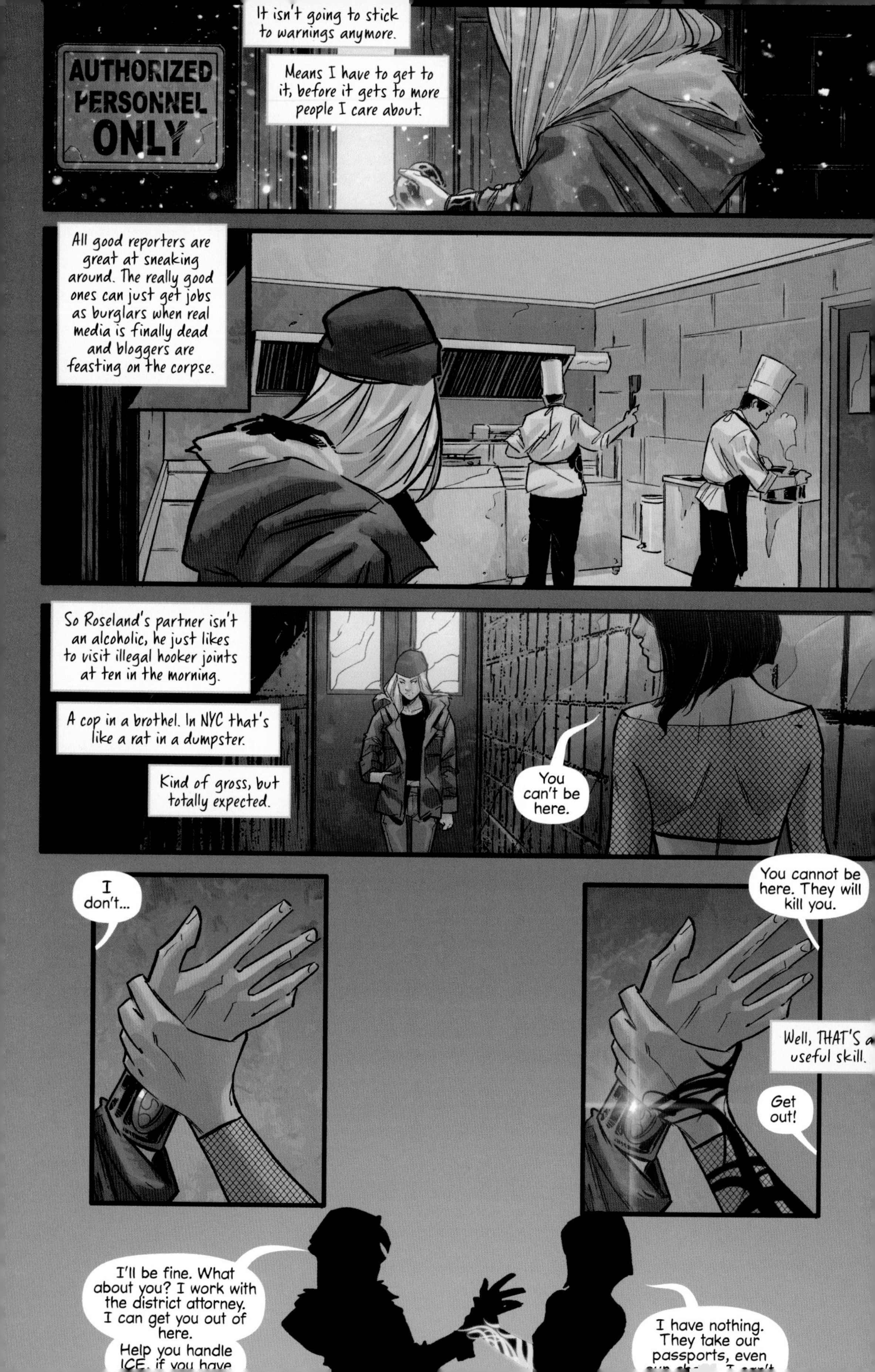
AUTHORIZED PERSONNEL ONLY
It isn't going to stick to warnings anymore.
Means I have to get to it, before it gets to more people I care about.
All good reporters are great at sneaking around. The really good ones can just get jobs as burglars when real media is finally dead and bloggers are feasting on the corpse.
So Roseland's partner isn't an alcoholic, he just likes to visit illegal hooker joints at ten in the morning.
A cop in a brothel. In NYC that's like a rat in a dumpster.
Kind of gross, but totally expected.
You can't be here.
I don't...
You cannot be here. They will kill you.
Well, THAT'S a useful skill.
Get out!
I'll be fine. What about you? I work with the district attorney. I can get you out of here.
Help you handle ICE, if you have
I have nothing. They take our passports, even

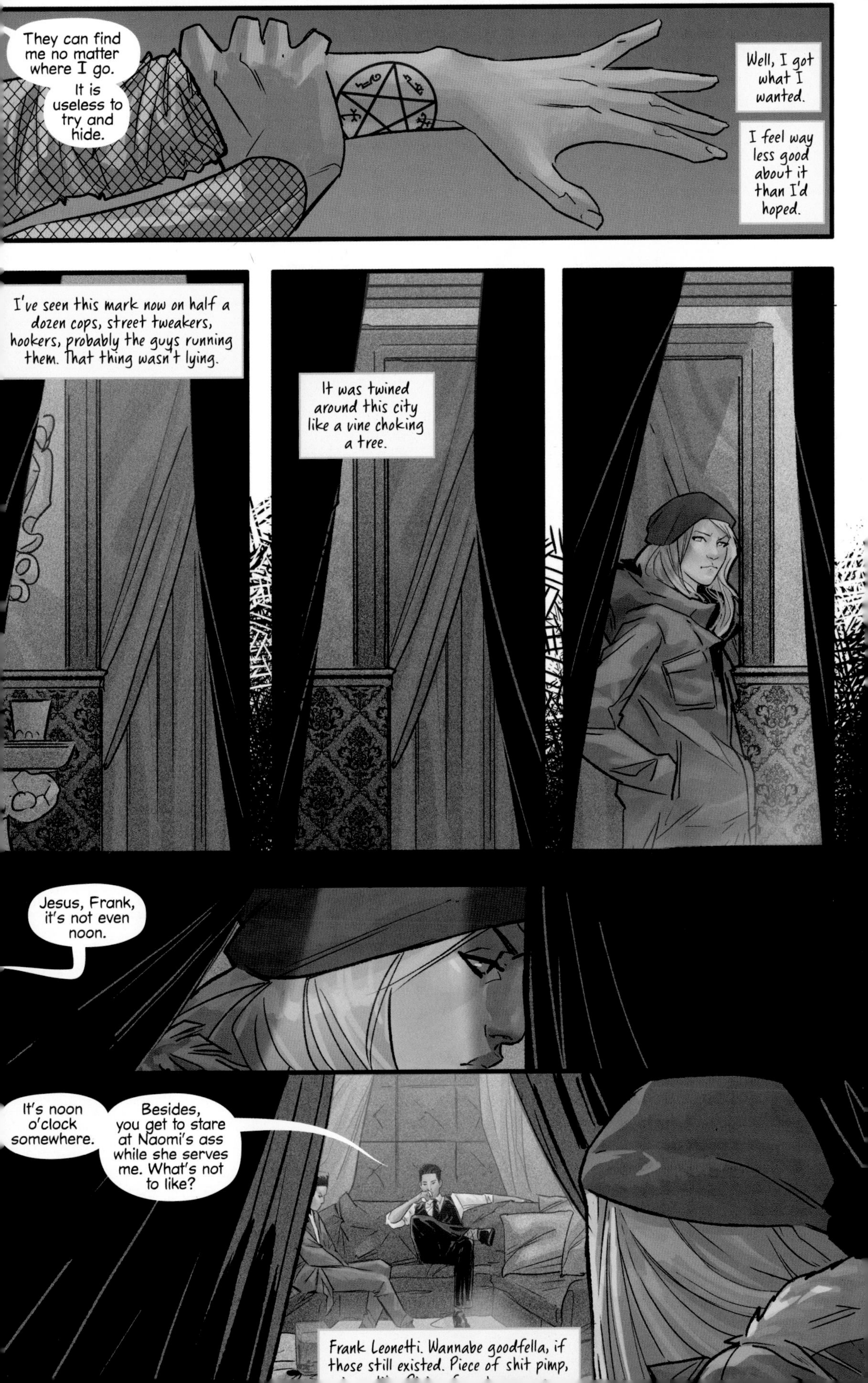
They can find me no matter where I go.
It is useless to try and hide.
Well, I got what I wanted.
I feel way less good about it than I'd hoped.
I've seen this mark now on half a dozen cops, street tweakers, hookers, probably the guys running them. That thing wasn't lying.
It was twined around this city like a vine choking a tree.
Jesus, Frank, it's not even noon.
It's noon o'clock somewhere.
Besides, you get to stare at Naomi's ass while she serves me. What's not to like?
Frank Leonetti. Wannabe goodfella, if those still existed. Piece of shit pimp,

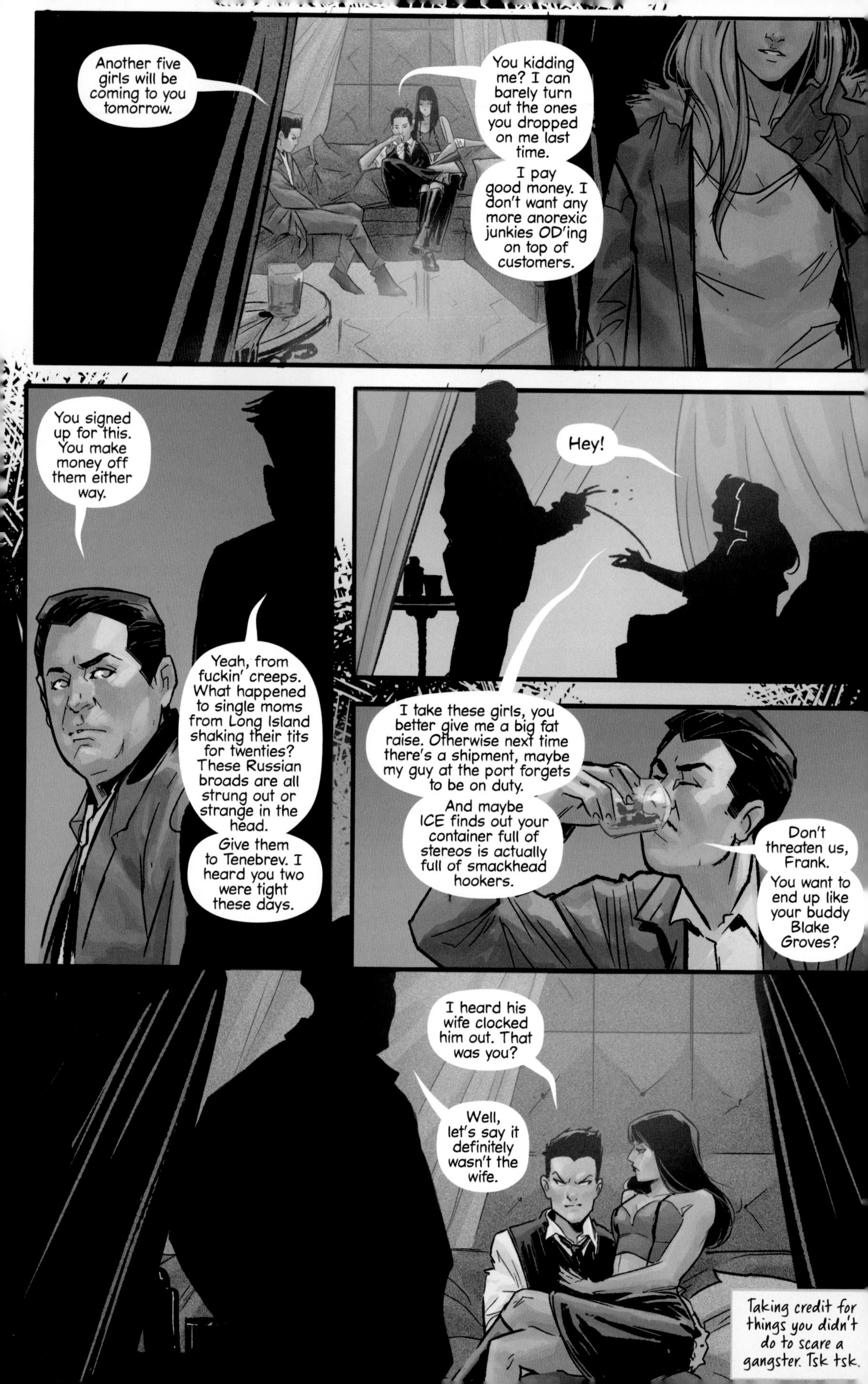
Another five girls will be coming to you tomorrow.
You kidding me? I can barely turn out the ones you dropped on me last time.
I pay good money. I don't want any more anorexic junkies OD'ing on top of customers.
You signed up for this. You make money off them either way.
Yeah, from fuckin' creeps. What happened to single moms from Long Island shaking their tits for twenties? These Russian broads are all strung out or strange in the head.
Give them to Tenebrev. I heard you two were tight these days.
Hey!
I take these girls, you better give me a big fat raise. Otherwise next time there's a shipment, maybe my guy at the port forgets to be on duty.
And maybe ICE finds out your container full of stereos is actually full of smackhead hookers.
Don't threaten us, Frank.
You want to end up like your buddy Blake Groves?
I heard his wife clocked him out. That was you?
Well, let's say it definitely wasn't the wife.
Taking credit for things you didn't do to scare a gangster. Tsk tsk.

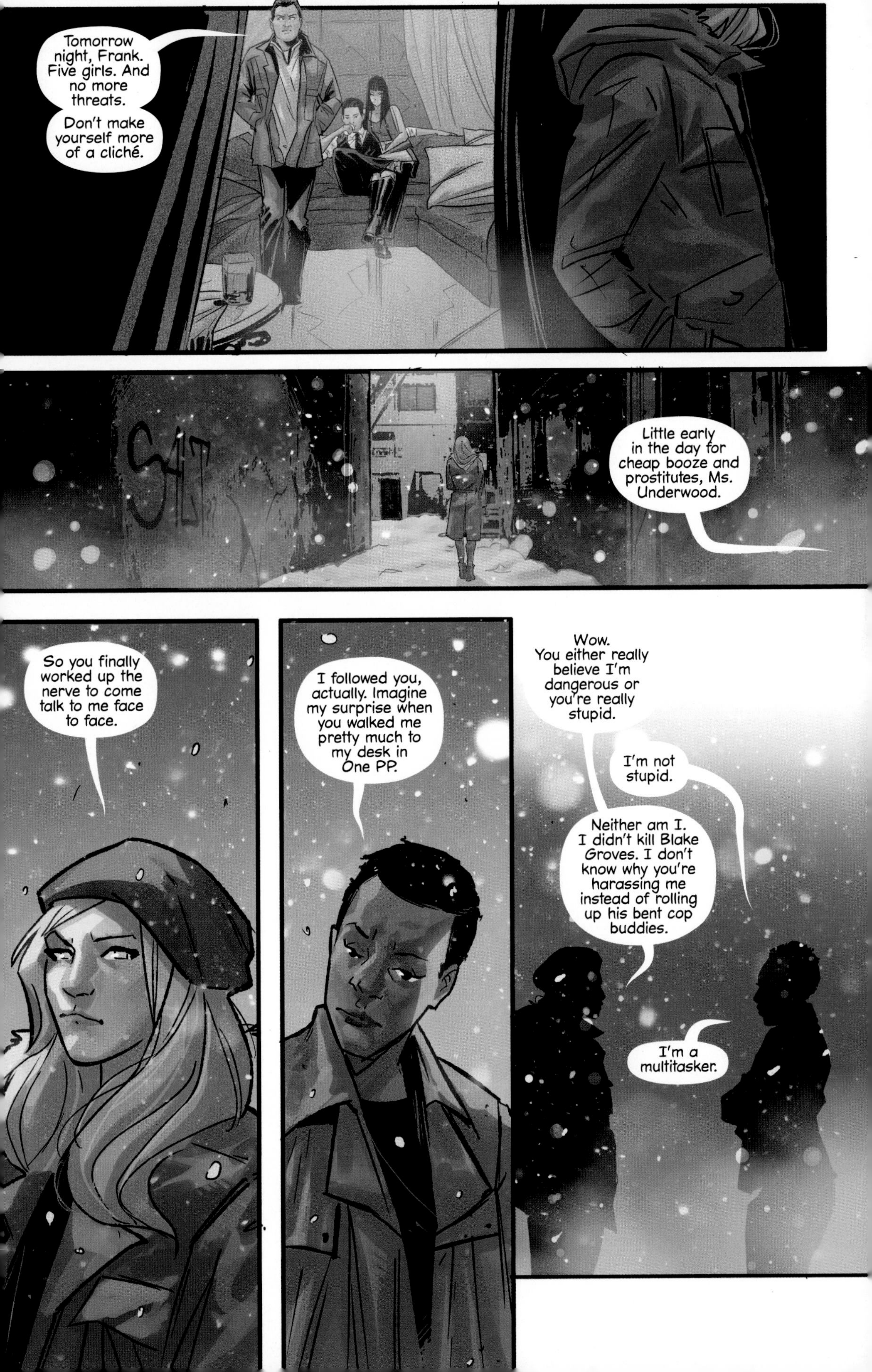
Tomorrow night, Frank. Five girls. And no more threats.
Don't make yourself more of a cliché.
Little early in the day for cheap booze and prostitutes, Ms. Underwood.
So you finally worked up the nerve to come talk to me face to face.
I followed you, actually. Imagine my surprise when you walked me pretty much to my desk in One PP.
Wow. You either really believe I'm dangerous or you're really stupid.
I'm not stupid.
Neither am I. I didn't kill Blake Groves. I don't know why you're harassing me instead of rolling up his bent cop buddies.
I'm a multitasker.

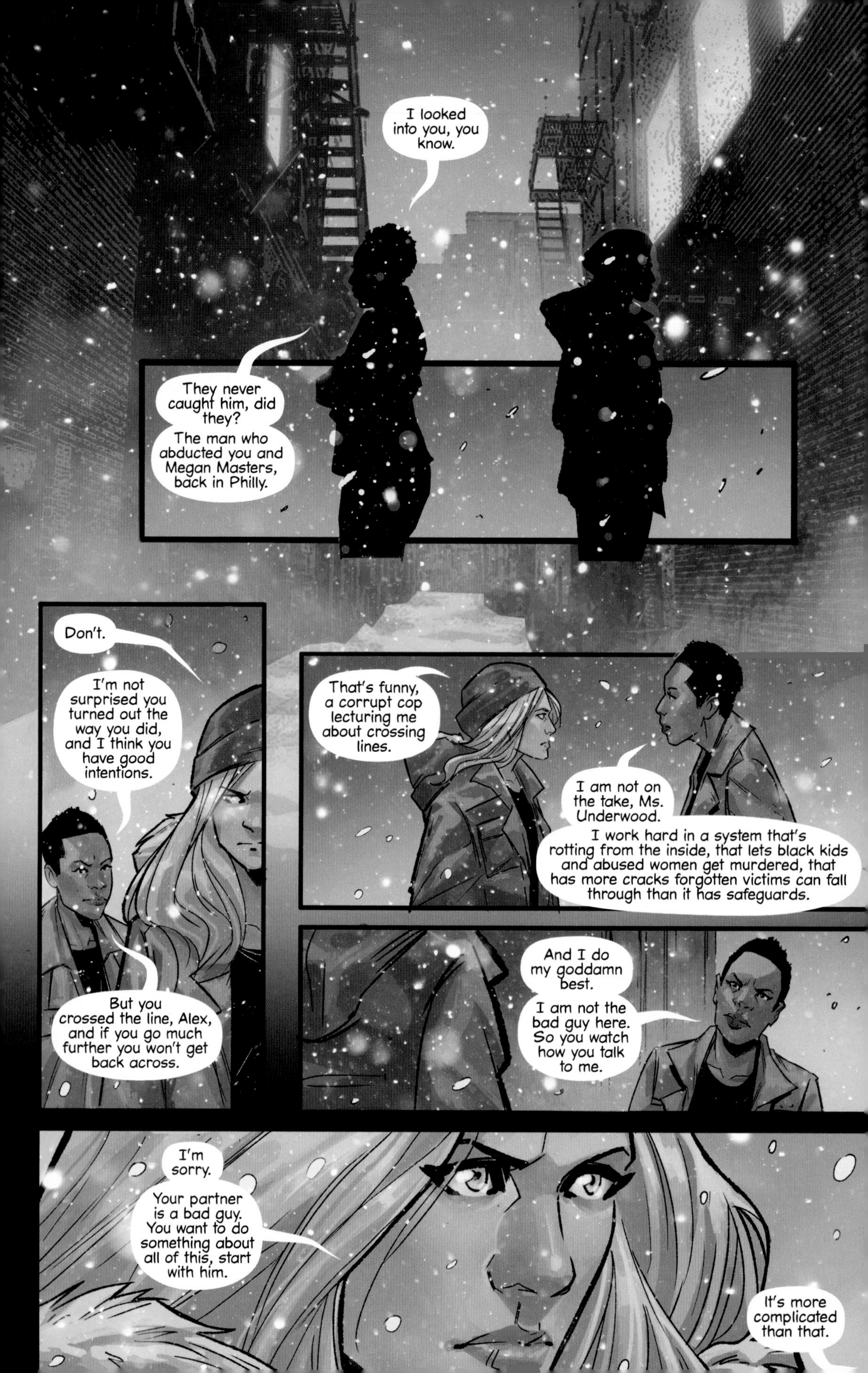
I looked into you, you know.
They never caught him, did they?
The man who abducted you and Megan Masters, back in Philly.
Don't.
I'm not surprised you turned out the way you did, and I think you have good intentions.
But you crossed the line, Alex, and if you go much further you won't get back across.
That's funny, a corrupt cop lecturing me about crossing lines.
I am not on the take, Ms. Underwood.
I work hard in a system that's rotting from the inside, that lets black kids and abused women get murdered, that has more cracks forgotten victims can fall through than it has safeguards.
And I do my goddamn best.
I am not the bad guy here. So you watch how you talk to me.
I'm sorry.
Your partner is a bad guy. You want to do something about all of this, start with him.
It's more complicated than that.

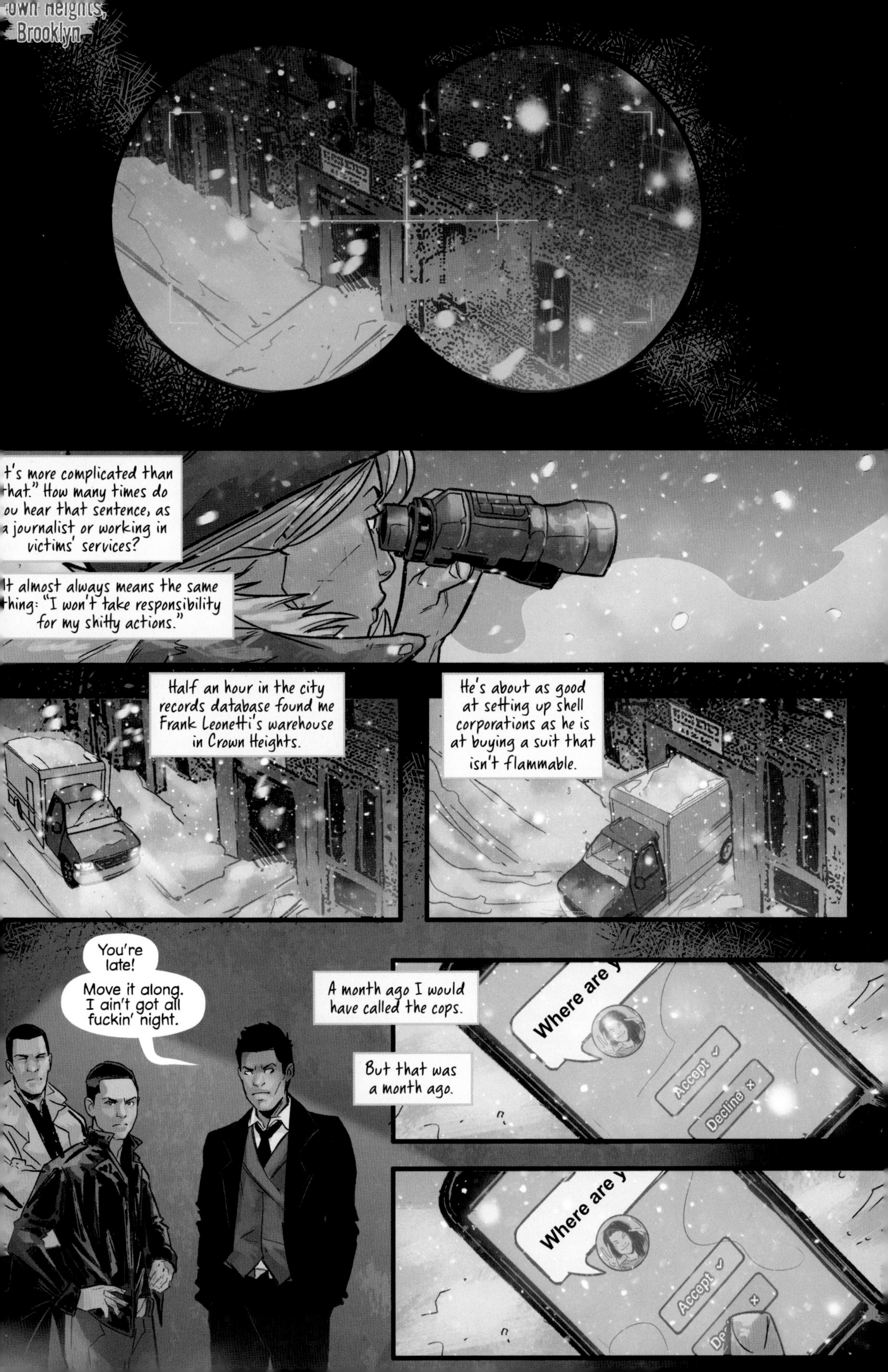

own Heights,
Brooklyn
t's more complicated than hat." How many times do ou hear that sentence, as a journalist or working in victims' services?
It almost always means the same thing: "I won't take responsibility for my shitty actions."
Half an hour in the city records database found me Frank Leonetti's warehouse in Crown Heights.
He's about as good at setting up shell corporations as he is at buying a suit that isn't flammable.
You're late!
Move it along. I ain't got all fuckin' night.
A month ago I would have called the cops.
But that was a month ago.
Where are y
Accept
Decline
Where are y
Accept

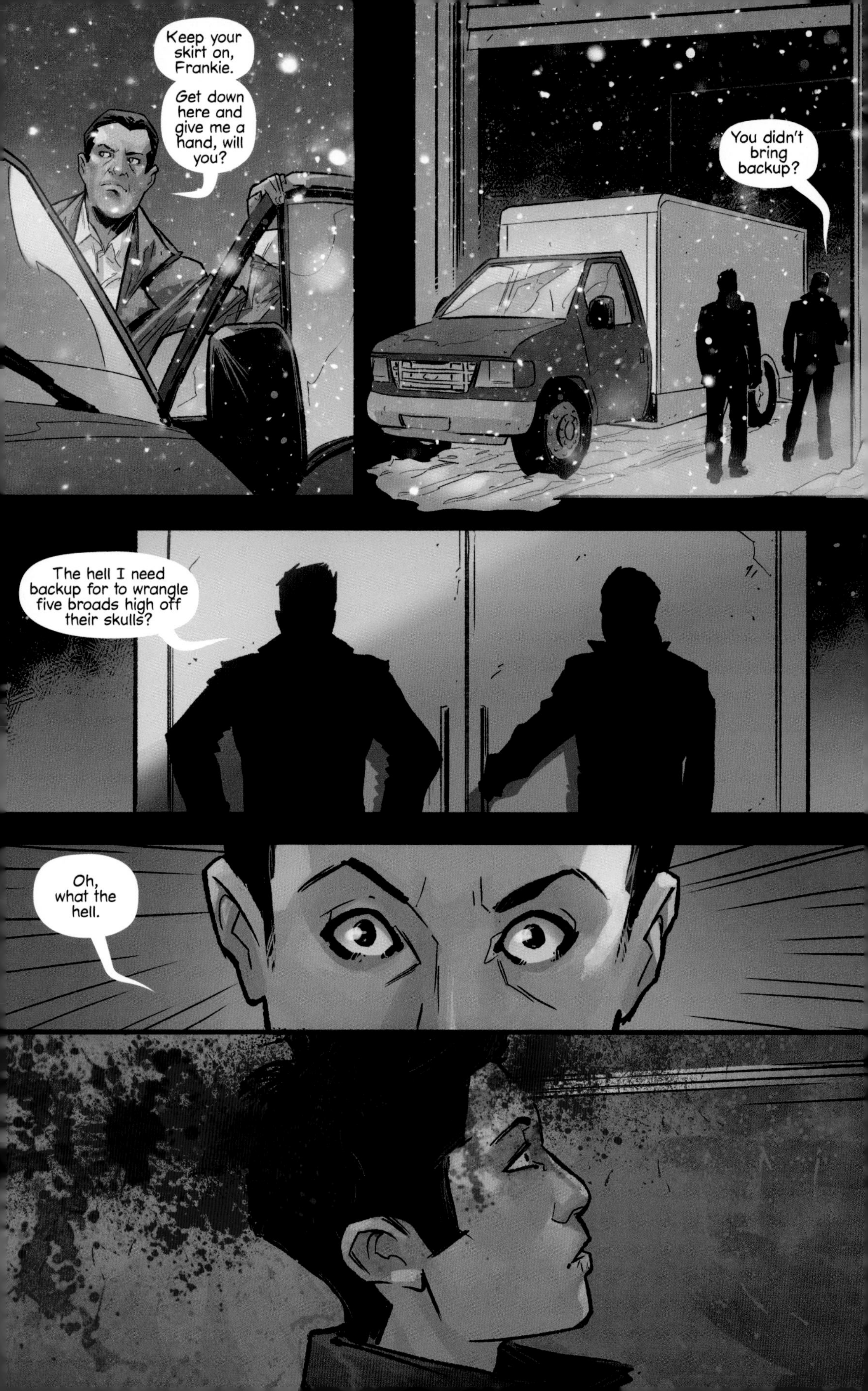
Keep your skirt on, Frankie.
Get down here and give me a hand, will you?
You didn't bring backup?
The hell I need backup for to wrangle five broads high off their skulls?
Oh, what the hell.

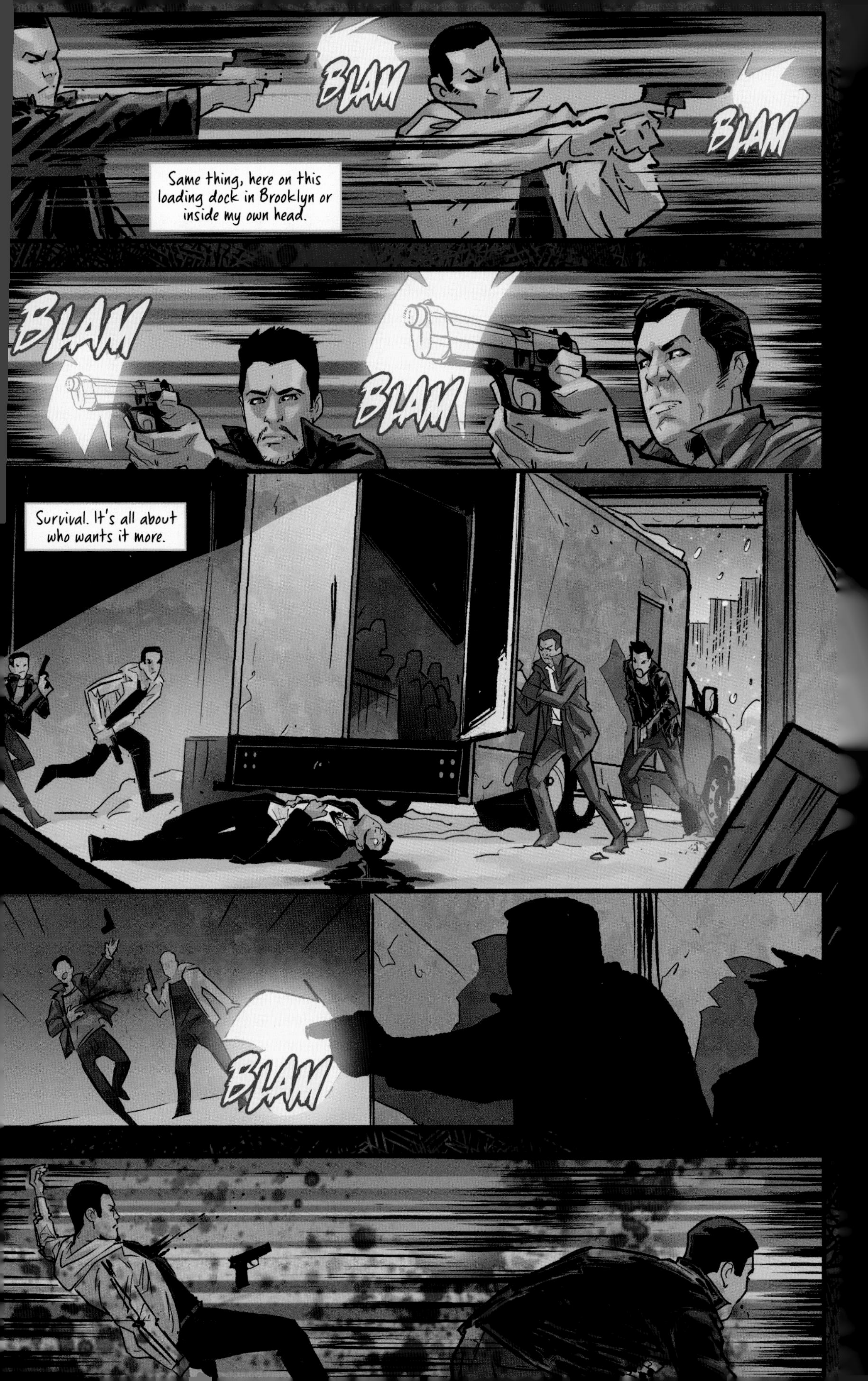
BLAM
BLAM
Same thing, here on this loading dock in Brooklyn or inside my own head.
BLAM
BLAM
Survival. It's all about who wants it more.
BLAM

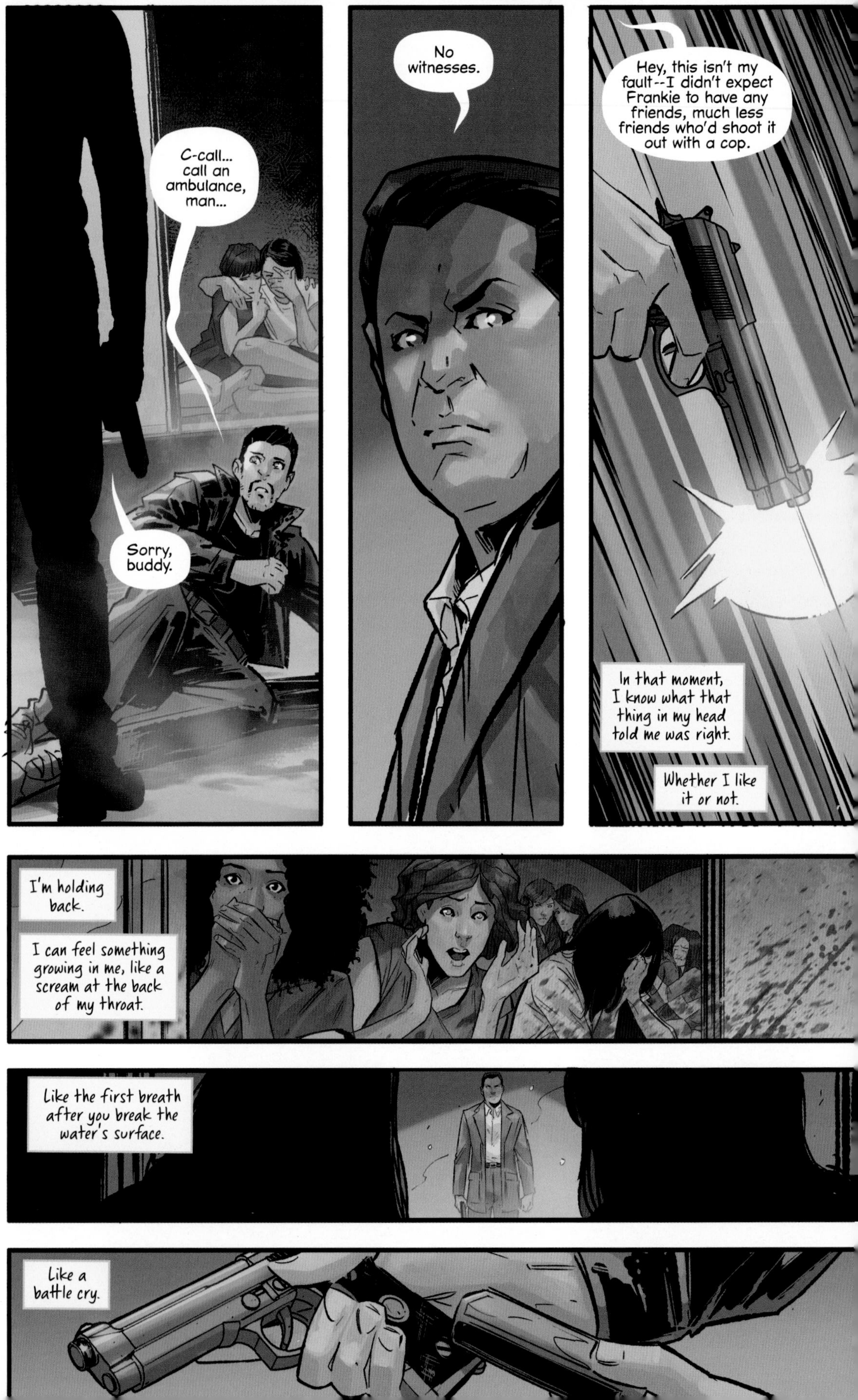
C-call... call an ambulance, man...
Sorry, buddy.
No witnesses.
Hey, this isn't my fault--I didn't expect Frankie to have any friends, much less friends who'd shoot it out with a cop.
In that moment, I know what that thing in my head told me was right.
Whether I like it or not.
I'm holding back.
I can feel something growing in me, like a scream at the back of my throat.
Like the first breath after you break the water's surface.
Like a battle cry.

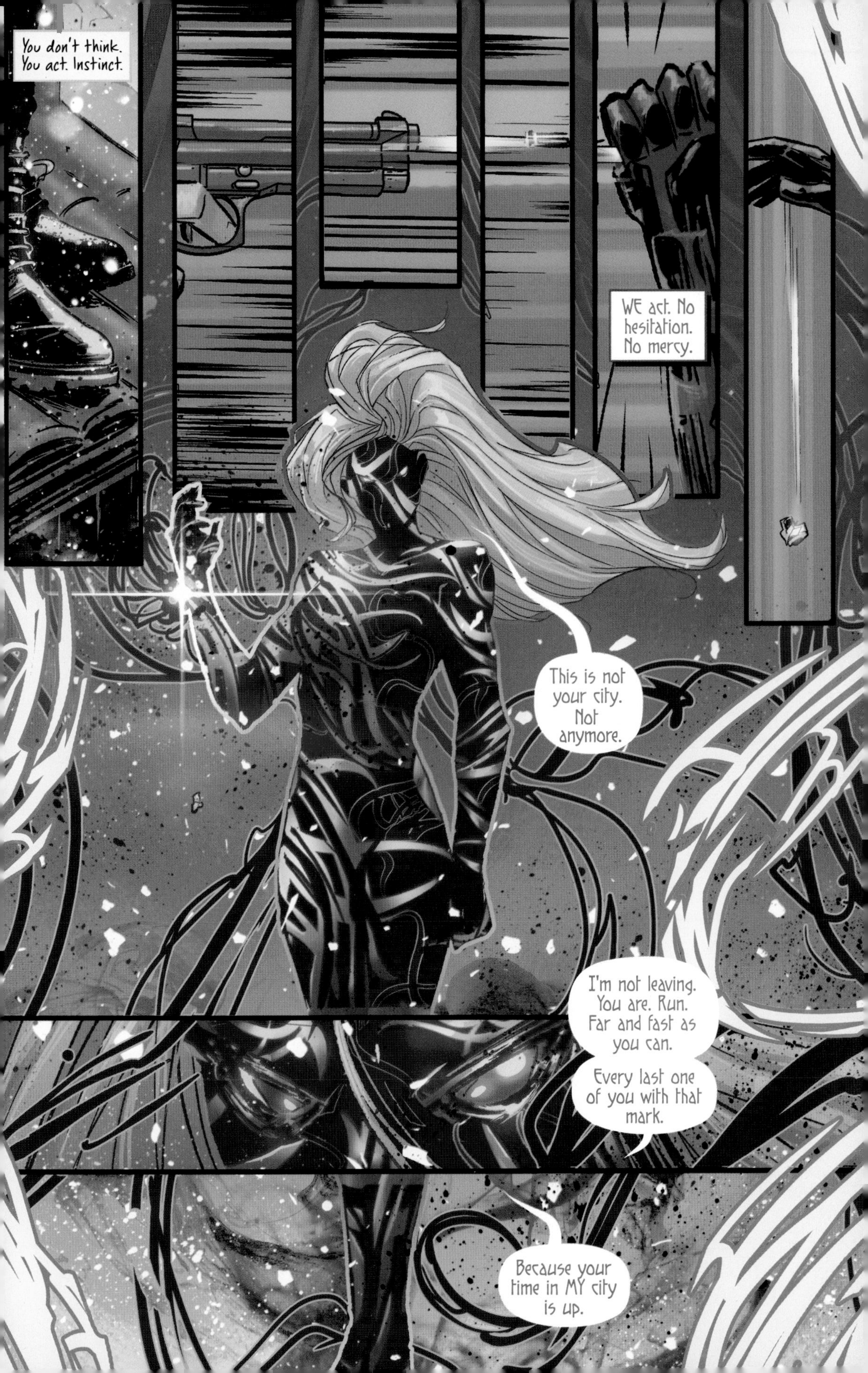
You don't think. You act. Instinct.
WE act. No hesitation. No mercy.
This is not your city. Not anymore.
I'm not leaving. You are. Run. Far and fast as you can.
Every last one of you with that mark.
Because your time in MY city is up.

CHAPTER SIX

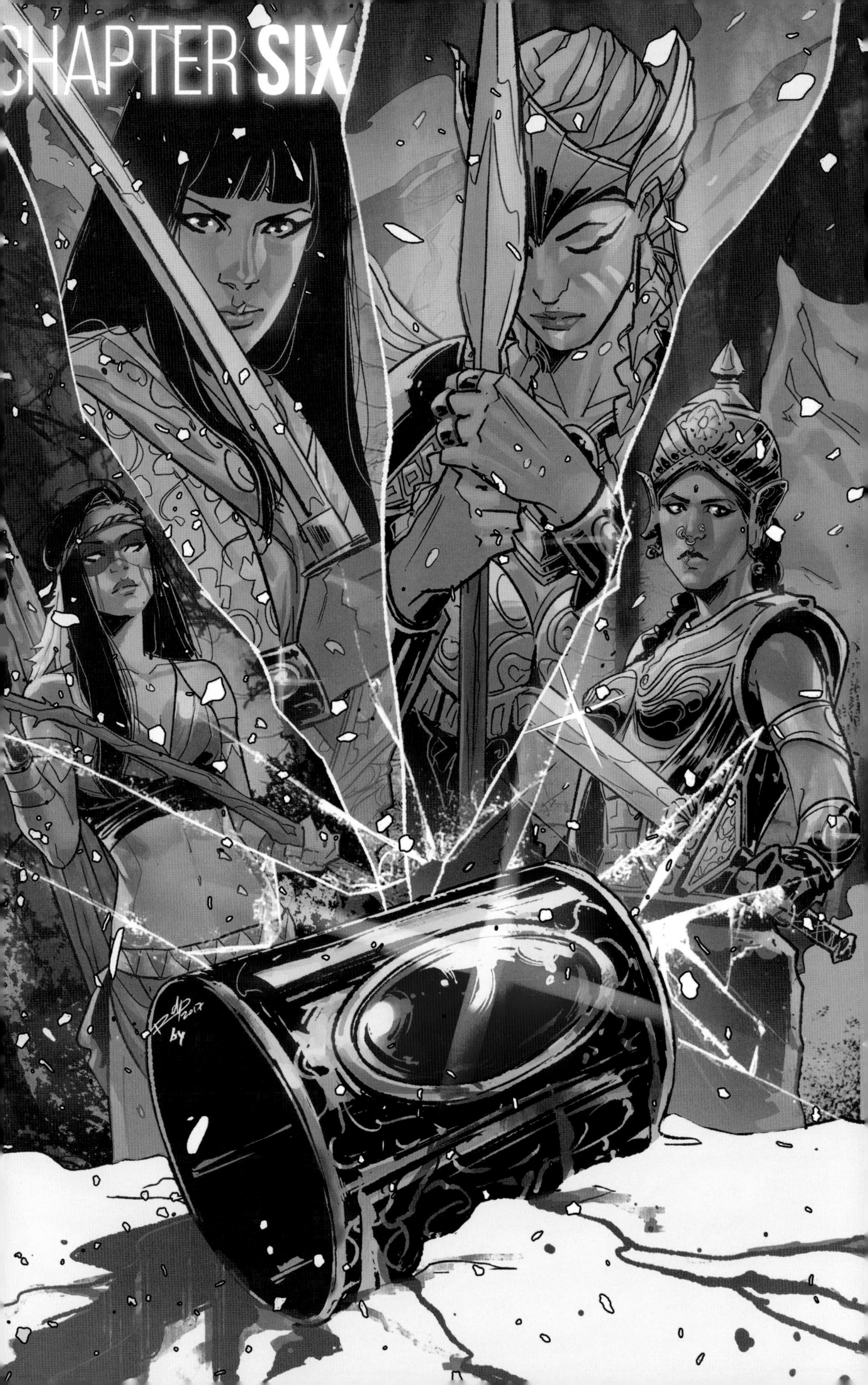

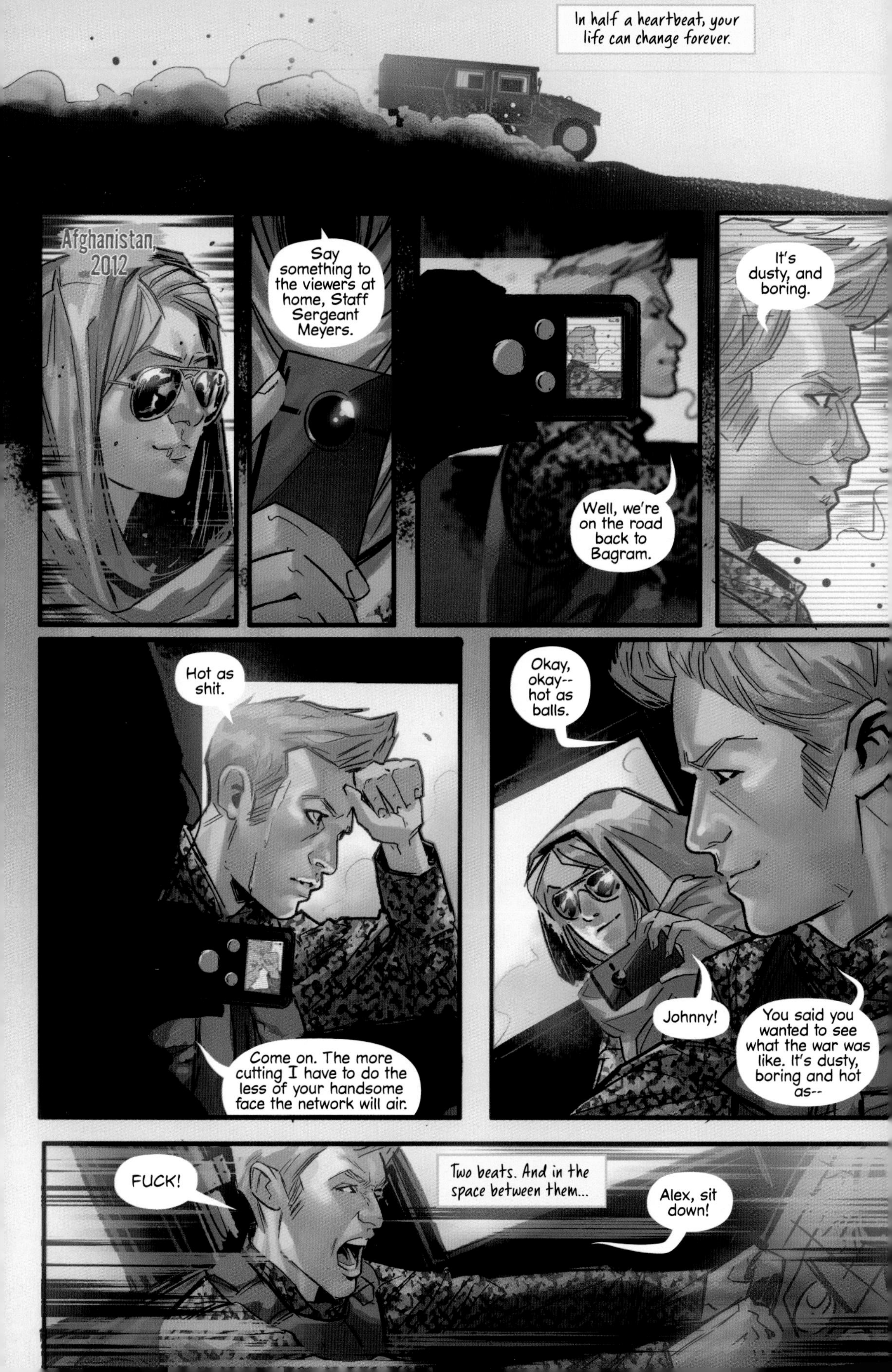
In half a heartbeat, your life can change forever.
Afghanistan, 2012
Say something to the viewers at home, Staff Sergeant Meyers.
Well, we're on the road back to Bagram.
It's dusty, and boring.
Hot as shit.
Come on. The more cutting I have to do the less of your handsome face the network will air.
Okay, okay-- hot as balls.
Johnny!
You said you wanted to see what the war was like. It's dusty, boring and hot as--
FUCK!
Two beats. And in the space between them...
Alex, sit down!

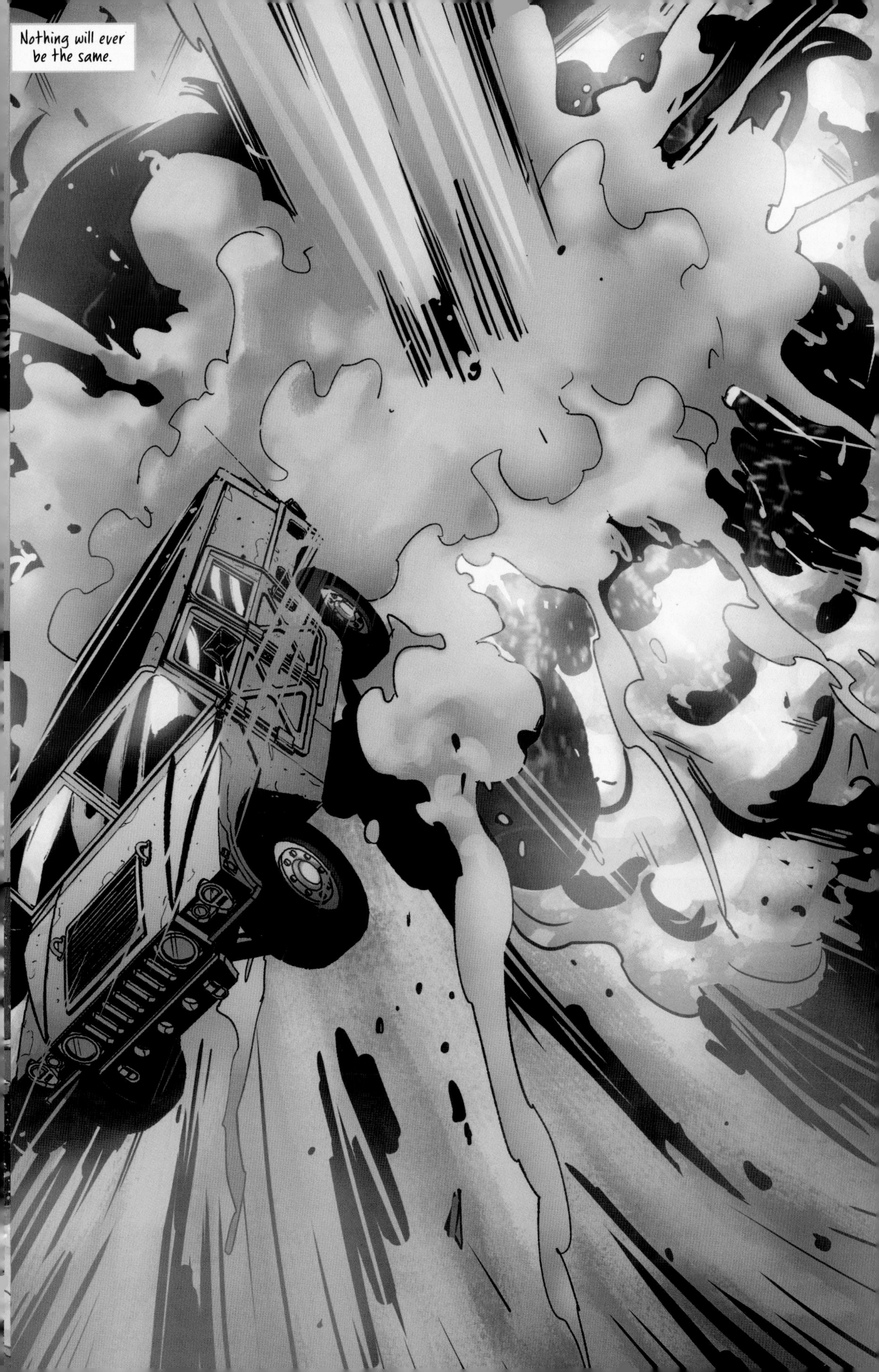
Nothing will ever be the same.

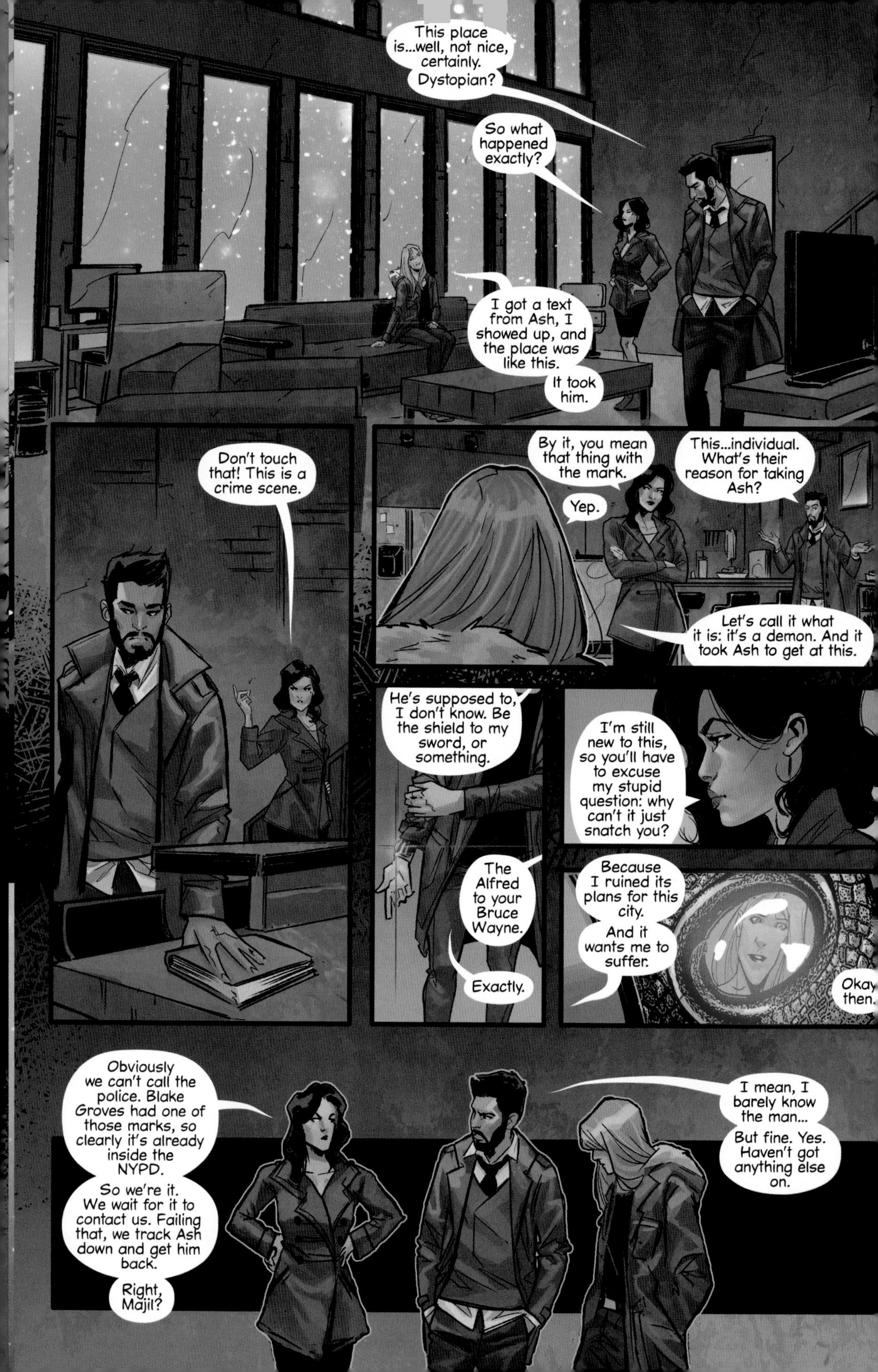
This place is...well, not nice, certainly. Dystopian?
So what happened exactly?
I got a text from Ash, I showed up, and the place was like this.
It took him.
Don't touch that! This is a crime scene.
By it, you mean that thing with the mark.
Yep.
This...individual. What's their reason for taking Ash?
Let's call it what it is: it's a demon. And it took Ash to get at this.
He's supposed to, I don't know. Be the shield to my sword, or something.
The Alfred to your Bruce Wayne.
Exactly.
I'm still new to this, so you'll have to excuse my stupid question: why can't it just snatch you?
Because I ruined its plans for this city.
And it wants me to suffer.
Okay then.
Obviously we can't call the police. Blake Groves had one of those marks, so clearly it's already inside the NYPD.
So we're it. We wait for it to contact us. Failing that, we track Ash down and get him back.
Right, Majil?
I mean, I barely know the man...
But fine. Yes. Haven't got anything else on.

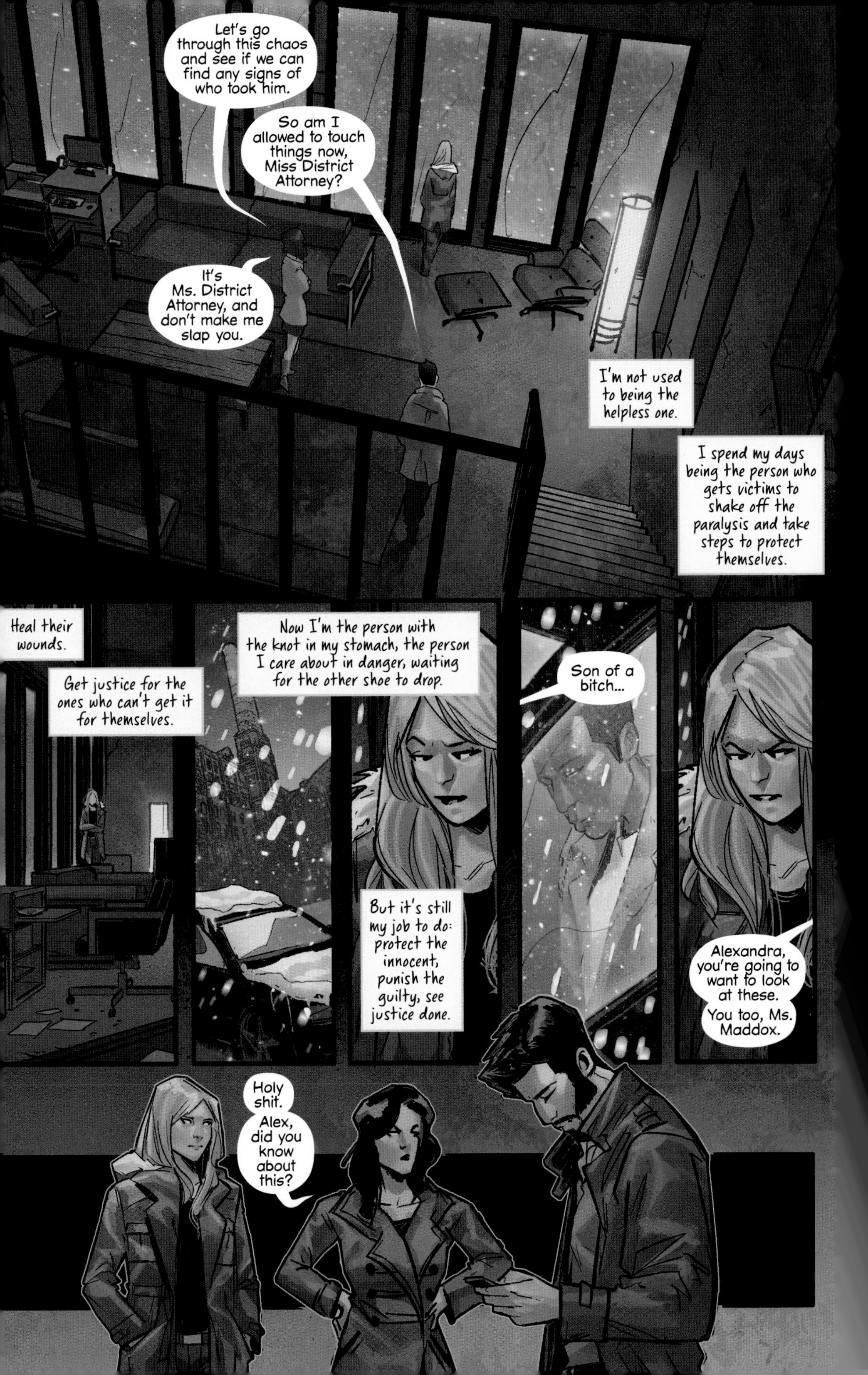
Let's go through this chaos and see if we can find any signs of who took him.
So am I allowed to touch things now, Miss District Attorney?
It's Ms. District Attorney, and don't make me slap you.
I'm not used to being the helpless one.
I spend my days being the person who gets victims to shake off the paralysis and take steps to protect themselves.
Heal their wounds.
Get justice for the ones who can't get it for themselves.
Now I'm the person with the knot in my stomach, the person I care about in danger, waiting for the other shoe to drop.
But it's still my job to do: protect the innocent, punish the guilty, see justice done.
Son of a bitch...
Alexandra, you're going to want to look at these.
You too, Ms. Maddox.
Holy shit.
Alex, did you know about this?

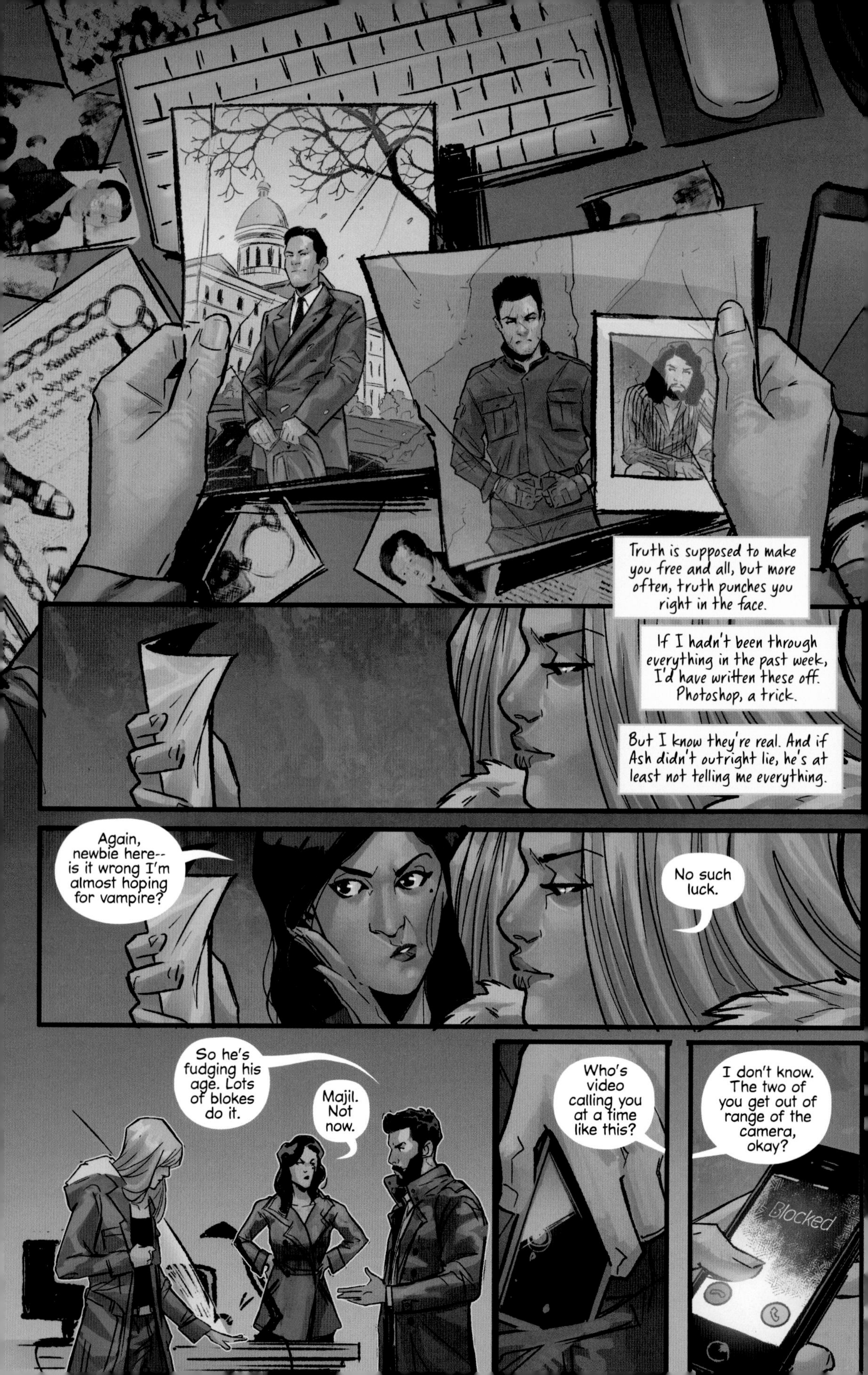
Truth is supposed to make you free and all, but more often, truth punches you right in the face.
If I hadn't been through everything in the past week, I'd have written these off. Photoshop, a trick.
But I know they're real. And if Ash didn't outright lie, he's at least not telling me everything.
Again, newbie here-- is it wrong I'm almost hoping for vampire?
No such luck.
So he's fudging his age. Lots of blokes do it.
Majil. Not now.
Who's video calling you at a time like this?
I don't know. The two of you get out of range of the camera, okay?
Blocked

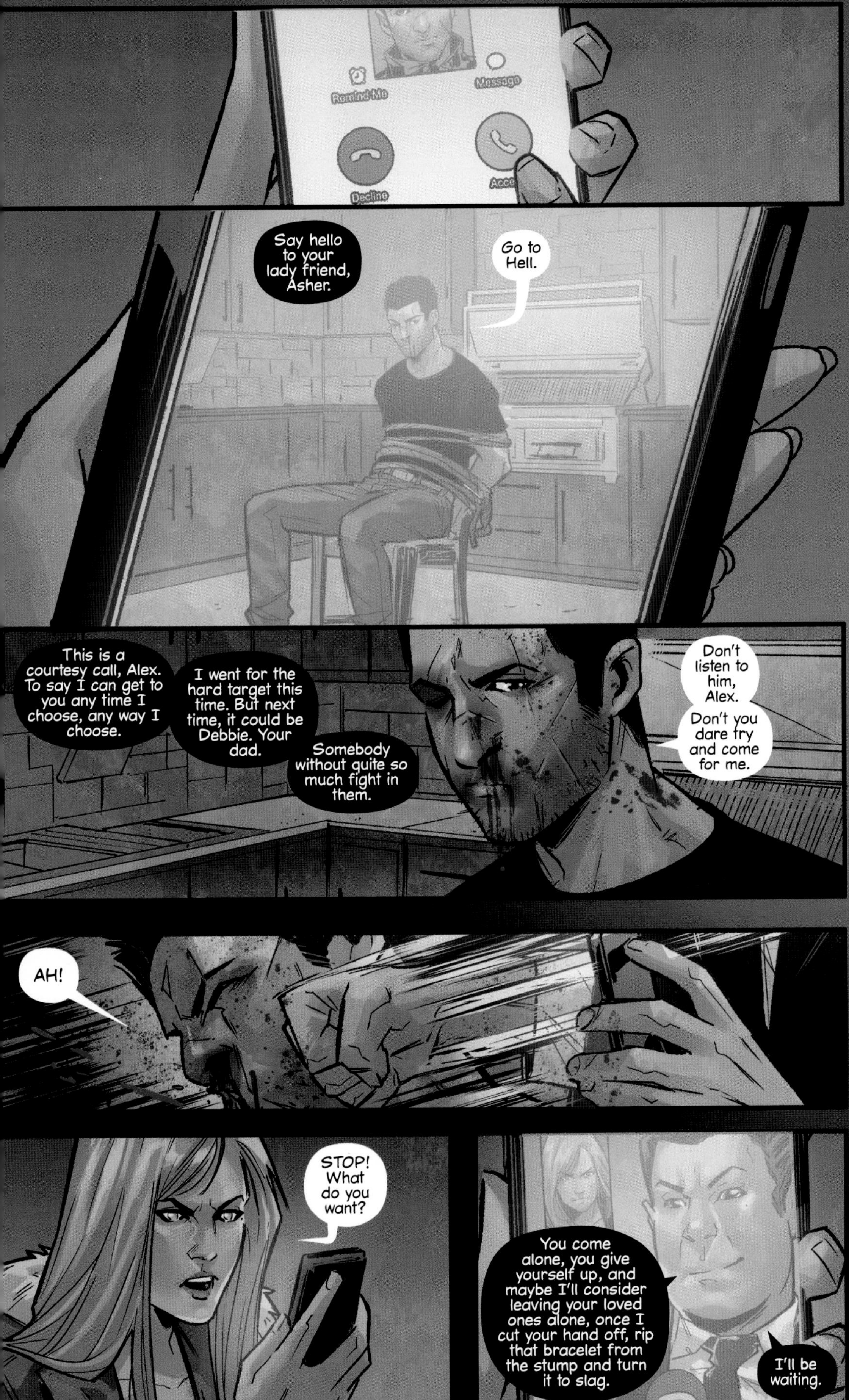
Remind Me
Message
Decline
Say hello to your lady friend, Asher.
Go to Hell.
This is a courtesy call, Alex. To say I can get to you any time I choose, any way I choose.
I went for the hard target this time. But next time, it could be Debbie. Your dad.
Somebody without quite so much fight in them.
Don't listen to him, Alex.
Don't you dare try and come for me.
AH!
STOP! What do you want?
You come alone, you give yourself up, and maybe I'll consider leaving your loved ones alone, once I cut your hand off, rip that bracelet from the stump and turn it to slag.
I'll be waiting.

I think we sent the message loud and clear.

Let's see how long it takes your lady friend to try and be a hero.

You're a tough nut, aren't you? Strong silent type?

What is it? Ex-special forces? Private military?

Because you put up quite a fight. Good thing this body is just a temporary ride, or I'd be pissed.

Not military, then. CIA?

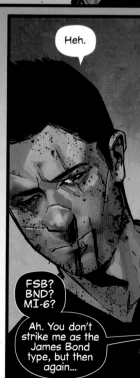

Heh.

FSB? BND? MI-6?

Ah. You don't strike me as the James Bond type, but then again...

Appearances and all that.

You going to tell me why an MI-6 operative is in New York playing mystical butler?

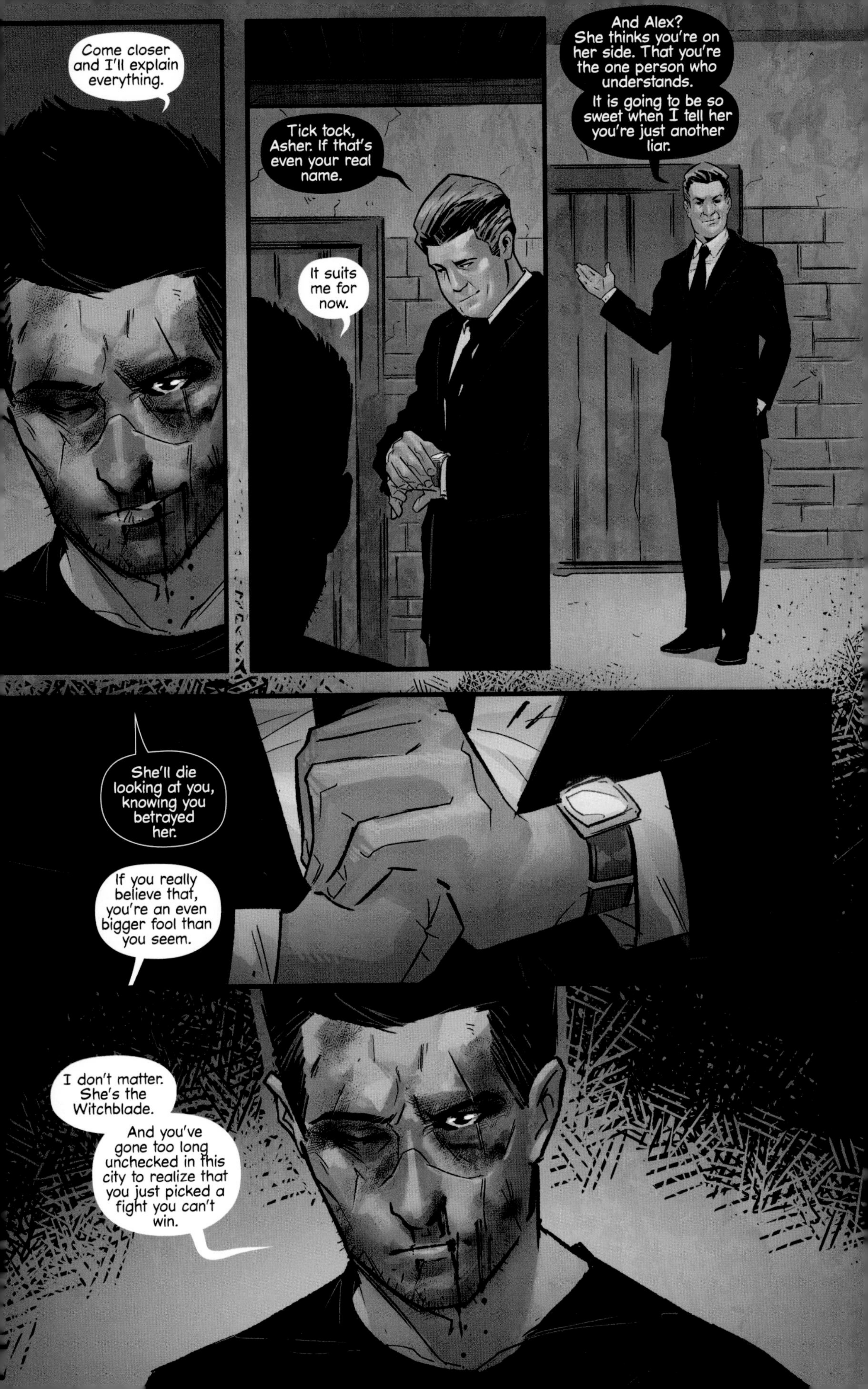
Come closer and I'll explain everything.
Tick tock, Asher. If that's even your real name.
It suits me for now.
And Alex? She thinks you're on her side. That you're the one person who understands.
It is going to be so sweet when I tell her you're just another liar.
She'll die looking at you, knowing you betrayed her.
If you really believe that, you're an even bigger fool than you seem.
I don't matter. She's the Witchblade.
And you've gone too long unchecked in this city to realize that you just picked a fight you can't win.

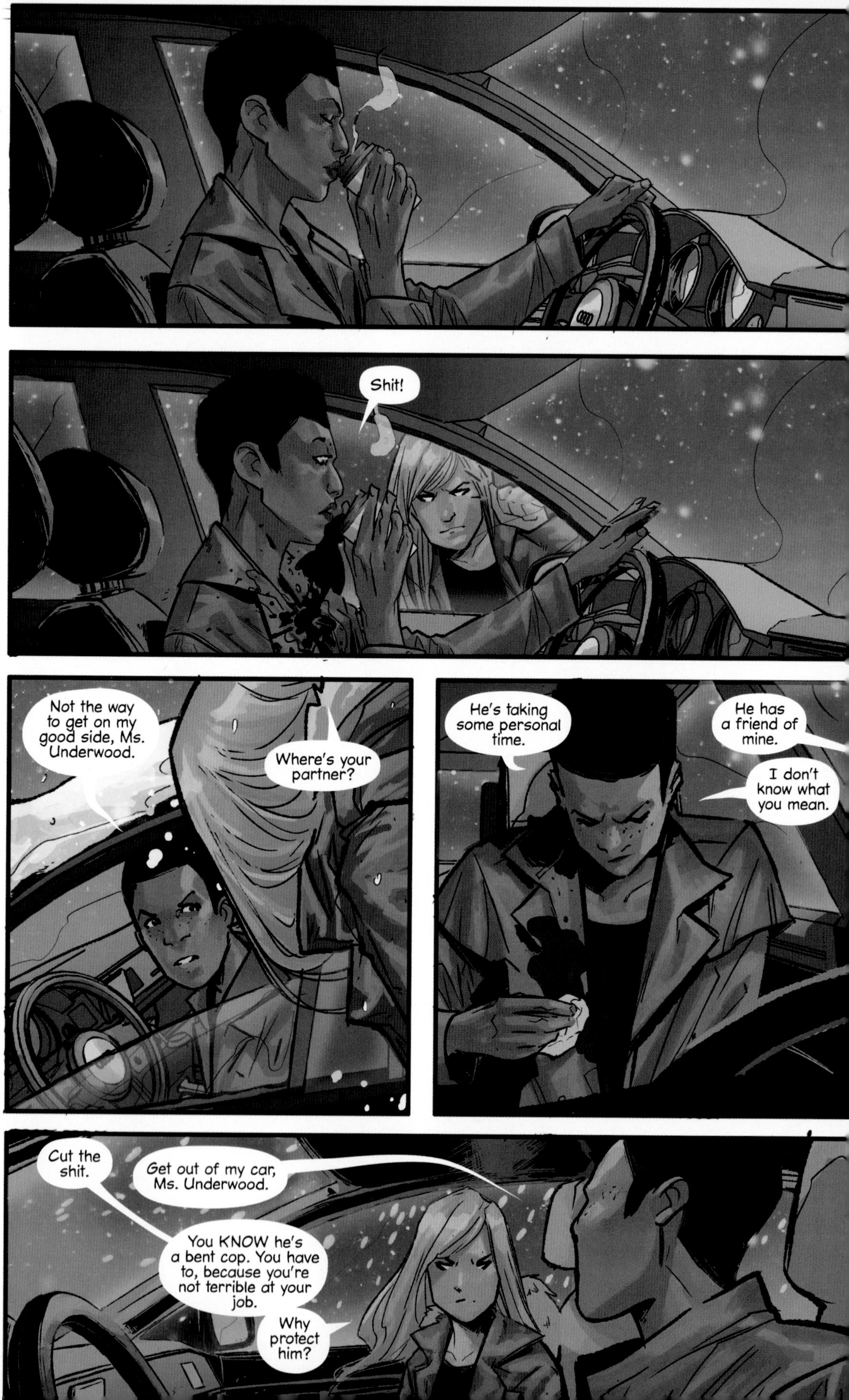
Shit!
Not the way to get on my good side, Ms. Underwood.
Where's your partner?
He's taking some personal time.
He has a friend of mine.
I don't know what you mean.
Cut the shit.
Get out of my car, Ms. Underwood.
You KNOW he's a bent cop. You have to, because you're not terrible at your job.
Why protect him?

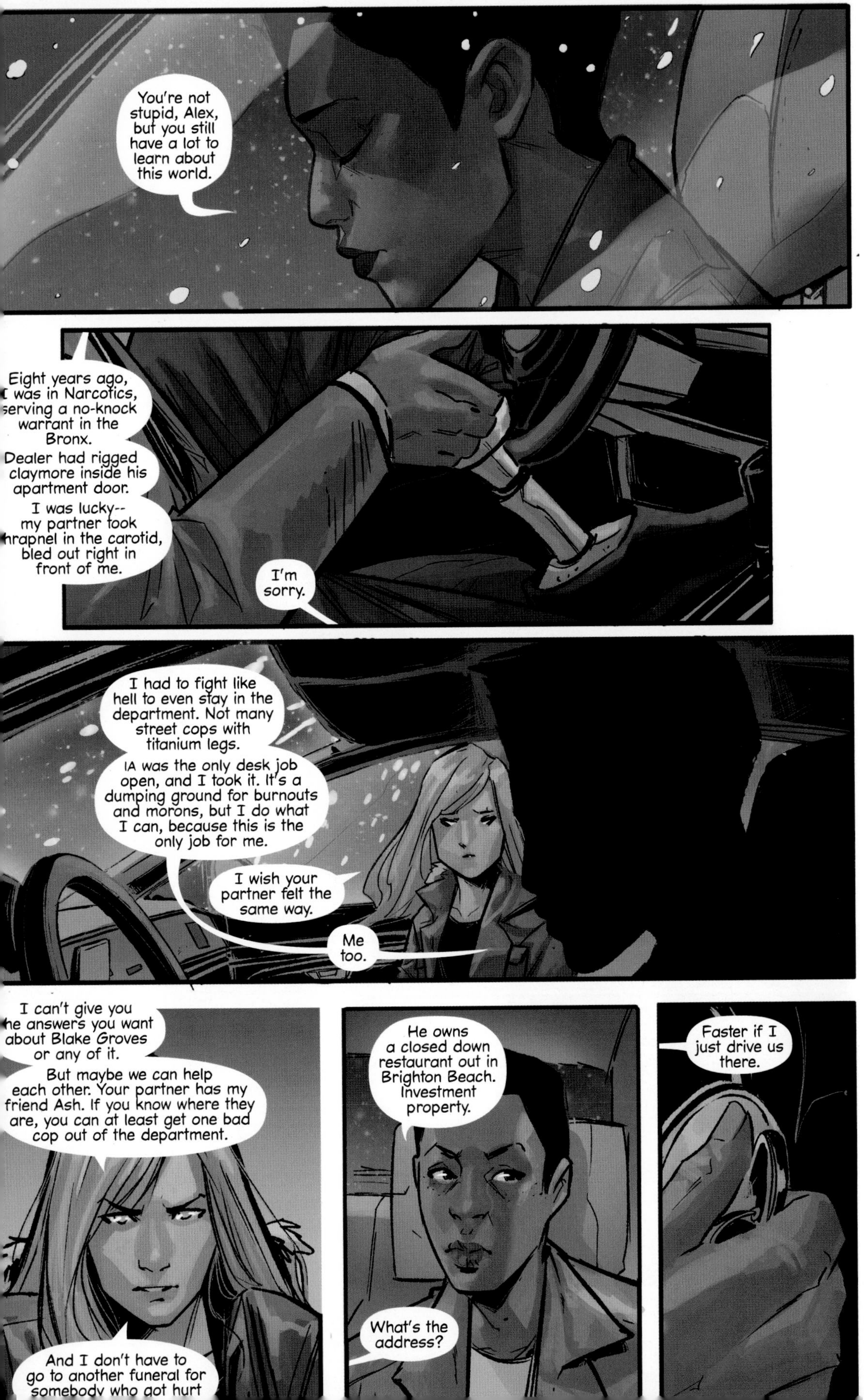
You're not stupid, Alex, but you still have a lot to learn about this world.
Eight years ago, I was in Narcotics, serving a no-knock warrant in the Bronx.
Dealer had rigged claymore inside his apartment door.
I was lucky-- my partner took hrapnel in the carotid, bled out right in front of me.
I'm sorry.
I had to fight like hell to even stay in the department. Not many street cops with titanium legs.
IA was the only desk job open, and I took it. It's a dumping ground for burnouts and morons, but I do what I can, because this is the only job for me.
I wish your partner felt the same way.
Me too.
I can't give you he answers you want about Blake Groves or any of it.
But maybe we can help each other. Your partner has my friend Ash. If you know where they are, you can at least get one bad cop out of the department.
And I don't have to go to another funeral for somebody who got hurt
He owns a closed down restaurant out in Brighton Beach. Investment property.
What's the address?
Faster if I just drive us there.

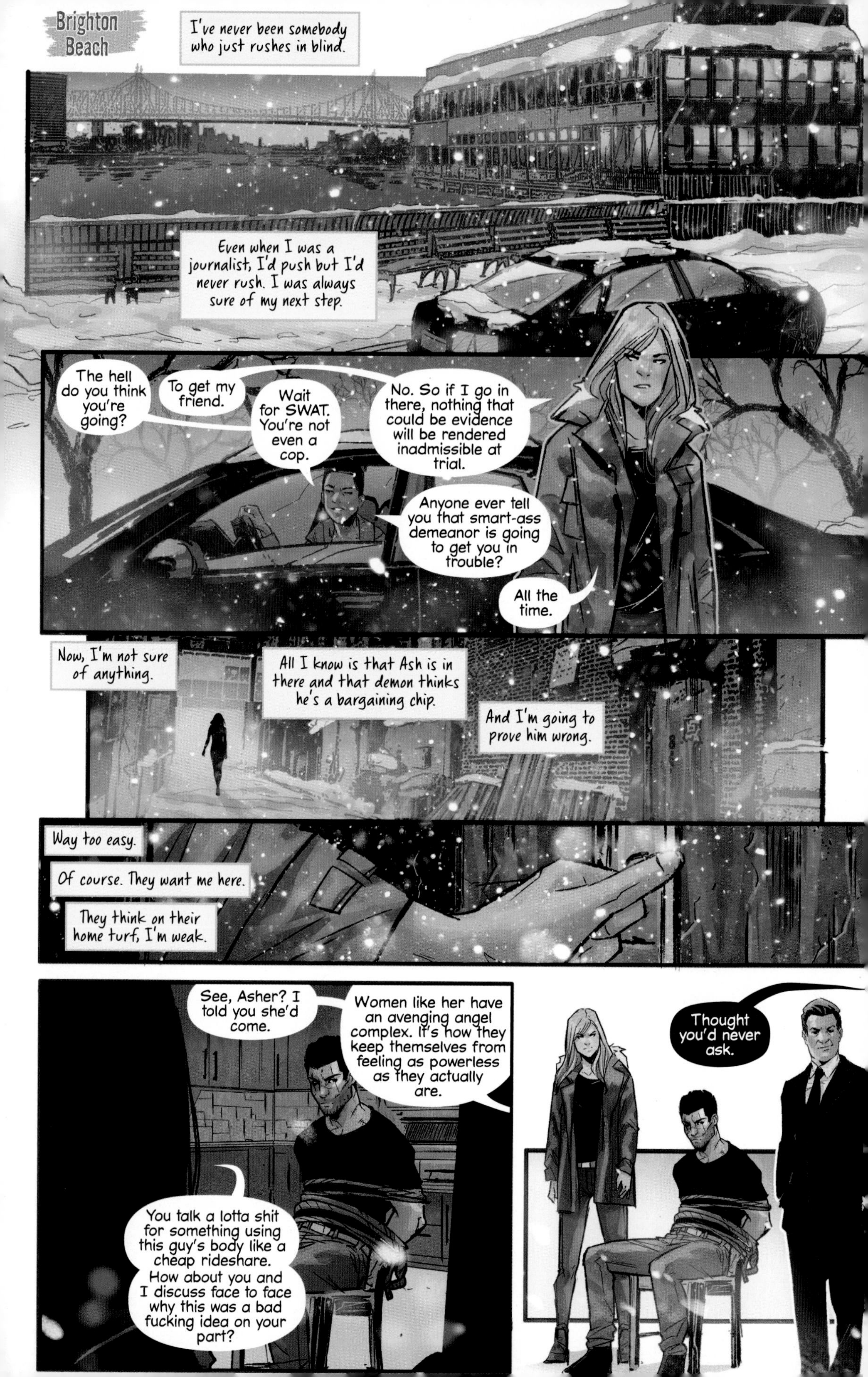
Brighton Beach
I've never been somebody who just rushes in blind.
Even when I was a journalist, I'd push but I'd never rush. I was always sure of my next step.
The hell do you think you're going?
To get my friend.
Wait for SWAT. You're not even a cop.
No. So if I go in there, nothing that could be evidence will be rendered inadmissible at trial.
Anyone ever tell you that smart-ass demeanor is going to get you in trouble?
All the time.
Now, I'm not sure of anything.
All I know is that Ash is in there and that demon thinks he's a bargaining chip.
And I'm going to prove him wrong.
Way too easy.
Of course. They want me here.
They think on their home turf, I'm weak.
See, Asher? I told you she'd come.
Women like her have an avenging angel complex. It's how they keep themselves from feeling as powerless as they actually are.
You talk a lotta shit for something using this guy's body like a cheap rideshare. How about you and I discuss face to face why this was a bad fucking idea on your part?
Thought you'd never ask.

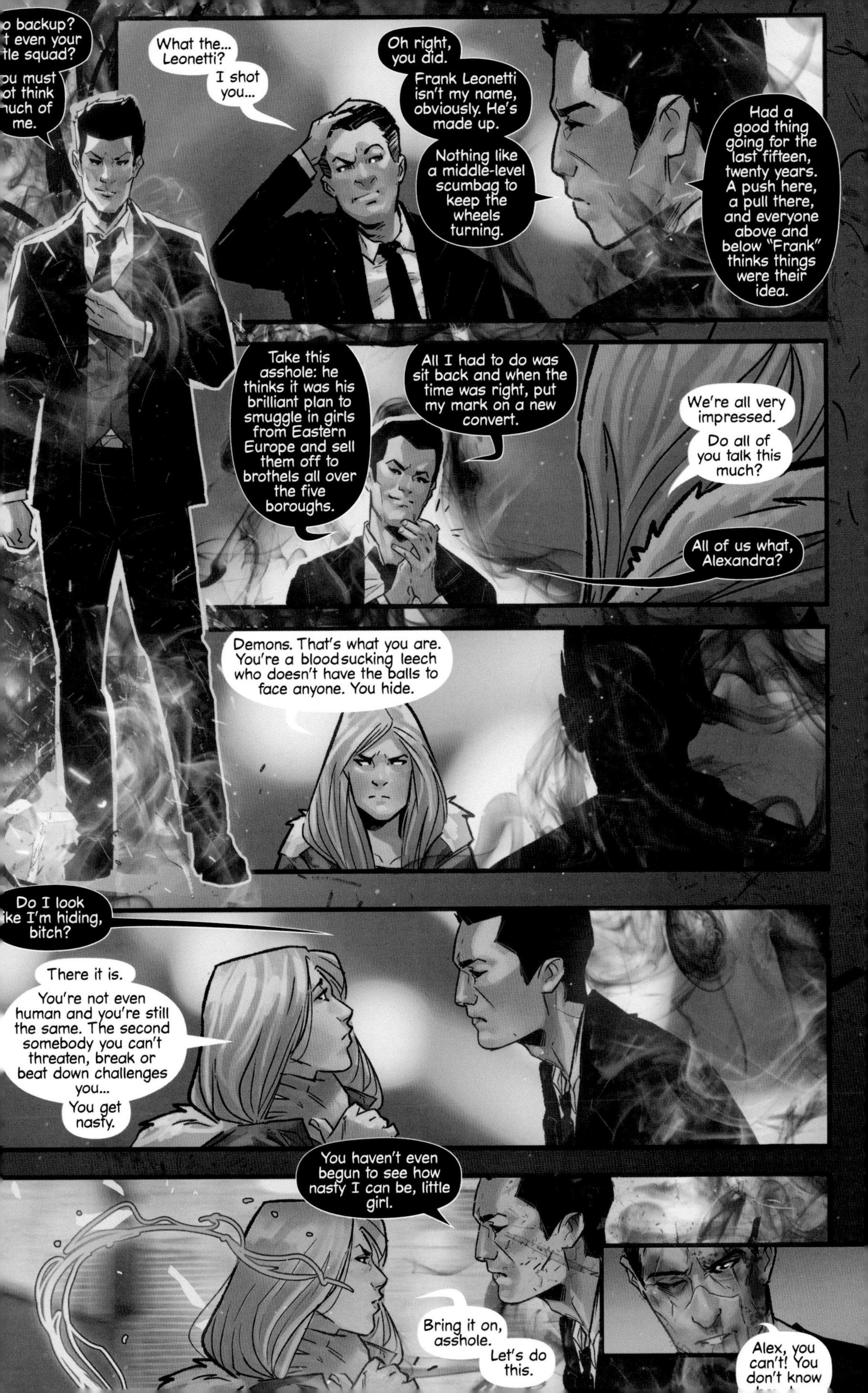

o backup? t even your tle squad?
ou must ot think nuch of me.
What the... Leonetti?
I shot you...
Oh right, you did.
Frank Leonetti isn't my name, obviously. He's made up.
Nothing like a middle-level scumbag to keep the wheels turning.
Had a good thing going for the last fifteen, twenty years. A push here, a pull there, and everyone above and below "Frank" thinks things were their idea.
Take this asshole: he thinks it was his brilliant plan to smuggle in girls from Eastern Europe and sell them off to brothels all over the five boroughs.
All I had to do was sit back and when the time was right, put my mark on a new convert.
We're all very impressed.
Do all of you talk this much?
All of us what, Alexandra?
Demons. That's what you are. You're a bloodsucking leech who doesn't have the balls to face anyone. You hide.
Do I look ike I'm hiding, bitch?
There it is.
You're not even human and you're still the same. The second somebody you can't threaten, break or beat down challenges you...
You get nasty.
You haven't even begun to see how nasty I can be, little girl.
Bring it on, asshole.
Let's do this.
Alex, you can't! You don't know

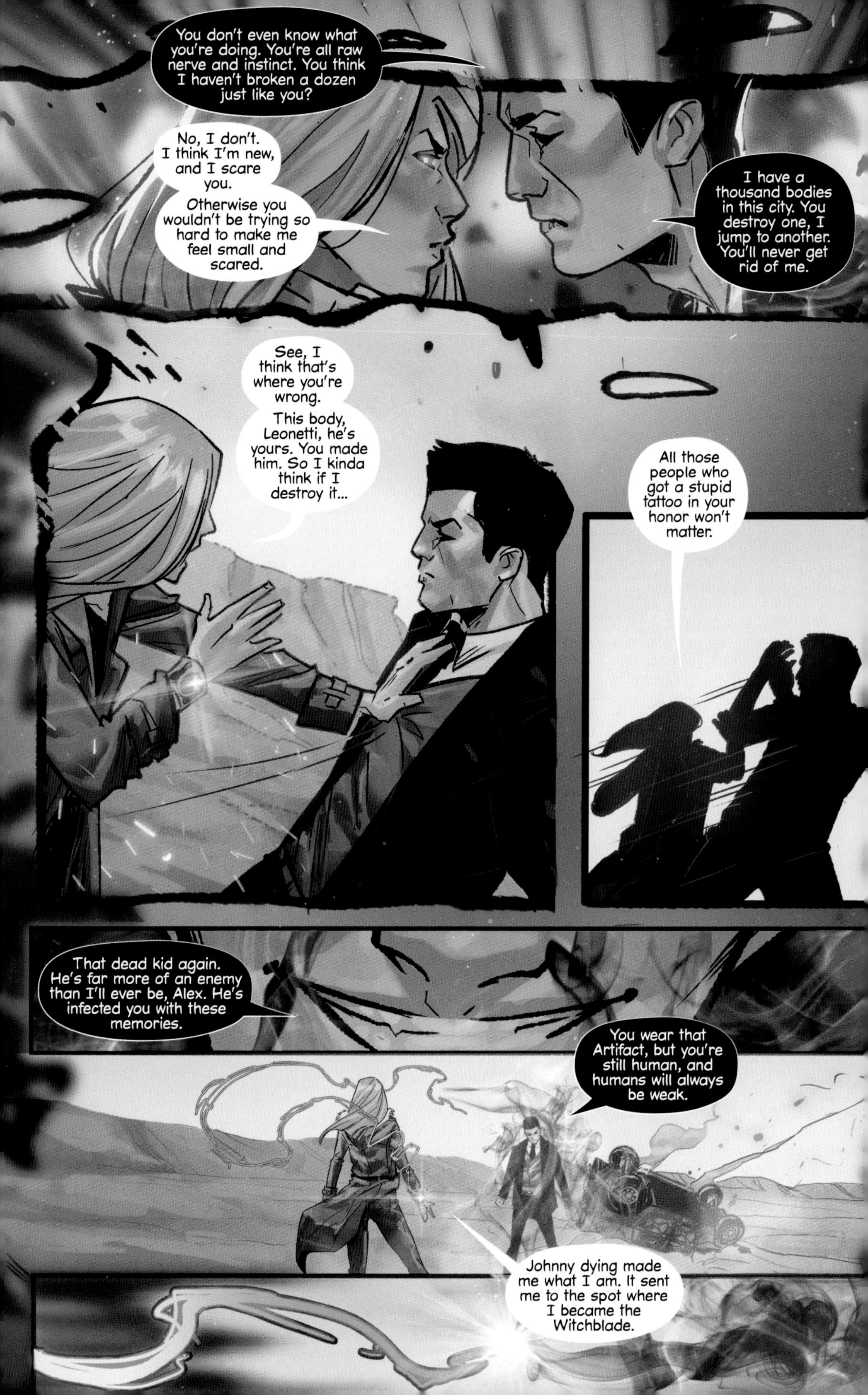
You don't even know what you're doing. You're all raw nerve and instinct. You think I haven't broken a dozen just like you?
No, I don't. I think I'm new, and I scare you.
Otherwise you wouldn't be trying so hard to make me feel small and scared.
I have a thousand bodies in this city. You destroy one, I jump to another. You'll never get rid of me.
See, I think that's where you're wrong.
This body, Leonetti, he's yours. You made him. So I kinda think if I destroy it...
All those people who got a stupid tattoo in your honor won't matter.
That dead kid again. He's far more of an enemy than I'll ever be, Alex. He's infected you with these memories.
You wear that Artifact, but you're still human, and humans will always be weak.
Johnny dying made me what I am. It sent me to the spot where I became the Witchblade.

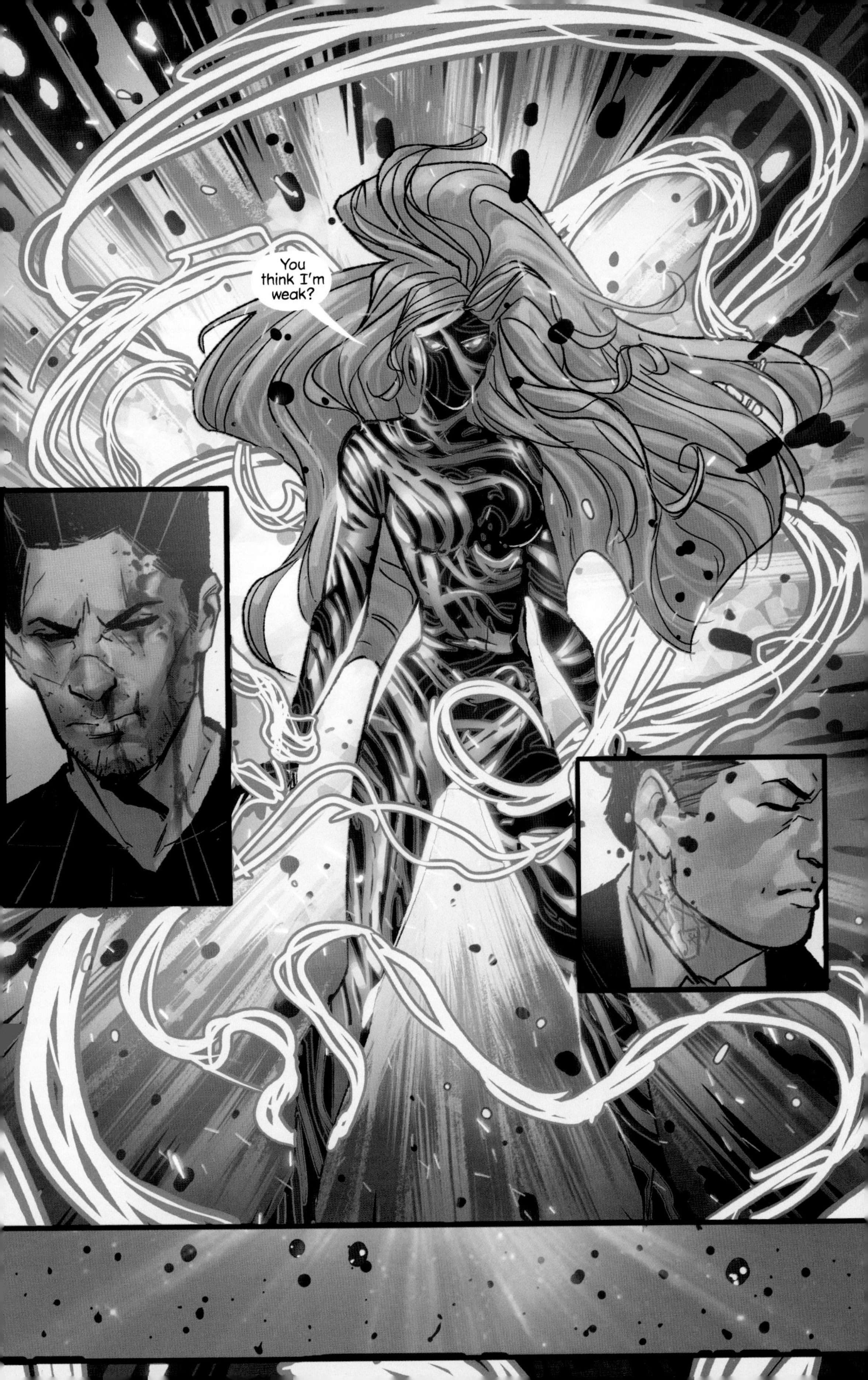
You think I'm weak?

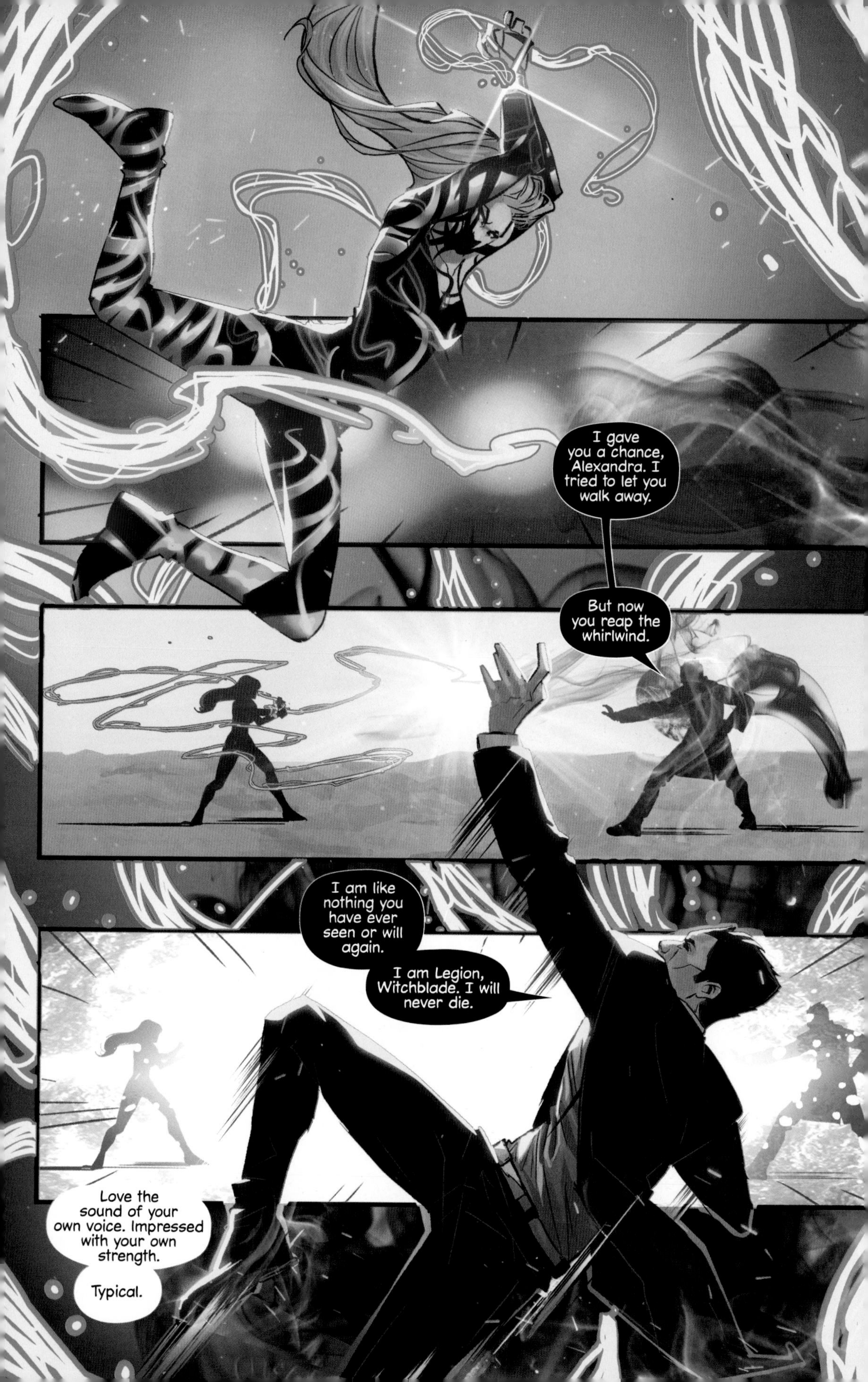
I gave you a chance, Alexandra. I tried to let you walk away.
But now you reap the whirlwind.
I am like nothing you have ever seen or will again.
I am Legion, Witchblade. I will never die.
Love the sound of your own voice. Impressed with your own strength.
Typical.

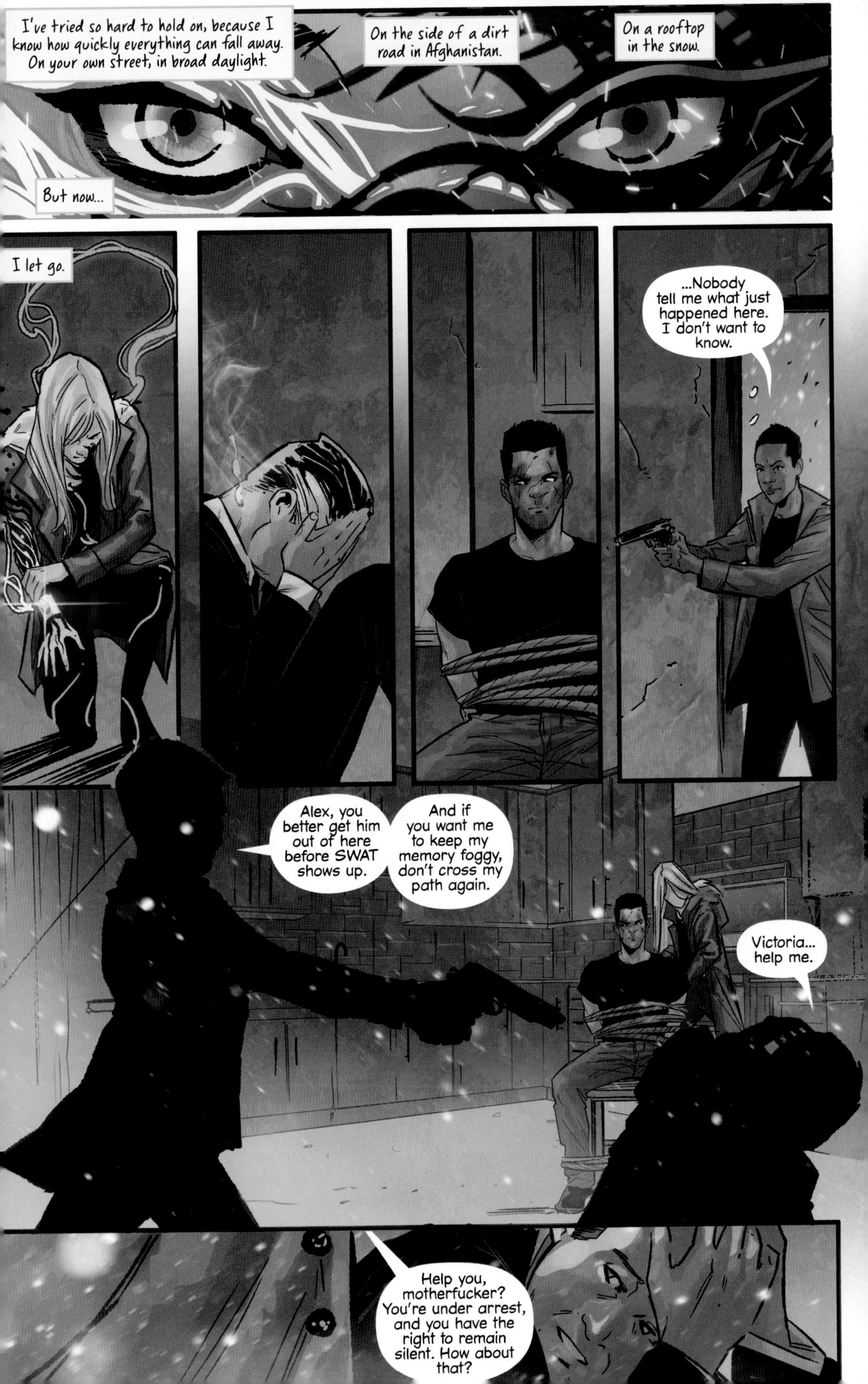
I've tried so hard to hold on, because I know how quickly everything can fall away. On your own street, in broad daylight.
On the side of a dirt road in Afghanistan.
On a rooftop in the snow.
But now...
I let go.
...Nobody tell me what just happened here. I don't want to know.
Alex, you better get him out of here before SWAT shows up.
And if you want me to keep my memory foggy, don't cross my path again.
Victoria... help me.
Help you, motherfucker? You're under arrest, and you have the right to remain silent. How about that?

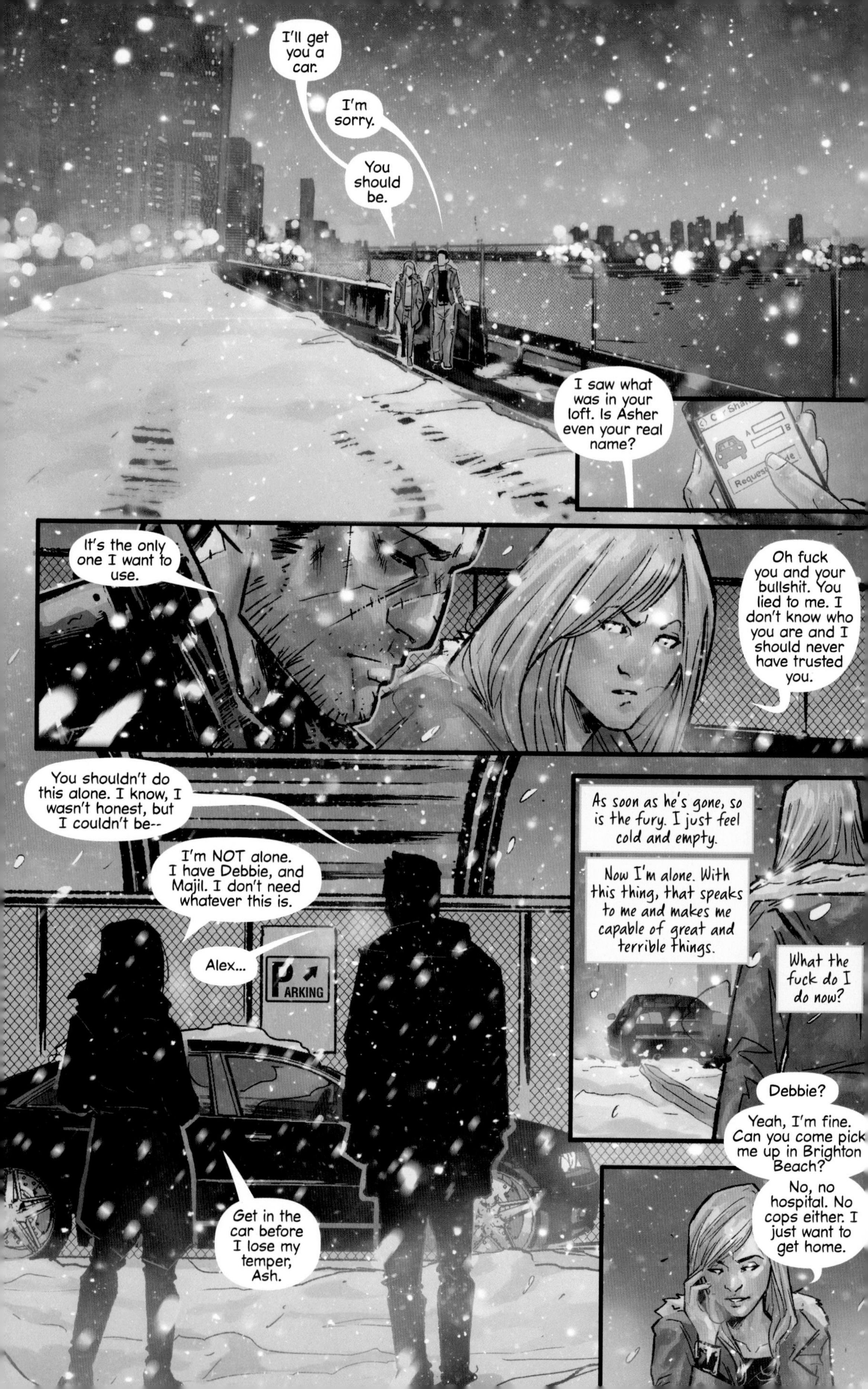
I'll get you a car.
I'm sorry.
You should be.
I saw what was in your loft. Is Asher even your real name?
It's the only one I want to use.
Oh fuck you and your bullshit. You lied to me. I don't know who you are and I should never have trusted you.
You shouldn't do this alone. I know, I wasn't honest, but I couldn't be--
I'm NOT alone. I have Debbie, and Majil. I don't need whatever this is.
Alex...
PARKING
Get in the car before I lose my temper, Ash.
As soon as he's gone, so is the fury. I just feel cold and empty.
Now I'm alone. With this thing, that speaks to me and makes me capable of great and terrible things.
What the fuck do I do now?
Debbie?
Yeah, I'm fine. Can you come pick me up in Brighton Beach?
No, no hospital. No cops either. I just want to get home.

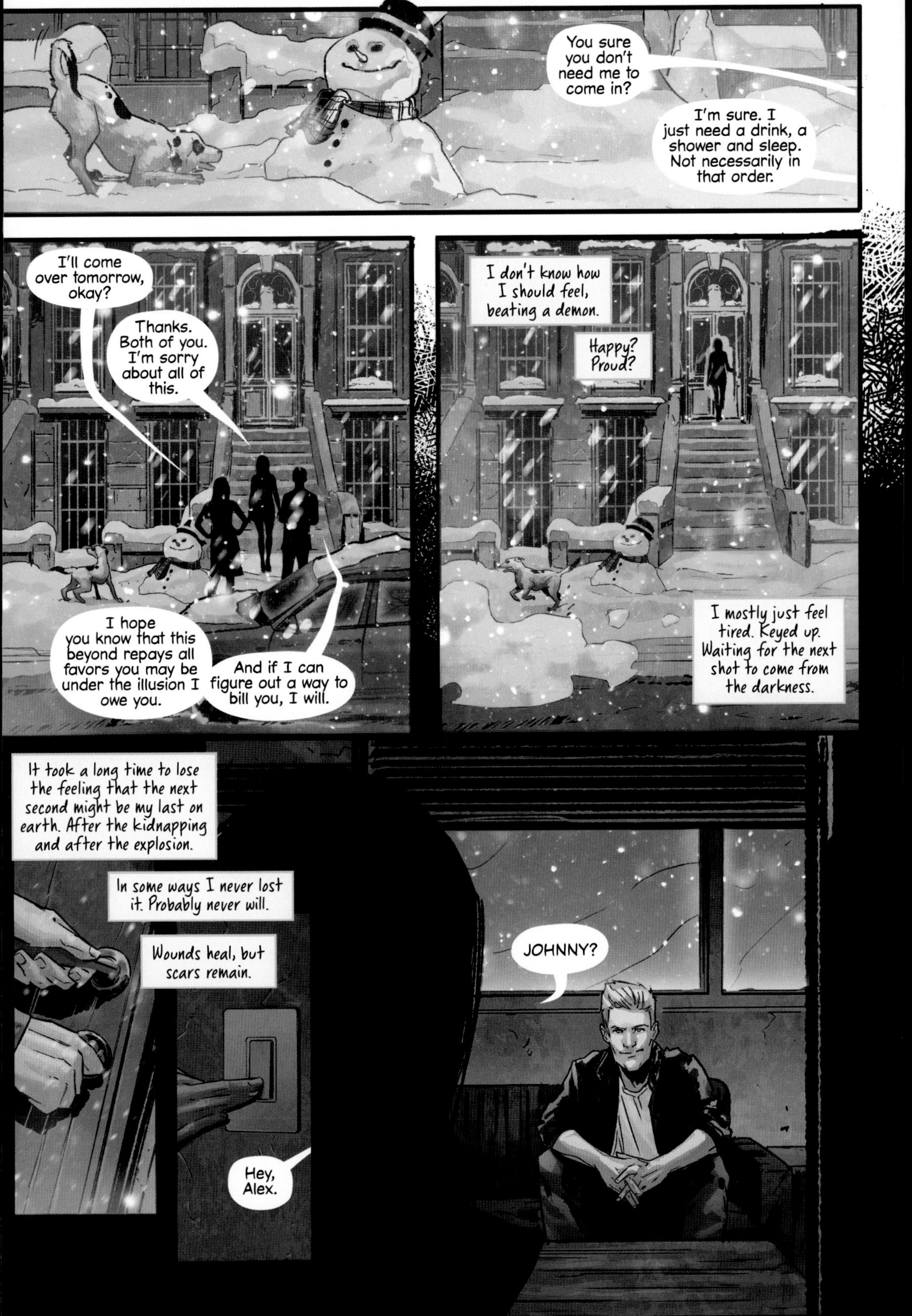
You sure you don't need me to come in?
I'm sure. I just need a drink, a shower and sleep. Not necessarily in that order.
I'll come over tomorrow, okay?
Thanks. Both of you. I'm sorry about all of this.
I hope you know that this beyond repays all favors you may be under the illusion I owe you.
And if I can figure out a way to bill you, I will.
I don't know how I should feel, beating a demon.
Happy? Proud?
I mostly just feel tired. Keyed up. Waiting for the next shot to come from the darkness.
It took a long time to lose the feeling that the next second might be my last on earth. After the kidnapping and after the explosion.
In some ways I never lost it. Probably never will.
Wounds heal, but scars remain.
JOHNNY?
Hey, Alex.

COVER GALLERY

ISSUE 1 **COVER A** — ROBERTA **INGRANATA**, BRYAN **VALENZA**

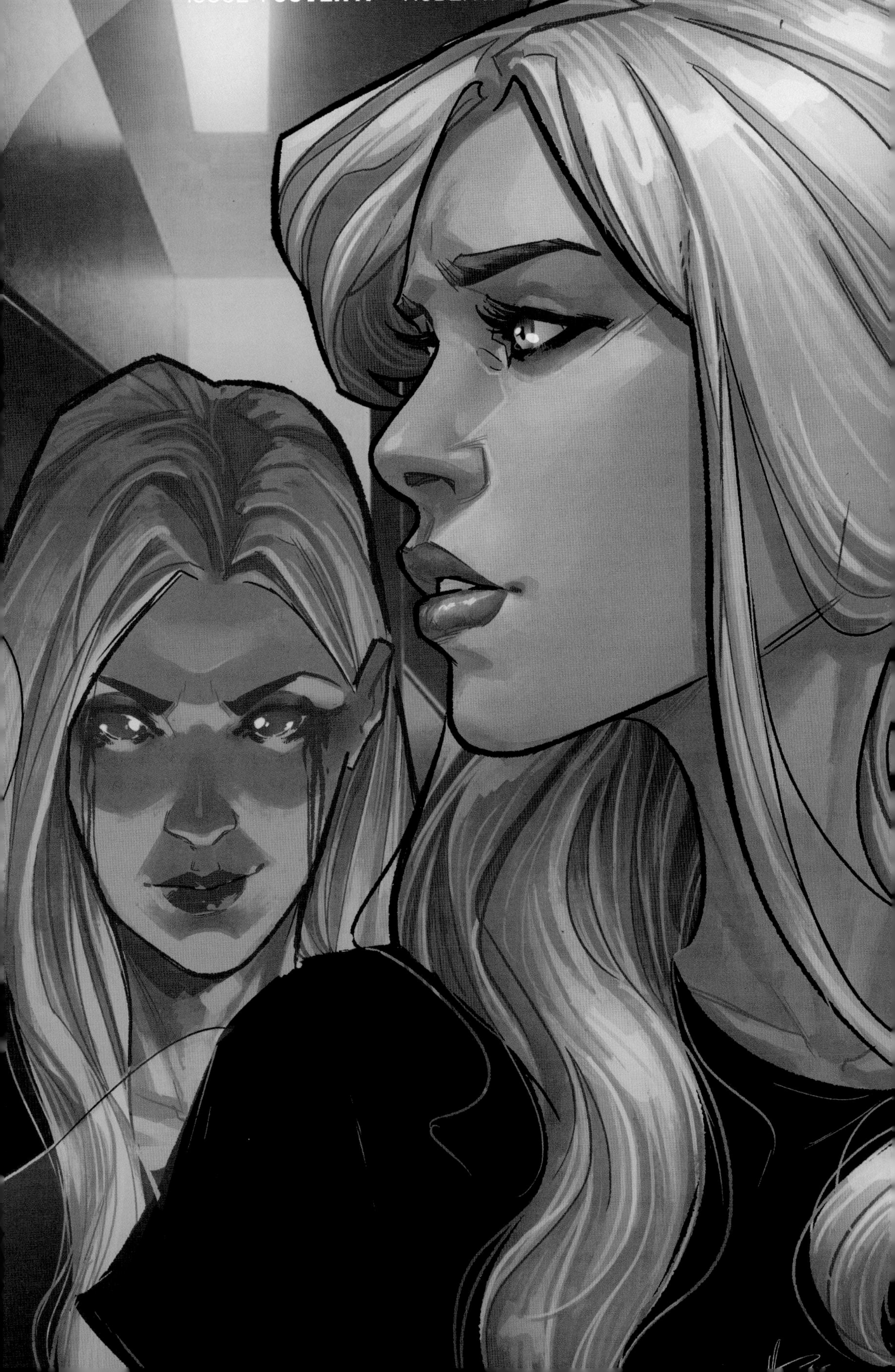

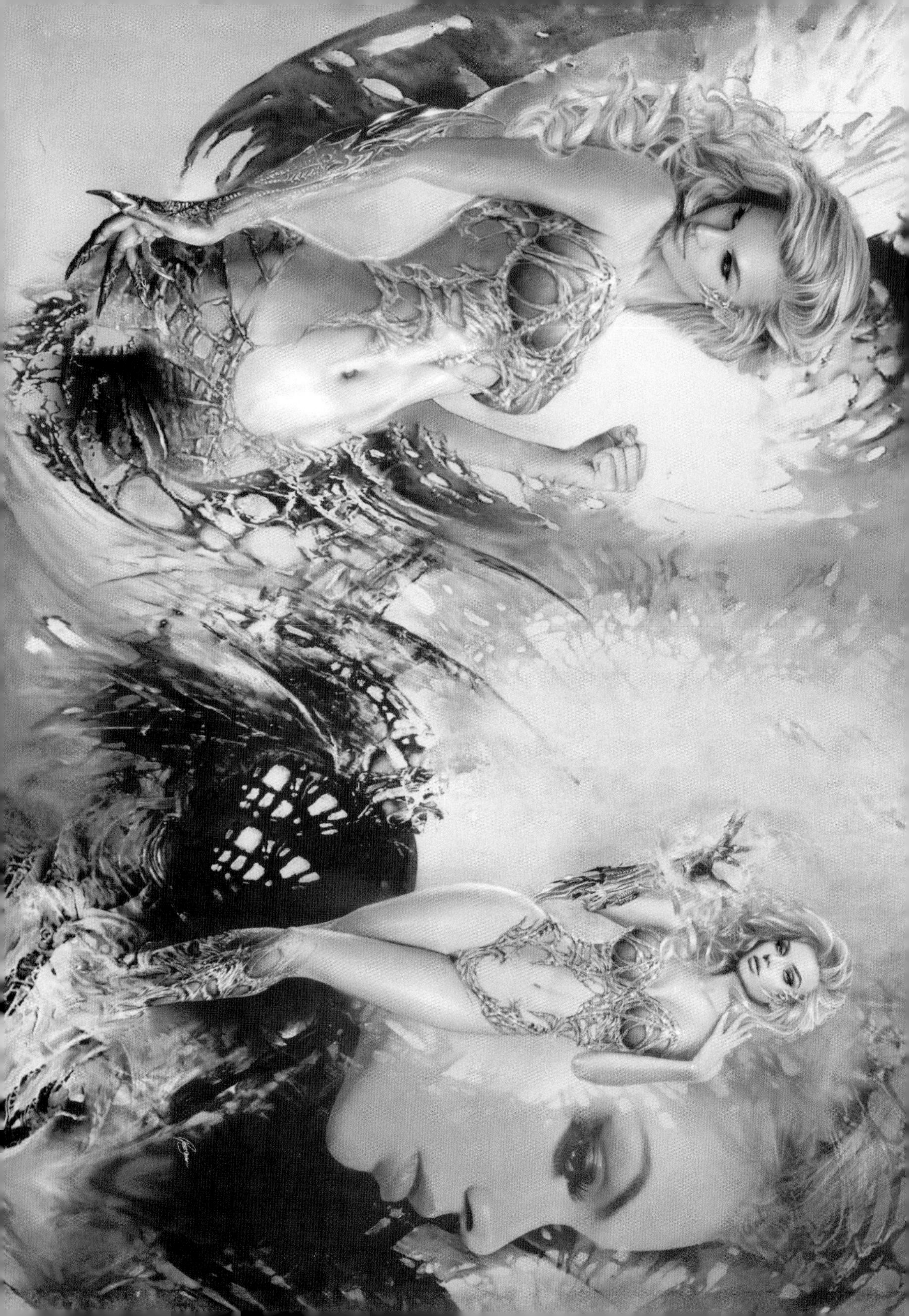

ISSUE 2 **COVER —** ROBERTA **INGRANATA** , BRYAN **VALENZA**

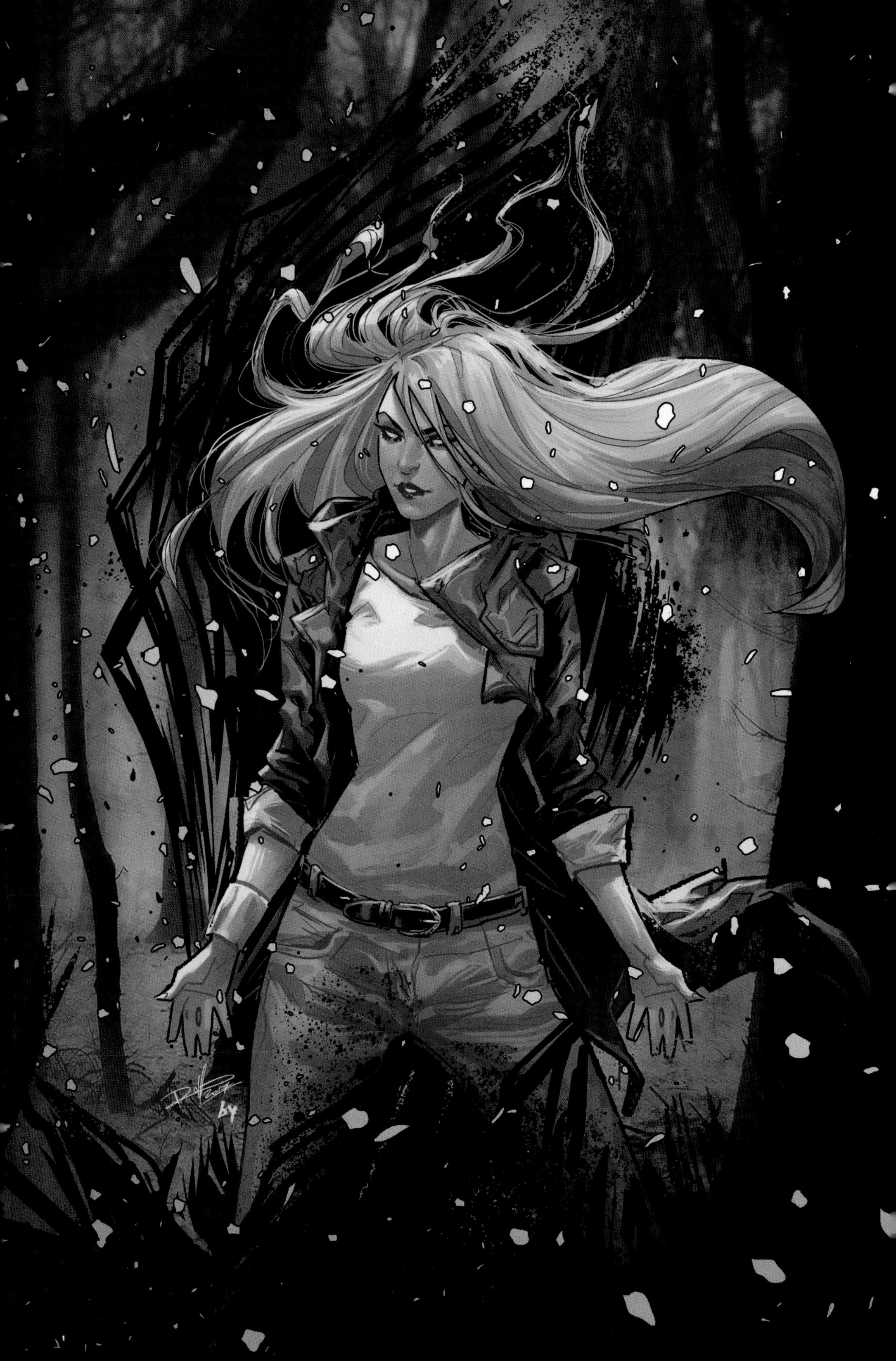

ISSUE 3 **COVER** — ROBERTA **INGRANATA** , BRYAN **VALENZ**

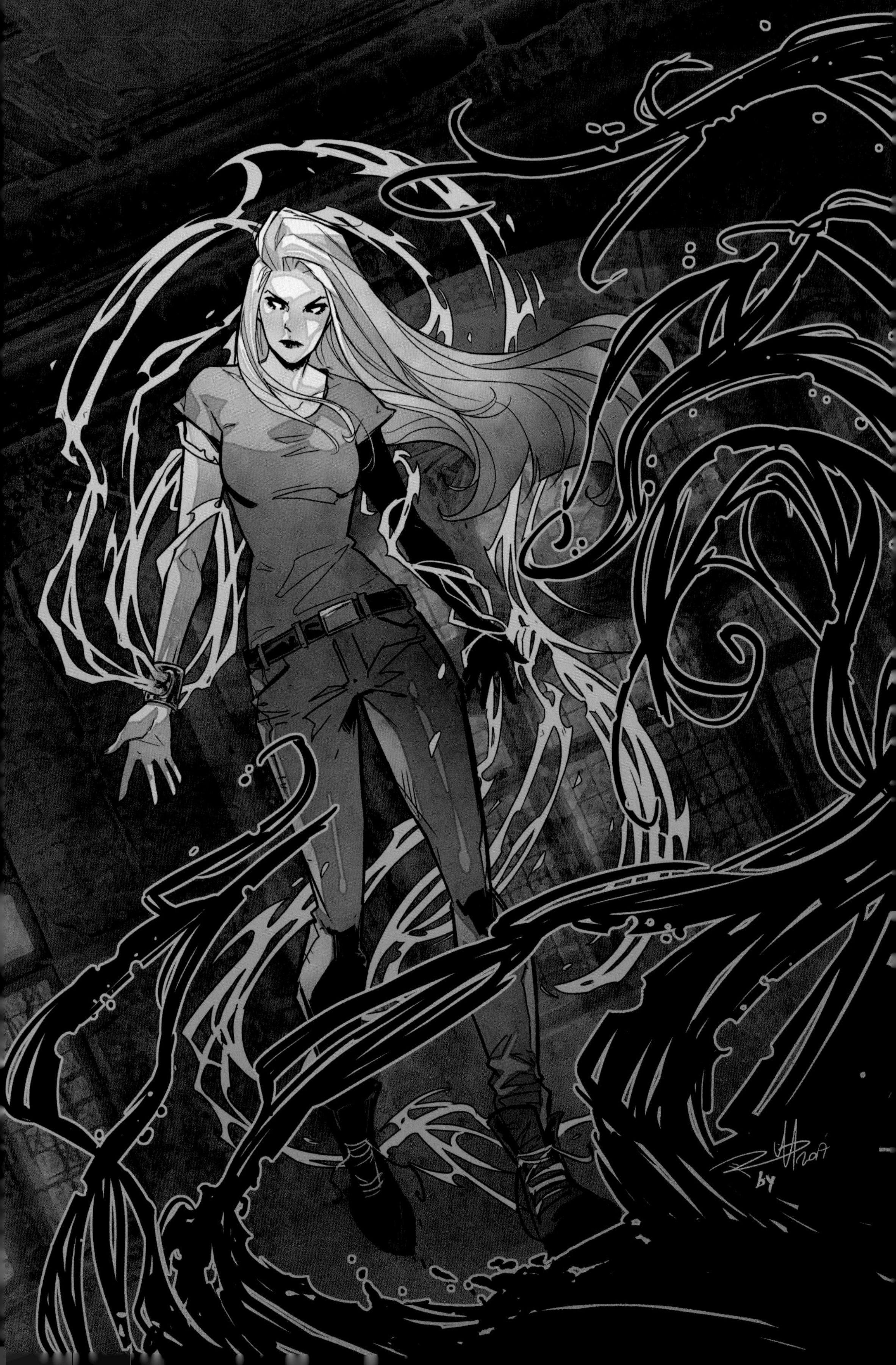

ISSUE 4 **COVER A** — ROBERTA **INGRANATA** , BRYAN **VALENZA**

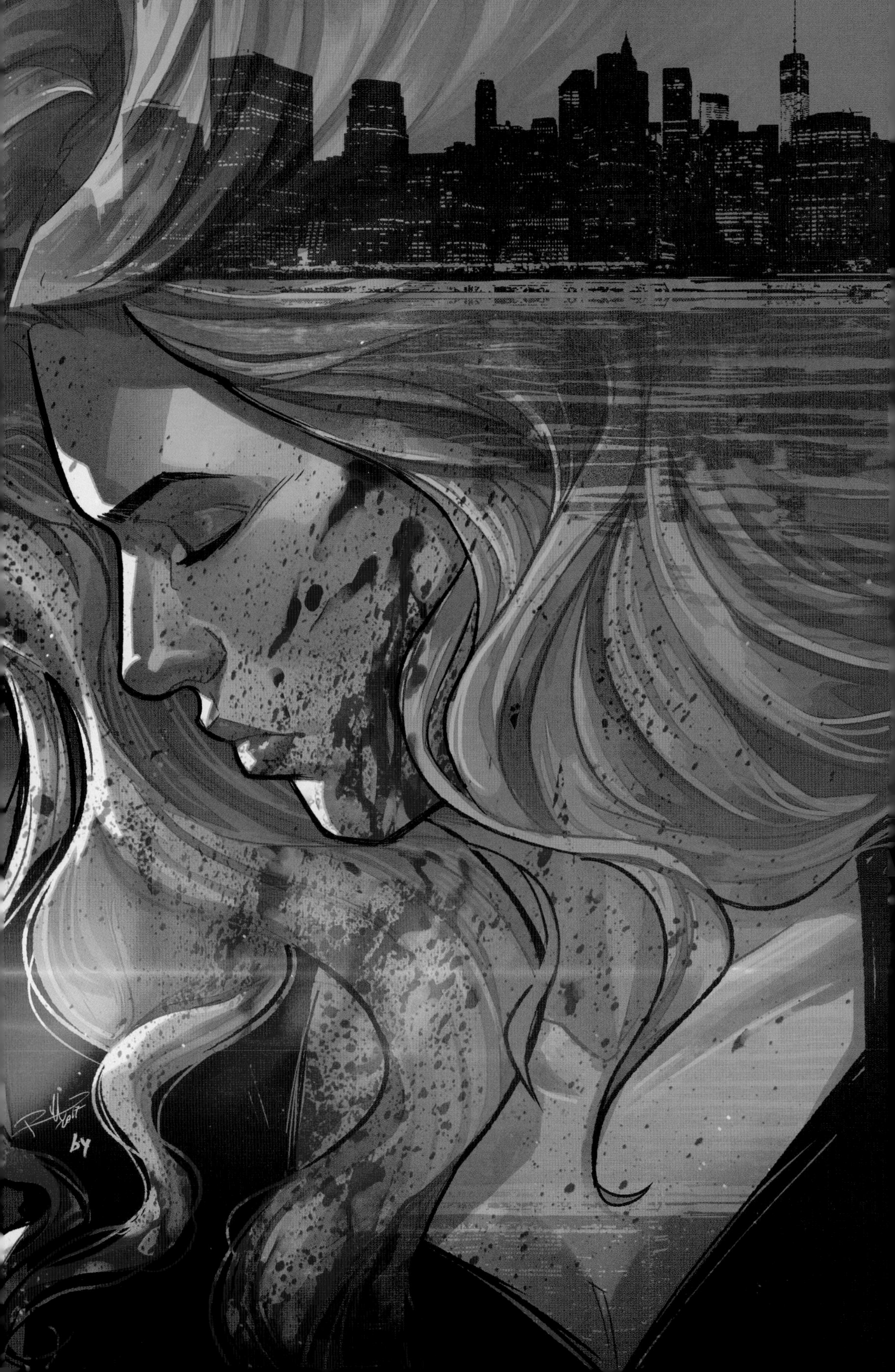

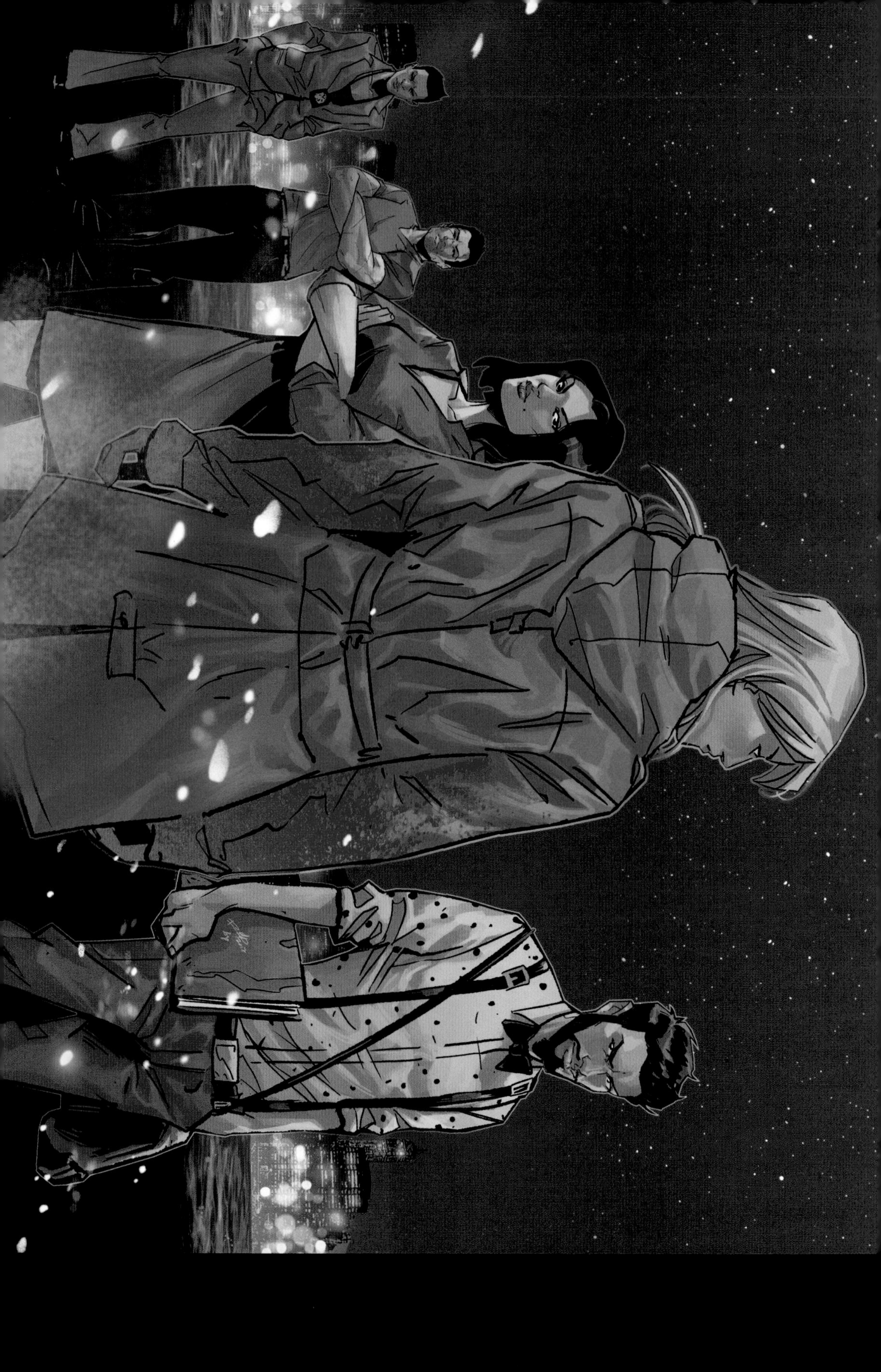

ISSUE 4 **COVER B** — ROBERTA **INGRANATA** BRYAN **VALENZ**

ISSUE 5 COVER — ROBERTA INGRANATA, BRYAN VALENZA

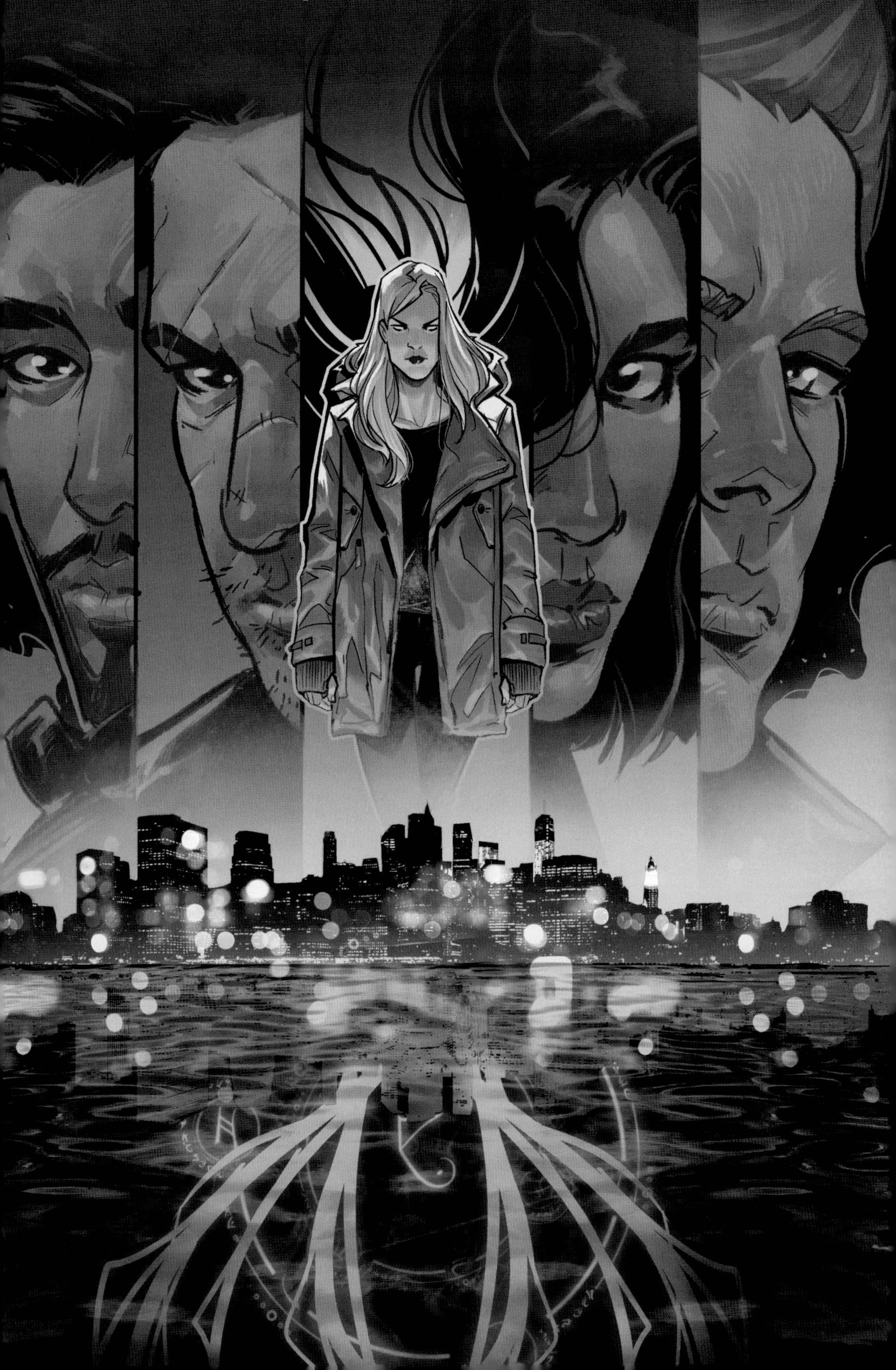

ISSUE 6 **COVER** — ROBERTA **INGRANATA** , BRYAN **VALENZ**

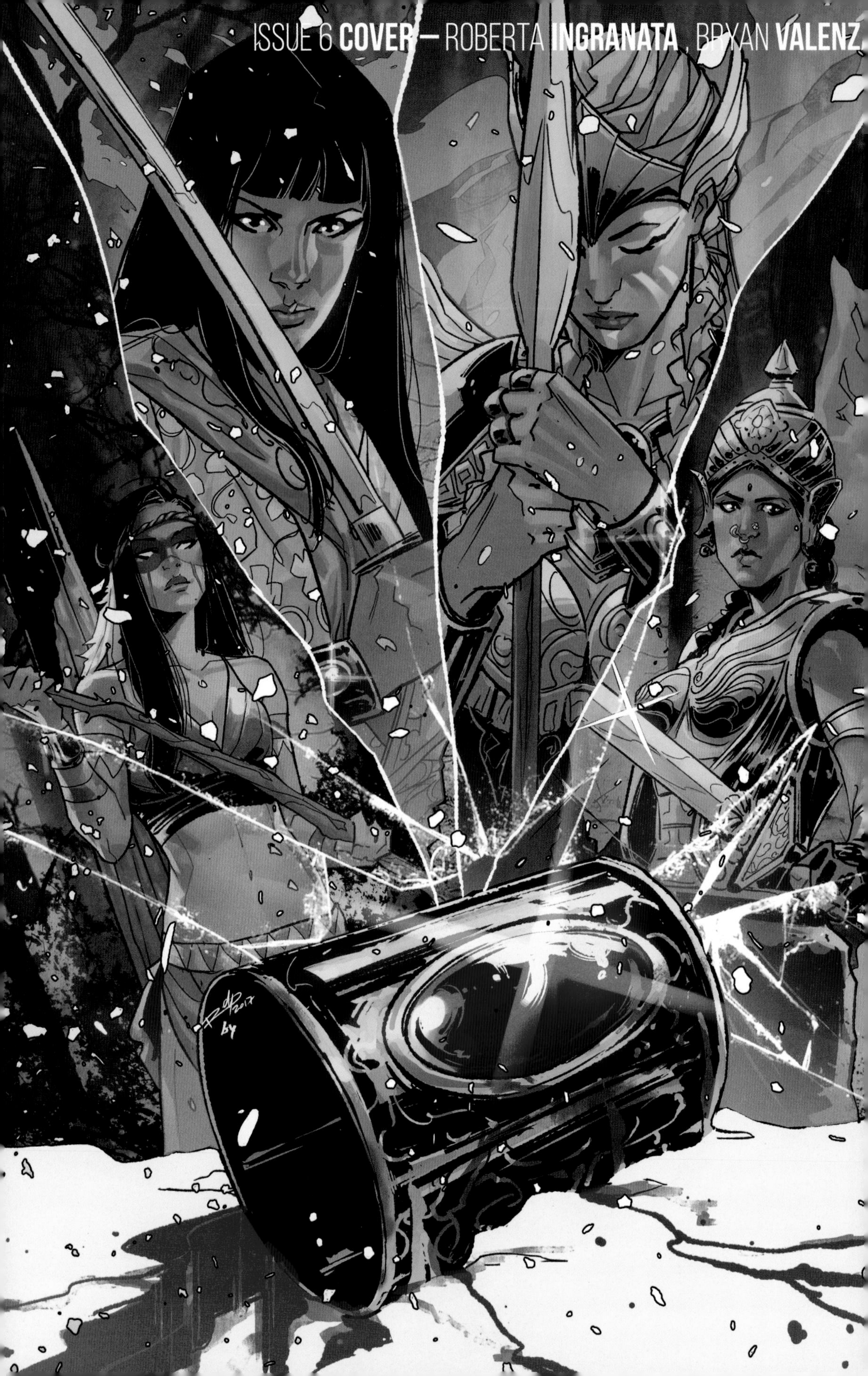

The Top Cow essentials checklist:

For more ISBN and ordering information on our latest collections go to:
www.topcow.com
Ask your retailer about our catalogue of collected editions,
digests, and hard covers or check the listings at:
Barnes and Noble, Amazon.com,
and other fine retailers.

To find your nearest comic shop go to:
www.comicshoplocator.com

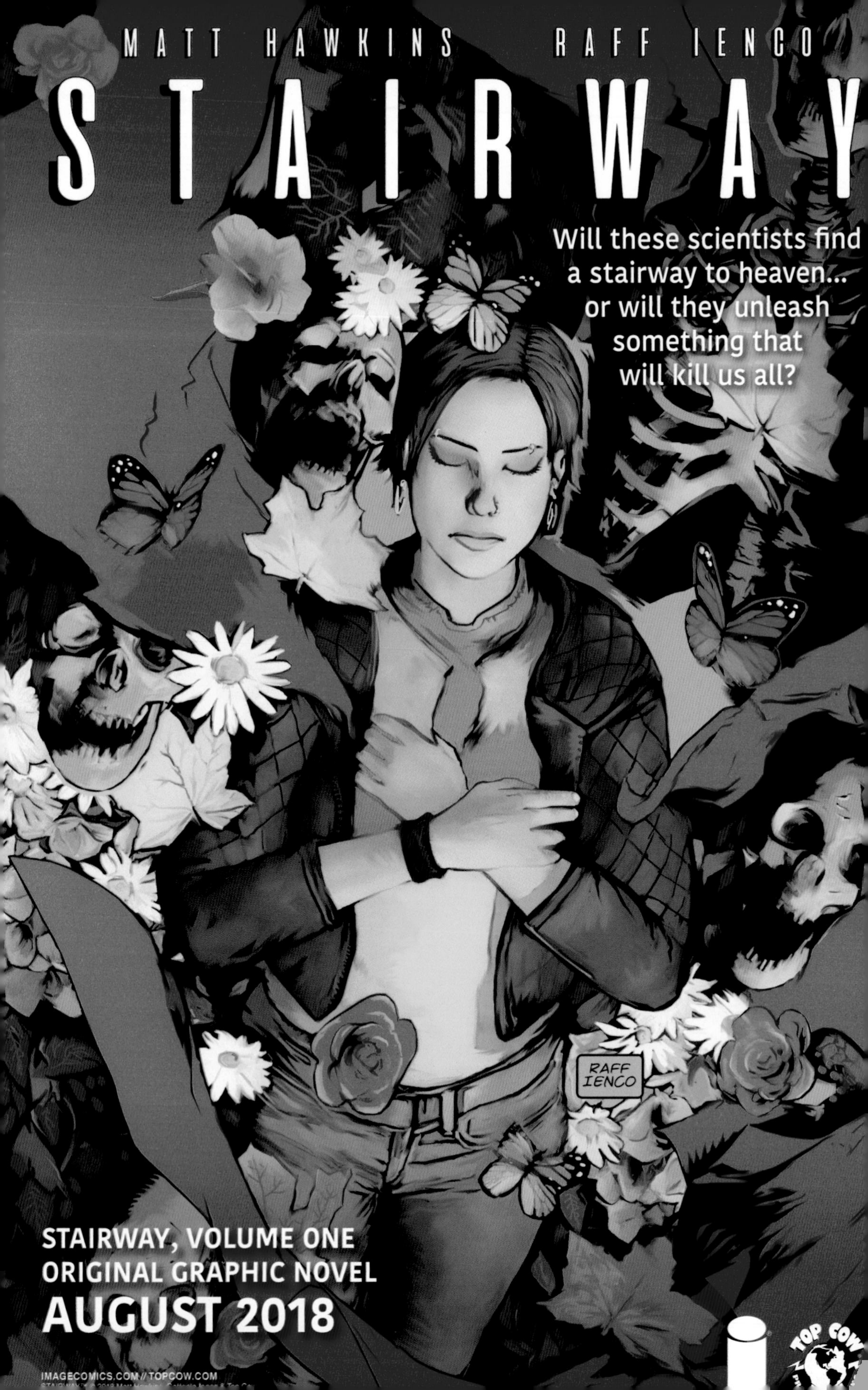

MATT HAWKINS
RAFF IENCO
STAIRWAY
Will these scientists find a stairway to heaven... or will they unleash something that will kill us all?
RAFF IENCO
STAIRWAY, VOLUME ONE
ORIGINAL GRAPHIC NOVEL
AUGUST 2018
IMAGECOMICS.COM // TOPCOW.COM
TOP COW